To Angie

GW01402661

The Lost Journey Homeward

Much love from Eve x

Eve Bonham

Onwards and Upwards Publishers,
Berkeley House,
11 Nightingale Crescent,
West Horsley,
Surrey,
KT24 6PD

www.onwardsandupwards.org

---

copyright © Eve Bonham 2015

The right of Eve Bonham to be identified as the author of this work has been asserted by the author in accordance with the Copyright, Designs and Patents Act 1988.

All rights reserved.

No part of this publication may be reproduced or transmitted in any form or by any means, electronic or mechanical, including photocopy, recording or any information storage and retrieval system, without permission in writing from the author or publisher.

Cover design: LM Graphic Design

ISBN: 978-1-910197-57-8

Printed in the UK by 4edge Limited

For Jack and Claire

PART ONE

"I struck the board and cried, 'No more;
I will abroad!
What? Shall I ever sigh and pine?
My lines and life are free, free as the road,
Loose as the wind, as large as store.'"

From 'The Collar'
by George Herbert

1

Hidden in the shadows, the watcher saw the woman stumble. She looked down, stopping in the midst of the dancers as if disconnected from the charge that kept them all moving. She lifted her head and looked around, startled by her sudden lack of equilibrium. A confused look came over her face as she glanced down again to try and fathom out why the floor was moving.

The club was cavernous with large areas of semi-darkness broken up with pools of colour. The bar area and its occupants were bathed with a greenish light. The low tables and tub chairs were lit from above with lamps that cast a red glow, and the crowded dance floor was illuminated by the changing colours of the disco lights as dancers gyrated to the music. A haze of smoke from cigarettes and joints drifted up from the darker corners, and the place reeked of mingling perfumes, pungent and sweet, and the sweaty smell of the unwashed and the unclean.

The lone woman had not moved, though she was now swaying slightly, a static figure in the midst of wild delirium, her halo of tangled, bleached hair framing a white face, her eyes mere black shadows. She looked scared. Lost.

"It's beginning to take effect," he spoke quietly into his mobile. "She's disorientated already and it's going to get worse. No-one cares and if they notice, they'll think her drunk." The club was swamped with a deluge of noise as the revellers enjoyed their temporary escape from the reality of the harsh world outside. Ross, silently observing his victim from a dim recess, despised them all.

Kate was dizzy. Euphoria and balance had both deserted her, and she tried to focus on a way to extricate herself from the pack encircling her. When a gap opened she staggered off the floor and, after smiling giddily at a couple sitting at their table near the dance floor, she looked across to the corner of the room. Karl was still sitting there, with his legs sprawled out in front of him, his watchful eyes mere slits in the gloom, and his shiny head catching glints from the strobe lights. His lean body, bony face and shaven head both attracted and repelled her. Sometimes she was unwilling to do the things he made her do, but she ached for his approval and needed the protection she gained from being Karl's woman.

Kate paused on her way to him and, leaning against a metal pillar, pushed her matted hair back. She felt muzzy and tried to steady herself so Karl would not think she was drunk. She wanted to be beautiful for him and avoid making him ashamed of her. She was often uneasy about his commitment to her, but drink helped to drown her worries and help her cope with his unkind remarks and her feeling of being excluded from Karl's inner circle of friends. She often felt despised by them.

Luckily she had her own friends – she could see Layla, in a red cropped top over her narrow jeans, sitting at a table with others, her pad and pencil in hand so she could entertain with her cartoon sketches of them. Standing at the bar was Josh, leaning aggressively towards another man, with whom he would soon pick an argument and swing a punch. Josh's quick temper aroused by alcohol was legendary, but when sober he was amusing and not unkind. Unlike many of her group, he still had work as a porter in a hotel. It was a nowhere job but it was better than Layla's occupation.

Needing a cigarette, Kate pulled a crumpled packet from her pocket. Unable to quell her rising panic, her fingers felt numb as she worked the lighter. She took a drag and exhaled, closing her eyes. Karl would look after her. He loved her. She was grateful for the advice he gave her about her investments.

Karl caught sight of Kate as she smoked and tried to dispel her dizziness. He felt a savage delight that she had signed up that day. He had given her a good time and pretended she was special to him. That afternoon she had placed her funds in his control. At last. She had asked him to come to the club with her friends this evening and he'd gone along with her – she had a good body and was a good lay – but there had been, and would be, many others.

He turned to another man in the shadows beside him and they laughed at Kate, myopically weaving her way across the club to them.

"The fool relies on me and says she loves me," he said. He had refused to dance with her and, disappointed, she had gone to the floor alone. *And alone is where she'll end up,* he thought. He didn't care – he had her money – a return on the investment of his time and ingenuity. During the day she had asked about the investments he proposed. He was evasive and plausible – persuasion was his stock in trade. Now he would no longer have to play the smooth-tongued advisor. He would take the funds out of the account tomorrow and disappear. She would lose everything but her future no longer bothered him. No doubt she would find another lover – she was pretty enough. It was time to move on – his scams might start to catch up on him. There were many other European cities to live in and many other fools to fleece! So long as he managed to evade Ator.

"I slipped the stuff into her glass half an hour ago," his companion said. "She'll soon pass out."

"I'll leave," said Karl, "and you can pick up the pieces."

He smiled at Kate as she approached their table, his lips curving into a simulation of pleasure. The other man melted away. Kate sat down beside him and tried to focus on his face. Karl put his glass down sharply on the sticky table beside her empty glass and placed his hand on her wrist, grasping her bare arm possessively. On this occasion he would not slide his hand along to her elbow and suggest in a low voice that they leave together. Instead he slowly uncurled himself from the dusty seat, removed his hand and stood up, wiping his palm on his jeans and looking down at her with a cold expression.

"Karl, where are you going?" she asked, confused by his behaviour. She was slurring her words.

"Too bad but I have to leave, Kat," he drawled without any pretence of regret. "I have business to transact and won't get back tonight."

"Don't leave me here alone." The woman wanted reassurance – she was pathetic. "I'll come with you."

"No way. This is something I do on my own. You know the rules, Kat. No interference and all will be OK. Ross is here and will see you safely to the flat." Ross was Karl's new recruit who was reliable and always available to do the odd little job which his boss found too dull or distasteful. Kate had not met him though Ross knew what she looked like. The flat was a modern apartment with one bedroom, which Kate thought Karl owned, but which in fact he rented and to which he had no intention of returning after that night. Karl knew that the rent was paid until the end of the week, and he reflected with some pleasure that the landlord was a hard man who never extended even a day without payment. Kate had no money left. She'd managed to unload a lot of her inheritance from her dead papa before they'd met and he would now relieve her of the rest. She had trusted him in a world where it was sensible to trust nobody. Karl was a man who never expected affection and never gave any. He did not bother to conceal his contempt for this creature he had ruined.

Karl gave Kate one last measured look to satisfy himself that she would be unable to follow and walked off without looking back.

From the bedside clock Ross could see it was 3.20 am. He stared down at the inert body of the woman on the unmade bed. She was a pretty girl even with her tangled hair, dark mascara-smudged eyes and puffy face – and she had a good body. He stared at her full breasts in the slinky top and ran a gloved finger down her leg, noting that there was a jagged tear in her tights and a purplish graze showing through the ruptured black nylon – sustained where he had caught her on the edge of the car door. The bruise would be the least of her worries. She was on the way down. Leaving her with one pale arm hanging over the edge of the mattress, he turned away and began to look round the untidy room.

There was a large cupboard with the doors open and disarrayed clothing inside. The dressing table had a single smeared mirror and a clutter of pots and jars on its top surface. He pulled open a couple of drawers, crammed with cosmetics, and in a third he found a collection of papers, which he riffled though. Pocketing some money he found tucked into an envelope, he paused when he saw a couple of letters, which were signed 'Daddy'. Karl had told him that she had no family. Someone was telling lies round here, but then few people he met these days told the truth. Like him they were either concealing information or spreading misinformation.

Rapidly reading one of the letters, he snorted derision and then glanced at the figure on the bed. But Kate was oblivious to his presence. There seemed to be a brother too, but they lived in a different country. It was evident that the father was worried about her. With some cause! He pushed the letters into his jacket pocket.

Moving silently through the flat, he could see that the desk in the living room was clear and he checked that none of Karl's other belongings had been left behind. Karl had effected his departure swiftly whilst Ross waited at the club for an hour, as instructed, to ensure Kate's passive 'compliance', before transporting her back to a flat which would soon cease to be her home.

Ross had been here only once before, to collect his boss and drive him to an appointment, and Kate had not been present. The place had sleek functional furniture and no frills, though the girl, after moving in, had tried to make a bit of a home of it by hanging up a couple of framed art posters, putting a large blue pottery bowl on the table and throwing some colourful cushions on the grey sofa.

The mobile in his pocket emitted a muffled summons and he answered it without saying anything.

He heard Karl's voice say cautiously, "Ross, is that you?"

"Yeah. I'm at your flat. Kat's unconscious on the bed. She passed out at the club – as you said she would – and I brought her back here. Job done."

"Good. Get the key to the place out of her bag and take her credit cards and mobile, and bring them to me here together with the key I gave you. I'm at the hotel I told you about – in room number 314. I'm finishing a bit of work and then I'm off on a business trip. Get over here in an hour and then drive me to the airport for a 7 am flight."

Ross could visualize his new boss, sitting in the featureless room, tapping at his laptop, working with cool concentration, just as if he had woken up from a good night's sleep and hadn't spent the last four hours at a club. The man was clever, resourceful and ruthless. Ross had hoped to learn more about the man's business affairs but Karl was about to jump ship and terminate their association. He would abandon Kate, having fleeced her, and move on to pastures new.

"Right. I'll do that. See you shortly."

"At 4.30. Not before." Karl cut the connection.

Ross looked thoughtful as he slid his mobile into his hip pocket. The fact that he never drank alcohol in any form and functioned efficiently at any time of the day or night made him useful. He would find other work with those who appreciated his talent for discretion, his unmemorable features and his ability to speak a number of languages. His quiet efficiency masked his self-interest. His loyalty to those who employed him was provisional on their usefulness to his game plan.

Karl's departure would be of interest to Ator, whose long arms of power and influence stretched to encircle those he wished to control. It was almost impossible to elude his attention – and disloyalty was never tolerated. Going away would merely buy time and Karl, clever as he was, would not be able to escape that easily.

He picked up Kate's bag, which he had brought back from the club with her, and his gloved hands explored the contents, extracting the items Karl had mentioned, including her wallet, which he would be allowed to keep. He left her passport, surprised that Karl had not told him to get rid of it. Now he would deal with the girl.

He went through to the bedroom and pulled the pillow out from under her head. He bent over and turned her on to her side so that her face was not pushed into the dented pillow and he could hear her breathing. It would be so easy to suffocate her but that was not in his instructions. His eyes fastened on an unusual ring on the finger of her dangling hand. He knelt down to look at the stone in its gold setting and then tugged at it. It was tight and her knuckle was in the way. He gave a brutal pull and Kate gave a low moan as the finger bone snapped. Wrenching the ring off, he held the jewel up to the light to examine it whilst Kate's plundered hand flopped down and became still again.

With her keys, mobile phone, cards and ring in his pocket, Ross left the apartment and silently shut the door behind him.

Kate groaned and opened her sticky eyelids. Her head felt thick and ached horribly and her hand was hot and painful. The blind was up and the hard afternoon light, slanting across the room, hurt her eyes. She tried to focus on her hand and, when she moved it, gave a gasp of pain. Her finger was swollen and in agony. She suddenly felt sick, and lurching from the bed to the bathroom, holding her injured hand to her chest, she vomited convulsively. Afterwards she slithered to the floor and sat there, stunned, trying to recall what had happened the night before.

An hour later, having drunk some water and splashed her face, she was sitting miserably on a chair trying to quell the bouts of nausea and get a cup of coffee down. Still cradling her painful hand, she wondered why she had such a pounding headache. There had been binges before – probably too many – but she had never felt as bad as this. What had she been drinking? At the club they had celebrated the conclusion of a business transaction involving the investment of her capital. She remembered Karl had left her at the club and said that someone would take her back to the flat

Why had Karl not reappeared? He often went out at night but was always back around dawn. She looked around and for the first time noticed that all his things had gone. She got to her feet and, wincing as her thigh brushed the edge of the table, saw the ugly black bruise on her leg. She went over to the desk and registered that its surface was cleared – the laptop was gone together with the files, including the buff folder which contained her share certificates, the signed deed and bank information. Pulling the drawers open with her left hand, she found them all empty. There must be a reason – perhaps Karl had needed them at the office.

She stumbled into the bedroom and tore open the cupboard door. All his clothes and shoes had gone too. He had not said he was going away – surely he wouldn't abandon her! In a panic, she picked up her bag from the carpet and fumbled for her mobile. When she couldn't find it, she ran back into the living area and, dumping the contents on the desk, frantically searched through them. It was not there. Someone at the night club must have stolen it.

Clammy fears washed over her. She decided to take a taxi to the hotel which Karl had been using as an office for the past month. He made a habit of using hotel rooms as offices – they were conveniently vacated when cities or circumstances changed. Karl discouraged her from coming to where he worked, so she had not been to the most recent 'office' but she had heard the name of the hotel mentioned and had noted it down on the calendar. Narrowing her eyes, she focussed on the scrawled name, cursing the fact that she'd never found her lost glasses.

Still dressed in the clothes she had worn the night before, unable to change her black skirt and shredded tights because her hand was hurting too much, and puzzled as to how she had sustained such a large bruise on her leg and the injury to her finger, she threw a coat over her shoulders. With one clumsy hand she scooped the contents into her bag again and stumbled out of the flat. The door clicked shut behind her.

Her mind felt soggy and her thudding head and throbbing finger were hampering her progress but she managed to get downstairs and let herself out of the front door into a wintry afternoon. After a while she managed to flag down a taxi, told him the name of the hotel and awkwardly climbed inside, trying to shield her finger from contact with anything. Slumping down, she closed her eyes and didn't open them until twenty minutes later, when the taxi stopped.

The taxi-driver said something which Kate didn't understand but saw they had arrived at the hotel. He looked at his distressed passenger with some concern as he pointed at the meter.

Kate fumbled in her bag with one hand for money to pay him and realised with horror than her wallet was missing. Nor could she locate her credit cards – she had no money on her.

"Could you wait for a few minutes? I'll go in and ask for my friend to come down," she pleaded. The taxi driver nodded and switched off the engine. Kate got out and glancing up at the glass and concrete monster, went into its soulless entrance lobby and across to the gleaming reception desk where an elegantly suited woman with perfect make-up and arched eyebrows observed the dishevelled creature in front of her.

Taking a calming breath, Kate mentioned Karl's name and asked the receptionist if she would ring and ask him to come down. The woman calmly consulted the screen in front of her and then, giving the agitated young woman a cool stare, informed her that their client had checked out of the hotel.

"Surely not," Kate protested. "You must be mistaken. He uses the room as an office and has done for over a month."

"I assure you that he left early this morning and has not indicated that he will be returning. The room has been cleaned and now has another occupant."

Kate turned away with a cry of distress and stood in the centre of the lobby, shaking with indecision, her finger throbbing with pain.

"Are you alright, miss?" This time the question came from the hall porter. "Do you need help?"

What Kate needed was a friend and, with a surge of relief, she remembered Layla. She shook her head and went out, cradling her injured hand.

The taxi was still there. Trying to sound calm, she told the driver that she would now like to go to a different address. He helped her inside and then drove her on. She was so grateful for his patience and unspoken sympathy. *Please, Layla, be there for me*, she mouthed silently. She had no money and no one else to turn to.

She had conveniently erased the existence of a father and a brother. And now she ached with her need of the only people who might still care about her. She wondered if her father was still searching for her and knew that if he had turned his back on her, she fully deserved it. She had a sour taste in her mouth and bitter regret in her heart.

Layla opened the door wearing a purple dressing gown, her dark hair tied up with a saffron coloured scarf. "What the hell has happened to you?" she asked, but when Kate started sobbing she paid off the curious taxi driver, thanked him and helped her friend inside. Layla's rented house, which she shared with Josh, was chilly, untidy and full of colour. Layla had painted artistic murals on the walls, even though at the previous flat she had done the same with felt-tipped pens and been thrown out by the irate landlord when he discovered them.

Before asking any questions she put Kate's hand into a sling made with her scarf and took her off to see the local doctor whose surgery was a few minutes' walk away. He announced the finger broken and strapped it up firmly, giving his patient something to reduce the pain. Kate was submissive as Layla paid the doctor, took her friend back to the flat and put her into her own bed.

Kate, unused to female solidarity and touched by Layla's kindness, finally gave in to utter despair and her tears came. Karl had left her. For weeks she had suppressed her suspicion that his interest in her was waning or, even worse, simulated. Now she had to face the truth – he had gone. She rolled on her side facing the wall, turning her back on the harsh world.

Layla let her howl into the pillow for a while, and finally decided it was time for some home truths. She went through to the kitchen, made two cups of mint tea, and returned to the bedroom.

"Kat, calm down. Drink this." Layla seated herself on the end of the bed and drank her tea thoughtfully, looking at her friend who, having ignored the tea, was now lying on her back, staring at the ceiling in utter misery, her cheeks shiny with dried tears.

Layla put down her cup with a decisive clink. "Let's talk," she said leaning forward. "Kat, you and I have rollicked around together ever since you poled up in this mad city, with your inheritance burning a hole in your pocket. You know the scene now." She paused but there was no response. "You've had men like Karl before, who can spot a honeypot from afar and take advantage of her. You pay – with money or sexual favours – and they give you their protection in this dangerous world before deserting you. You told me that Karl's the latest in a succession of faithless men."

"Why do they always leave? Why do the men I meet have no love? No loyalty." Kate's pale face was a mask of despair, her voice whining with self-pity.

"Wake up, kid," said Layla, patting Kate's feet. "Face up to the situation. Karl's dumped you. Accept it."

Kate didn't want to accept Layla's bleak view of life. "All men can't be like that. There have to be some good guys around. But I never meet them."

"You won't meet them in this twilight world. It's too dark for nice people. Anyway, you'd probably find them boring. Good people are dull – they avoid danger and darkness. They spoil things by switching on searchlights and showing all of us up for what we really are. I don't like harsh lights, guilt trips or being made to feel dirty. Keep me away from do-gooders." Layla put out a hand to ward off unwanted intrusions that might undermine her resilience.

"So I'm on my own again." Kate looked anxious.

"You've got me," Layla said with mock reproach. "And I paid the doctor!"

Kate glanced up gratefully. "Yes, you did. But I've got nothing to repay you with. I've lost so much."

"Let's hope that includes your illusions!" said Layla as she got to her feet. "You can't have many more to lose!" Kate started to sob again. "Cheer up. I'll find out the full picture – maybe it's not as bad as you think." Though Layla knew that it was worse. Karl had a reputation for being a ruthless con-man.

"He's also taken my mobile, credit cards and the bank documents. He persuaded me to transfer the rest of my money into some investments."

Layla saw that Kate was becoming aware of the extent of the damage. "Trust and Karl don't go together," she said drily. "You're a gullible idiot. He'll have swindled you out of it."

Kate moaned, "I thought he loved me."

Layla cut in quickly. "No you didn't think that. You know he's incapable of love. You didn't love him either. You needed protection and admiration. What he wanted from you was sex and money."

"He cheated and robbed me," Kate said angrily.

"Anger's good, better than self-pity," Layla said with a grin. "Stop seeing yourself as a victim. When we first met you had a reputation of being gutsy. You seemed to have lots of money and we were all happy to help you spend it. We had fun. Like the rest of us you probably told a pack of lies about your past but we accepted you."

Kate kept silent and looked down at her bandaged hand. Layla remembered her telling them that she was an orphan.

"I don't know why yesterday evening seems so hazy." Kate put a hand to her matted hair. "I feel dreadful."

"You *look* dreadful. If you can't remember what happened, Karl probably spiked your drink – he's been known to do that. It gave him time to take your money and run. I'll get Josh to find out if he's still in town."

Kate gave a low, desolate moan. She sagged back against the pillows. Her skin looked pale and waxy against the grimy purple bed linen. She whispered, "Maybe he hasn't gone and there'll be an explanation."

"Better get some sleep." Layla bent down and gave the pallid girl a kiss on the forehead. "You stink. When you wake up, take a bath."

Leaving the bedroom, Layla went into the sitting room and telephoned Josh, putting him quickly in the picture. "We saw it coming and tried to warn her. See if you can find out if Karl has left town."

"I'll also check out the flat they shared," said Josh. "How's Kat?"

"Her finger's broken but that's the least of her problems."

"I'll call by later," said Josh and rang off.

Layla smiled as she put down the phone, looking at a cartoon drawing she had made of Josh on the wall opposite. They had known each other for years and she knew she could rely on him. Their relationship was close but not physical. He wasn't her pimp and he wasn't her lover. She didn't do lovers in her line of work. They enjoyed each other's company and laughed and partied together. But on a deeper level they were allies – friends who gave each other support. Josh offered Layla some degree of protection without any obligation and was happy to act as escort or messenger. Layla offered Josh uncomplicated sisterly companionship without jealous demands, a domestic haven and the occasional alibi. Josh was a professional thief of considerable skill and Layla a discreet and highly paid call-girl.

Layla went into the bathroom and began to apply make-up. She had two 'clients' that evening and wondered what they saw in her face. Looking at her reflection in the mirror, she saw her features were still beautiful but there was a hint of desperation in her eyes that no amount of mascara could hide. She often felt trapped, but Josh – her confidante, her partner in crime, her brother in damnation – kept her sane with his buoyant grin and buccaneer insouciance. She drew eyeliner along her eyelids with a practised hand. It was sad that the only thing she painted these days was her face. She picked up her lipstick, applied it thickly and pouted at herself. With her mask back in place, she was ready to face the world.

As she dressed she wondered if Josh would be able to track down Karl. She hoped he wouldn't stop at Caz's Bar and get deflected by drink. Sober, he was reliable and remarkably effective. He never drank when he was working and so he was rarely caught. He'd learned his lesson after a couple of spells in prison in other countries. He always moved on, as she did, when things got difficult or dull. Josh's problem was that in his cups he lost his balance and his temper. He became aggressive and this got him into more trouble than his thieving. His physical and mental scars were the result of brawls rather than punishment. Layla knew to avoid Josh when he'd been drinking. "Please, Josh, not today," she pleaded silently.

When Josh arrived, having made no detour to any bar, much to Layla's relief, he told her that a few enquiries 'on the grapevine' had indeed confirmed that Karl had left the country. "This time Kat's not telling lies. He's picked her clean. There's no hope of her retrieving anything. Karl's clever and covers his tracks well. Our little heiress is now skint and alone in the world."

"She's not alone – she's got us," Layla said quietly.

"For the time being. But she'll have to learn how to survive on her own. I've got itchy feet and I don't want be hampered by someone who's not only short-sighted but short of resources. It's a hard life and we don't need extra burdens."

"Kat's a friend, not a burden – and we've lived off her for months!" protested Layla.

"So I'm prepared to carry her for a while. But I'm practical and I don't need extra baggage." He grinned. "You're quite enough."

Layla laughed and smacked him on the arm. "Let's go and break the news to her! I suspect it won't come as a surprise."

Kate was awake. "Hi doll," Josh said to her. "As we thought, Karl has done a runner and cleaned you out. I had to use an unorthodox method to gain entry – but the place is deserted and all traces of him have disappeared."

"So I'm penniless," Kate said in a small voice, looking down at her hands. "I can't even sell my ring, because it's gone missing from my finger."

"With no rent coming in, it won't be long before the landlord repossesses and sells anything left behind to defray lost rent. So I grabbed as many of your clothes and shoes as I could and brought them back with me." Josh dropped a large bin liner on to the bed and gave her an encouraging smile. "I also removed the television and sound system from the flat. Thieving's my trade and I never let a good opportunity slip."

Kate looked at the plastic bag with dismay, all of them realising that this pathetic bundle was all she now possessed in the world. "It seems I'm homeless too."

"You'll have to be like the rest of us – and live by your wits." Layla's voice sounded brittle. "You can stay here for a while, till you find yourself a job. I don't advise embarking on my kind of work – you're not tough enough – even if the money's good. I expect there's bar or waitressing work you could do though it's lousily paid. You won't be able to buy yourself so many clothes or eat such good food but you'll probably manage."

As she listened to this, Kate realised she had to face up to a grim future. "I used to love giving money to people who had none, but now it's all gone I must learn to live without." She was disgusted with herself. The past three years in Europe seemed hollow and heartless, a reckless waster of her time and talents. She closed her mind to the image of home where life had been simple and love had existed, knowing she had lost the key to it, along with her father's letters. She could never go back.

Kate shook her head to free herself from such painful introspection, sat upright and turned to her friends who were watching her. They were sympathetic now but their patience would not be unlimited. Having lost her innocence and her illusions, she was adrift in a cruel, loveless world. In a measured voice she said, "I'm OK now. I accept the situation and I'll manage. Thanks for your help – you've been straight with me."

She saw Josh, leaning against the door jamb, dart a glance at Lyla and then give her a thumbs up to show he was aware she had turned the corner and come to terms with her changed situation.

"That's more like the Kat I know," he drawled, a crooked half-smile on his lips. "Welcome back, kid."

"I'm lucky to have friends like you," said Kate, unsure if she could trust them. She looked at Layla who was sitting in an upright chair near the small window. Her face, in spite of her heavy make-up, was remarkably beautiful, its oval shape accentuated by her abundant hair tied up in an untidy knot on top of her head. Seeing Kate's appraising glance, Layla raised her eyebrows and gave an encouraging smile. "You've never told me why you live in this city," Kate asked, to change the subject. "It's so far from where you come from."

"That is precisely why I am here." Layla's tone was lightly ironic. "I'd hate to run into anyone I used to know when I was a pure young thing. What a ghastly surprise it would be for them. It's useful living where you don't understand much of the language. I can ignore what I don't want to hear: criticism and disapproval. It blurs the truth when you're never quite sure what people are saying. That suits me. When you're down and living on dregs – or drugs, as we are – it's better if you don't listen to people telling you how low you've fallen. You're a fool, Kat. You could have stayed on top if you'd been smarter and less gullible."

"I may have hit rock bottom but at least I've never sold myself," Kate was stung into saying, but she regretted the words as soon as they were uttered.

"Hey," said Josh with mock admiration, "she's made a quick comeback to the lass we know and love – the one with the biting repartee and the barbed comment!"

"OK, sunshine." Layla's voice cut across the room. "So here are some home truths. I may have come from the gutter whilst you had a cosy childhood cushioned by wealth, but now we're level. The difference is that I'm smart and you're stupid. You did crazy things like giving that fat gold bracelet to a stinking tramp on the bridge."

"He needed it then more than me," muttered Kate, remembering her joy and the man's astonished face. She recalled how good it had felt to crouch down so her face was level with his and to put the gift into his grimy hand. To show him that she cared that he had nowhere to put his head at night, whilst she was sleeping on silk sheets and plump pillows. She had wanted to give him something of value – her sympathy as well as her jewellery.

Layla pointed a scarlet fingernail at her sister in crime. "You may not be peddling your body but you certainly parted with your assets – you're no better than me."

"You're right. I'm so sorry, Layla," Kate wailed. "I didn't mean to insult you. You're the only friend I've got. Karl's left me and I feel used and dirty."

"You certainly need a wash," said Layla crisply. "Take a bath – but hold your hand out of the water. I'll help you out of those wrecked clothes. Josh, take yourself off – have a drink and we'll see you shortly."

Obediently Kate climbed out of bed. Josh, saying he was hungry and needed to eat, left the room.

Whilst helping her friend undress, Layla whistled, "How on earth did you get that ugly bruise? When you're clean you can borrow a pair of my jeans – the pink ones you bought me – we can all go out for a drink to drown your sorrows. After that I have a couple of clients to go and see. If I drink enough, I might be able to ignore what they look like and what they want." She gave a harsh laugh, "I ought to be short-sighted like you. My life would be better lived out of focus."

Kate quietly put her hand on Layla's arm. "Thank you, Layla. One day I'll do the same for you."

2

"I'm off to the hospital – I think it's broken and there's quite a bit of bleeding." David told his father.

"What can I do to help?" Theo asked.

"There a delivery of tiles due between 5 and 6 pm. The contractors will have left by then and I won't get back in time. Can you possibly get over here, meet the lorry and ensure they unload them in the compound?" David sounded as if he was in a hurry.

"No problem. I'll be there," Theo reassured him. "Get Andrew to a doctor as soon as possible. See you later."

The call ended and glancing at the clock, Theo turned to his visitor. "That was David, down at Homeward House."

"Has there been an accident?"

"Not to my son. A young man called Andrew has had a blow to his face."

"Was he in a fight?"

"Nothing like that, Francis," Theo laughed. "He never gets angry. He's the architect for the new wing at the hotel. He was near the scaffolding and one of the workmen erecting it accidentally clouted his face with a scaffold pole. David thinks he's broken his nose. There's lots of blood. He's taking Andrew to hospital and wants me to be there in half an hour to await a delivery."

"I must be off then." The man put on his suit jacket.

"No need to hurry – it's only five minutes down the hill."

"It must be quite disruptive living at the house whilst the new wing is being built," Francis said as he picked up some papers from the table and placed them in his briefcase.

"It's not too bad – I escape up here to my studio during the day."

Francis looked around at the old stone barn, with its south-facing doors converted into a huge window overlooking the valley below. "Marvellous view."

"Much better than my old workroom, which was demolished when work started on the new wing. David felt quite guilty about my having to move everything out, but now that I've been here a few months I'm very content and find this quiet hill very conducive to creation."

Frances took a final look at the large sculpture at the other end of the barn. "You've nearly finished it, Theo. It's magnificent." He snapped the briefcase shut and put his glasses neatly into their case. "Thanks so much for listening to my concerns about the bank and the borrowing. I do worry occasionally that David's enthusiasm for his new project blinds him to the stern reality about

19

the financial side of things. He's borrowed a lot of money and there's nothing coming in with the hotel closed during the building work. I worry because the house – your home – is held by the bank as security for the loan."

Theo looked at his old friend with affection and thought how lucky the business was to have him as their accountant. He was nearing retirement from a firm in town but worked assiduously and gave his clients wise advice. The bank had requested for the deeds to the property to be lodged with them as part of the loan agreement. Frances had come to see Theo because, though David ran the business, he lived in the house and on the land which was held in trust for his son.

"Don't be too worried, Francis. David has an ambition to run a larger hotel and will work hard to achieve it. I'll keep an eye on the project and the costs. Andrew tells us that we're running to budget, though there may be some overspend later on. He's talented and professional even though he's newly qualified. Let's hope his nose isn't broken."

"I did carefully suggest to David," Francis persisted, "that he might consider selling off some of the land that is not required for the hotel grounds, to raise funds. But he wouldn't hear of it."

"He loves the fields and water meadows and would feel he was a failure if he had to sell them. But thank you, Francis, for your advice."

After Francis had left, Theo stood still in the centre of his barn. He was not alone. The stallion he had created stood immobile, his massive body poised to move forward, one leg lifted from the ground, his head alert and his muscles gleaming through his flanks. With larger pieces the sculptor worked in clay, and the brown surface glistened wetly. Over many months his horse had become a companion. It would soon be finished, and later, when it was dry, he would send it to his foundry for casting into bronze.

His children were also with him. There were two finished sculptures on the oak chest in which he stored his drawings. He had made them six years before and had had them cast into bronze. Unique – and not for sale – they were portrait heads of his son and daughter; David had been twenty-one and Kate eighteen – a time when they had all been living together. Sadly they were not together now and hadn't been for almost three years. He had no idea where Kate was – somewhere out there in the world unwilling, or unable, to communicate with her father or brother. He wondered why.

He walked over to the window and gazed out. The simple stone building stood at the top of the lower slope of a hill, with dense trees above and behind, with the fields extending below. He could make out their family house that had become a hotel, and his eyes followed the river as it passed through some woodland and flowed towards the town – a little further off to the east. Beyond and around the valley were the hills, their purple contours familiar as the faces of old friends. It was a peaceful scene but as Theo was well aware, the sad reality was that even in this beautiful part of Britain there were people who were not at peace with themselves or the world they lived in.

His daughter had always been restless, unable to appreciate the fields they owned and always seeking greener pastures. His son was diligent and ambitious but was never satisfied with what he had achieved and always wanting to do more.

He glanced at his watch, picked up a jacket and left the barn. David needed him back at home – and it was rare that his son asked for help.

Later that evening, David drove Andrew from the hospital to his flat and dropped him off.

Andrew's bandaged face made him look like the victim of a mugging. "I hope my neighbours don't think I've been in a fight."

"Worried that your professional image might get tarnished?" David helped him out of the car. "Do you want a hand inside?"

"I'll be fine. I have a dreadful headache and I'll just crash out."

"Don't crash on to your face. It might hurt."

"It already does. A lot." Andrew tried to grin and winced in pain. Noticing this, David patted him gently on the shoulder. They had been friends since college days and always looked out for each other.

"Are you sure you'll be alright on your own?" David asked, looking concerned. "The nurses say the bruising will be considerable by the morning. With black eyes, broken nose and stitches in your cheek, you're going to be no oil painting."

"In that case, nothing changes." Andrew always regarded himself as an ugly man – his large nose was crooked and now it had been broken it might be worse. His round face had to contend with freckles and glasses, and he was slightly overweight. He hoped good manners and hard work would divert attention from his unpromising features and they had won him respect and friendship. But he saw that women did not find him attractive. It was David who got their attention.

He looked at his friend and wondered, not for the first time, how it was that David was so completely unaware of his physical impact on others. He was a tall man with a habit of standing stiffly upright but with a controlled effort as if he was itching to move off. His thick, midnight black hair was a strange contrast to his milky pale skin and startling blue eyes.

Andrew located his key and let himself into the entrance door. "Thanks for the lift – sorry to cause you so much trouble. You've been so kind."

"No problem. I'll ring you tomorrow. Don't even think about coming on site."

Standing in the open doorway, Andrew watched his friend walk back to his car. There was with a distinctive springiness to his walking which betrayed his compressed energy. He gave a wave as David drove off, then turned and went inside. His face radiated pain.

Some weeks later, Theo returned home early from working in his studio to meet Olga, who had been interviewed by David for the post of duty manager and who would, while the hotel was closed, assist in getting everything ready for its re-opening. She was a tall, neatly-dressed woman with clear, grey eyes and a calm manner. David had said she was experienced, astute and perfect for the job, but wanted Theo's approbation before he finally took her on. After they had chatted for a while, Theo realised that Olga would be ideal – a vital support to his overworked son.

"My son finds delegating difficult and you may have to persuade him to let you take over some of the tasks and responsibilities. He is ambitious to succeed and create a bigger, better hotel – and he really needs help."

"I expect I'd be able to manage that alright. I would love the job."

"Has David told you about our family?"

Olga smiled. "Not a lot. He's quite reticent."

"Let me fill you in. Since childhood, David has had a real affinity with this house and the land. He has always had a dream to live and work here and to run it as a hotel. Do you know he has a sister, Kate?"

Olga was surprised. "He's not mentioned her. Where does she live?"

"Kate's been overseas for about two and a half years." He didn't say they had no idea where she was nor how much he missed her. "Some years back, the house and family chattels were placed into a trust for the two children, which meant that at twenty-one everything came in their ownership. When she turned twenty-one, my daughter wanted to take her share of the family wealth to go travelling and then to set up her own business. I gently tried to dissuade her but she was adamant. It was her choice, so we acceded. In order to raise the capital to buy her out, a huge mortgage was taken out on the house and the plan to convert it into a hotel was put on hold. Kate took the money and left home."

"That must have been hard."

"It was – for David who had finished his studies in hotel management but had to defer the hotel project whilst he got work, gained experience and saved to pay off the debt. He spent two years in a junior management role in a large modern city hotel. The time came when the deferred hotel project could proceed." Theo chose not to mention that it was proceeds from the sale of his sculptures that raised the funds to repay the mortgage and get the plan back on track, nor that David had gone to the banks and obtained a large loan to convert the old house and transform it into a viable hotel.

"The hotel opened with only eight bedrooms," Theo continued. "It soon became apparent that we needed to enlarge it, and we decided to use a young architect who had been at university with David and was working at an architect's practice in the town. Andrew was grateful to be given such a prestigious job. His design for a new wing to provide more bedrooms and a new kitchen is both imaginative and practical."

"David has told me that construction has been enabled by a loan from the bank. He tells me it's going to be hard work to get the hotel into profit, but also challenging and exciting. His enthusiasm is catching! I'd love to be involved."

"Welcome aboard." Theo put out his hand to shake hers.

"I look forward to it," Olga said, putting her small hand in his massive one and smiling into his deep blue eyes.

Theo put down his tools and stood back to look at his sculpture. He had been working on it for some time and it was now finished. It would be expensive to cast into bronze but he knew it would sell. He decided to declare an edition of three and instruct his agent to offer the first for sale. He gave one last pensive look at the huge animal then turned away, wiping his palette knife on his overall. He walked over to a long workbench where he proceeded to clear away his tools, wash them in the adjacent sink and place them in order along the surface. He felt satisfied, elated and calm all at once, as he always did when he completed a piece.

He had been a sculptor for many years but had been involved in other activities too. Although he lived in the country, his work was widely known, and for years his agent in the city had been selling his bronzes to clients in many countries.

The telephone rang in the studio and Theo strode across to answer. It was David.

"Hi Theo." His son had for a long time called him Theo. "I've had a strange telephone call and want to tell you about it. Perhaps we could meet up for lunch?" This happened rarely since Theo had relocated his studio and David often took no break.

"I've finished the horse," said Theo, "as I'd expected to do today. So I'll walk down and join you – in about half an hour?"

"I have a better idea. Why don't I get some sandwiches and a couple of beers, and I'll drive up and join you in the studio? Then I can see the sculpture and tell you about my call."

"Good plan, David. See you soon." Theo put the phone down, poured himself a glass of water and then walked over to the window, wondering what it was that had upset his son.

He looked across at the far hills, purple and green below leaden-grey clouds. Rain began to sweep across the valley and envelop parts of it in mist. A heavy shower passed over the fields below with the farmhouse and outbuildings and then the river which snaked its way across the meadow and reached Homeward House. The men on the scaffolding would get wet.

As he was watching, a pale blue car left the hotel, and he saw it move along the main road to the turn-off for the track which wound its way up the hill to his studio. David was on his way. Theo had an intimation of what David might be going to tell him. Whilst he waited he looked at his sculpture. The horse, immobile but alert, stared back as if he too could hear the crunch of tyres on the dirt track and the silence when the engine was cut. The car door banged, and a few seconds later David opened the large wooden door and came in.

Theo stood smiling as David, dressed in a well-cut suit he usually wore as proprietor of a hotel, came towards him and placed a carrier bag on the floor, before giving his father a brief hug. His son, now twenty-seven, always looked older than his years. Normally restive, today he looked tired and anxious.

"Hello, David. What's up?"

"Hi, Theo. I've had a strange telephone call from a guy called Jakob. He says he has some unpleasant news for us."

"Is it personal or business?" asked Theo. "Or could it be about Kate?"

"Of course it's about bloody Kate!" said David in exasperation. "Any bad news we get is always about Kate."

"Is she alright?" Theo looked intently into his son's face.

"It seems she's alive."

"Is she ill? Injured?" The pain he felt was reflected in his son's eyes.

"He didn't say. I got the impression the problem isn't to do with health."

Theo leaned forward and put a hand on his son's arm. "David, tell me, is she coming home?"

"That indeed would be bad news as far as I'm concerned." Theo winced so David continued in a softer tone. "I don't know. Jakob has news of her but wants to come and tell us in person. She's obviously in trouble – nothing changes – and it seems she's almost destitute. I can't believe she's squandered everything."

At this point he noticed the completed sculpture that his father had been working on for so many months and broke off to have a look at it. "You've finished the stallion! Well done – it's superb. Breathtaking. One of your best."

"I've grown to like him too," Theo said following his son's gaze before returning to the worrying issue of his daughter's welfare. "Does this Jakob have a message for us from Kate?"

"He wouldn't say."

"We must meet him," Theo said firmly. "How do we make contact?"

"He didn't give me any number."

"That's a pity. Did you ask him where Kate is?"

"I did but he wouldn't say. I got the impression he thinks what he's going to tell us will shock us."

"I'm unshockable as far as Kate is concerned," said his father grimly.

"We'll just have to wait and see. He said he was travelling and he would call again later."

"Later today or later this week?"

"I don't know, Theo," said David wearily. He did not share his father's patience with his sister and her escapades. "We'll just have to wait." He picked up the bag. "How about a sandwich?"

"And a beer!"

They sat companionably side by side on the wooden bench in front of the window with their backs to the view. They were silent as they ate, facing the sculpture but focussing on something else – each mulling over a vision of Kate, earlier in their lives.

Theo was recalling his daughter's eighteenth birthday, which they had celebrated at their home with a huge summer garden party, when most of her friends had gathered together. She had been doing holiday work helping out in the primary school, where her lively sense of fun had made her a favourite with the children. Her ability to see things through the lens of a child's eyes made people feel that she was innocent and immature. But her trusting nature was one of the things Theo loved most – untouched by material concerns she never succumbed to negative thinking.

David voiced his thoughts. "I used to think of Kate as headstrong, but I envied her high spirits. We're as different as the earth and sky. I can work towards a goal but Kate has a short attention span. I remember how upset you were when she dropped out of college and never managed to hold a job down. Her only success was working with children – perhaps because she'd never truly grown up herself." He paused, recalling the last time he had seen Kate. "Do you remember the day she left?"

"As if it were yesterday," the older man sighed.

"She took only a small suitcase and a lightweight rucksack slung over her shoulder, saying she wanted to travel light."

"She looked thin and ethereal," said Theo.

"She was stubborn and selfish," said David, "and well aware of the stress and financial problems that her demand for her share of the trust fund had caused us. The moment she turned twenty-one she told us she wanted to make her own way in the world and 'find her destiny'." He swallowed the rest of his beer and added, "All she had with her was a ticket, her bag and her bravado, but she had a large sum of money stashed away in her bank. She wouldn't let us drive her to the station, and ordered a taxi. Then she was gone."

Theo said reflectively, "Kate wanted to shed the weight of our expectations. She misunderstood us. She thought we were disappointed in her and told me she needed to cut free from the emotional shackles."

"She never listened to us."

"She wanted to search for meaning and purpose. But she's encountered the wild world and lost sight of the truth." Theo sighed.

"She's well and truly lost."

"I won't give up on her." Theo stood up. "She may yet find her way home. I worry about what Jakob has to tell us but we must be patient until we hear from him again."

David looked at his watch and bounced to his feet, quivering with his habitual tense energy. "I must get back to work. I'm sorting out staffing requirements and I'm interviewing a young woman for a job in reception."

"You work too hard, David. Try to relax more." Theo's smile hid his sadness that his son never spent long with him – their priorities were very different.

"There's a lot to do," said David picking up his car keys.

"I've finished for the day, so I'll come back with you." Theo always had time for David. He put an arm around his son's shoulders and together they left the studio, switching out the lights and leaving the horse in the silent barn.

A month passed and neither of them mentioned that nothing had been heard from Jakob. One morning they were having breakfast together. Recently David had shifted them out of their large bedrooms in the old house, which had extensive views over the gardens, to use the spacious rooms as his luxury suites.

He and his father were now accommodated in comfortable though much smaller rooms in the owner's private flat at the rear of the hotel, looking out over the courtyard and the new wing opposite, still under construction. Theo missed the space and the views. He had thought of moving out and living nearby but stayed because it provided opportunity to enjoy his son's company, even though David tended to use the flat mainly for sleeping. He worked all hours, constantly taking decisions and making plans for the re-opening of the hotel, and urging on the pace of the building work and the renovation of the old family house.

The telephone rang and Theo answered.

A voice he did not recognise said abruptly, "This is Jakob here. Who are you?"

Theo felt his hackles rise but replied calmly, "I'm Theo. A few weeks ago you spoke to my son and said you had news of Kate."

"I'm in the area and can call in this afternoon. About 4 pm. I'll tell you about Kate then." He paused and Theo kept silent. "Will that be convenient?" The question came with a hint of mockery.

"Yes, of course." Theo wondered what his motives were in coming to see them and what his relationship might have been with his daughter.

Jakob rang off without another word. He had not asked for any directions. It was almost as if the man felt obliged to see them about Kate and was undertaking a task. Theo's apprehension about Kate deepened. He looked across at his son. "That was Jakob – he's coming here this afternoon."

David stirred his coffee. "I'll be here so we can see him together. This morning I'm tied up."

"How is the recruitment of staff going?" Theo asked. "Did you take on the receptionist you saw a while back?"

"No, but last week I interviewed another applicant and I've taken her on. She's intelligent, neatly dressed and has a quiet confidence. Surprisingly suitable."

"Why is that a surprise?"

"Because she's trained and worked as a district nurse."

"Why does she want to work in a hotel?"

"She's looking for something calmer and less stressful. I gather she had a rather unpleasant experience when one of the patients that she was visiting set his dog on her and she was bitten. She didn't say too much about it but I think she wants a change."

"I hope she finds working here less traumatic. But she'll need to be resourceful and resilient coping with hard-to-please guests. What's her name?"

"Maria. She'll start two weeks before the hotel opens. As it happens, she's coming here today to see Olga, who will give her a tour round and discuss her duties." He paused, recalling her calm eyes. "I think she'll fit in well."

"I look forward to meeting the young woman who's gained your approval."

David stood up. "I've got to go. See you this afternoon, Theo. I feel rather apprehensive about what Jakob's going to tell us. Let's talk to him in the library

– it's already redecorated and quiet – and I'm less likely to be interrupted than in my office."

As David left the room, Theo knew he should return to the studio and his new sculpture of a young girl reading a letter but he felt reluctant to continue work on a depiction of his daughter when he was unsure what sort of person she had become.

He had written to Kate regularly for three years but rarely got a reply. She had requested they keep in touch by letter and sent him new addresses as and when she moved. During the first year or two she had responded infrequently but her rare letters had been enthusiastic, full of details of places she had seen and the fascinating people she met. She even sent them the occasional photograph. Then there were worrying gaps and the brief communications she sent were evasive and vague. In one letter she said she was a disappointment to him and her brother. In another she admitted she'd been drawn into a way of life which she rather regretted. Theo sensed she was concealing the truth about her situation. He wrote again asking if he could come and visit her.

After a long time she replied saying she did not want her family to come looking for her, interfering in her decisions and cramping her style. Soon after that she started giving them accommodation addresses and PO box numbers. Theo thought it likely that many of his letters did not reach her. Often he was unsure which country she was in but he kept on writing to the last known address, giving her news of home and gently reminding her that he missed her and wanted so much to see her. She had no mobile and had made it clear from the start that she wouldn't call, as it might make her homesick. She had never telephoned but he didn't give up hope and he kept on writing. His new sculpture was his way to visualise her reading his letters. One day she might feel ready to come home.

Theo made himself another cup of coffee, and sat down at the table again with a sheet of writing paper. He would write to Kate, whilst waiting to meet a man who would give them news of her. He did not know where to send the letter but perhaps this Jakob might have a current address for her. He wanted to reassure his daughter that whatever she'd done, he still loved her and always would. He picked up his pen.

Theo felt instinctive mistrust. The man sauntered into the room wearing a pale linen jacket over a dark shirt. He was probably in his forties and sported a suntan and cropped hair. He had a smile lurking on his face as his eyes roamed round the room but would not meet those of the men whose hands he shook. There was shrewdness in his surface affability that made Theo wary.

David politely invited him to be seated and the man sat down in one of the comfortable library chairs, commenting, "Nice house you got here. I hear you're converting it into a hotel. Building work can be so costly, don't you agree?"

"The existing hotel is to be enlarged," said David as he too sat down. He had no wish to indulge in small talk. "So what news of Kate?"

Ignoring the burning question, the visitor said, "I'm Jakob and I'm having an extended holiday in this country and looking around for a new situation. I've discovered that the person I know of as Kat is a relative of yours."

"She might be," said Theo who had remained standing. "How do you know her?"

"I worked for a while in the same city, in a bar where she and her crowd used to meet up. They were noisy and indiscreet about their affairs. So those of us who worked for a living listened and got to know a lot about them. It was clear that little rich girl was being fleeced by a nasty predator." He paused hoping to get a reaction from his listeners. Getting none, he grinned – white teeth in a tanned face. "I tried – we all tried to warn her and help her. But you know Kat – she has to have her own way!" Another jaunty smile.

David and Theo shrugged their shoulders and glanced at each other with eyebrows raised. Slightly discomposed by their silence, Jakob continued by giving a damning catalogue of Kate's wild misdemeanours and extravagances, followed by an account of how he had last seen her, about six months before, at a party in a night club. "Her current lover, a shrewd operator called Karl, had stitched her up and cheated her out of her remaining capital. Having bled her dry, he dumped her and absconded. She was probably on dope and didn't realise until after he'd gone."

"So you are saying that this man called Karl cheated her out of everything?" There was a sharp edge to David's voice.

"I rather think she'd lost most of it before he appeared on the scene. I'm told the man was the last in a long list of con men who'd abused her generosity. I've since heard that she's living in another city and is penniless."

"So why exactly have you taken all this trouble to come so far to tell us rumours that may be inaccurate?" David's suppressed irritation was evident.

"They're true enough," Jakob said with breezy assurance. "It was no secret. But later on, news about Kat did get a bit confused. We heard reports that she'd died of an overdose but later found out this was untrue. I thought you might be relieved to know that she's alive."

"How did you find out about us and where we live?" Theo asked.

Jakob looked at him carefully and replied, "I ran into a man called Ross who used to work for Karl. He said that Kat had been lying when she told us she had no family, because he'd found some of her papers and letters with your name and address on them."

"So how did my letters come into his hands?"

"When she did a runner from an apartment without paying the rent arrears, she threw a batch of unimportant papers into the waste bin and your letters were amongst them. Ross retrieved them thinking the writer might not want some irate landlord to whom Kat owed money contacting him to make restitution for her."

"How considerate of Ross!" David's voice was loaded with sarcasm. "And how do we know that either of you are telling the truth?"

"Why should I lie? I've chucked in my job over there and as I happen to be in this country, I thought you might be worried and appreciate some news of

Kat. Or you might like these back." The man put his hand in his jacket inner pocket, pulled out some crumpled air-mail letters and threw them on the table. "Ross gave me these letters and I got your address from them."

Theo glanced down at them and recognised his own handwriting. His heart lurched; he closed his eyes and ran a hand through his hair in anguish. When he looked up, he saw David's troubled gaze fixed on the wall opposite at a photograph of his sister wearing a floppy sunhat and laughing at the camera.

"Where is she?" David asked. He spoke without looking at Jakob, his eyes still on the photograph. Theo could see he was trying to control the painful waves of anxiety and anger that pulsed through him.

"I've no idea where she is now. The last time I heard, two months back, she was living at the house of a known prostitute and her pimp. I heard they'd all been caught stealing but that Kat evaded arrest and left the country. At any rate that's the story that was going around. No-one is quite sure where any of them are – they might be in prison or hundreds of miles away." He paused and then continued in a sympathetic tone. "I realise this news might be upsetting and I'm sorry."

The insincerity needled Theo but he spoke in a measured way. "From what you say it appears that Kate was alive two months ago. But right now you have no more idea of her whereabouts or if she's alright than we do. That's not much comfort."

Jakob flashed his teeth in a parody of a smile. "I wouldn't worry too much – Kat's a girl who knows a bit about the wicked world. She'll be OK even if she has no money. She's tough and smart. Anyway, bad pennies always turn up."

"Get out," said David leaping to his feet. "You disgust me." His pale skin was blotched red with anger.

Jakob leaned back in the comfortable chair, goading the younger man with a teasing smile. "So this is the all the thanks I get for bringing news that your sister's alive."

"Get out," repeated David with intimidating calm. "You're a liar and you've insulted my sister."

Theo stared at his son in admiration.

Jakob gave a harsh triumphant bark and wagged his finger in a gesture intended to infuriate. "Poor little rich boy is now getting touchy – this could be a big mistake." He uncurled himself slowly and then suddenly sprang to his feet.

"Out!" David rarely lost his temper but when he did it was impressive. He gave no sign that he was intimidated by the other man's threatening move.

"Going to throw me out, are you?" said Jakob with a sneer, rocking on his toes as if poised for an aggressive punch.

Theo stepped forward and opened his hands in a silent gesture intended to defuse the situation. Whether Jakob misconstrued the conciliatory move or whether he realised that he was in a room with two men on their own territory, he backed off and retreated to the door.

"You called me a liar," Jakob spoke to David in a menacing whisper. "You might regret that." Then he left.

Both men remained still for a few seconds. Theo, beside the window, watched Jakob emerge from the main entrance and stride across to his car. There was the distant sound of the engine starting and the car moving off down the drive. He turned to his son, "Sometimes, David, you really surprise me."

David was still smouldering. "I so nearly hit him. He was getting pleasure from telling us disgusting things about Kate, whether they were true or not. It's one thing for a brother to bad-mouth his stupid sister but it really makes me angry to hear a stranger do it."

"I wonder what his motive was in coming here," Theo said thoughtfully.

"He intended to upset us with his horrible news about Kate. Why on earth does he have a grudge against us?"

As Theo looked down at the table and the letters which he had written to his wayward daughter, he wondered if his old adversary was behind Jakob's visit.

"At least we know Kate's alive even if we don't know where she is," David said. "I'll just hold on to that for the moment. We've had bad news about her before. Two years ago we heard she'd been severely injured in a car accident but that turned out to be exaggerated. We felt despair when there was no news at all. I'm used to the downward spiral in my sister's life. The latest episode in her disastrous story has been delivered by someone who relished being offensive. We just have to get on with our own lives and Kate has to live with the mess she has created for herself."

The young man's fury had abated. He was already putting the distasteful meeting behind him and was making for the door. "I've got to meet Andrew about the drainage problem. Let's talk later."

And Theo was left in the library alone with his suspicions.

There was a ringing tone, a click, the usual unnerving pause, and then a familiar rasping voice said curtly, "Ator speaking."

Jakob's mouth felt dry – as it often did when he had to talk to his employer. He cleared his throat, saying, "I've seen the family – the father and brother. I had a good look round the place before the meeting. They were upset to hear my news of Kate's ruin. Following your orders, I rubbed salt into their wounds. The brother's a bit of a hothead and lost his temper."

"What about the father?" Ator asked tersely.

Remembering Theo's penetrating gaze which had made him uncomfortable, Jakob said, "He was broken up when I brought out his letters that she'd thrown away."

"Satisfactory." Ator was always curt and Jakob knew better than to expect any thanks.

"Send me a report about the family property. I'll give you instructions about that later. Firstly we need to find the woman and put her out of circulation."

"Do you want me to kill her?" Jakob was unwise enough to ask.

"Don't interrupt." Ator snapped. "Listen and do what I say. That's why I pay you. Eliminating a person is easy. Making her life hell serves my purpose better. Do the family know where she is?"

"They have no idea."

"Get Laslo to track her down and arrange for her to be deprived of her freedom. When Theo hears the bad news, I hope it chokes him."

"It may take a bit of time to find her."

"Do it. Report back." The telephone clicked. Ator had disconnected. He never talked for long.

Jakob put his mobile in his pocket, itching with discontent. He was efficient, obedient and well paid. One day he'd stop working for the evil bastard. As he set off on his next assignment, he smiled at the prospect of freedom.

3

She had lost another job and was desperate with worry as to how she would find the money to pay the rent for her tiny apartment above a grocery shop. The girl had complained once too often to her manager about the abuse she received from the men working in the packing department. He refused to believe her or do anything about it and eventually told her to find another job. She was unable to obtain other work, got in arrears with the rent and was kicked out of the apartment three weeks later. So she moved on again.

Tamay exhaled a stream of smoke into the humid atmosphere. It was stifling – they needed an electrician to get the extractor fan working. She called across to her assistant. "Kelly, have you got that lot from the club done yet? They're calling for it at six tonight. You'd better get a move on. They've all got to be ironed." Leaning back she patted her frizzy hair. She really must get a haircut soon when she had time. She was run off her feet most days although things had got better of late with this new assistant.

Watching the girl unloading the washing machines, Tamay, who managed the laundrette, smoked contentedly feeling no shred of guilt. The evening before she had said to her sister, "This girl's a lot better than the last one. She is thin as a scarecrow but works hard, doesn't say too much and takes a load off my shoulders. I wonder where she puts her head at night." She glanced at her fingers holding the cigarette, noticed that one of her nails was slightly jagged and began to search for a nail file in her bag after depositing her cigarette in the overflowing saucer she used as an ashtray.

Having dealt with her nail, she took another drag as she watched Kelly working. The young woman picked up another huge bag of dirty clothing and, tipping it out on to the floor of the laundrette, she bent down and began to stuff the muddy clothes into the gaping mouth of a large washing machine. The other five machines were all in the midst of their cycle, and the noise of sloshing water and the whine and whirr of the spins were interposed with the noise of traffic on the road outside and the occasional sighs of the tired worker, who straightened up her aching back and slammed the door closed on another load of smelly football shirts.

Tamay felt a stab of guilt and called across to the girl, "Take a five minute break, Kelly, and make yourself a coffee." When her assistant was sitting on a stool with a cup she looked so sad that Tamay said, "Why is a nice girl like you with a bit of education working in a place like this?"

To her surprise she got an answer. "I've been unlucky. A year ago I lost my rag with the lecherous sous-chef in a restaurant kitchen where I was employed to do the washing up and within five minutes found myself on the pavement minus a job. More recently, while working in a factory, I tried to get fair treatment for a woman whose medical condition caused her absences from work – but I was labelled as a troublemaker and we both got fired." The girl stared morosely at the floor as she spoke about her past jobs and drank her coffee.

Tamay looked out of the window and was surprised to see the same man as she had seen the day before walking slowly past. His immaculate, dark coat was out of place in the street. He looked like a businessman and she wondered what he was doing in this predominantly retail area.

"I've got no complaints, Kelly," Tamay said. "Machine number two has finished – better get on." She stubbed out her cigarette and muttered, "I can't believe the price of these. I've got to give up soon. I can't afford it."

Kate made no answer since she had heard this refrain often and knew that in her own case real necessity had forced her to give up smoking. As she unloaded the garments into a large plastic basket she remembered other jobs she'd had. After the split up with Layla and Josh, she had managed to get a job working in a shop but the pay was abysmal so she moved on. For a time she had answered the telephone in a taxi firm, but got fed up with the clients shouting down the phone at her when the drivers didn't turn up. The jobs gradually got worse but her tolerance of them improved. Kate learned not to protest about unfairness, in order to keep her job – and she badly needed the money. Mere existence was so hard. She ate the cheapest food and bought second hand clothes – her own garments had long since worn out. She had learned not to spend all her wages in the first three days and never went to restaurants or bars. Seeing a film was a rare extravagance.

She changed her name as often as her jobs – Kat, Katrin, Kathy, Kelly – but she never seemed to find a new identity. Nor did a new name bring any success – it seemed as if she was haunted by all her past failures. Poverty bred loneliness, though she kept hoping she would meet someone who might be a friend and with whom she could share a conversation, a meal and perhaps a bed. She regarded the laundrette job as temporary until she found something better.

Glancing at the plastic clock on the wall opposite, she could see there were still two more hours until the end of her long day when she could go home. The word 'home' made her grimace, because the one room she rented in a grimy block nearby could hardly be described in this way. Suppressing the aches in her shoulders she started ironing the final items and thought about her real home. She wondered if David had managed to achieve his dream of making it into a hotel.

She remembered as children how excited they had become making family plans for the old house. Theo had talked of converting it into a hotel and the idea had caught their imagination. Their father had worked hard at his sculpture, making a name for himself, gaining respect and achieving better prices for his work. He was putting together the resources to help them achieve their dreams and their potential. Motherless, the pair of them had in their own individual ways managed very well. As schoolchildren they had often cooked meals and amused themselves, when their aunt, Rachel, was unable to do so.

David's ambition to be a hotelier had taken him off to college to study hotel management. Unlike her, he was hardworking and single-minded, and afterwards, to gain experience, he found a job in a large town where he learned about the hotel business and pursued his career. Theo had written and told her that David had now returned home, full of plans and enthusiasm. Kate had been unsure of what she wanted to do and though she dallied with the idea of working with children or in education, she decided she wanted to travel first. Theo's generosity had given her choice and she had selfishly danced out of their lives some years back. She had over time managed to suppress her guilt at abandoning them, and had persuaded herself she no longer missed them. Now, when going home was impossible, she was not so sure.

Shortly before closing time, Tamay took off her grubby overall, put on an overcoat and, telling Kate to lock up, she lumbered out of the door. When she left the laundrette, Kate looked at the grimy mirror near the door and a pale gaunt face stared back at her. She was no longer beautiful and had almost stopped feeling sorry for herself. At the end of each day, enveloped in steam and smell, she ached to get out into the fresh air.

As she trudged home, she passed the corner store where she stopped when she was too tired to walk the mile to the cheaper supermarket. The family who ran it were nice enough and the owner's wife would chat to her if the shop was not too busy. It was here that she had her 'accommodation' address though she rarely received letters. Recently, in a moment of acute loneliness, she had sent her father her contact address at this place even though she was convinced that he would have given up on his wayward daughter and stopped writing to her.

She went in to buy a tin of soup, which she could heat on the single ring in her room. Standing at the counter, she hesitated about asking for her mail, not wanting to risk disappointment.

"Oh, Kelly, there's a letter come for you," Vanisha said in her soft lilting voice. "It's been here for over a week." She handed it over. "Pretty foreign stamp. Nice handwriting too."

Kate took it and her eyes blurred with tears when she saw the familiar writing. Her father had not forgotten her. "It's from Daddy," she told Vanisha. "He's always kept in touch – when I've let him know where I am."

"Why aren't you living at home?" Vanisha asked. "Why do you live in a different country so far from your family? We work here in a country that's not ours but we all stay together as a family. Very supportive and nice. It's no good to be on your own."

"You're right, Vanisha," Kate responded. "It's horrid being alone. But I can't go back to my family. I'm the rotten apple, the black sheep, and there's no way I can wipe out all the mistakes I've made."

"Black sheep – what do you mean?" Vanisha was puzzled.

"It's a long story," said Kate wearily, "and a miserable one. But now I'm going to go and read my letter."

"I think if your Daddy is writing to you, he must still care about you. You ought to consider going back. You don't look well and you never look happy. Do you eat enough?" Vanisha asked, the concern in her voice mixed with curiosity.

"I'm alright. Thanks for the letter and the advice. I'll buy this bread too." Kate paid and turned to go.

"Bye, Kelly. See you soon." Vanisha watched the young woman go out of the shop and sighed. "What a sad one, that girl is," she said to her husband, who was stocking the shelf opposite with packets of rice and pasta.

"Sad and bad," Sanjay commented, surprising his wife as he normally kept his opinions to himself. "She doesn't look like a good girl to me." He lowered his voice. "A foreign man came into the shop recently and asked about a young woman called Kate who is missing. He was trying to discover where she lives."

"Do you think the missing girl might be Kelly?"

"His description could fit her but I did not divulge my suspicions. She has a guilt-ridden look and might have a shady past. But I don't pass on information. My discretion means I'm trusted by my customers and that's good for business."

Kate decided to stop in the public gardens on her way home. Some children were playing tag on a patch of dusty grass, watched by their mothers, sitting on a bench chatting to each other. Seating herself on another bench, beside an overflowing litter bin, she took the letter out of her bag and opened it.

Dear Kate,

I hope you are in good health and happy. I was so pleased to get your card with an address where I might contact you. A year of silence has been so dreadfully worrying. I see you have travelled a long way from your last place though you gave me no reason and no news. But I'm encouraged by the fact that you wrote at all. I'd no idea where you were and my last two letters have been returned to me. I was deeply saddened that you appeared not to want to remain in touch. Now you have broken the silence, I'm overjoyed.

I hope you are still interested in us here in this beautiful corner of the world. The hotel is now flourishing – it took a while to get the business going, but David works as hard as ever and has loyal staff. You will be unaware that your brother has met a wonderful young woman and they have become engaged. Her name is Maria and I'm hoping that under her influence David will take time off from his relentless work schedule, slow down and relax more. I love him dearly but as you know he is very driven to achieve the success he craves.

I am still making my sculptures and they seem to be well received, since they continue to sell, although now I use an agent. Last year I decided to undertake fewer commissions. I prefer to create work from nature and my own imagination – it is more satisfying. I still involve myself in activities connected to the local school and this gives me much pleasure for, as you know, I dearly love children.

I often wonder how and where you are. I have never made demands nor put pressure on you as I believe that adult children should make their own decisions. David and I miss you and hope you are happy. It is now four long years since you left here and since I've seen you. I love you and I always will. Whatever you have done and wherever you are, I will always be your father and I hope so very much that you will come home.

Your loving father.

Kate's eyes filled with tears and she gave a stifled sob. She looked up and saw that someone had sat down at the other end of the bench and that he was looking at her with a concerned expression on his face.

"Not bad news, I hope," he said gently.

Kate shook her head and looked away. After a minute she folded up the letter, put it into her shoulder bag and glanced at the man who had spoken to her. He was bearded, wore glasses and was watching her with a kind smile.

"You seem troubled by your letter." He was hesitant. "I too had a difficult letter this week. Talking with someone about it can help to clarify things. Do you have a friend you can share your problems with?"

"I've got no-one." Kate rarely experienced sympathy and it dissolved her usual reticence. "There's no-one who cares what happens to me except my father who has written to me from home."

"Then why don't you go back?"

"You don't understand. I can never go back – I've burned my boats." There was a desperate note in Kate's voice.

"Then you need to go forward."

"I try to move on – I keep thinking things can't get any worse – but they do." She felt some relief telling this to a complete stranger. A caring listener was a rarity in her life, so she went on. "I want a decent job, some kind friends and a normal life. Things are so hard." She faltered and looked down at her rough and reddened hands. "I feel dragged down by the weight of the past and by my own mistakes."

"Perhaps you are one of these people who like to suffer, who wallow in their own misery and feel sorry for themselves all the time," he teased.

"No I don't. I just feel trapped and I'd like to be free." She stared across the gardens, embarrassed by her confession.

"What you need right now is a cup of coffee and I think I saw a café down the street over there." The man stood up, his well-cut overcoat emphasising his broad shoulders. Leaning down and putting his hand under her elbow, he exerted enough pressure to get her to stand up. "My name's Vadim."

Suppressing a tremor of apprehension and responding to firmness with compliance, Kate picked up her bag. "That's very kind of you."

They went to a café and he was kind. Distant but kind.

Meeting again two days later, in a street near where she lived, Kate was unsure whether be flattered by his making an effort to see her again or whether the encounter was just by chance. They chatted and when he asked if she would like to join him for a drink, it had seemed impolite to refuse. After a couple of glasses of wine she relaxed a little and when he asked her if she was hungry and would care for something to eat, she realised she was very hungry and saw no reason to refuse.

Over a meal in a restaurant, he told her that he was in the city for a couple of weeks on business and implied he was lonely. He seemed as glad of her company as she was of his. Kate relaxed. When they finished eating he paid her a compliment. "If you ate a good meal more regularly, became less thin and if you laughed a bit more often you would be quite attractive."

Kate stiffened – not because she was unappreciative of the compliment but because she sensed the emptiness behind it. She looked at him carefully but he avoided her gaze and called for the bill.

Vadim walked her back to the front door of the building where she had her room. "Perhaps I can see you again."

"That's very kind of you," Kate said gracefully, "but as you're going to be leaving the city very soon, I don't think there's much point in meeting again."

He inclined his head. "Thank you for your company," he said and shook her hand in a friendly way. Relief flooded through her as he turned away – there was something strange about him and his attention to a poor, unimportant woman. His charity appeared motiveless and she knew she did not want to find herself alone with this man.

She turned to put her key in the door and, hearing his step behind her, looked quickly over her shoulder. He was standing close to her and she shrank back against the door with a look of alarm as he said, "Don't worry, Kelly. I'm not going to touch you or proposition you. I only want to ask if you will do something for me."

Kate looked at him warily. "What would that be?" Trust in his motives had evaporated.

"I always take something home for a special friend when I go on business trips." This was a hint there was a wife or partner, but Kate was absolutely convinced that he was a loner. Vadim continued, "I always find it so hard to choose something. Would you help me buy a gift?"

It seemed such an innocent request and feeling it would be uncivil to refuse, she reluctantly agreed to meet him in a smart shopping mall after work the next day. He thanked her and having agreed the time and place, he walked away without looking back. She went inside and climbed the communal stairs, dismayed at her acquiescence but reassured that there would be plenty of people around when they met. There was no reason why he should wish her harm – yet she felt threatened by him.

The next day at the laundrette she worked hard and was touched when Tamay came back from her extended lunch break with a large ham roll she had bought for her assistant. "Here you are, Kelly. You need to eat something. Take a few minutes' break and I'll do some ironing." She indicated the chair and Kate thankfully sat down and took a bite out of the roll.

She watched the large woman reflectively and wondered what sort of life she led. It occurred to Kate that she was so wrapped up in her own misery that she rebuffed sympathy from others.

Tamay, when not smoking, chewed gum to try and disguise the smell of her cigarettes. As she ironed, her jaws worked constantly except when she transferred the pink substance visibly from one side of her mouth to the other. Kate smiled in amused disgust and, as if on cue, the woman looked up and with a toothy grin said, "Nice to see you smiling for a change, Kelly."

"Thanks, Tamay. How's your Tomas keeping then?" And Kate listened for another ten minutes to wheezy complaints about the woman's lazy, drunken, husband. The familiar torrent of words washed over her, almost comforting in their predictability. So why did she feel apprehensive? Was it worry about meeting Vadim after work?

Five hours later, as she sat locked in a small bare room in an unknown part of the city, she knew her instincts had been right. Vadim had intended to harm her. The faint menace that emanated from him and her intuitive mistrust had been justified. Why had she not obeyed her gut instinct to avoid this man?

Sitting on a wooden chair, with head in her hands and her elbows on the metal table in front of her, Kate tried to make sense of the sequence of events that had just taken place.

She had met Vadim as arranged and he took her in a taxi to the shopping mall. She felt nervous to be enclosed in a vehicle with him – but he had been pleasant and reassuringly aloof. It seemed as if he was avoiding touching her and she felt some guilt about repulsing his overtures of friendship. They arrived at the store and Kate was relieved to be amongst crowds of other shoppers.

Keen to help him choose the gift for his 'friend' and be able to escape home, Kate pretended an enthusiasm she did not feel. Assuming the recipient was female she suggested a bottle of perfume, a silk scarf or a piece of jewellery. He bent his head, as if considering, and said that a bracelet might be nice. They took the escalator up to the first floor jewellery department. They approached a female shop assistant standing behind a glass counter and asked to look at gold bracelets. Vadim suggested Kate sit down on a chair by the counter. Tired from a long day's work on her feet, she sat down with relief, placing her cheap handbag over the back of the chair, where its shabbiness might not be seen by the well-groomed assistant. Vadim stood slightly behind her as they bent over the tray of items presented to them. They spent about twenty minutes examining the various bracelets and trying to decide whether 18 carat might be better than 9 carat gold and whether this clasp might be more secure than that.

Although they had not mentioned who the recipient was, the sales assistant clearly assumed it was a gift for her.

"Would madam like to try on any of the bracelets?" she smoothly enquired.

"No thanks," Kate swiftly replied. "We're buying for someone else." She felt embarrassed by her creased and shabby work clothes, well aware of the condescending attitude of the shop assistant towards her and the ingratiating smile on the woman's face when she spoke Vadim.

"The young lady is giving me some help in choosing a gift for a special friend." He looked across at the sales assistant over Kate's head and gave a smile of complicity.

"So the gift is for another ... lady," said the assistant, pausing slightly before the word 'lady', to indicate her doubt that the person on the chair qualified for that courtesy.

Aware of the older woman's scrutiny, Kate suddenly realised that Vadim could very well have enlisted the shop assistant in selecting a gift and was puzzled why he had asked her to come along.

They finally selected a thin bracelet from those displayed on the velvet base of the '9 carat' drawer. The sales assistant removed it and placed in on the counter, whilst she returned the drawer to the display cabinet. Vadim was still looking – almost absent-mindedly – at the 18 carat selection, which was then also returned to the cabinet by the assistant.

Stroking his dark beard as if in doubt, Vadim said, "I'm not really quite sure about this purchase. I want to be certain that it's the right decision." He smiled across at the assistant from where he stood behind Kate, giving a minute shake of his head, as if he'd decided against buying such a costly gift for such a miserable looking creature.

"Very well, sir." The shop assistant nodded with a small smile of approval rather than disappointment.

Leaning over Kate's shoulder, Vadim murmured, "Perhaps perfume after all." Surprised, Kate rose to her feet, grabbed her bag and they walked away. "Rather too expensive – that bracelet," he said, but Kate did not believe him.

Downstairs at the perfume counters, Vadim ignored Kate's vague suggestions and quickly chose a bottle of "Poison" Eau de Toilette by Dior. He asked for it to be gift-wrapped and paid for it with cash, pulling four twenty-dollar notes from his wallet, whilst Kate, standing awkwardly beside him, remembered the money she had squandered on expensive perfume in years gone by and how much eighty dollars would mean to her now.

They moved without speaking towards the front door of the store. Kate was uneasy and impatient to get away from the man. On the pavement outside the large open doors, whilst other shoppers flowed in and out, Vadim paused and with a smile thanked Kate for her help and said how much he had enjoyed her company. The smile did not reach his eyes, as he handed to her the small chic carrier bag containing the perfume and said formally, "Please accept this as a parting gift and token of friendship." The insincerity sent a jangling frisson down Kate's spine.

"I can't do that," she protested. "You've bought it for your friend. I was happy to accompany you though I've been very little help."

Vadim, rather than trying to persuade her to take the bag, was looking back into the shop, and Kate was surprised to see a cruel sneer distort his face. Kate spun round. Three men were running purposefully towards the entrance. She squinted and saw they were heading towards them. Confused, she turned back to Vadim and saw him walking quickly away through the crowds, having left the bag at her feet. She stared at the bag – the poison he had left behind.

Someone roughly grasped her arm, and a voice said, "Please, come with us, miss. We've reason to believe that you have taken something that you have not paid for."

Another voice: "Where's your bearded accomplice?"

"I don't know what you're talking about," Kate protested. "I've not bought anything or taken anything from your shop. And I certainly don't have any accomplice!" she added angrily, trying to shake off the man's grip. "And if you're talking about this perfume," she said kicking the bag with her foot, "I think you'll find that it's been paid for."

"Please come quietly. We don't want to make a fuss out here in front of everyone," said the tallest of the men, who was wearing a dark suit, whilst his uniformed companions took both her arms firmly and forced her to go with them.

A few minutes later they were in a small room at the rear of the ground floor. The man in the suit was standing in front of her and one of the uniformed men was leaning against the closed door. The bag of perfume and her handbag were on a small table. "You have stolen something from us," he said coldly.

"How dare you accuse me! I've stolen nothing. I was given the perfume by a horrid man and I didn't want it anyway," she protested.

"We are not talking about perfume. We are talking about an 18 carat gold bracelet worth over $2500."

Kate stared at him in amazement.

There was a knock and the door opened to admit the shop assistant from the jewellery department, with her crimson lipstick and smart crisp suit. "That's her. She's the thief."

Then it hit Kate. With sudden clarity she recalled Vadim casually looking at the tray of more expensive gold bracelets, the assistant turning away, him leaning over her, the handbag with its broken zip hanging over the back of the chair, open to receive what he had covertly removed from the tray. She exhaled sharply and her shoulders sagged. To the men, it seemed like an admission of guilt.

Vadim had framed her, but why? What reasons could he have to do this to her? She watched with horror as the man picked up her handbag, grimacing with distaste at the cheap plastic and torn zip, and upended it on to the table. The contents clattered out: a packet of aspirin, a set of two keys, a small cloth purse, a tube of hand cream, an opened letter, a pen, some paper handkerchiefs, a small notebook and an incriminating heavy gold bracelet. She remembered thinking how vulgar it was when she had seen it in the tray.

Silently the man picked up the item between thumb and forefinger and held it in front of her face. His expression was grim. "You took this. You had no intention of paying for it. You are a thief," he said in an acid tone.

Panicking, Kate whimpered, "It wasn't me. It was him." But it was no good. The evidence had been found in her possession and her companion had disappeared. Who would believe her unlikely story? Who would listen to her stammered excuses? No one did.

Now she was at a police station, sitting in a locked interrogation room. She had been questioned by two different people and made a statement but it was obvious that they thought she was lying. She had no lawyer, no friend to vouch for her character – and no hope of escaping the inevitable. She was well aware that a night in a cell confronted her and after that a longer spell in prison. She was trapped. She would lose her job and when her rent was unpaid, she would lose her room and all her meagre possessions. She felt as if she was sliding back again down the black hole towards despair.

Kate stared through the grimy window as darkness fell. She had wilfully lost her innocence and her inheritance long ago. Her health and her self-respect had gone more recently but she still had her freedom. Now she would be deprived of that too. She had been tricked and would be found guilty. There was no hope of a reprieve – the evidence was against her. Her 'accomplice' had disappeared. Conviction was certain.

Later she came to the conclusion that Vadim was a thief who had planted the bracelet on her so she would be the one at risk when taking it out of the shop. He'd used her and she had taken the rap.

After conviction and having been given a sentence of six months, Kate was transferred to a huge woman's penitentiary, situated in a grey soulless building some long distance from where she had not committed her crime. She resolved to try and avoid self-pity, aware that she was guilty of other wrongdoings for which she had not been punished. Soon the problems of dealing with bullying from other prisoners and the unpleasant indignities of incarceration blotted out any further self-searching enquiry into why this had happened to her.

The other inmates were for the most part unfriendly, or worse still unkind, to the foreigner in their midst, and Kate felt isolated – and vulnerable. After a couple of weeks she found herself working alongside a woman of about forty with a blotchy careworn face, who said, "I'm Donna. You're not from here, are you? What's your name?"

"Kelly." The lie was by now habitual. Her real name was the only thing she could keep as an unblemished secret. "I've been living in this country for a while." This was the first time anyone had shown any interest in her and Kate was grateful. The inevitable question came next.

"What are you in here for?" Donna bent down to pick up another pile of sheets. They were both working in the prison laundry – exhausting work but familiar to Kate.

"Robbery. I didn't do it."

"They all say that. Not me though. I'm inside for stealing a car – I was on drugs, otherwise I'd never have had the nerve. The stupid owner left the keys in and it seemed so easy. Until I crashed it. I ran into a pedestrian and badly injured him – he died later. Bad luck for me – and him too. So I deserve to be here," she said with resignation. "It's not the first time either."

"But I don't deserve to be here," Kate retorted throwing towels into a large tub. "Not for a crime I didn't commit. Some cruel bastard called Vadim set me up by planting the item he stole in my bag. I've no idea why he was so vindictive – I'd done nothing to him. I hardly knew him."

"What did you nick then?"

"A gold bracelet. I didn't steal it."

"If you say so." Donna didn't care either way.

"But I am guilty of leading an irresponsible and selfish life, so I deserve punishment," Kate said bitterly.

"Tell me about your wicked life then. It sounds fun," Donna grinned as she folded a greyish sheet of rough cotton.

Kate straightened her back and looked down the corridor of her life. "It was fun for a while, until I lost everything. I talked my dad into giving me my share of family money. Off I went abroad to spend it and do as I pleased. I roamed around and ended up in the proverbial 'big bad city' where I met some good life people like myself. We all did parties, sex and drugs, and for a while it was riotously enjoyable."

"It's always exciting to break free from the restrictions of home." Donna picked up another sheet. "It bored me rotten."

"I was stupid enough to run away from the safety and the love that surrounded me at home. I bought my friendships by splashing my money around, throwing parties for people I hardly knew and trashing rented apartments. I was unkind and cruel and behaved so badly," she ended up, a look of self-disgust on her face.

"Sounds like you had a wild time."

"Until I fell for a handsome shit called Karl who managed to cheat me out of what was left of my money," Kate said as she wiped the steam from her glasses. "He disappeared after arranging for one of his thugs to rob me. Then came the lean times – tears and remorse, hunger and loneliness. I had a couple of good friends called Layla and Josh but they abandoned me." Here Kate's voice faltered. At the time it seemed like a betrayal but perhaps they had been cruel to be kind and had left her so they would not drag her down. How she missed Layla's quick humour and Josh's bear hugs. "I felt desperate when I knew they'd gone without me – and I was on my own. I've been slipping downwards ever since."

"In here, there's no further you can fall. It happens." Donna shrugged.

Kate felt a sharp pang of irritation at the older woman's blind acceptance of her situation. She felt contaminated by the experience and cut off from normal humanity. Incarceration with criminals was humiliating. And frightening.

About a month later, Kate was cornered in the exercise area.

Three days before she had accidentally stumbled in the canteen and had knocked a tray of food out of the hands of a large woman who was called Claudine. The woman had sworn at her in filthy language and Kate had lost her rag and snapped back. She received a black look before one of the warders interrupted and told them to go back to their tables.

Claudine and two other female inmates managed to accost her against a wall, a long way from the prison officer who was overseeing the exercise hour. A sick feeling washed over Kate as she recalled how badly one of the inmates had been beaten up about a week before. A stinging blow to the side of her head and a savage kick on her shin made her gasp. She was about to cry out when the one standing behind her put an arm round her neck and her hand over her mouth. They tore off her glasses, threw them down and stamped on them. They pushed her face against the wall and Kate, who knew what was coming, was terrified.

Suddenly she was released and the three women melted away. Kate remained frozen for a few seconds and as she turned round, a prison officer strode up to her. "Who were they?" she asked in a crisp voice, noticing the smashed glasses on the ground and Kate cowering in terror. Kate opened her mouth, but seeing Donna who was standing nearby shake her head, she stuttered that she didn't know who they were. The officer, whom Donna had alerted, gave her a hard look and walked away.

A week later, Donna 'fell' down some stairs and broke her leg.

The time passed and Kate learned resilience. But when the day of her release came, she felt anxious about the prospect of her expulsion into a world that had not been kind to her for some while. She was taken into a small room, told to change back into her old clothes and was handed back her battered bag with her personal items inside. She signed a form and listened without attention to some unwanted advice. The gate opened and she walked out into the threatening void.

The day was overcast and there was a light drizzle of rain. Kate had been given a small amount of money she had earned in prison, so she took a bus to the town where she had lived, to see if she might be able to retrieve her few possessions. During the journey she opened her bag and glanced through the contents. Her eyes fell on the letter from her father. Did he still care? In the absence of any other plan, she decided to go to the Indian corner shop and see if there were any further letters waiting for her.

About three hours later she stood outside and taking a breath to calm herself, she opened the door. When she entered the shop, Sanjay was talking to a customer but he broke off and shouted at her. "You get out of here, you dirty thief. You've been in prison, so get out of my shop." Surprised and dismayed by his venom, Kate stumbled outside, trembling with shame and disappointment. She would have no chance to discover whether her father was still trying to communicate.

She rounded the corner and walked blindly along, unable to achieve the only plan she had been able to fix her mind on. She heard running footsteps behind her, and fearing some sort of attack she shrank back against a wall. It was Vanisha, holding up her sari as she ran with a look of furtive worry on her face.

She stopped in front of Kate and glancing over her shoulder, she spoke rapidly. "Kelly, I don't condone what you did. But I want you to know that we have had three letters for you – perhaps from your Daddy. Sanjay made me send two of them back to the sender's address. But this one arrived only two days ago, and ... here it is." She pulled out a crumpled envelope from the pocket of a cardigan that she wore over her sari and thrust it into Kate's hand. "I must go. My husband would be angry with me for talking to you. Don't come back to the shop. Go home, Kelly. That's what you should do." She gave a quick encouraging smile, turned and scampered back.

Kate had no time to thank Vanisha before the kind Indian woman disappeared round the corner. She put on her new glasses and looked down at the envelope – it was from her father. What did he feel when she never replied, when his letters were returned? Did he think she might be dead? How cruel she had been to him – how thoughtless of the pain she had caused! Angry with herself, she ripped open the envelope, and a single sheet of paper seemed to echo what Vanisha had said. The few words on it read:

Kate. My daughter. Where are you? I forgive you. Come home. I love you. Daddy.

She made up her mind instantly, saying, "Yes, I will." A huge rock seemed to roll away and open a path that had always been there but had been hidden by her own blind obstinacy. "I'll go home. I'll ask Daddy to forgive me and I'll make it up to David – somehow. I'll work and won't be a burden on the family."

Realising she had spoken aloud, she glanced round. No-one was in sight – she was on her own. The momentous decision had been taken but she had no idea how to achieve it. She had no money and many thousands of miles to travel. She would have to work to pay for her journey back, and getting a job and accommodation now she had a prison record would be hard. She had nothing except the freedom to move in the right direction.

It was Kate, no longer Kelly, who took a deep breath and set off down the narrow street.

4

It was the music that intrigued him. Driving up the winding drive through the wood, David had become aware of it – faint at first, then louder. It was the first sign that something extraordinary was happening. He couldn't understand why there should be music as the hotel had no booking that day for a wedding or party.

The last of the daylight was draining out of the western sky, visible through gaps in the trees, and darkness was surging in to take its place as David turned the final corner and emerged into the wide front courtyard where he pulled up and got out of his car. Looking up at his hotel he saw all the lights burning – each window luminous with a peach-coloured glow. There appeared to be many people inside. Normally when he returned to the hotel, it was quiet and peaceful, but now there were voices, laughter and vibrant music.

Why was he in the dark? He was bemused. It was his business and he should have been told what was happening. He has been away only three days and yet some important change had taken place. Without his knowledge or authority. The atmosphere was charged with excitement – he could feel it as he climbed up the steps to the entrance.

He hesitated before going inside – he felt like an outsider. The door opened and a wave of sound surged out as someone emerged, almost colliding with him. He registered that it was his cousin, Jamie, who farmed the adjoining land. Why was he dressed in a suit?

"David. At last. That's marvellous. We knew you'd be back today and we've been waiting for you."

"What's going on?" David knew he sounded aggrieved.

"It's wonderful news. We're all so pleased." Jamie clutched his arm.

"Will you kindly tell me the reason for all this festivity?" David demanded, shaking off his hand.

"Your sister's returned. Two days ago. She's alive and she's come home. Your father's so happy. Come on in. We've got family and friends in to celebrate, arranged a band at short notice and there's a big dinner tonight in her honour. I'll tell them you've arrived." He darted back inside and left David on the doorstep.

So that was the reason. His sister Kate! With a pulse of relief he realised that she was not dead as they had feared after almost two years of silence. This moment of brotherly affection was followed by a wave of apprehension. She had come home. With her messed-up life, dramas and disasters. He felt a surge of savage anger against this lost and luckless sibling of his. He was pleased she was alive, but no way did he want her around. She would crawl underneath the protective skin of his ordered existence and irritate him. It had been much less complicated since she had left home. Now she was back, their lives would be disrupted again.

He unclenched his hands, took a deep breath and turned on his heel. He walked through the garden down to the old summer house and stopped beneath the beech tree beside it. He looked up, unobserved, at the hotel that he had created and tried to imagine the scene in the well-lit reception room. His father had arranged the party without his help. Everyone would be making a fuss of his beautiful sister. After five years away she would be the centre of attention. He would feel excluded.

Why did he feel so disturbed? Why could he not celebrate that his sister had come home? He turned his back on the house and stared across the long grass to the stream and the rickety plank bridge that was just visible in the evening haze. A crowd of small flies rose up from the water and hovered for a few seconds before moving off in a shimmering swarm to the other bank. His distracted thoughts dwelt on his childhood and settled on a painful incident that had taken place one spring day many years before, when he must have been about ten and his sister seven years old.

The two of them had been outside playing a game. Each of them in turn dared the other to do something. The initial 'dares' involved throwing sticks high into a tree, jumping over the narrow part of the stream and swinging from branches or standing on a gate post. If one of them was unable to do the task, then the other would have to do it to show it was possible. Kate's 'dares' for David became more risky and challenging. His were designed to be easier as she was younger and smaller.

They were playing near the wooden summerhouse, beside the stream where it widened out into a pond. Kate made David climb up on to the roof and stand upright waving his arms. He nearly fell – and she taunted him from below.

David climbed down saying, "My next dare for you is to lob a stone at that large leaf over there and hit it." He pointed to one on the other side of the pond.

Annoyed, because accuracy was not her strong point, but determined to try anyway, Kate picked up a knobbly, grey stone. David watched her as she stood on the bank, her small lithe figure under the trees, dappled with light. Without pausing to assess the distance, she hurled the stone across the pond, where it missed the water completely and hit the grass on the far side.

David sniggered. "You need glasses."

"OK, Mr Clever," she snapped. "You do it then. Bet you can't."

David bent down and searched until he located a smooth, round stone, then he looked across at the lily to gauge its position. Taking aim, he smoothly threw his stone across to it, where it landed beside the leaf and disappeared making a neat hole in the opaque green algae on the surface of the water. He turned to his sister with a look of triumph.

"Well done," Kate said grudgingly, "but it was easier for you – your arm is longer than mine." David didn't bother to point out this was absurd. He was used to her always having the last word and undermining any sense of victory he might feel. He watched with fascination as the slick of green slime gradually closed over the hole, repelled that it had swallowed his stone and left no trace. The leaf remained entangled in the slime but would soon get waterlogged and be sucked down. The gardener had told them that lurking in the pond was a horrible monster who would eat them if they fell in. They didn't believe him but felt uneasy about the pond and its dark secrets.

"My turn now," said his sister. "I want you to walk the plank!"

A narrow plank bridged the lower end of the pond from where the stream flowed on its way down the valley. She looked at David to gauge his reaction since this was something their father had expressly forbidden. His prohibition seemed unreasonable to Kate but quite sensible to David. She loved flouting rules.

"We're not allowed to do that. Dad's said it could tip up and we'd fall in," David said.

"And you always do what you're told," his sister jeered. "Or perhaps the real reason is that you're afraid." She turned away in disgust. "I've got an older brother who's frightened of water." They both knew he hated swimming. "Coward!" she called over her shoulder, goading him to abandon common sense.

"I'll do it," David said angrily.

"In bare feet," she threw in.

"Alright!" He slowly took his shoes off, trying to control his nervousness. He thought of the stone sinking through the green algae and his heart beat faster. He walked slowly over the bank and taking a deep breath, he edged out on to the slender bridge, with his feet at right angles to the plank. He took small sideways steps along the mottled wood, looking down at his feet, trying to avoid looking at the slime. Then suddenly he heard a plop and transferred his gaze to the water, where a gap had opened up beneath him showing a dark hole in the green surface. To distract him, Kate had thrown a stone at the water below the bridge. David wobbled, lost his balance and with a wail of terror he fell backwards into the waiting water.

Unable to swim and forgetting that the water was not deep, he panicked, and slipped below the opaque surface. For an agonising few seconds he thought he might drown. Then he scraped his shin on a submerged branch stuck in thick mud and realised he could stand on the bottom. With revulsion he pushed his feet into the oozing sludge, straightened his torso and emerged. As his head broke the surface, he saw Kate, whose worried frown was replaced by a grin.

"Oh, there you are David. So the pond monster didn't eat you?" She shrieked with laughter. "You've got green yuck on your head and you look so silly." His humiliation was complete.

David's fear gave way to anger, as he waded his way to the bank and pulled himself out, his wet clothes clinging to him. He snarled at his sister, "I bet you couldn't have done it."

Kate tilted her head, raised her eyebrows and, with an impish grin, she kicked off her shoes and sauntered over to the slimy plank. Before he could stop her, with a cheeky little wave, she set her foot on the bridge and to her brother's horror darted across at a run. In the middle she skidded a bit, teetered for a theatrical moment and, regaining her balance with her arms out wide, carried on. A few seconds later she was across and fell forward on to the grass. Jumping to her feet, and waving her arm triumphantly, she called across at her defeated brother. "See. I did it. No problem."

David, outmanoeuvred again, felt a bitter sickness well up inside his throat. "You're crazy, Kate. You're not as tall as me and you'd have been out of your depth if you'd fallen in."

"You forget that I can swim and you can't," she shouted back. She was wrong – he was never allowed to forget it. "I'm braver and better than you are," she yelled.

David picked up his shoes and with water still trickling down him, began to trudge back towards the house, the game and his tolerance at an end. His sister's shrill derision pursued him, hyena-like, as he plodded back up the slope. And yet he adored her. She was a carefree little girl, always smiling and skipping about. Protecting her was an honour and one of his greatest pleasures even though she did not appreciate his concern. Her laughter had been so galling, and in the pit of his stomach he remembered the fear. And the shame.

She would be laughing now. All the sounds of a lively party wafted down to him as he stood in the dusk, hidden and apart. His father would want him to go in and welcome his sister. His delay was perverse. He stood hesitating, leaning against the tree and running his fingers along the bark, picking at a small knot in the wood. He wanted to go in and take part in the long-awaited family reunion and yet he had to demonstrate his disapproval by hanging back, upset by his father's spontaneous generosity towards a worthless daughter.

This dilemma made his head ache, the pain creeping in, clouding his judgement, taking the edge off his concentration. He felt torn, aching to earn approval from his father, angry with his sister but needing reconciliation. He leaned over and put his forehead against the trunk of the tree, the corrugated surface scratching his skin, as if to tease out his ill humour. He heard someone shouting his name and, wrenching his head away, he staggered off balance.

The wind blew through the tree. "What shall I do?" he whispered to the rustling leaves. He heard his father's voice, deep and resonant, calling him. A stab of hope was followed immediately by a wave of irritation. He knew so well how persuasive his father was. He remained silent.

"David, can you hear me?" The older man would know to look for his son in the place where as a child the lad had often hidden. Unable to stop himself, David moved out from under the deep shade of the tree and on to the path, where his pale skin would be visible under the stars.

Theo stopped in front of his silent son. "Jamie told me you'd arrived. Why are you out here?" There was no hint of reproach. "Don't you know that Kate's come back? We've invited friends and family and are giving a party." He spread his arms expansively. "We've been expecting you home for two hours."

"I've been working. I managed to get that contract we wanted for a big conference. I've done a good deal and you'll be pleased."

"David, of course I'm interested in how you've done and delighted you've been successful. We can talk about that later. But the momentous news is that Kate's home – after five years away. She's thin and looks unwell, but her health will improve. Do come in to welcome her home." He put his arm round his son's shoulders, his warm hand clasping the young man's upper arm.

David reacted as if he'd been burnt, shaking his father's hand off. "Why do you expect me to be pleased? Think of all the heartache Kate has caused." He remembered the anguish when news had come that she had been in a car accident and the relief when they discovered she was unhurt. "You and I worried when there was bad news and despaired when there was no news."

"I never felt despair," his father interrupted him gently. "I always felt that she would realize she was going in the wrong direction and would come back to us. I never gave up hope."

"My sister has been leading a riotous, wicked, depraved life." David spoke quickly and jerkily, almost coughing in his fury. "She's wasted everything – her money, her health, her integrity. Her rotten friends have deserted her, so she decides to return home. It will throw our lives into turmoil. She'll bring back all the mess and mayhem we used to put up with. And I'm meant to be pleased?" He raised his splayed hand above his head in a gesture of outrage. "You're asking me to welcome her! Well, I can't." Appalled by his own words, David knew his father would be upset by such bitter resentment against his sibling.

Theo looked up at the stars and then at his son. "Some people thought that Kate might be dead – we hadn't heard from her for over two years – and then she came home unexpectedly. I was overjoyed, but she was crying and saying how guilt-ridden she felt and how she didn't deserve to be welcomed back into the family." Theo paused, watching David's averted face and hoping to see some remorse for his jealous outburst, and then went on. "I love Kate – she's my long lost daughter. Whatever she's done, I forgive her. I'm so happy to have her back."

David nodded jerkily, as if trying to swallow his medicine. "Alright. You're pleased she's alive... and so am I. But why do we have to go to the extravagance of throwing her a big party? Whatever is all this costing – the musicians, the food and wine?"

Theo sighed. "The cost doesn't matter, David. What matters is compassion and love. This evening is a demonstration of our delight that she's chosen to come home and seek reconciliation. She's no longer lost."

Ignoring this and feeling ill-treated, David stared across at the house, saying, "I'm thirty and you've never thrown me a big party. I've worked long and hard for you and the family business and you've never spent this sort of money on me."

"David, snap out of it. This is petty. When you and Maria became engaged I wanted to celebrate with everyone to show how happy I was for you both. You said you'd prefer to rather have a small, special dinner party – which we did. I respected your choice, your way of doing things. You like to plan and do things quietly. Your sister has always been more spontaneous – and reckless. An impromptu party would show her how much we love her, but I delayed it until today when I knew you were returning." Theo's measured tone was an attempt to defuse his son's anger.

David, still simmering, turned to look directly at his father. "You love Kate so much that you forget what she's done. Five years ago she demanded to have her share of the family trust. She couldn't wait for it – she wanted it then and there. To everyone's amazement, and with some considerable effort and sacrifice by us to get the sum together, you gave it to her."

Theo nodded. "It was her choice. She wanted to go and you wanted to stay. I respected both choices."

"Off she went without a backward glance to another country," David swept on and nothing would stop him, "to a city that could cater for her self-indulgent appetite, where she spent it on extravagant living, expensive clothes and faithless friends and lovers. When it's all gone, she comes home begging for forgiveness and you shower her with love and throw her a huge party." He took a deep breath. "I've stayed here, worked hard and managed to pay back the debt that she got us into. I've tried to be a good son and we've enjoyed life together over the years. This lavish hospitality on the return of a spendthrift daughter is over the top. That's why I'm so hacked off."

"David, you know I love you and everything here is yours. You've no reason to feel insecure. You're my son – a man of integrity. Show it now and come with me."

A wave of acceptance broke over David as the pull of his father's love worked its change. He would do it – not for Kate but for Theo. "Alright. You win. I'll come." The pain and resentment ebbed from him as they walked back to join the party. He could sense the happiness radiating from his father. They reached the door and went in together.

The warm light from the large chandelier shone down on the heads of the two men as they entered the hall, the son's short dark hair and his father's shaggy grey mane. Soft reflected light glinted off the polished furniture and on the varnished oil paintings on the wall. The entrance hall of the old house was large without being austere, and fine wooden stairs ascended to the first floor. A balcony overlooked the staircase, creating a feeling of space and elegance, and some of the larger and more luxurious bedrooms opened off this landing. There were further rooms in the new wing, down a spacious, well-lit corridor, at the far end of which there was a door marked 'Private', which led to the flat that father and son now occupied.

David took his coat off and glanced round the lobby and reception area to check that all was in order, tidy and welcoming for guests. He loved this house where he had lived most of his life. Peace enveloped him as it always had on his return from school, college or work to this refuge where he could close the door on the uncertainty of the outside world. He breathed in the protective aura of his home and felt release of the tension that had built up in him during the altercation with his father in the garden. The muscles of his face relaxed and he breathed out slowly as if trying to exhale his ill humour.

"It always feels good getting back," David said with a smile of genuine relief. "If this house is a haven for me after only three days away, I wonder how my sister reacted after five years' absence." He turned to his father with his eyebrows raised.

Theo stood waiting and watching his son. When their eyes met, he said gently, "David, I should warn that Kate's not looking so well." Knowing his father to be a master of understatement, David prepared himself for a distressing change in his sister.

The shock of Kate's appearance was immense. When he entered the large reception room, he observed many people and was distracted by many voices. For a moment David didn't realise where his sister was and he had a stab of panic that he wouldn't identify her at all. As his gaze searched the sea of faces, he felt a gentle touch on his arm and registered that his father was trying to alert him to his sister's presence in the corner of the room. A familiar profile caught his attention and, with a jolt of recognition, he realised it was Kate. She was standing next to their aunt, Rachel, her face averted, listening to the other woman. David visibly flinched – he could hardly recognise his sibling.

A slight hush descended as the people around him saw his stunned reaction. Sensing the decrease in volume of the conversation, Kate turned and saw her brother and father standing in the centre of the room. Theo went over to her but David stood still, shocked by the alteration in her appearance. He closed his eyes briefly to shut out the present and a picture of Kate on her eighteenth birthday swam into his head – small, poised, radiantly healthy and beautiful.

He opened his eyes and saw her walking across the room towards him. This was a mockery, an almost unrecognisable ghost of her former self, with haggard face and emaciated body. Her long, dark hair had gone and her thin face was framed by listless, bleached straw. The bones round her neck were scrawny; her skin was blotchy with a pallid greyish tinge to it. She looked much older – and ill. She was wearing a beautiful white dress that hung loosely on her gaunt frame.

Kate paused in front of him, seeing the dismay in his face. "Hello, David. I see my return and my appearance have upset you. I look a wreck!" She put a tentative hand on his arm and reached up to kiss his cheek. "Please try to forgive me," she whispered.

David, making an effort not to recoil, put one arm round her bony shoulder as her dry lips brushed his face. He leaned down and briefly put his lips on her forehead in a gesture of affection that he could not feel. Feeling embarrassed, he looked over her head and saw his father a few yards away watching him with an expression of sympathy and approval. Theo must have had a similar shock when he had first seen Kate; the change in her would have devastated him. Some affection for his little sister surfaced and he tried to quell the resentment that lurked below.

"Hello, Kate. Long time no see. You've become very thin," David said with what he hoped was a note of concern.

"What you mean is that I'm ugly and sick, which is true. And it's self-inflicted."

David remained silent, unable to refute this.

"Daddy has been so amazingly kind and forgiving – I don't deserve it."

No you don't, thought David.

Kate read this in his eyes, saying, "I've made a mess of my life, but I'm so relieved to be home."

David didn't trust himself to respond, so Kate went on. "I want to prove to you that I've changed. I don't want you or Daddy to support me – I'll work for my living and manage my life properly. I want to try and win back your respect." David saw a spark of resolution in her eyes, even though she was ill and exhausted. She faltered, fearing rejection. "But I won't stay if you don't want me to."

Her brother shook his head in confusion. "I don't know what to think. I need time." Remembering his promise to his father, he forced a smile and managed to say, "Anyhow, welcome home."

His father walked over to his cherished children and, putting one arm round each of them, he smiled warmly. Encircled in his father's love but trapped by his own resentment, David felt immensely self-conscious. Aware that a number of people were watching the scene with curiosity, he ached to retreat from all the family emotion. He had not yet seen his fiancée and, needing an excuse to break away, he looked round for her.

"Maria's over there," his father said. "By the window." Catching his eyes, she came across and taking David's hand, she put her arm round his neck and embraced him. David, embarrassed again by another open demonstration of affection in front of everyone, responded somewhat stiffly and gave her a formal kiss on the cheek.

Maria, who knew him to be reserved in public though warm and loving in private, removed her hand from his shoulder and took his arm, saying "Isn't it wonderful that Kate's come back?" She smiled warmly at her future sister-in-law. "We're all going to look after her and help her regain her health," she said linking her arm with Kate's so that she had one sibling on each side of her. David was proud of her tact and kindness.

"When I'm stronger, I intend to earn my keep. I'm going to reform," said Kate firmly, turning to her father. "I have a lot to prove."

"Let's think about the future tomorrow," Theo said gently. "This is a night for celebration. Let's go in to dinner now your brother's here." Tucking Kate's arm in his, like a strong father supporting an ailing child, he moved off towards the open doors of the dining room, followed by David and Maria and the other guests.

Embarrassed by the large and generous party her father was throwing for her, Kate felt subdued at dinner. She had a long hard road ahead to repair her fractured relationship with her brother and gain his respect. Sitting next to her father, she listened to him as he told her about friends who had married and children who had been born during her absence. She was grateful he did not ask her questions and he was clearly aware of her need to listen and not to talk.

After the first course her father rose to his feet to wander round and ensure all his guests were enjoying themselves. Kate watched him as he circulated and put people at ease with gentle courtesy and kind words – he radiated goodwill. She became aware of a young man on her other side who was trying to talk to her. He had been introduced to her as a friend of David's, and the architect who had designed the extension to the hotel. Politely, she turned to him and tried to focus on what he was saying.

"I'm so sorry. I didn't quite catch that?" she gave him a faint smile.

"I've got your attention at last," he said with an answering grin. "I realise this can't be easy for you – having been away so long – and seeing so many people and friends again."

"How long have you known my family?" She noticed he had a crooked nose and a kind smile.

"I met your father about three years ago – when my firm was asked to design the new hotel wing. I respect your father, who has been so encouraging, and like him very much. I've known David for a few years – we were at college together. There's a sensitive person concealed beneath the industrious persona he portrays to the world. He's always available to discuss problems and careful not to make rash decisions. I always know where I am with your brother – he's a fair man and I trust him. He works too hard but that's his way." He looked across his friend who was sitting further down the table beside Maria. Kate's eyes followed his.

David was listening to his fiancée with a frown of concentration. The couple seemed oblivious to those around them and Maria seemed to be trying to persuade him to agree with her.

"What's Maria like?" Kate asked. "I met her yesterday for the first time. Is she good for David?"

"She is a lovely person – cheerful and unselfish. She works as receptionist in the hotel and is brilliant with the hotel guests, but quite reticent about herself. I expect you'll get to know her well since she's going to marry your brother." He paused and Kate detected a trace of doubt in his voice as he said, "I hope they'll be happy together."

Needing to change the subject, Kate asked, "Tell me about yourself and where you come from."

Andrew told her about his family who lived in a different part of the country. After seven years of study and training, as a newly qualified architect he had joined a practice in the local town. "I had some doubts about whether I had been wise coming to work in a rural area where there might not be large commissions and exciting design projects for architects. But I met up with David again, and he and I hit it off. He had faith in my ability and gave me my first big commission – a project to provide more accommodation for this hotel. It's led on to other jobs – a canteen and dining hall for the local school, and more recently upgrading a residential block for nurses from the local hospital. It was David who started the ball rolling."

Warming to his enthusiasm, Kate said, "I've had a look at the new wing and the bedrooms and bathrooms. I've also seen the redesigned kitchen. The hotel looks really smart."

"The project has changed the look of the old house and it must seem strange to find your home open to the public. Does it bother you?" Andrew asked, sensitive of her feelings.

"Not a bit," Kate responded quickly, even though it did. "I went away for a long time and nothing stands still." She liked Andrew for his openness and enthusiasm; his lack of cynicism was refreshing. He did not enquire about her life or show any disapproval. No doubt he had already been told that she was the black sheep of the family and was being tactful!

She was feeling emotionally drained after a tearful and distressing afternoon, when, after gentle probing, her father had elicited from his daughter the details of her long and difficult odyssey back home. He had not probed further back than the day of her release from prison and decision to return, but had encouraged her to speak about her inward voyage and her outward journey. She told Theo it had taken almost a year to earn the money but did not mention the many privations she had endured in her endeavours to save as much as possible. At one stage she had been robbed of her savings and this cruel blow set her back many months. Illness had struck and, unable to afford medical care, she could not work and lost her job. In destitution she developed a tenacious ability to cope with hardship and a steadfast resolve to drag herself onward that she had never possessed in her days of wealth and self-indulgence.

She had fallen silent and found Andrew watching her, so she said, "The way home was tough and testing but my determination won through and here I am. I had no possessions to weigh me down," though she had carried with her heavy guilt for her selfish hedonism. "When I arrived in this country, I was forced to beg from a stranger the cost of a train ticket northwards, and a kind woman paid for my final bus fare. I walked the last few miles – an appropriate final humility." Here Kate stopped, her heart full, and she was unable to tell her companion about the amazing love her father had shown his undeserving child when she finally reached home.

Her brother's attitude was different. Would he forgive her for the pain she'd caused? She looked across at David and her eyes filled with tears. She would try to win back his love and respect, but it seemed hopeless.

During the dinner, Maria could see that David felt tired and isolated and, though he tried hard to dispel his sombre mood, he could not let himself relax and enjoy the evening. He smiled tightly at those around him, tried to join in the conversation and hoped, as she did, they did not notice his lack of spontaneity. Maria was well aware of his disquiet as she tried to distract him by talking about the hotel and the progress in creating a garden for guests' children, a project which she had devised. He said little and she wondered yet again what married life with him would be like. She found it hard to visualise and this made her uneasy. She saw uncertainty in his eyes. Was this only because of Kate's return? Or he was unsure about their future together?

Dinner was over. Theo had made a short speech expressing his happiness over his daughter's return home after five long years away. Everyone was well aware that Theo had forgiven his wayward child. Many guests took their leave whilst some stayed for coffee and a brief chat with the prodigal daughter. The musicians finished playing and were packing up ready to go.

David said to Maria that he needed some fresh air. She went with him out on to the terrace and they leaned over the wall, savouring the fragrant smell of the summer garden.

"I couldn't stay in there another minute," said David. "Everyone avoided mentioning what we all know – that my sister's led a wild and selfish life and has wrecked her health too."

"Kate's exhausted. She will get better when she can eat properly and get some sleep," ventured Maria soothingly.

"She looks as if she's half starved – that garment was hanging off her. Of course I realise that it's the lovely dress that I gave you to celebrate our engagement."

"I lent it to her – she arrived home with nothing but what she stood up in – a torn pair of jeans and a tattered T-shirt. She needed something better for her welcome home party."

"It was a special gift for a special occasion," David said reproachfully. "My scarlet sister is wearing that white dress so it's tainted. I never want you to wear it again."

"I won't because I plan to give it to her. It's a special gift to someone who really needs the hand of friendship." Maria sounded piqued. "I'm sorry I've upset you – I'd no idea that you'd mind so much."

"I do mind that my beautiful fiancée – a respectable woman – has got so intimate with my disreputable sister that she can lend her clothes."

"Oh, for goodness sake, David! She's going to be my sister-in-law!" Maria burst out in exasperation. "Unless I can't put up with your prejudice." She turned away from him and the heels of her shoes echoed her irritation as she stalked angrily back indoors.

The outside door banged behind her. David winced and looking moodily in through the windows at the few remaining guests, he saw Maria re-emerge in the room and walk across to join his sister and father. Why did he feel so resentful? He turned his back on the scene, struck the balustrade with his fist and stared into the darkness.

Just below him in the garden, half hidden in the foliage, a dark figure was watching the angry man on the terrace illuminated by the lights from the room behind him. A look of sly satisfaction passed across the face of the intruder. It was a pity the daughter had made it home and the father hadn't thrown her out. But jealousy had flared up and there were signs of cracks in the relationship between the son and his fiancée. This would be welcome news to Ator. Family harmony wasn't the only thing that would go up in smoke. Soon all the guests would leave and the family go to bed. Then it would be time for him to act. Ator would be pleased with his night's work.

Three hours later, the moon rose from behind the hills in a circle of luminous light. If anyone had been awake in the valley at that hour, they might have heard the sound of an owl screeching, the sighing of the trees in the rising wind, and the quiet sound of a car as it passed stealthily along the country road. A few minutes later, they might have observed a thin spiral of smoke curling upwards from amongst the trees.

But there was no-one awake to see it. Soon an orange flame became visible on the hillside and the sound of crackling disturbed some of the animals that lived in the vicinity and that ran from it in fear. Some birds rose up and flew off and two mice scurried away from the barn.

In the building, sitting on the workbench, the bronze eagle that had been delivered that day from the foundry seemed to watch impassively as the flames licked upwards from the corner of the building and took hold along the wooden beams. An unfinished model of a leaping hare and a portrait head in clay ready for despatch to the foundry began to soften and drip on to the floor. Here was work in progress – Theo's studio was on fire.

Theo was woken in the early hours by a telephone call from the police. A cowman, doing the first milking of the day in a local dairy farm, had seen the burning barn and called the fire brigade. David woke up and within minutes they were on their way, leaving an exhausted Kate asleep in one of the hotel rooms.

Soon they were on the scene, watching the firemen tackle the blaze. It took a few more hours to get it under control and fully damped down. Theo saw that the old barn was a blackened ruin and his tools destroyed, but he was relieved that only possessions had been lost. No-one had been hurt and the fire had not spread to set the surrounding trees alight. He saw that David was horrified by the destruction and upset over the loss of his father's sculptures.

Theo, still aglow with pleasure over his daughter's homecoming, decided he would not let the disaster steal his contentment in her return. Most of the bronzes he created were sold or in a gallery – it was work in progress that had gone up in smoke. And his studio. David was being practical and dealing with the departing fire team. He appreciated his son's sympathy and help.

They returned home that morning with grimy faces, their clothes smelling of ash and smoke. Kate was still asleep but, whilst David was making some tea, she appeared. When they told her the news, she became distressed and burst into tears. Theo sat her down at the kitchen table, gave her a cup of tea and put his arm round her shoulders.

He spoke to them both. "Let's not allow this unfortunate fire to dampen our spirits and wipe out the real joy of Kate's return to her family and her home. I may have lost my studio but I've found my daughter." He glanced up at David, whose impassive expression told him more than words.

5

Theo and Kate looked up to watch for the first strands of smoke to appear. When some wisps emerged from the chimney and wafted upwards into the pale azure sky, they both hugged one another in delight.

"There you are, Daddy. Smoke from your own hearth. It confirms that you are now living in your new home." Kate threw her thin arms wide and called out to the valley below and its resident population of birds and small animals, "Please welcome my father to his new abode, Home Barn."

The sounds of subdued tweeting and birdcalls continued unabated from the surrounding trees. Theo laughed and said, "Business as usual."

"I hope it will be," said Kate. "The birds will always be here. But you need to get back to work. You must be itching to make something new."

"I may not have had a studio for over a year but I've been thinking about what I might do. I've made a couple of models on David's kitchen table. I've been able to spend time with the galleries marketing my work and encourage them to sell editions of earlier sculptures. This has brought cash into the bank to help me rebuild the barn." They both gazed in pleasure at the newly finished stone building, which now comprised a new studio and an adjacent annexe as a dwelling for the sculptor.

Kate put her arm through her father's. "Let's go in and see how warm it gets with the new stove."

They entered through a tall door which led into the studio. The barn had been resurrected after the fire, which had damaged the old structure but not entirely destroyed it. The new roof was supported by four new wooden beams in pale oak and two older blackened ones that had survived. Theo had wanted to incorporate as much as possible from the burned-out building to ensure continuity from the past. The old stone walls had been cleaned and re-pointed but stones that were badly damaged had been replaced.

Theo was pleased. "It's much less draughty and damp. It used to be so cold in the winter months. The wood burner should enable me to work throughout the year."

"It's throwing out a lot of heat." Kate watched the flames through the open door and felt a corresponding warmth in her heart. A lot had happened in the intervening year since her return and the dramatic night of her welcome party and the barn fire.

Theo strode over to the huge window which looked out over his world – the peaceful valley below and the hills beyond. "How I love the view! For years I've watched the seasons pass from up here."

Kate joined him and as they gazed at the familiar landscape, she said, "Daddy, I hope you realize how grateful I am to you and David for accepting me back into your lives."

"Of course I do, my little one," Theo said with a smile. "You keep telling us!"

"I'm never quite certain that David is as enthusiastic as you are about my return."

"Don't worry about him – he'll come round. You promised me not to dwell on what's past and forgiven, so let's go forward together, you in a new job and me in my new studio. Let's make a cup of coffee in my new cottage to celebrate."

They went through a small connecting door on the other side of the studio into the extension, which provided a large open-plan sitting area and dining space. Here stood a battered but attractive old wooden table and chairs in front of the window. Wooden stairs led up to a large bedroom in the roof space and a shower room.

Kate put on the kettle in a small kitchen at the rear. She was relieved that David and Theo no longer had to share the apartment in the hotel. It had become very overcrowded with three of them, and the confined living space had exacerbated disagreement about her role in the family, what she might do and where she would live. In her anxiety to made amends and earn her own living in any modest job, Kate had offered to work in the hotel as a chambermaid. David said he would find it difficult having his sister in menial employment in a business that he owned and ran, but she thought his problem was the thought of having his bohemian sister on the staff. Although the siblings appeared to be on good terms on the surface, there were tricky undercurrents of resentment on his part and guilt on hers.

In the end, Kate had gone her own way. She did farm work for her cousin, Jamie, for a few months and recently found a job working in the kitchen of a local pub called The Crown, where there was a restaurant. She wanted to be independent, and rented a small, inexpensive house nearby and shared it with another woman.

Kate emerged from the kitchen with a coffee pot and took down two mugs from an old kitchen dresser which she had found in a shop in town. She saw her father looking at a fine pair of landscapes which David had given him and hung on the cottage walls.

"Thanks for helping me move in and assemble everything," said Theo taking his mug of coffee from her. "I couldn't have done it without you and David. He managed to move my huge collection of books." He pointed to a towering bookcase, crammed with his library.

"You once said that where your books are is where home is," Kate reminded him. "All that's left for you to do is drive down the hill to Homeward House and collect the couple of cases with all your clothes."

"I suppose I do need a few sweaters, socks and things," Theo said vaguely. Kate smiled – everyone knew how little personal appearance mattered to him. "It will be peaceful here," he said looking across at his daughter over the rim of his cup as he drank.

"You need your own home. I think Andrew has done a great job getting the barn rebuilt and designing the annexe."

"He's a talented young man. I'm grateful to him."

"David and he often chat animatedly about art and architecture. Maria gets on well with Andrew too. She and I have become good friends which puzzles my brother who wonders what we have in common. He thinks we're as wide apart as day and night."

"For that matter, David and Maria are very different. They share compassion for others and a genuine affection for each other, but..." Theo tailed off.

"There's a lack of passion," Kate put it into words.

"It's been a long engagement." Theo avoided the questions in both their minds: what was the reason for delay; would the marriage actually take place?

Kate rose to her feet. "Daddy, I should be off to work soon."

"You're doing alright," said Theo giving her a kiss, "and I'm proud of you."

"I can't see any reason why you should be."

"Because you've changed, Kate. Now you think of others first. That's why I'm pleased – it has taken determination to turn yourself around!"

"Your encouragement has helped, Daddy. But I'm by no means totally reformed. Perfection will take a little longer." This was said with a cheeky smile. She picked up her bag and slung it round her shoulder. "Bye – see you Thursday."

She set off down the track to the road below. It was nearly two miles to the pub and she usually walked. When she reached the main road, she turned and waved, knowing he would be watching even if she couldn't see him through the window. He raised his hand as if in blessing.

Theo stood there thinking about his children. Kate was making progress, her sunny personality re-emerging after her traumatic time overseas. He was more concerned about his son whose restless energy meant that he never relaxed. He gazed down at the hotel far below and felt apprehensive for its success. David needed income to pay off his large loans and he needed a supportive wife to help him through this critical period.

David's blue car appeared on the lower road, and turned up the track to Home Barn. Theo was not expecting his son but perhaps David felt the need to see him. He walked through the connecting door into the studio and stood there waiting.

The car came to a halt, scrunching on the new gravel outside, and a car door banged.

Theo turned to greet David with a smile but this faded when he saw his son's furious face. "David, what's the matter?"

"Maria's broken off our engagement. I can't believe it!"

"Tell me about it," Theo said sitting down on a wooden bench and indicating the space beside him to encourage his distraught son to sit down too.

David was too upset. He paced angrily around the studio as he spoke. "You may have suspected things haven't been right with me and Maria for a few months. I thought it was my fault – because I've had little time to spend with her. There's so much going on at the hotel – I'm snowed under with functions and the forthcoming conference. She's been involved in staff training too, so I see less of her than when she was in reception. But now I find that my closest friend, Andrew, whom I've always trusted, has been undermining Maria's commitment to me. He's always singing her praises and saying how lucky I am. For all I know, he wants to step into my shoes with her. Or maybe he's already climbed into her bed!"

"Calm down, David. It's unthinkable that Maria would be unfaithful whilst engaged to be married. She's not that sort of girl. Andrew may admire Maria – we all do – she's a lovely person, but you don't have grounds for this jealousy."

"Then why has she handed me back the ring and said she can't marry me?"

"If you lost your rag and accused her of something she's not done, then I can sympathize with her response." Theo's disapproval was evident.

"I'm going to have it out with Andrew. If it's true, it'll be the end of our friendship. At least now this building project is completed, he won't be forever hanging around here or the hotel."

"Andrew doesn't 'hang around' – he's a hard worker – like you, which is why you both respect each other. I'd think very carefully before you confront him. Don't cause a rift that you might regret."

David gave a sigh of exasperation and sat down heavily on the bench beside his father.

Theo continued, "I suggest you wait until your anger subsides and consider whether you have overreacted, or if there is a deeper underlying problem. I'm sorry that Maria has made this decision but you must have given her provocation – not just today but during these past months." He put a hand round his son's hunched shoulders and spoke gently. "David, I've seen that all's not well between you both. You don't seem like a young couple hoping to spend the rest of their lives together. Why have you both allowed your wedding to be postponed for so long? Do you really want to go through with this marriage? Examine your feelings. That's what Maria has been doing. Don't fly into a rage and pretend to be jealous. It's unfair on Andrew."

There was silence before David said slowly, "You may be right. As always you get to the heart of the matter. I have had doubts but I'm upset that Maria hasn't voiced her misgivings before now."

"She has done today and although you know it's the right decision, you don't like it because your pride's hurt. Don't drag in unwarranted suspicions of Andrew in order to find someone else to blame."

"I'm not convinced that Andrew has no interest in Maria," said David, his face tense, "and I still love her."

"Perhaps you do, or you think you do. Better to make a break now and reconsider, before embarking on a marriage that might be unhappy for both of you." Theo paused before saying, "I'm very fond of Maria and I expect she's upset too. I hope you can remain friends."

David sighed and got to his feet. In an effort to focus on something other than the misery of his broken engagement, he caught sight of a large bronze eagle, which had been delivered from the foundry a week before. "It's back!" he exclaimed with genuine delight. "It looks great. I can't believe it survived." The bronze had been in the studio on the night of the fire.

"Bronze is tough and hard to destroy. When I found my blackened eagle in the charred ruins of the barn, I had to save it."

Theo walked over to the bronze and ran his hand over the outstretched wings of the imperious bird, poised for flight on its huge claws, its curved beak craning forward. "It's good to see it again. It could have been a total write-off after the fire. But the heat wasn't too intense in that corner and I sent it back to the foundry, where they sandblasted it. A couple of months ago, I went up there and did the patination. As you can see, the colour is darker and richer now – rather different from the pale golden colour it was before the fire. I had intended to declare an edition of six but now I've decided to keep it as a unique piece and never cast another. This eagle went through fire and has been reborn." He did not mention that the bronze portrait heads of his children had been destroyed.

"It's like a phoenix rising from the ashes – very symbolic." David touched the piece thoughtfully and turned to his father, choosing his words. "I'm sure you'll be happy in this peaceful place. I hope there's no hard feelings about my wanting to live on my own."

"David," said his father with a smile, "you needn't feel bad that it's me who's flown the nest rather than you. It'll be better for us both and when we do meet up it will be because we want to spend time together and not because we're sharing accommodation and can't avoid each other."

David nodded, took a deep breath and said, "I need to get back to the hotel. And try not to think about the broken pieces of my personal life." He gave his father a quick hug and left.

Theo reflected how fortunate he was that his children still came to him for advice, though they had to make their own choices and live with the consequences. Later that day he drove to the hotel to collect his remaining bags and clothes. He returned to his new home, unpacked and then ate a simple meal. He gazed contentedly across at his full bookshelves relieved that his books had survived. He had always kept them in the hotel library because the old studio had been damp. He took down one of his favourite volumes, sat beside his glowing wood burner and read.

"A month ago! You and David broke off your engagement then." Kate was hurt. "Why haven't I heard before now? I thought we were friends."

Maria was standing on the doorstep of Kate's house. "Can I come in? We'll talk about it inside." She was less comfortable than Kate about airing private information in public. When the door had closed behind them, she asked, "How did you hear?"

"David telephoned me earlier today and happened to mention it casually. Important news about his life – and it just comes out in conversation. You didn't say anything either!"

Maria, touched by the concern on Kate's face, realised she had offended her. "We decided not to broadcast the news until I've finished working at the hotel. It will be easier for both of us if I'm not in reception day after day where everyone might feel embarrassed about what to say to me – or to him. I'm leaving at the end of this week."

"So you've lost your job too. That's awful. How could David do this?" Kate flared up.

"You've jumped to the wrong conclusion. He didn't want me to go – but I do. I persuaded him it would be difficult to stay on. In any case, I've been at the hotel for four years and I feel that it's time to go back to my original vocation – nursing."

"You're just saying that to make out he's not a tyrant. You're so bloody nice!" Kate got to her feet, angrily saying, "I need a drink," and went through to the small cottage kitchen to get a bottle of wine.

Maria followed her and stood in the doorway whilst Kate searched for a bottle of red wine she knew was lurking in the untidy cupboard. "David's no tyrant," she said soothingly. "In fact he's one of the kindest men I've ever met. That's what attracted me to him in the first place. He doesn't choose to let the world know that underneath all that hard work and efficiency there's a sensitive and generous man trying to conceal what he regards as a weakness."

"He's certainly fooled me. Though now I come to think of it, he's always been over-sensitive and wary about showing his feelings. Not like me; I wear my heart on my sleeve, blurt it all out and have no secrets. We're not very close anymore so I ought not to be surprised that he didn't tell me he isn't going to marry the woman he claims to love. But you and I are friends, Maria, so I'm sorry you felt unable to let me know."

In response to this reproach, Maria explained, "I couldn't tell you before David did, and he chose to delay talking about it. Your father knew – but he never breaks confidences."

Kate had eventually located the corkscrew skulking behind a pile of unwashed crockery. "Pity that my reformed way of life doesn't seem to have improved my dreadful untidiness," she said, opening the bottle.

Maria, who didn't want any wine, accepted the glass to mollify her friend and took a small sip. Kate took a gulp and, going back into the small sitting room, lowered herself into a sagging sofa. Maria sat in a chair and said tentatively, "I do hope my not marrying your brother won't affect our friendship."

"We're like chalk and cheese, you and me – pale, pure chalk and mouldy old cheese," Kate said with a laugh. "But somehow we get on together. I haven't had a real female friend since…" She paused, deciding not to mention

Layla's name, and then continued, "…a call-girl that I knew in my wicked past who really helped me when I was desperate, down and out!"

"Mouldy old cheese! Why do you describe yourself in such disparaging terms?" Maria said choosing to ignore Kate's reference to the past and avoid eliciting a flood of embarrassing details. "You're not old – only twenty-seven, a couple of years older than me. And your skin looks marvellous now you're eating properly."

"I can't afford the rubbish takeaway meals or expensive convenience food that I used to gobble down without a thought, so I have to cook and eat simple stuff."

"Your hair is so lovely now – thick and dark just like David's."

Kate was pleased with this compliment. She had been growing out her dyed blonde hair for so long, feeling embarrassed about the dark roots that were becoming so visible. A couple of months before she had taken the plunge and paid to have the rest of the dry ends cut off, and now had a short dark bob. She looked at her friend's clear complexion and sleek fair hair that she always wore tied back.

"And you look as you always do – beautiful."

Maria blushed modestly, saying, "That's the sort of thing my mother says." She still lived with her mother who suffered from back pain.

"Is she upset about your breaking off with David?"

"She's disappointed, though to be honest she never felt that we were ideally suited. He and I are alike, both diffident and reserved, but I'm not driven like David. I regard quality time together as a priority but he can't always see the need for it. He's self-effacing which makes it hard for him to be a hotelier and he has to push himself to be at ease with guests. My mother thinks I'd be happier with someone less introverted who would draw me out of my shell."

"I'm not sure I agree. But do go on with your defence of my brother's character."

"I don't think he needs defending – I just want you to see another side of him. He's honest and fair with all his employees, taking great care to ensure they feel appreciated and encouraged. He listens to their problems at work and tries to involve them in the solutions. Even though the hotel is only marginally in profit, he feels compulsion to help local charities, but he does this in a low-key, unostentatious way. He prefers to be generous in secret."

"That sounds like the good deeds that my father does."

"Like father like son, perhaps."

"Not really, Maria. He doesn't have our father's wonderful calmness of spirit. Theo loves everyone but David lacks passion. Passionate love is what a woman wants from the man she's marrying. I'm so sad that he doesn't love you like that."

"Perhaps I'm not the right woman to stir up strong feelings in David," Maria sighed. "And it's just as well we discovered it now. He's feeling bruised about it and so am I. We know it wouldn't have worked and need to put some space between us. And I have to find another job."

"That reminds me," said Kate glancing at a red clock sitting jauntily on a shelf with dog-eared books and chipped pottery ornaments. "I'll have to dash – I'm on an evening shift at the pub." She grabbed her coat and bag.

Maria stood up too. "I'm on my way home – I'll give you a lift."

Later that evening, the kitchen at the The Crown was less frenetic than it had been an hour earlier when the rush to produce meals had been at its height. Kate was still busy stowing plates in the dishwasher and washing up all the pans in the sink. She never wore gloves and at the end of a long shift her hands were bleached and wrinkled. Her glasses steamed up, so she always took them off, not minding that the filthy crockery was out of focus. Her back was aching as she picked up a tray of clean wine glasses and walked through to the area behind the bar. The chef had gone home, one waitress had already left and the other was serving coffees. Colin and Amy, the licensees, were still serving drinks to customers as she came through.

"Hi Kate. How's it going?" Amy's chirpy question needed no response – they could see she was exhausted. "There's a couple who came in earlier asking after you."

"Really?" Kate showed no interest.

"They seemed to know you work here. But I didn't let on you were in this evening in case you want to avoid them. And you might."

Kate looked up sharply from stacking glasses on a shelf. "Why do you think that?"

"I dunno. Just a feeling about the guy – he's sort of sinister. Are they still here, Colin?"

"Nah, I think they've left." He was pulling a pint and didn't look up.

"You're wrong." Amy dug Kate in the ribs. "They're over there in the far corner by the fire. A tall, dark chap and a woman with long hair."

Kate turned and, putting on her glasses, looked in the direction Amy indicated. A couple were chatting animatedly together sitting at a small table. She immediately recognised them – the past had collided with the present! At that moment the woman glanced up and their eyes met. Layla. And Josh! Appalled, Kate dived back into the safety of the kitchen. She leaned over her sink, a griping pain in her gut, and took a few large breaths.

How can Josh and Layla be here in this country? It can't be a coincidence. They must have tracked me down. Her thoughts were in turmoil and she felt panic at the havoc they might cause. She had managed to forge a new life, salvaged from the wreckage of her past. The pair were unconventional and reckless, and Kate shuddered, feeling a cold premonition they would disrupt her life again. She knew them well – they had been through a lot together. At best they would disclose embarrassing revelations and at worst they might tempt her to abandon her good resolutions. Kate straightened up, and as she tried to calm her racing heart, she remembered what fun they once had had together and how wickedly amusing they could be. She must not underestimate their magnetism.

"Your friend's at the bar and says she wants to see you," Colin's voice broke in on her thoughts.

"Tell her I've gone home. And please, Colin, don't tell her where that is," Kate said urgently. "I'll just finish up my work and go home when the pub's closed."

"OK, darlin'. Trust in me. By the way, I love the new hairstyle." And he disappeared back to the bar.

An hour and a half later, well after closing time and much later than usual, Kate left by the back entrance. Colin, who lived over the pub, was still checking beer barrels and doing the final jobs before locking up. She told him she'd been given a lift to work and left her bike at home, hoping he might offer to run her home, but Colin just shrugged and asked if she wanted him to call a taxi. Since the cost of a taxi at this time of night would make a serious dent in her meagre wages, she opted to walk home – it was only a couple of miles.

Kate peered out, heaved a sigh of relief when she saw the car park was empty, and took off her glasses. Layla and Josh had left. She wondered where they were staying and knew that if they really wanted to find her, for whatever reason that might be, they wouldn't give up. She tied the belt round her coat, slung her bag over her shoulder and set off down the country road. She had learned how to survive in dangerous areas in big cities so a dark walk home on a dry, starlit night posed no problems. What made her nervous was the prospect that she would soon have to confront her disreputable friends. She needed time to work out how she would deal with them and with temptations they would bring into her life. She was already relishing the forbidden pleasure of seeing them again.

As she walked along she remembered that although Josh and Layla had helped to fleece her and in the end abandoned her, they had taken care of her when Karl absconded with the rest of her money. She was curious to hear what had happened to them in the intervening years and had to admit that when she had caught sight of them across the bar, she felt a surge of affection that would be difficult to repress when they met. How could she deny their charm and reject their company? Face to face, would she have the strength to renounce them? Perhaps she didn't have to.

She had denied herself so much. It was hard, even with the help and encouragement of her father, to conquer her laziness, suppress her appetite for possessions and to come to terms with her guilt about her selfish behaviour. There were times when she was tempted to give up and go back to a less morally demanding life. Her job was menial and sometimes she regretted not accepting help. Things were difficult. Money was scarce. She shared a cold two-bedroomed house with a dull woman and some very tatty furniture. Her health was better now she was back home in the country with a supportive family nearby. But where was she going? What did the future hold?

She recalled that she had told Layla and Josh that her family were all dead. They would find out that this wasn't the case, if they hadn't already done so.

66

Unashamedly inquisitive, they might want to meet her brother and father – she shuddered at the thought.

At this point she heard the sound of a car on the road behind her and, since she was wearing a dark coat and had no torch, she stopped and stepped back off the road on to the grass verge in case the driver could not see her. As the car approached, she realised it was going very slowly and a sudden horrifying thought occurred to her: it was them. Looking for her.

Needing time to compose herself and now desperate not to be seen, she shrank back into the hedge as they came alongside.

The headlights illuminated the empty road ahead as the vehicle stopped. She heard the passenger window wind down and a deep, familiar voice said laughingly, "Would this be a damsel in distress?" It was Josh. "Could this be our pal, Kat?"

Another mellifluous voice chimed in, "Are you hiding from us? Surely not. When we want so much to see you." Layla's.

When Josh opened the passenger door to get out and the inside light came on, Kate, even though her vision was blurred, could see Layla in the driving seat, leaning across with a wide and welcoming smile on her face. Feeling slightly embarrassed by her unjustified fear of them, Kate stepped forward and stood frozen with uncertainty whilst Josh came over to her and pulled her into his arms. "Hey, girl, you look great," he said, giving her a big kiss on the lips and an enormous hug.

Kate's reaction was slow. She realised she hadn't been kissed on the lips for a long while and she stood still, savouring it, immobilised by the sudden intimacy, a remembrance of things past. She could say nothing.

"Layla, here's Kat – the blonde bombshell – our Kat. And she's really a brunette!" shouted Josh, kindly choosing to ignore Kate's silence.

"I knew that all along," said Layla, climbing out of the car and leaving it in the middle of the road, lights blazing. She came across and when Josh had released Kate, she hugged her too. "Why didn't you want to say hello to us back there in the pub? Are you ashamed of us?" She held Kate at arm's length and looked into her face.

"I'm ashamed of myself," said Kate swiftly gathering her wits. "I didn't imagine I would evade you two for long and I wanted to get home, remove my skivvy working clothes and pop on my mascara and fishnets before you confronted me."

"Yeah. It's our Kat of the quick repartee and the flashing eyes," Josh said, grinning in delight. "And those long, beautiful legs, even without the fishnets. You look good, even in the dark. May we give you a lift, lovely lady?"

Kate smiled, in spite of her misgivings. "It is good to see you both again. We go back a long way and I've missed your wicked sense of humour."

They dropped her back at the dark little house where Jane was sound asleep, and returned to their cheap hotel in the town a few miles away. Kate was thankful as she was bone tired and needed to sleep. And to think.

Kate's intuition told her that her quiet life would be disrupted and might never get back on course. She would need some strength of character and ingenuity to deflect them from whatever their purpose was in coming here. And she was as certain as she could be that it was not just for old friendship's sake that this couple had travelled so far. There was always an ulterior – often a predatory – motive in all that Josh and Layla did.

As she fell asleep in her cluttered bedroom, she remembered them saying they'd come by in the afternoon the next day when she had finished her lunchtime shift. They wanted to catch up on her life, to tell her their news and to share a bottle of good wine. And who knew what would happen after that?

PART TWO

"Out of the mud two strangers came...

Nothing on either side was said.
They knew they had but to stay their stay
And all their logic would fill my head:
As that I had no right to play
With what was another man's work for gain.
My right might be love but theirs was need.
And where the two exist in twain
Theirs was the better right – agreed."

From 'Two Tramps in Mud Time'
by Robert Frost

6

Kate quietly crept down the staircase and, to avoid waking Josh, tiptoed through the sitting room into the kitchen. While the kettle boiled she surveyed the dirty crockery, some piled on the draining board and the rest swimming in the murky water of the sink. Jane usually undertook this chore, knowing that Kate spent many of her working hours washing dishes. But the woman had moved out three weeks before because she was fed up with the two lodgers – or 'spongers' as she called them. The kitchen had deteriorated in her absence. Jane had paid half the monthly rent and Kate would soon have to find another to share the cost or else she would slide into debt. Or get evicted.

There were no clean mugs in the cluttered cupboard so with a sigh of distaste she dipped her fingers into the cold, scummy water and found one, which she rinsed under the tap before spooning in some instant coffee. She felt tired – she wasn't getting enough sleep. Life might get more difficult and problems were looming but in spite of the risks it was more fun.

Still in her nightshirt she stood on the cold flagstones in her bare feet, sipping the hot liquid, and looked out through the smeary window pane at the back garden and the yew tree. The sun was already high in the sky, dispelling the dew on the grass. A splash of orange attracted her attention and she realised it was a shawl that Layla had left hanging over a bush last night, after she had danced sinuously across the patch of unkempt grass, flapping her hands to show Josh how butterflies fluttered. They hadn't gone to bed until after 3 am.

Kate sighed. Her family would disapprove of her friends and she couldn't keep the pair's presence secret for long. They were too flamboyant. She wanted them to go – they were weakening her resolve. But she wanted them to stay – they made her laugh and brought colour back into her life. The risk was huge – they were also selfish and disruptive.

She glanced at the clock – it was after 11 am and her shift at the pub started at noon – so she needed to get dressed and go to work. She walked back through to the sitting room where Josh was sleeping on the sofa under a rug, his grubby feet sticking out at one end. Not wanting to wake him, she crept past but his arm shot out and grasped her leg, arresting her progress.

"Dream maiden, you are mine," he murmured sleepily, closing his eyes again but still gripping her with long, bony fingers.

"Josh, stop that," Kate said irritably. "I'm in a rush – you'll make me late."

"Don't leave me here all cold and alone," Josh implored in mock desperation.

"Don't be silly, Josh, let me go. I've got to have a shower and go to work," Kate pleaded, acutely aware of his warm hand on her calf.

Josh sat up and grabbed her arm with his other hand. "I've got a grip on the situation. You're tired but you're lonely. A cuddle at dawn is better than a yawn."

"It's way past dawn," said Kate, smiling as she looked down at his eyes gleaming with laughter in an unshaven face. She pulled away from him and staggered backwards as he suddenly released her. "You're such a joker," she called as she darted upstairs.

Josh lay back on the sofa, pulled the rug round him, and listened to the soft footsteps pattering across the floor above. She couldn't elude them – they were already halfway towards winning her back again. Layla would be awake soon and they needed to talk about their next move.

Theo was sitting on a wooden bench in the small park, enjoying the warmth of the June sunshine. He'd come into town to attend a governors' meeting at the school and now he was waiting to meet someone.

Theo had things on his mind. He hadn't seen his daughter for over four weeks which was unusual. He never intruded uninvited into his children's lives, hoping they would get in touch when they wanted to see him. He'd heard that Jane had moved out and had been worried that Kate was lonely, so a few days ago he'd telephoned. Kate had answered and he could hear the sound of music and conversation in the background. She did not want to talk and it was obvious she had friends around. He felt uneasy because she had sounded guarded, as if she was concealing some kind of trouble. Kate had a couple of hours off between her lunchtime shift and the start of the evening one at The Crown, so he resolved to call in briefly on his way home from the town in the afternoon – to see if all was well.

There was another young woman about whom he was concerned and he could see her gliding across the grass towards him with an angelic smile on her face. He rose to his feet.

"Theo, how lovely to see you." Maria reached up and gave him a gentle kiss on the cheek. "How kind of you to suggest we meet. I've brought some sandwiches for us."

"Great idea," said Theo as they sat down on the bench together. "How's the new job?"

"I enjoy working in a hospital again. I'd forgotten how satisfying nursing can be – and how tiring. I need a lot of patience, tact and stamina."

"Just as you had at the hotel. Looking after people requires kindness. I think the change is doing you good." Maria's perfect skin was always pale but she looked well and Theo was glad she was getting on with her life after her broken engagement to his son.

Maria did not dodge the obvious question. "How's David?" she asked looking directly into Theo's face.

"He's alright. He knows your decision was the right one but he's feeling bruised. He walks round from time to time with a slightly tragic look but it's wearing off and he's as busy as ever. Too busy – but you know all about that." Theo smiled and Maria nodded, her blonde hair framing her heart-shaped face.

"He'll recover soon and I hope he'll learn to relax more and enjoy life." Maria said. "It's unfortunate that he seems to have fallen out with his best friend too. Andrew can't understand why – neither can I. We met up the other day and Andrew told me that he thought he had offended David but could not think how."

"Have you seen Kate?" Theo asked, to steer the conversation into easier waters.

"Not recently. She doesn't come into town that much. I wonder why she continues working in that mindless job at the pub. She must have scrubbed off her guilt by now along with most of the skin on her hands! She ought to look for something better."

"She wants to live in the country and there aren't too many jobs about. I, too, wish she would think about the future instead of washing away the past. She always said she'd like to work with children and I've been trying to encourage her to do some training." Theo paused, and then added thoughtfully, "I'm also a little concerned because she's avoiding me and David for some reason. We usually meet up once a week for a chat or a meal but she's not been in touch. I'm going to drop in and see her on my way home."

"Do give her my love." Maria opened the paper bag and offered it to Theo. "How's your work going?"

"Thank you," he said taking a sandwich. "I like living next door to my work. It's peaceful up there in my barn and this helps my creativity." He took a bite and they sat there together eating companionably. "I miss seeing you at the hotel."

"I miss you, too, Theo. I don't remember my own father. I think I've adopted you as a substitute," she said softly.

Theo gently touched the top of the young woman's head with his large hand, and said, "I adopted you long ago, Maria. If ever you need help, just ask. I won't let you down."

Josh was sitting at the wooden table, a mug of coffee in front of him, sifting through various letters and papers that Kate had left crammed untidily into the drawer.

"You're nosy, always rooting about in other people's things." Layla spoke in mock reproof as she wandered round the room with a faded red silk dressing gown carelessly wrapped round her. Josh was wearing a pair of torn black jeans, but had no shirt on. His ribs were visible in his gaunt frame. *He always looks hungry*, Layla thought.

"The habit dies hard," Josh said without a trace of guilt. "There's nothing here of any value but the information is useful." He picked up couple of documents and waved them at her. "Here is a demand for rent arrears and an unpaid electricity bill. It's clear Kat's got no money of her own and lives from one week's miserable pay packet to the next."

Layla flicked one of his dirty socks off a kitchen chair and sat down. "Many people slave away in mundane menial jobs to scrape together enough to live on."

"But not us. We're smarter than that." Josh looked thoughtful as he read one of Kate's letters.

"Not at the moment. We're skint and living off poor Kat who can't afford it."

"That's never bothered us much in the past," said Josh, putting down the letter he had read and tapping it with his finger. "The writer of this letter approves of Kat's wish to try and redeem herself by earning her own living but would be prepared to help her if things get tough."

"She never used to have these guilt trips but she seems to have caught 'remorse' like an illness." Layla sounded puzzled.

"The letter's signed 'David'. He's her brother, isn't he?"

"Yes. We know she's got family – a father and a brother – and they're both wealthy. One's a famous sculptor whose work sells worldwide and the other's got a big hotel – that posh one a few miles up the road. A few years ago, when we first met, she told us about her inheritance. We assumed that meant her dad was dead, and she didn't deny it. Now we've discovered he's very much alive. We've even seen his new studio barn conversion on the side of the hill."

"We helped her spend her first 'inheritance' but it seems there might be more. As we suspected, our Kat has got expectations. Her family love her and would bail her out if she got into debt. For some reason she doesn't want to ask them." Josh grinned wide, showing a broken tooth. "But she may have to."

"I have a nasty feeling you're concocting some wicked little plan." Layla leaned across to him and said, "But don't do anything that will physically harm Kat. She's my friend and I care about her."

"I adore our lovely Kat. She's potentially our gold mine." Josh began to laugh.

At that moment the doorbell emitted a croaky buzz and they both looked at each other with raised eyebrows. Josh pulled the papers together and pushed them back into the open drawer whilst Layla got to her feet and slowly walked across the room, waiting until Josh had closed the drawer before opening the door.

A giant of a man with shaggy grey hair stood there looking down at her, a benign expression on his broad face. "Is Kate in?" he inquired politely.

"Sorry but she isn't. She had to stay longer at work this afternoon to do a stock-take of the stores. She'll probably be back in an hour." Layla didn't invite him in but she looked him squarely in the face.

"By the way, I'm Theo – Kate's father." Through the open door he could see Josh lounging at the table, bare-chested. He gave the man a brief wave and then transferred his gaze to the woman, giving her a smile of genuine warmth. "It's good to meet some of Kate's friends," he said.

74

"I'm Layla." She felt an irrepressible urge to offer her hand to him, which he took in a firm but gentle grip, his large fingers enveloping her small ones. She looked up at his azure blue eyes and thought, *here's a force to be reckoned with.*

With strange reluctance, she withdrew her hand and pointed over her shoulder. "That's Josh. He and I have known Kat – I mean, *Kate* – for a long while. We're visiting for a few days."

"I hope you enjoy your stay. Perhaps we'll meet again." Theo bestowed on her another wide smile, turned and walked down the path, the sunlight glinting on his head. At the gate, he gave a friendly wave before walking across the road to a car parked on the verge. As he drove off, the sun went behind a cloud and Layla went back into the house.

"Who was it?" Josh called. "The landlord come to collect what's due?"

"No. I've just met Kat's father." Her hand still felt warm from his grip and she said quietly, "His name's Theo and I have a feeling he won't be a soft touch."

"All dads love their girls – he must be concerned about her or he wouldn't have come round. Everyone has their weaknesses." Josh got to his feet, grabbed a crumpled shirt off the back of the sofa and sniffed it.

"You wouldn't care to wash this for me?" he asked holding it out to Layla.

"Wash it yourself. I don't skivvy for you – or anyone," she retorted crisply. "You know the rules, Josh. I'm not your wife, lover or servant."

"I know. We're just friends – and business partners."

"You got it. When we don't need or like each other anymore, then we can split," Layla said and went upstairs to get dressed. She sat down on the bed in the room that had been Jane's and looked out of the window. The leaves of the tree outside shimmered in the light and the breeze made them flicker on the bedroom walls. There were times when Layla caught a glimpse of a different kind of life, one that embraced trust and hope, but it always seemed elusive.

Josh sat down to put on his shoes, looking around for his missing sock. He was bored with sleeping in the living room and would have preferred to be in a luxury hotel room! They needed a plan of action. It was time to think about tapping into some of Kat's brother's resources. If his sister was in dire need, David would help her. Perhaps they could get her blamed for something bad enough to get her sacked from the pub. Then she'd have to turn to her family. An alternative plan of action might be if Kat could put in a good word for him so he could get a job at the hotel. Then he'd be on the inside and with affluent guests around there might be opportunities. But right now he was hungry again and went through to the kitchen to forage.

Another puncture! Kate swore under her breath and pushed the bicycle back against the wall of the yard at the rear of The Crown. She would have to walk home again – and today there was less time between her lunchtime and evening shifts because Colin had asked her to check the food stocks in the store and freezers. Wearily she slung her bag over her shoulder and set off.

After a few minutes she heard a car coming along the lane. As it passed, the driver slowed down and stopped. It was Andrew. He got out and called to her. "Want a lift home, Kate?"

"Yes, please! My bike's got a flat tyre again."

Andrew opened the passenger door for her and Kate got in, wondering to herself how many men she knew who still opened car doors – apart from her dad and brother, who always did.

As he slid back into his seat and set off, she gave him a grateful smile, saying, "What are you doing out this way?"

"I wanted to see your father and check up on the solar panels on the barn studio roof. It would be useful to know how effective they are. He wasn't there but as I was leaving he got back from town – I think he said he had a school governors' meeting. I've had a look at the installation and I'm heading back."

"I haven't had time to see Daddy for a while – I feel a bit bad about it." Kate sounded guilty.

Andrew glanced across at her. "I like the new haircut – it suits you," but it was her green eyes that fascinated him.

"Thanks. Perhaps my dark hair suits my reformed character better than dyed blonde."

They were nearly at the cottage and Andrew was braking. Kate, not wanting him to meet her new 'lodgers', said hurriedly, "Just drop me off – don't get out."

As the car stopped by her gate she was dismayed to see Josh sprawling in a canvas deckchair on the small patch of grass in front of the cottage. He was wearing his battered straw hat at a rakish angle and grinning at her. "I've got friends visiting," she said to Andrew and jumped out. "Thanks so much. See you soon."

She darted through the gate without noticing Andrew's cheery wave as he put the car into gear and drove on.

"Josh, how many times have I asked you not to flaunt yourself outside the front of the house – there's the garden out the back if you want to sit in the sun." Kate stood over him frowning.

"Don't be angry with me, Kat, my love," drawled Josh. "I feel a bit solitary in this little rural backwater and I need to see some life. The odd modest car and the occasional muddy tractor seem so exciting!"

"I still haven't told people you're staying here," protested Kate.

"What's the matter? Are you ashamed of us?" Layla asked, having appeared round the corner of the house with a half-eaten apple in her hand.

"When you say 'people', do you mean your family?" Josh put the knife in. Kate stared at them in horror.

"Kat, do you really think we don't know about your brother and his hotel? Was that him, by the way?"

"No. That was a friend – an architect who lives in town." They were both looking expectantly at her. "Look," Kate stammered, "I know I should have told you about David – but we don't get on very well. He's my only sibling and we're very different."

Layla sat down on the grass and threw the apple core into the hedge. "We also know another secret of yours – you and your brother aren't orphans either." She gave Kate a cheeky smile. "There's 'Daddy' too."

Kate sighed in dismay.

"All those late night, sympathy-seeking confessions long ago – 'I'm all on my own in the world'," Josh said mimicking a woman's voice. "All lies and evasions."

"It didn't matter to you two whether I had family or not – you were happy to help me spend my money until it ran out," Kate responded stingingly.

"Not quite true, my darling. You lost the last part without our assistance." Layla patted the ground beside her and Kate sat down miserably. "We're your mates who took you in and helped you after Karl dumped you – when you were destitute. We were very fond of you."

"And still are," said Josh with a leer.

Kate put her head in her hands. "I know all that and I'm grateful. We have fun – and there's not too much of that in my life at the moment. But I'm trying to turn over a new leaf and not sponge on people and not tell lies. I'm trying to be less selfish."

"And we're a part of your wicked old life that you aren't proud of, so we get tarred with the same brush. Is that fair?" Layla hoped she sounded hurt.

"Kat, look at you." Josh spoke in his teasing way. "Slaving away at that rubbish job. Living on a pittance. This hair-shirt lark isn't for you. Stop beating yourself up and loosen up. You're young and need to live. I'm sure your father would understand that."

"Leave my father out of this. He's a kind and loving parent and only wants the best for me." She was near to tears. Josh and Layla exchanged glances.

"I think I met him this afternoon," Layla said airily. "Big man with a lovely smile. Calls himself Theo – he said to tell you he'd called by."

Kate put her face in her hands and gave a low moan.

"Come on, girl," Josh said getting up and crouching down beside her with his arm round her shoulders. "You were never going to keep them a secret. We always find things out."

"And you can't keep us hidden for much longer either," Layla giggled and put her arm round Kate's other shoulder. "Don't worry, darling. We won't disgrace you. We won't cause any problems."

Yes, you will, Kate thought, *and if I'm not careful you'll mess up my life again.* She gave them a weak smile, saying, "Sorry, guys. It's just that you turn up out of the blue and I need time to adjust."

"Has it occurred to you that we too might want to straighten our lives out?" said Layla putting a pious expression on her face.

"I'm thinking of getting a job locally," said Josh, with a suspect note of sincerity in his voice. "Can't live on you for much longer – we need to contribute."

Kate grimaced and got to her feet. She knew only too well that Josh was dreadfully dishonest and that Layla rarely told the truth. "I'm going to put the kettle on – I need a cup of tea."

Josh followed her into the cottage. "To hell with tea! Do we have any of that rot-gut wine left?"

"Have you completed the assignment?" The voice sounded impatient. "Give me a report."

Jakob spoke quietly into his mobile. "As you instructed, I tracked down the thief and the hooker in another city. I got drinking with them both in a dark club and they had no inkling that I was anything other than another drifter. I gave the thief information about a lucrative target, who happened to be one of the hooker's clients. The woman got him access to her rich client's hotel room and he did the job. I slipped the police enough information to get on their track, but also managed to warn them so they both escaped without being caught. They needed to disappear and I persuaded a friend to feed them news about Kate living near rich relatives in another country, where they could lie low for a while. They took the bait and they've now been with her for a month. She's panicking because she knows they're big trouble and if they start telling tales about her past, it'll mess up her new cosiness with her family." Jakob ended, knowing Ator well enough not to expect any words of approval.

"Would these two recognize you?"

"They might. That's why I've drafted in Ross. His English is excellent. He also knows what Kate looks like and what her weaknesses are."

"Will she recognize him?"

"No chance. She never saw him – she was unconscious."

"What about the others?"

"They don't know Ross – they were once at the same nightclub but it was crowded and they were high."

"Another operative means more expense. Tell him I'll brief him direct. He'll hear from me."

Jakob was annoyed at being excluded from the next step in his employer's plan. He had no idea why the pig had so much hatred for the target family. "And what about me?"

"You have another assignment. Instructions and funds in the usual place." The line went dead.

Jakob threw his mobile down on the hotel bed in a fury. Ator never gave him any credit for ingenuity. And never gave him the full picture. He hadn't even met his detestable employer. Always curt telephone calls and payment by discreet means. How he wanted to find out where Ator was, get a look at him and tell him what he thought of him! But it was unlikely he would ever have the chance and it would be most unwise. Jacob's work was an infernal servitude to a powerful individual whose disembodied voice dominated his life.

David was dog-tired. It had been an exhausting week at the hotel – a conference, a wedding, a huge dinner party and all the rooms full. There had been problems with the PA system and delays with deliveries.

"Two of the staff are ill, my sous-chef is on holiday and, to make matters worse, the head barman has announced he will be leaving."

He was having his weekly meeting with Olga, who asked, "Can we manage with one barman? It would keep costs down."

"We must have a head barman – the other bar staff doubles as a waitress."

"Francis has been saying we should try to reduce staff costs," Olga reminded him.

"He tells me that I'm good at hiring but not at firing. I'm used to him issuing dire warnings, but I do think it's useful to have an accountant who's a pessimist," David grinned.

After the meeting was over, he felt he needed a bit of space and decided to take a walk. There had been a report that the fencing along the lower meadow had been damaged by a large branch which had fallen off one of the trees, so he decided to walk down to have a look. On the way he could check on the lawns and the grounds.

The farmland adjacent to the hotel grounds was owned by his cousin, Jamie, who was married with two small boys. He had a large herd of cattle and a few hundred acres of grazing and arable land, and lived in an old farmhouse a few miles away. David had always been on good terms with his cousin. In his late teens, Jamie had fallen for Kate but she had not reciprocated his adoration, so he transferred his affection to Penny, who wanted to be married to a farmer and had since made Jamie a very contented man.

David was faintly envious of his friend's situation and remembered the summers when as a student he had helped out at the farm, working alongside Jamie, enjoying the outdoor life.

As he walked along in the warm sunshine, he felt his tiredness evaporate and serenity envelop him. He looked around at the peaceful scene – the beautiful trees, the water meadows, the river glinting in the distance, the familiar line of hills – and he began to unwind. He loved this place and never wanted to leave it. But it was lonely. Though there were many guests in residence, as proprietor of the hotel he often felt isolated and had few real friends. He missed having his father around in the evenings. Theo's unconditional affection and calm common sense were a balm when the pressure got too much. Kate had taken herself off to a dingy house and a dreary job, so the return of his only sibling had not really impacted his life that much. Sadly it seemed there was no way back to a closer relationship with her. Maria had gone too and the prospect of a happy married life had for the present receded. What was the matter with him? Why couldn't he be settled like Jamie?

At the lower meadow he could see that one of the old willows had lost a large limb, which had flattened some of the wire fencing. Willows often split and it had happened before. He decided to walk across a few fields to the farm and ask Jamie if he could move it with his tractor in a day or two. There was no stock in the adjacent field but he ought to warn his cousin not to put cattle in there until the job was done. He climbed over a stile and set off in the direction of the farm.

The cottage was quiet. Josh had caught a local bus and gone into the town to "look for work". Layla thought it more likely he'd gone to find a congenial pub and some company. He was a social animal, at ease with a drink in his hand and a friendly face beside him. She hoped he wouldn't drink too much and would remember to bring back a couple of bottles with him. Their wine had run out – again.

Layla was restless and wondered whether she could stay here for much longer. The house was dire but the area was beautiful though isolated. She wanted a change, to never have to return to her previous profession, but what work could she do here? She was disinclined to try and persuade Kate to obtain funds from her family to help them all along. She stared out of the window at the glorious day and decided to go for a walk. She couldn't be bothered to change out of her long, red skirt but she grabbed her black jacket from a peg by the door as she went out. Twisting her dark mane of hair into a knot at the back of her neck, she set off down the road.

After a while there was a sign on the left indicating a footpath and, looking down the narrow track, she could see a field and a clump of trees in the distance, which she decided to head for. The sun felt warm on her head and she could hear birdsong and the rustling sound of the wind in the leaves. There were wildflowers growing along the edge of the path and she began to think all things might be possible. Perhaps this time she could break free and start afresh in a clean world far from her sordid past. She admired Kate who had turned her back on her mistakes and was trying to be honest and hard-working.

In the midst of this reflection Layla tripped over a stone and realised how unsuitable her flimsy shoes were for a ramble. What hope did she have of making a go of it? She was urban with hard-won experience of fending for herself in big cities. She was ill-equipped for life in the country.

The path took a turn to the left, but directly ahead, on the far side of a large meadow, she could see the glint of water in the sun. She wanted to walk along the bank of a river and, scrambling over the fence, she dropped down into the rough grass and set off. Halfway across, she became aware that there were some cattle grazing at one end of the field. Unaccustomed to livestock, she felt a little uneasy but, as far as she knew, cows didn't attack humans, and though they looked quite large, she decided to press on and ignore them.

The animals were starting to move about and Layla saw that seven or eight of them were cantering in her direction. She felt frightened they might knock her down and injure her so she looked round for her best route of escape. She ran for the edge of the field nearest to her but her long skirt hampered her progress. Hearing the thundering feet of the cattle as they stampeded towards her, she gathered her skirt up and dashed for safety. In a blind panic, her breath rasping in her lungs, she looked over her shoulder and stumbled on a rut in the ground. As she fell, the frisky herd of young bullocks veered to avoid her and raced on past her and round the edge of the field. Terrified, but determined to get out of the field, she tried to get up and gave a sharp cry as her ankle gave way. She dragged herself along for a few miserable yards and then collapsed from the pain.

The afternoon was getting hot, and when he reached the lane, David stopped under a tree and gazed at the view. He could see the farm buildings about a mile away to his left and the copse adjacent to the barns. A large expanse of pasture lay in front of him, and the river beyond, with some cattle grazing. He reached the metal gate and as he opened it, David caught sight of a person, dressed in red and black, running across the field some way off. A few bullocks had broken away from the main herd and were cantering towards the fleeing figure. As they got closer, the figure fell. A feminine shriek echoed across the field. David started to run. The large animals dashed past and ran on down to the river, turning and then stopping in a group. He saw her trying to crawl to safety.

"Are you alright?" he called as he came up to her, though it was obvious she was not.

She turned, the terror in her face giving way to relief. "Keep them off. They'll trample on me."

Crouching down beside her, he saw a frightened face surrounded by dark, tangled hair.

"They won't harm you. They're just lively and curious," David said soothingly.

"I'm not convinced. I want to get the hell out of here," the woman swore.

David blinked in surprise but said calmly, "I assure you the cattle won't attack you even though they may seem threatening."

"They looked bloody dangerous to me." She was trying to get up again, but gasped and sank back on to the ground. "I think I've broken my ankle." She tried to move her left foot and winced.

"Stop moving," David said sternly and then, in a more gentle tone, "Let me have a look at it." He noticed that the woman had lost one of her shoes and carefully took the other off the injured foot, felt the ankle and gently moved it. She flinched in pain but made no sound. "No, you've not broken it – I'd say it was just sprained."

"It hurts when I try to walk on it."

"Don't worry. I'll help you." He put his arm round her waist and pulling her up said, "Put your arm round my shoulder." They hobbled for a few ungainly steps, the woman swearing under her breath. Then David said, "Look, if you don't mind, it will be easier to carry you to the lane. Then you can wait by the gate and I'll go to the farm and see if I can borrow the four-by-four to come back for you and drive you to the local doctor's surgery."

Without waiting for her to reply, he scooped her up and set off across the field. Glancing down at her face, his eyes met hers as she looked at him for the first time. Embarrassed by her scrutiny he looked away, saying, "Not far now."

"I must be getting heavy for you."

"You're as light as apple blossom."

"A real knight in shining armour," she said softly.

"You've lost your shoes." He averted his gaze to her muddy feet.

"Those horrid animals are coming closer again," Layla said nervously, looking over his shoulder at them.

"Don't worry. They're young bullocks which have been inside all winter and are now out in the fields and cantering about, feeling frisky in their new-found freedom. A heifer might attack you if you approached her when she had a new calf with her but this lot aren't dangerous."

"You seem to know a lot about it. Are you the farmer?"

"No, but I used to work on this farm as a boy."

They reached the gate and he gently put her down on the grass verge beside the rutted tracks of the lane. David glanced down at her red skirt – almost as colourful as her language. "Wait here. Don't attempt to walk on that foot. I'll be back." And he set off, wondering where on earth she'd come from and whether he'd ever seen such amazing eyes before.

After half an hour, he returned and helped her into a new but mud-spattered Land Rover. "Where to now? I could run you into town to a doctor's surgery, but I'd have to leave you there because I must get back to work."

"A doctor will just strap my ankle up and tell me to rest it and take some painkillers. I might as well go back to where I'm staying and do that myself."

"If you're sure. Where to?"

"Not far from here – small house called 'Dunrovin' on the road from The Crown to the junction near the bridge over the river." She was twisting her long hair back from her face and did not notice the man flinch with surprise. "I'm staying with a good friend who lives there. Do you know it?"

"I know it. It's got a wooden porch."

"That's the one. I've arrived from abroad with a friend and we thought we'd come and see our pal, Kat. It's been a while but we go back a long way. She works at The Crown."

Her companion said nothing.

After a few minutes, David pulled up outside the gate and helped the woman from the vehicle down the path to the cottage. Her close proximity bothered him and he wanted to get away quietly. He hoped his sister would still be at work and was dismayed when he saw the door opening. A strange man emerged and stood in the doorway. Wearing black jeans with a dirty white T-shirt that contrasted with his dark skin, he looked gaunt, grubby and disreputable.

"What happened, Layla?" His words were slightly slurred. "Why are you barefoot?"

"Hi Josh. I was running away from some cows and I fell and messed up my ankle. But I've been rescued and kindly delivered home." She leaned against the porch and relinquished the arm of her rescuer. "Thanks very much for your help – we'll manage now." She smiled at him warmly.

"Fine. Take care of that ankle. Bye." David's voice and face were devoid of expression as he turned and went.

Layla looked puzzled as she watched the car drive off. "Come on, Josh, give me a hand indoors and then find me some paracetamol. It hurts like hell." As he helped her in, she said in disgust, "You've been drinking. I can smell it on your breath." She sank down on the sofa.

"Who's the dark, handsome fella?" Josh sneered, looking down at her, with that slightly thick sound he had when he'd spent the day in a bar. "Nice watch, expensive shirt, big car – is he local?"

"I've no idea. I didn't ask his name." Layla frowned realising he had not inquired about hers either. "He saw me and came to help. It was very kind of him." She was annoyed with herself for not finding out his name or where he lived. She must be losing her touch.

Theo had finished the deer he was modelling in clay and felt the need for some fresh air. He loved animals and enjoyed recreating them in sculpture. They became a part of him and his family. He put away his tools, washed his hands and his thoughts turned to his human children. He could no longer mould their lives – they had to mature and grow on their own. They still asked for his guidance from time to time but recently both had seemed very preoccupied and he'd seen little of them. His daughter had been avoiding him and since he had met the couple staying with her, he understood why. His son had a few financial worries and was immersed in hotel work, to the detriment of his relationships. Theo decided to go down and see how things were with David.

It was a fine day so Theo chose to walk to the hotel, striding along beneath the trees, with the light filtering down through the leaves, casting patterns on the ground. When he turned the final corner and the building came into view, he stopped to take in the scene – his old and much-loved home in its garden setting. A couple of guests were unloading cases from their car. A man emerged from the entrance, walked down the steps and stopped to examine the front of the hotel before going to a car and opening the door.

As Theo approached, the man looked up and their eyes met. His stare was as hard as stone. Before Theo could utter a friendly greeting, the man climbed into the driving seat, closed the door firmly and drove off. Theo looked thoughtfully at the receding car before going into the hotel.

"I haven't seen you for a while." David, who was seated in his office, rose and went across to hug his father.

"I'm making good progress on the deer I'm working on, but I need a break and some company so I thought I'd disturb you."

"You never disturb me. I'm really glad to see you. Take a seat and I'll get one of the staff to bring us a cold drink."

When they were settled in two chairs in front of the window that faced westwards over the lawns and rose garden, David told his father about his walk the day before and his encounter with the strange woman in red and black who had sprained her ankle.

"I was surprised to discover that she's staying with my sister together with a very shady looking man whom I saw when I dropped the woman off."

"Do you know her name?" Theo asked.

"He called her Layla – it sounds foreign. I'm not sure I want to know her, if she's one of Kate's seedy friends from the past."

"Don't judge her without knowing anything about her," Theo interrupted gently. "I thought she was very beautiful."

David looked at his father in surprise. "You've met her too. When?"

"About a week ago when I called by to say hello to Kate and she answered the door. Her companion is called Josh, though I didn't speak with him. I think they've been staying there for almost a month now."

"Kate's been avoiding us – so clearly she doesn't want us to meet them. If she really wants to turn over a new leaf and put her horrible past behind her, Kate should have the strength of character to tell them to go."

"Kate has always been a friendly soul and perhaps these friends have been kind to her."

"You're so good-natured. You always give people the benefit of the doubt. I expect we'll find out, as we're sure to run into them again."

"Tell me about the hotel." Theo was keen to hear how business was going and listened with interest as David put him in the picture.

"We do have some financial worries – though business is picking up. Francis is still concerned that we're not reducing our borrowing and that we need more income. I've told him we have good occupancy and another big conference booked in later this summer which could really put us on the map. We'll need to hire a marquee and extra staff. Olga worries that staff levels are too high. Staff wages are a huge cost in this business."

"By the way," Theo asked casually, "who was the person leaving as I came in? Dressed in black with close cropped hair. He didn't look like a guest."

"He applied for the post of restaurant manager and I've just finished interviewing him. Though somewhat reserved, I think he'll do. I haven't got much time to find anyone else. Alex gave us little notice and leaves next week. There's no time to advertise and the agency only sent me two candidates. The other never turned up for an interview."

"It's quite a responsible position, David. You need to be sure you can trust him," Theo said, careful to give no hint that he was offering advice.

"He's experienced – his references seem alright. The problem is that I think Tracy, who helps in the bar, is soon going to leave as well. I'll soon be looking for someone to replace her, so the sooner I get the new manager in place, the better. Staffing problems in a hotel seem to be never-ending!" David sighed in exasperation.

"What's his name?"

"Sergio. Unusual name. I think he said his mother was Italian. I'll take him on if his references check out."

Theo, not wanting to interfere, tried to quell his doubts. He gave his son an affectionate smile and said in his mild teasing way, "Why don't we invite Kate and her friends over for a meal?"

7

Kate was in a flat panic. The evening would be a huge trial and she was dreading every minute of it. She was upstairs in her house, getting dressed for the dinner in the hotel restaurant to which her father and brother had invited them all. Now that her visitors' presence was no longer a secret, the problem of damage limitation – restraining her friends' unconventional opinions – loomed large. Theo, who had met Layla briefly and glimpsed Josh through the door, must have mentioned it to David. Her brother had not met them, otherwise he would never have suggested they come for dinner. He would be appalled if he ever discovered what amoral lives they had led.

The night before she plucked up courage to face Layla and Josh and tell them that they had to be polite, be careful and be normal. "You mustn't swear, nor refer to the past. And don't talk too loudly and too long," she had implored. They had laughed at her anxiety and with straight faces solemnly promised to behave, before dissolving into laughter again. Kate knew that Josh could not be relied upon to stay sober and Layla would be bound to come out with some outrageous revelation. They were completely impossible, Kate thought as she put the finishing touches to her make-up and picked up her hair brush, but she loved them. They were fond of her and surely they wouldn't want to upset her by messing up tonight.

During the last month she had enjoyed having her bohemian friends around. Their affection for her was genuine but Kate knew they were opportunists who always took what was offered and more. She wondered what her father's reaction would be to her unorthodox companions, though he was always kind and took people as he found them. He always saw the best in people not the worst and his attitude tended to elicit their best.

Kate hoped her father would persuade David to be tolerant tonight, to understand that she could not cast her friends adrift without shelter and food, that she owed them for the time when they had looked after her and saved her from despair.

"Kat, come on," Layla called from downstairs. "You insisted that we were ready on time and now you're the one who's going to make us late."

"Coming," Kate yelled back, feeling flustered as she slipped a green dress over her head and pulled it down. She yanked a brush through her hair and grabbing her shoes and bag, she went downstairs.

Josh was standing in the small room below, his gaunt height accentuated further by a pair of scuffed Cuban-heel boots. He wore a creased white silk shirt tucked into his narrow trousers with an embroidered waistcoat over the top. He looked rakish and buccaneer.

"Josh, my darling, you look awesome!" she said, giving him a kiss on the cheek. "Be good as gold tonight, please."

He struck an 'awesome' pose and gazed over her head, hand on hip. "Your wish is my absolute command," he murmured grabbing her round the waist and looking into her green eyes with a roguish smile.

"Who did you say was going to give us a lift to the hotel?" Layla asked in her languid drawl. Kate turned to look at her friend, who was reclining on the old sofa, magnificent in a crimson blouse and a black skirt with an uneven feathery hem. Her heavy hair was piled up on the top of her head, designed to look as if it would tumble down any second. She was heavily made up – with her full lips a scarlet red, her olive skin faintly gleaming and with a black smudged look round her remarkable eyes. Kate almost shook with apprehension – and admiration. Layla was going for gold in her effort to create an impression.

"I like the lipstick." But Kate spoke with too little conviction.

"I wear bright red on my lips to distract attention from my knockers," said Layla tartly.

"You could just wear a less revealing shirt," Josh commented.

"You look wonderful, Layla. They'll all fall in love with you," Kate said and hoped fervently they would. "Andrew will collect us. I've mentioned him to you – he's the architect who gave me a lift back from work one day. He caught sight of Josh looking rather the worse for wear. So you'd better be ready to act like a responsible citizen this time."

"Josh never looks respectable," Layla said pulling a gaudy tasselled shawl about her shoulders.

Nor do you, thought Kate, putting on her shoes. The doorbell rang. "That'll be our lift."

"Let's go, sweetheart," said Josh. "We'll follow you meekly."

"I wish that were true," said Kate under her breath, giving him a nervous smile.

Andrew greeted them with his habitual friendliness. Layla sat in the front passenger seat of his car, noticing the young man's crooked nose and plain features in profile. Kate was in the back with Josh who was whispering into her ear that he would "be a good boy", making her giggle.

When they turned off the main road on to the drive, Layla noticed the large sign and read it out loud: "Homeward House – that sounds welcoming. How long has your brother been running the place?"

Kate fell into the trap and replied, "It's always been in the family. It was my childhood home and after I left the country, David and Dad transformed it into a hotel. David trained in hotel management – it was always his dream to run his own place."

"He's a marvellous hotelier," said Andrew, "and aims to make the place very special to attract discerning guests. Here we are." And the car rounded the corner and the hotel came into view. The old stone walls of the front façade were bathed with soft evening sunlight and the windows, lit within, looked inviting.

"Very nice, Kat," said Josh with a low whistle. "Not your average family house, then. It's huge." When the car stopped he leapt out to walk round and help her out.

"It wasn't always this big," Kate said nodding her approval at his courteous gesture. "Andrew designed the new wing."

"How talented to be able to create buildings," Layla said as Andrew opened the door for her.

"I'm not so sure about the talent – but it took seven years of hard work to qualify," he replied with a grin.

As they walked up the steps to the hotel entrance, Layla glanced at Kate and it dawned on her that this was where she belonged – even though she no longer owned her share of it. This was Kate's home. "We won't let you down, Kat. Stop looking so anxious – it's all going to be OK," she said quietly.

In the hall the receptionist greeted them and showed them into the lounge, where Theo was waiting. He came towards them, impressively tall in a velvet jacket. He kissed Layla on the cheek, greeting her warmly, shook Josh firmly by the hand and said how pleased he was to meet him. He hugged Kate, saying, "Lovely to see you, darling. Your brother will be through in a minute. He's just greeting a party of guests who have booked the private dining room. Andrew, good to see you."

Within a few minutes Theo had put them all at ease and at this point his son arrived wearing a dark blue suit and a practised welcoming smile. Layla was startled for a moment when she recognised him and then gave a soft peal of laughter. "My best friend's brother turns out to be the hero who rescued me from the trampling herd of cattle. What a surprise!" She held out her hand, smiling up at him, confident that she now looked very different from the bedraggled creature who had lost her shoes along with her dignity.

David took it and murmured politely, "Good to meet again. How's the ankle?"

Kate was amazed. "You've already met! Why didn't you say so?"

"I've had no chance. We haven't seen you recently." David gave his sister a kiss on the cheek and smiled at her. "You look very pretty tonight – that dress suits you."

Then he turned and shook hands with Josh and gave Andrew a brotherly hug.

"Tell me why you didn't let on that Kate was your sister when you dropped me at her home," Layla asked David.

He went over and sat down beside her. "Because I like keeping my powder dry," he said looking into her extraordinary eyes.

In the main dining room they were seated at a large round table in the bay window, set apart from the other guests. Outside night had fallen and the gardens were attractive, lit from hidden spotlights. Pale green illuminated branches and trees made the shadowy depths between the lights even darker. Inside the lighting was discreet, with candles on each table casting a soft glow on the faces of the guests.

The meal had been excellent and the conversation animated. Theo noticed that, after an initial hesitation, Layla had succeeded in navigating her way round the array of cutlery by covertly watching Kate. Over coffee his daughter began to relax for the first time that evening. Sitting between him and Josh, she let the waiter refill her glass. It was clear to Theo that Josh had been making a big effort all through dinner not to drink too much wine. His daughter seemed so relieved that she picked up her glass and took another large sip. Josh gave her a nudge and whispered in a prim voice, "Don't overdo it, Kat." Kate gave a smothered laugh and almost choked.

Theo was watching them in amusement. He was certain that Kate wasn't having an affair with Josh – their body language didn't indicate this. She was comfortable with the man and his teasing was almost brotherly. What he couldn't understand was the nature of the relationship between Josh and Layla. He had caught a couple of meaningful glances the pair had exchanged. There was affection, to be sure, but love was absent; it was almost as if they were business partners. There was a lack of spontaneity in Josh which made Theo suspicious – the man was making a serious effort to be agreeable but he could sense that under the surface charm there was deviousness.

He glanced across at David, who was listening with reluctant fascination to Layla's description of the exotic masks worn at a carnival in some foreign city. Then she borrowed a pen to draw on a linen napkin and David managed not to protest. She was a beguiling woman and he was dazzled by her, but Theo could detect in his son a distrust of her contrived vivacity and her garish beauty.

Theo had his own idea as to what the visitors' motives might be for their extended visit to Kate. It was a testing time for her resolve to turn away from self-indulgence. Would she be able to withstand the considerable charms this worldly couple possessed? He watched his daughter with concern as she finished her wine and put the glass down a shade too heavily on the table.

Theo was aware that Andrew was not impressed with the newcomers and saw him watching Kate, who was leaning towards Josh and laughing at a something he had said her. Theo wondered why selfish, irresponsible charmers always fascinated women, whilst kind and trustworthy men were ignored.

Kate felt Andrew's gaze and smiled at him. His face lit up and she decided that he was not as dull or ugly as Layla thought. She turned to her father and said, "I'm so grateful to David for inviting my friends. They've been good to me in the past. I've been feeling bad about not seeing you recently but it's been busy in the pub and with Josh and Layla staying, there's been a lot going on…" She tailed off and gave him a lopsided guilty grin, nodding to a waiter who filled up her glass.

Theo smiled down at her, "There's no need to apologise. I've been occupied with my work. I always love to see you but there's never any obligation. We're a family but don't have to live in each other's pockets."

"I heard you'd called at the house and felt bad I hadn't told you they were staying with me. Josh and Layla were supportive when I was at a low ebb. I'll tell you about it another time."

"Whenever you want. I'm always happy to listen. Or give help if you need it."

"You're my Rock of Gibraltar, Daddy. Now *there's* one place I haven't been."

"My Children's Advice Bureau never closes."

Kate was feeling unsteady. She had drunk more wine than usual and when they all rose from the table, she felt off balance. Her vision blurred and as she lurched backwards, her wine glass was jolted over the edge and smashed on the polished wood floor.

A waiter came running to the scene and immediately started picking up the pieces and wiping up the spilt red wine. Josh steadied Kate on her feet and Theo put an arm round her trembling shoulders and gave her a forgiving hug.

Distraught, Kate apologised to her brother, "How careless of me. I didn't have my glasses on and misjudged the distance."

"Not to worry. These things happen," said David smoothly. "Let's leave the table and go through to the lounge."

Kate detected the note of reproach in her brother's voice that he could not quite conceal. Miserably she pulled away from her father and, finding Layla quietly beside her, said with a nervous laugh, "That was clumsy of me." The two women linked arms as they all left the dining room, Kate focussing on her feet.

In the lounge, David offered his guests a liqueur before they left. Andrew declined – he rarely drank alcohol – and Kate, the wayward sister, shook her head. But the others accepted. Layla sat beside Kate on the sofa and chatted to her about the meal in an effort to defuse her friend's embarrassment.

Josh leaned over the back of the sofa as he passed on his way to accept the glass of brandy he was being offered by David and whispered, "Clumsy Kat." He slurred the words, and he could barely restrain himself from laughing out loud. Kate gave him a savage look, angry with herself for spoiling what until then had been a successful evening.

To steady herself, she looked round for her father and saw him and Andrew standing in the bay window talking amicably together. While she watched the two men, Theo caught her eye and smiled with encouragement. Perversely, she averted her eyes and noticing Josh and David chatting together, turned back to Layla and said bitterly, "I warned you both to negotiate your way carefully through tonight's pitfalls and then I go and fall into them myself! How stupid is that!"

"Easily done, honey child," Layla replied, patting the arm of her mortified friend. "You were nervous – and that can often make one hit the bottle."

"I did not hit the bottle," hissed Kate in humiliation. "I just had one glass of wine too many – not surprising when I was so worried, thinking of what you two might do."

"On this occasion we were models of self-control. Because we knew it mattered to you."

"I'm so annoyed with myself."

"Don't beat yourself up about it. No one will remember tomorrow." Layla spoke calmly, trying to defuse her volatile friend.

"Oh yes. One person will," Kate said between her teeth, thinking of her brother and how she wanted to gain his approbation but never seemed able to.

At this point, Josh and David burst out laughing. Kate stared at them in amazement, wondering how these two men, such total opposites, had enough in common to be able to share a joke. Assuming they were laughing at her, she went red with shame and fell silent.

The evening came to an end soon afterwards. Just before their departure, David excused himself, saying he had to see two of his staff before they went home. Theo, who was staying in his son's apartment for the night, went to the front entrance to say goodbye. He enveloped his daughter in a fatherly hug, trying to dispel her low spirits. She muttered her thanks, stiff with chagrin.

Andrew drove the trio home to the cottage, in silent sympathy for the hapless Kate, and then left for his flat in town. Josh and Layla tiptoed tactfully about until Kate had flung herself upstairs and into bed. Then they opened a bottle of her wine and shared their impressions of the evening.

"How are your plans going to hook the big fish?" Josh asked Layla, a few days later. He was sitting on the old stone wall in Kate's garden, a stick in his hand, whipping off the heads of the nettles growing on the other side. "How are you going to tempt him to lend us money?"

Layla was lying in a faded deckchair that had seen better days. She was painting her nails a dark crimson colour, balancing the small bottle precariously on her stomach. She looked thoughtful. "I haven't yet worked out how I can painlessly relieve him of some of his wealth and get some capital together so I can disappear to a sunny climate and set myself up comfortably in a nice home. I have a slight problem in that he's such a nice guy." She painted another nail and examined it carefully to ensure an even colour.

"But he's an easy touch – he knows nothing of our wily ways and those of the big bad world. The other night you had him eating out of the palm of your greedy little hand!"

Layla had finished the fingers on her right hand and held them up to dry, waggling them. "For that matter, how are *you* getting on insinuating yourself with our reserved hotelier?" Layla raised her plucked eyebrows questioningly.

"I've been very proactive," Josh announced proudly. "I've got a job at the hotel." He took another lunge at the nettles and decapitated five.

"How did you manage that?" In her surprise, Layla's stomach contracted and she scooped up the varnish bottle before it wobbled over. "Doing what?"

"I'm to be a waiter and barman, working for the restaurant manager – a new guy who started last week. You may have noticed him when we first went into the lounge – he brought the tray of drinks over to us. Very short hair and the practised non-committal expression that discreet employees always have."

"Can't say I recall him."

"The waitress who worked in the bar fell out with the new manager and left. Yesterday I managed to persuade David that I'm the man to fill the vacancy. He's under the impression he interviewed me but I talked him into giving me the job. It seems my good behaviour the other night paid off."

"You'll have to dress a bit more conservatively working in a country house hotel. I hope you'll manage to resist the temptation of all that alcohol."

Josh took another swipe at the nettles with his stick. "Count on me. Where self-interest is at stake, I can be quite disciplined."

Layla exhaled audibly, "Really?" She started to paint the fingernails on her left hand.

Josh continued, "I have a crafty plan. Whilst I was shown round, I got a good look round the place. There are loads of opportunities…" He tailed off. Layla took his meaning. Josh had worked before in bars; he was quick, dextrous and – when sober – efficient and polite. His light-fingered skills were useful for more illicit activities.

The pair remained silent, each revolving devious schemes to rob Kate's brother of money, valuables and peace of mind. The beheaded nettles looked forlorn and ragged.

"Do you ever wonder, Josh, whether we are beyond guilt?" Layla said thoughtfully. "We seem to have no remorse." Theo's face swam into her mind and made her feel deeply uncomfortable.

"I start work on Monday," he said, ignoring her question. "Are *you* thinking of getting some work? I'd like to know when you're going to dirty your pretty little hands?" Josh gave her a wicked smile.

"I might take up painting again. David admires creativity and loves art." She was looking down at the tiny brush in her right hand as it dispensed an oval lozenge of colour.

"Can you paint?" Josh was surprised. "I know you draw. I've seen you do cartoon figures many times."

"In my innocent youth, I went to art college, but dropped out because I met a magnetically attractive man who led me astray. I've always wanted to paint again, but life got in the way." She carefully screwed the top on the bottle and tossed it on to the grass. She looked at her handiwork, before turning her palms inward and holding up the gleaming red talons for Josh to see. "I'm one colourful lady with a hidden talent."

Josh laughed and moved further along the wall, slashing at some tall wild flowers.

"Don't do that, Josh. They're flowers."

"They're weeds."

"As the saying goes, Josh, weeds are merely flowers growing in the wrong place. Rather like me at the moment. Those weeds are beautiful."

"As you are, Layla." Josh threw the backhanded compliment over his shoulder but continued with his massacre.

At this moment a small car drew up outside the garden fence. Josh glanced at the road and, tossing the stick to the ground, watched a young woman in a pale blue dress emerge and approach the gate.

The visitor saw them both looking at her and paused, her puzzled frown swiftly erased and replaced by a shy smile. "Hello. I'm looking for Kate."

Josh ran a hand over his unshaven chin and stared at the slender, blonde-haired apparition. He slid off the wall and gallantly opened the rickety gate for her. "Welcome to our modest garden and abode," he said with a practised smile and a bow.

The woman gave him a wary look and approached uncertainly, her eyes on the beautiful creature reclining in a deckchair waving an elegant hand at her companion. "He's called Josh."

"Are you friends of Kate's?"

"We certainly are," Layla said in a mellow voice.

"We've known the lovely Kate for years," Josh drawled, dropping the nickname Kat, "and been through thick and thin together!"

"I'm Layla." Layla gave a dazzling smile that did not reach her eyes.

"And who do we have the pleasure of meeting?" Josh gave an encouraging grin.

"I'm Maria – I've known the family for a while." Her voice was soft. "I used to work up at their hotel. As a receptionist."

"Why no longer? Did you get fired?" Josh asked as he gazed at her translucent skin.

Maria was startled and looked up at his dark face. "Of course I didn't," she stammered. "I just... changed jobs."

Irritated by Josh's obvious admiration for their visitor, Layla said, "He's so inquisitive."

Maria smiled carefully and said, "I assume Kate's not at home. I'll come back later." She took a step back.

"Don't go, Maria." Josh took her arm and smiled disarmingly down at her. "Any friend of Kate's is a friend of ours. I have a favour to ask. I've just got a job at the hotel you used to work for and I'd love to know more about the place. How about a cup of tea?"

Layla pursed her lips as Josh steered a reluctant Maria into the house.

"Why have we taken on this new guy?" Olga asked. "With his hollow cheeks and black hair he looks quite sinister. Do we really need another barman – it's another salary to find."

"I think we do. He's polite and pleasant with the guests and is a good waiter too."

David was in his office at the rear of the hotel, discussing the staff with his manager. "We have a good team now that Francis is in charge of our finances and you've persuaded the unflappable Maggie to stay on as head housekeeper."

Olga looked thoughtful. "Emily, our new receptionist, lacks experience and isn't as courteous or efficient as Maria was." She paused and David knew she was curious about whether her boss had got over his broken engagement. He had seen little of Maria. She was a fine person and she would find someone else who would cherish her more than he had been able to.

After Olga had left his office, David needed to talk to his chef. As he walked over to the kitchens, he saw the leaves of the large chestnut tree behind the new wing were beginning to turn. Another summer was coming to an end and he hoped guest numbers would be enough to keep things rolling on during the autumn and winter. On his way back he noticed his latest employee, Josh, was checking the incoming stock that had just been delivered to the back entrance of the bar. He had taken a risk when he had agreed to give his sister's disreputable friend a trial, but Josh had knuckled down and worked well alongside the laconic Sergio.

He wondered what Layla was doing. He felt relaxed in her company even though he knew her past might not bear too much scrutiny. She was a flirt and yet she was fun. As he sat down at his desk, her mellow laughter lingered in his head and her ripe strawberry lips in his mind's eye. He didn't approve of her kind of woman – but he wanted to see her again.

As the office door closed behind David, Josh looked up from stacking crates. He had noticed his boss but decided to keep his head down. He knew that a steady attention to the job in hand would carry more weight than a cheery wave and he very much wanted to be seen working assiduously. Josh respected David, who was astute and observant. Other staff called him a workaholic who rarely relaxed, and they said he had given too little time to the woman who had been his fiancée.

Josh was enchanted by Maria. Unlike any woman he had known, she was modest, reticent and gentle. He was touched by her innocence, fascinated by her pale beauty. After their tea together, he felt he was floating. Layla teased him that he had Maria eating out of the palm of his hand but he knew she regarded him with suspicion.

Josh wanted to know more about her and after he had started work at Homeward House it had been easy to inquire about the young woman who had once worked in reception. Soon he was regaled with the story of her lengthy engagement to the young proprietor and he was curious as to why it had come to an end. David was clearly a good catch and therefore it appeared Maria was not self-seeking. She had principles, something which Josh knew he didn't possess. He found people with integrity and moral values intriguing. He had managed to get Maria's address in the local town and was determined to track her down and lay siege. To break down her reserve would be a challenge.

Sergio opened the door and surveyed his tall assistant. "Haven't you finished yet?" he asked curtly. Josh looked at him and nodded. Wiping his hands on a cloth he followed him into the bar. Sergio was a surly man of few words but two could play at that game.

Layla felt restless. Now that Josh and Kate were both working, she was often on her own and needed an occupation. Josh had managed to get himself in a position where he might contrive to use his particular talents. She should be thinking of ways to further their grand plan and help them move on.

She decided to get some fresh air, threw on a jacket and left the dingy cottage. It was a fine windy October day, and hoping to get a view over the valley, she headed up the hill. There was birdsong in the hedgerows and she felt the breeze in her hair. Country life was seductive, enticing her to stay and vegetate. But she couldn't afford to do that.

She couldn't afford to do anything at all. Their lack of money was beginning to annoy her. Josh was earning a small wage now but he had no intention of sharing it with her. He made a tiny contribution towards food but seemed to spend the rest with his newfound friends in the bar in town where he went to chill out. Kate's miserable earnings from that pub meant she had no surplus to lend to anyone and could hardly make ends meet as it was. The rent was in arrears and a letter threatening to cut off the electricity had arrived the other day. They had a hand-to-mouth existence, so it was imperative to tap into the family resources. She needed to contrive an appropriate excuse to see David, but how could she do this? What were his interests outside work?

Layla tried to recall what she and David had talked about at the dinner party. Apart from his passion for his hotel and the countryside around it, he had talked about art and his admiration for people of creativity and vision, such as his father. If she took up painting again, he might be persuaded to take an interest and support her in the role of beautiful, impoverished artist.

On reaching the top of the incline she stopped to pause for breath and found herself in a narrow lane on the brow of the hill. Some tall trees beckoned her in their direction and she set off towards them, glimpsing sweeping views through small gaps in the tall hedge bordering the lane. Her mood lifted and she envisaged having a brush in her hand and the challenge of trying to capture the essence of a place on canvas and reawaken the magic of painting a portrait.

Did she know David well enough to ask if she might borrow some money to set herself up? The next time they met she would plead poverty and ask for help. But how long could she wait? She had tried hard to make herself irresistible and though he had seemed captivated, he had not contacted her.

After a mile she reached the wooded area and through the trees glimpsed the stone walls of a large building. A few minutes later, as she turned a corner, she saw a small track leading to a recently converted barn.

Then it struck her that this was Theo's studio. She had seen it from far below when Kate had pointed it out to her. Layla was curious about the sculptor and his work and, on a whim, decided to call in.

As she approached, the door opened and Theo came out, wearing a long canvas work apron over his clothes. "Welcome, I'd been hoping to see you again." He had a broad smile on his lined face and held out a hand in greeting.

Layla was surprised. He behaved as if he was expecting her. She tried to assure him that her visit was purely by chance. "I was out walking and found myself in this lane, saw the barn and realised it was your studio."

"Perhaps you were led here," he ushered her through the door. "Come on in." He closed the wooden door behind her.

Layla stopped, gazing about her in surprised delight. The rectangular barn had a high roof and handsome stone walls. In the centre of the long wall facing south west was a huge window. She walked across to stand and stare at a breathtaking panorama across the valley of the distant hills. Below were forests, fields and hedgerows. Tiny, blurred white sheep dotted the distant pastures, and cattle grazed in the meadows by the river. To the west were cottages and farms and to the east she could see the church spire in the town. Clouds scudded across the sky and the wind whipped the autumnal foliage of the trees to and fro, and sent the leaves spiralling upwards into the air before falling earthwards. The world below was a picture of natural beauty encompassed in a wooden frame.

She turned when she heard Theo moving around – removing his canvas apron and putting various tools on a workbench on the other side of the studio. He was used to the effect the view had on those who saw it for the first time and she thought how sensitive he was to give people time to absorb the impact. The sunlight streamed in, filling the barn with light and shadow. In the centre of the floor space was a life-size clay maquette of a stag. Around the walls were various sculptures – some work in progress and others finished and cast into bronze. On a shelf high up on the rear wall a dark bronze eagle presided over the studio.

The stag was nearly finished, his muscles in his body taut, his head held proudly aloft. The animal's nose was sniffing the wind, his ears alerted to an unknown threat, one leg poised ready to move. Layla admired the ragged striated texture of his flanks and antlers that were a crown of jagged thorny bones. This animal would have to fight for his life.

She suddenly re-focussed on Theo watching her from the other side of his stag.

"It's so good," she said in awe of his skill as a sculptor

Theo nodded. "Thank you. It's almost finished and will soon be off to the foundry. The first bronze cast will be going to Canada, and my agent has already found someone interested in buying the second."

"What are you going to start on next?"

"I have a tall figure – a winged angel – to make, commissioned by a large insurance company. But what I am going to do right now is make a hot drink for us both. Let's go through to the cottage." He led her across to a wooden door in the wall of the barn and into his home.

Layla was enchanted by the simplicity and the charm of Theo's living area. The view was encapsulated in a smaller frame but it was still there – a part of his life. He invited her to sit down whilst he made coffee, and she looked round at the huge bookcases and a pair of handsome oil paintings on the wall opposite.

Theo noticed her looking at them, and said, "David found them for me. He took a lot of trouble trying to choose what I might want to live with. My son has excellent taste and I like them very much." He put the mugs down on a low oak table and sat down in a large wooden chair opposite her. "How enjoyable to have a visitor! Not many people drop in casually up here on my hill but it's a real pleasure when they do."

"Surely you like your solitude? Interruptions to your work must be distracting."

"Real people and living animals are more important. It's from them I get my inspiration. It's tranquil here and I enjoy gazing down over my part of the world but I need human contact. I love meeting people and finding out what makes them tick."

Normally this sort of remark would have made Layla feel apprehensive but she felt curiously at peace. Unguarded. A telephone rang in the studio but Theo ignored it.

"So tell me about yourself – where were you brought up? Are your parents still around?" Theo began.

Though Layla rarely talked about herself, she found it easy to tell Theo about her childhood. She had no siblings and no home. Her father was dead and she had long ago lost contact with her mother. She gave no reason, nor did she say that her mother had abandoned her. "My parents are far removed from me in time and space. Like an old photograph and with blurred rough edges," she concluded.

"What did you do when you left school?"

"I wasn't very academic but I loved drawing and painting. I went to a big city in a different country, learned a new language, got myself a waitressing job and put myself through art college." She decided not to mention her first lover who helped pay for the fees and then became jealous of the time she devoted to her painting, nor the man with whom she fell in love, who persuaded her to drop out and go travelling with him. That too didn't last. All she said was, "Although my tutors said I had potential, I didn't finish the course. I left before the end, missing my final exhibition and a degree. What a fool I was." She looked down at her idle hands with their gaudy nails.

Theo was positive. "Why don't you take it up again? It's never too late to return to something creative that you love doing."

Layla looked up quickly. "Recently I've been thinking of doing just that. I really need a job – but I've no qualifications. I thought I might see if I can get back into art, while I look around and decide what I'm going to do."

"My advice would be to stay here a while longer. Seek work – even if it's a modest occupation. But take up painting again. It'll be good for you."

"I used to work in oils and the materials I'd need are way beyond my means. Little can be done when you have no money and no prospects," said Layla with an artful smile. "Josh has now got a job in the hotel but poor Kate's still paying for my food and lodging."

"I believe there was a time when you did the same for her. That's what friends do – help each other out. My daughter is kind-hearted and she values your friendship."

Kate was independent and would never ask for his help so Layla decided it was time to let her father know about the dire situation at the cottage. "Her rent's in arrears and she can't pay the bills. There's a notice to cut off the electricity if we don't pay the final demand by next week. The little house is cold, dreary and winter's coming. For months she's been so generous. I feel bad about it." *And I feel bad about my plans to tap you and your son for money,* Layla admitted to herself as she looked across at Theo, who was listening intently. "Kate won't ask for assistance but she needs it. She slaves away at that menial job and never complains, but I know she's desperately worried."

"Thank you for telling me. I suspected she was having financial problems. I believe she's taken on longer hours at The Crown."

"That's because she's got two homeless people sponging off her," said Layla contriving to sound guilty.

"Josh has a job at the hotel. Does he help?"

"Not Josh! He earns a modest wage, and bought himself a second-hand motorbike to enable him to go into town and drink with his pals. Not that he ever drinks at work," she added hastily. "He never lifts a finger in the house and says he's fed up of sleeping on the broken-backed sofa in the living room. David has offered him extra hours and staff accommodation at the hotel so he's moving out next week. I don't blame him. It'll be warm and comfortable and close to his work. Kate and I are on our own and may soon be out on the streets – or country lanes!" Layla, hearing the rising wind in the trees, gave a despairing laugh. Surely a successful and wealthy man like Theo would help his own daughter?

Before Theo could reply, there was the sound of a car in low gear coming up the hill. They listened as it drew up and stopped outside the barn. A door banged as Theo rose to his feet, saying, "Another visitor – I'm very fortunate today." He went across the room and into the studio, leaving the connecting door open.

Layla heard a voice she recognised as David's. After a minute she got up and went nearer to listen.

David sounded agitated. "The couple concerned are some of my best regular clients. I've reassured them that the police have been contacted and are on their way. This is dreadful – we've never had a robbery before. I've asked Olga to tell all the staff to keep quiet about it because if the news gets out, it will be bad for business."

"Any idea who might be responsible?"

"Not yet," said David. Layla inwardly winced because she knew. "I did try to phone but you didn't answer, so I've come to ask if you'd come down and pour oil on troubled waters. You may recall meeting Mr and Mrs Lawrence – you had a long chat with them on the terrace during their last visit. They're both very upset – the jewellery that's gone is of great sentimental and monetary value. Can you talk to them whilst I deal with the police?"

"Of course I will. I've finished work for the day and was just having a cup of tea with a visitor."

At this point David became aware of the figure standing in the door that led into the cottage and with a look of astonishment he realised it was Layla.

Theo said, "The young lady was out for a walk and called in. She tells me she went to art school and I'm encouraging her to take up painting again."

"Hello David." Layla gave him a winning smile, painfully aware that she was wearing no make-up and her hair had been blown into a tangled mess during her windy walk. "Your father is so kind."

"Good to see you again. I'm sorry but there's a bit of a crisis at the hotel and I've got to get back." He turned to his father. "See you shortly, Theo."

"I won't be long – I'll drive Layla back and then come on to the hotel. I hope I can help."

"You always know what to say and how to calm people down. You're much better at it than I am – I don't have the time or the patience." He glanced at Layla, hesitated, gave her an apologetic smile and left.

She remembered Kate saying her brother never had time for the people who mattered most – even his father. He was always focussed on the hotel and pre-occupied with his guests' needs. How could she get under his skin and make him want to see her?

A few minutes later, Layla left the barn with Theo. He stopped at Kate's house and saw her to the door before driving on to Homeward House. Layla wondered if he would respond to her appeal for help. Though sympathetic, he had not revealed what was in his mind, but she had the unnerving feeling that he detected what was in hers.

As David drove back to his hotel, he was no longer thinking about his angry guests but about Layla. He had seen her again – looking natural and without artifice, as she had been when he had first encountered her in the field. This was the Layla he preferred – not the exotic creature who had appeared at his dinner party. He wanted to get to know her better but had not contacted her because of work pressures. He must find the time.

But not today. He turned into the hotel drive and the police arrived a few minutes afterwards. Theo would placate his outraged clients. He rarely asked his father to help but realised that the older man had a calm steadiness that was much needed at this moment.

Though the hotel was thriving there were potential problems that could derail its path to financial security. The possibility of failure haunted him. He had taken over the family home and he had to make the project a success.

This robbery was a shock. They were insured but their reputation might suffer. The hotel was known for charm and comfort in a peaceful country setting. Security and privacy were integral to its reputation. David got out of his car and stalked inside with a frown on his face, determined to find out who had committed this crime against his guests, his hotel and against him. Success in this business was vital and it was under threat.

8

"I haven't seen you in ages." Andrew had caught sight of Maria across the coffee shop and walked over to join her. "How is the nursing going?"

"It's hard work, but I really love it. Especially as I'm now doing community nursing. What's your news?"

"My firm managed to get the contract to build two new classrooms for the primary school and as they were my designs I've been given the project. It's not a big job but I like creating children's space."

"Have you heard that Kate wants to study to become a primary school teaching assistant? She's fed up with her mindless job in the pub and hopes to get a better one in town. She's going to move here."

Andrew looked delighted and said, "She's been there for too long and needs to move on. Is her friend Layla still living the cottage? She's pulling Kate down – and doesn't contribute much."

"I'm unsure what I think of Layla and I don't know what her motives are for remaining here." Maria had detected the disapproval in his voice. "Theo likes her but he likes everyone. She's an attractive woman. When I saw Kate recently she told me that David has taken Layla out to dinner a couple of times."

A woman who knows what she wants, thought Andrew as he asked, "What news of David?" He wondered if Maria had recovered from her broken engagement to his friend.

"He's fine as far as I know. There was some problem up at the hotel recently but I'm not sure what. Josh has got a job as a barman at the hotel, where he has staff accommodation. He's bought a motorbike and comes into town quite often to go drinking in The Anchor with friends." She smiled, "Shall I tell you something really funny? Josh has been besieging me – he declares himself passionately in love. I try to put him off but he only gets more attentive."

Andrew frowned. He no longer believed that Josh and Kate had ever had an affair, but he was puzzled as to the nature of the friendship between him and Layla. The thought of the unscrupulous Josh pursuing Maria made him uneasy.

Maria saw the concern in Andrew's face. "Don't worry about me – I'm not going to fall for a wolf in sheep's clothing. I'm able to take care of myself."

I'm not sure about that, thought Andrew, as he looked at Maria's face, radiating innocence. He had always liked her and didn't want her to be deceived.

She stood up. "Must dash now – I've got to get back."

Andrew watched her go, hoping that Josh would soon lose interest in her. She was pure gentleness – right out of his league. His thoughts turned to Kate and her long term plan to move into town and study. His spirits lifted – she would be nearer and there would be more chance of seeing her.

There had been a fine spell of weather at the beginning of November and Layla was itching to go outside and see if she could capture the autumn colours on canvas. She had managed a few sketches and only one small exploratory painting since the arrival of the gift.

A number of large packages had been delivered unexpectedly ten days before, sent from a specialist art shop but without any indication of who had ordered them and arranged their despatch direct to her. The comprehensive collection of artists' materials had been a lovely surprise. She remembered her student art kit; she had never possessed fine quality equipment like this. There was everything one might need: a wooden easel, various linen canvasses, a mahogany box full of tubes of artist's quality oil paints, two wooden palettes, a selection of hogs' hair and sable brushes, a palette knife, linseed oil and turpentine. There was a hard-backed sketchbook of good cartridge paper with pencils, charcoal and a putty rubber. The last objects she had unwrapped were a small folding stool and a large canvas shoulder bag. Surveying this superb array of materials, she had felt excited and empowered.

The anonymous donor was extraordinarily generous and Layla knew it had to be Theo. She would use it and produce a painting good enough to give him by way of thanks for his belief in her. It was hard to earn money as a painter, but if she improved and learned her craft, she might be able to maintain herself working at something she loved. Her earlier occupation disgusted her. This was a chance of a new direction for her in a new environment.

Slowly she unscrewed the top of the bottle of linseed oil and inhaled it – the nostalgic smell taking her back to art classes, hours at an easel and carefree student days, when she had felt the whole world was before her and imagined a life devoted to art. But it had all gone wrong – she had taken the wrong path, and ten years down it she wondered if she could find her way back, shake off the feeling of being unclean and erase the past. She fingered the top quality linen canvas and recalled that at college she had made her own stretchers with cotton canvas. Her future was a blank canvas, ready to be painted on.

An image of Theo smiling at her in his studio came to mind. He had encouraged her. She felt stirrings of hope – there was a better life to live, less selfish and more meaningful, if only she could get back on track.

Tying her hair up in a turquoise scarf, she put on a warm sweater and pulled on a pair of old boots. Taking her boxed easel and putting a sketch pad, oil paints, brushes, a palette and a small canvas in the carrying bag, she left the cottage and set off over the fields towards the river.

Ross felt oddly nervous as he checked his watch and then dialled the number that Jakob had given him. This number changed every week and he had to make the call on a specified day and time. After five rings the call was answered but the recipient did not speak. Ross cleared his throat and said, "Sergio reporting."

A hoarse voice: "Go ahead." It was Ator.

"Job done fifteen days ago. I managed to get undetected access for Krait to the designated building. Items successfully removed and Krait off the scene unobserved. No suspicion aroused. Still working for target." Ross had been told to be brief and oblique.

"Krait did confirm." There was a pause.

Ross waited. Jakob, whose cover name was Krait, had told Ross about Ator's tactics.

Ator continued, "Please leak news of this event to the press. Vital no-one knows where the information comes from." The rasping voice was unemotional but menacing.

"When should I do this?" Ross asked.

"Now." Ator cut the connection.

Ross thought rapidly as to how he might carry out these instructions and after ten minutes he made a few calls having ensured his number was withheld from the person to whom he spoke. He then left the room to start his shift in the restaurant in his role as Sergio. He wondered what had become of the stolen jewellery and where it would end up.

Ator commanded total obedience and Ross was loyal from fear rather than affection. Disloyalty was not an option – agents who disobeyed, or went to work for someone less ruthless, regretted it.

The cattle were nowhere to be seen as Layla cautiously opened the wooden gate and set off across the field. She was reminded of her first meeting with David. He had told her during their last dinner together how he liked walking over his land. She still had no idea whether he was keen to know her better. She found him attractive but was unsure whether to attribute his appeal to his good looks or his bank balance.

She reached the banks of the stream that meandered along the far side of the field, and looked about for a place to put her easel. It was a mild day with little wind. She found a spot near some sweet chestnut trees and set up her easel amongst the fallen husks and nuts. Pulling out her lightweight folding stool, she sat down, set her sketch pad on the easel and looked across at the view she had selected to paint. On the left side some trees still had autumnal foliage, there was a central vista across the field, and on the right there was the roof and half a front façade of a small cottage visible through some shrubs. She wondered who lived there. Having done a couple of sketches with which she was not entirely satisfied, she decided to move. The glimpse of the woodland dwelling was like a magnet and she set off to explore.

As she approached, Layla saw that the cottage had stone walls, a faded yellow door and a tiny overgrown garden. It was on one floor with a low roof in reasonable repair and a stubby chimney. She put down her kit and stood looking at it, wondering if it was occupied. Curiosity got the better of her.

There was a small fence and gate that she opened before going to knock on the door. No response, so she walked to the window and peered in. The main sitting room was simply furnished with a kitchen area to one side and two doors at the back, probably to a bedroom and bathroom – if there was any plumbing out here. The paint was peeling and there was no evidence of recent occupation. She noticed an oil lamp on a wooden table and a candle in a saucer on a battered dresser but there were no electric lights. *Romantic if a little primitive,* she thought. Wandering round the rear, she leaned over to look into a small window which revealed a tiny bedroom. Then she noticed a rough track wide enough for vehicles, leading away though the trees. Isolated but not inaccessible.

Returning to the front facade with the watery sunlight on its mellow walls, she decided to make a sketch and then paint. The trees behind the cottage were in late autumn colour and the composition was perfect. An easy subject to start with. She had the pleasurable feeling of anticipation. The scene was peaceful and isolated with just a hint of mystery about the abandoned dwelling. She set up her easel and her folding stool about thirty yards from the cottage and picked up her charcoal.

It was Josh's half-day off and he was in town. He parked his bike and headed into the pub.

He had spent the morning cleaning out the cellar and rearranging the bar to Sergio's instructions. The restaurant manager took delight in giving Josh unnecessary work whilst he made private telephone calls from the small room that he used as his office. At one point, when Josh was carrying crates to the bar, Sergio pulled open the door and stared at him, before closing it again firmly. It was as if he was trying to discover whether his barman was listening to his conversation.

Josh had a plan. He would first have a few drinks with his mates at The Anchor and later he would call on Maria to plead his undying love for her – yet again. She and her mother were amused by him but Maria showed no interest in protestations of affection. His role as spurned courtier was entertainingly novel and he planned to intensify his pursuit. She was worth the wait. She would be beautiful in bed!

At The Anchor he ordered his first drink, casually flirting with the barmaid, and listening to the general babble.

He felt annoyed with Layla, who had been very distant with him and had made it clear that she thought him responsible for the robbery at the hotel. Nothing had been said but Layla was waiting for him to confess – and let her know how much he'd got for selling the stolen jewellery. Since he was completely innocent, this was very irritating. It was particularly galling because a similar job which he had planned to do in a few weeks was now impossible. Security had been tightened and David was putting in new measures to ensure greater protection for his guests and their property. Josh was as furious as his boss! His wages were modest and he wanted more spending money. He needed to think of the future and had been in this backwater for long enough. Though he didn't find the place disagreeable, he was getting itchy feet and when Maria succumbed to his charm offensive, he planned to leave the country and resume his more lucrative profession in another big city.

But he had to have Maria first. His confidence had taken a dent but he would wear her down. The woman had got under his skin and she must be conquered before he went off again. To get Maria, he needed to win her mother's approval. Maria would not be home yet but her mother would be there. He was hungry as usual and she might give him something to eat. He finished his drink, combed his unruly hair with his fingers, and got to his feet.

It was getting chilly. Layla was walking about to warm herself up. She was satisfied with her sketch and had started putting on colour and shade, trying to capture the tones before the light faded. She wanted to have enough done so she could finish off back at the cottage, should the weather make it difficult for her to return.

Shortly after she settled herself back on her stool, she saw a movement in the corner of her eye. It was a dog. She picked up her palette and started to mix oils to get the right tone for the walls of the cottage. Seeing a figure emerge from the tree to her right, she decided to keep on painting, conscious of the impact on a walker of finding a lone artist working on a painting. Was it David? She pretended to be oblivious of his presence. Then the dog barked. Hearing footsteps, Layla turned brush in hand, fully aware of the effect she was creating.

A few yards away stood a man she had never seen before, wearing a green jacket and carrying a stick. His collie stood obediently at his heel. Layla awarded him one of her most practised dazzling smiles. Already amazed by this beautiful woman with her long dark hair tied up with a turquoise scarf, sitting at her easel holding a palette, he reeled from the impact.

"Hello," he said with a bemused expression. "What are you doing here?"

"I'm painting a picture," she responded, deliberately choosing to misunderstand him and turning back to the canvas.

"I meant, where are you from? You're a stranger." Layla glanced at him. The man was about thirty with a friendly face and tanned, freckled skin.

"I don't know you either. If we're into interrogations, I could demand who you are and what you're doing – but it's obvious you're walking the dog." Layla said this as she applied some colour to her canvas.

The young man laughed. "I belong here. This is my land – and you are trespassing!"

Layla turned and put down her brush. "Are you going to order me to leave?" she said raising her eyebrows and rapidly assessing the situation. Remembering David had talked about his work on the farm when he was younger, she realised this might be his cousin, the farmer who was married, but couldn't recall his name.

"That depends," he said, enjoying the encounter and the banter. "I have the right – but first I want to know your name. I warn you that if you don't reply and co-operate fully with information, I might set my dog on you." They both looked down at his dog, who was sitting on his haunches placidly watching them with his tongue lolling out.

Layla smiled again. "He doesn't look very fierce to me. Unlike your cows." This remark puzzled the farmer as there were no cows in the nearby fields. She went on, "But I won't risk incurring your dog's savage attack by refusing to identify myself. I'm Layla and I live a couple of miles away." She had finally dredged up his name. "You must be Jamie." She stuck out a hand smeared with paint.

He looked startled but took her hand. "Have we met?" He was sure he would have remembered.

"We haven't, but I've driven in your smart Land Rover." She was pleased to see he looked even more confused. "Can I have my hand back?" She extracted her small hand from his large one and, taking pity on him, explained. "I was the person that fell over in your field and sprained my ankle. Your cousin, David, who owns the hotel, rescued me and borrowed your vehicle to drive me home. I'm pleased that I can now say thank you!" She scooped up a strand of hair and tucked it into the scarf, looking up at him.

"So you're that woman. David didn't say much about you and I'm beginning to realise why. You're the exotic creature he's been seen with recently. News travels slowly in a small country community but it does eventually leak out."

Layla pretended to look offended. "I'm not sure I like being referred to as 'that woman' or 'creature'."

"No insult intended," Jamie said hastily. "And of course you're welcome to walk on my land and paint anytime you like."

"That's very kind but it's getting cold and I'm thinking of calling it a day." Layla rose to her feet and started putting her kit away. "By the way, who lives in that dear little place?"

As she predicted he replied, "No-one. I own it and in the summer months I occasionally let it out as a holiday cottage. But because there's no electricity here and it's a bit primitive, I don't get much rent for it."

Layla finished dismantling her easel. "I'm off now. Perhaps we'll meet up again. I'd love to come back sometime to paint." She gave him another of her captivating smiles.

"I'll walk back with you. And I could carry this." He picked up her boxed easel and the folding stool and fell into step beside her.

Layla thanked him, noticing his strong forearms and muscular calves. He was another useful contact – or conquest.

Theo stood in the lobby of the hotel, watching David talking to a police detective. His son desperately wanted to find out who was responsible so he could reassure his clients that all was being done to try and retrieve their valuable jewellery. Theo knew the chance of identifying the thief was slim and the chances of recovering the stolen items even slimmer.

The detective said a polite goodbye and David walked over to his father. "Progress is slow – I'm not convinced they are doing all they can." He spoke quietly as there were guests around.

"I'm sure they are doing their best." Theo was soothing but realistic. "Let's face it, David. No one has been injured or mugged. Theft is wrong and the thief should be found and punished, but you might have to accept that there are many unsolved crimes of this nature. The hotel's insurance will cover the value of your guest's lost items."

"I'm proud of my hotel and its reputation is at stake. This hotel is advertised as a safe, quiet and luxurious country retreat. If this gets out, it won't be good for business."

"People are more important than property. You have other guests who need your attention and I think you've spent enough time agonising over this incident. You have a hotel to run and I think you should try to put things in perspective," Theo said firmly.

David gave him a smile. "You're right. I'll leave it in the hands of the police and the insurance company, and get on with other things. I've got a meeting with the catering team in half an hour – we have a big wedding here next week. That might help cash flow."

"Thanks for lunch." Theo enjoyed their weekly lunches when he would catch up on the hotel's progress. He put his hand on his son's shoulder. "You're doing fine. Don't fret too much about what's past. No one blames you. Just focus on the present and the future."

Over lunch David had mentioned diffidently that he had seen Layla and taken her out for a meal. Theo was pleased to hear this and suggested that David invite her out for the day and drive to the city. His son had been noncommittal as always.

As he left, Theo saw two guests checking in at reception and gave them a welcoming smile. Through the door into the lounge, he caught sight of Sergio standing in the bar. Theo found him efficient but cold and reserved. Josh by contrast was popular with guests and, in spite of his rakish appearance, was attentive and surprisingly unobtrusive.

At that moment, Sergio looked up and caught his eye. They stared at each other for a few seconds. Theo detected the man's guarded insolence and felt he ought to warn David, but perhaps this was something his son would discover for himself. Waving a hand at the receptionist, he walked out into the autumnal sunshine.

"Don't plead innocence, Josh. I know you did the job," Layla sneered.

"How many times do I have to repeat that I am not responsible for the theft at the hotel?" Josh said wearily, sitting down on the arm of the sofa on which she was lying with a rug around her. He had called in on his way back from town after another frustrating evening getting nowhere with Maria. "This place is damp and cold but I'm pleased to get away from the hotel for a few hours. The atmosphere there is distinctly chilly."

"Why is that?"

She hadn't seen the newspapers so he told her. "The news is out. The robbery at the hotel is in the press and on local radio and television. The boss is incandescent about the bad publicity. We all had instructions not to talk about the matter but someone has spilt the beans. I wonder who it was." He gave Layla a suspicious look. "You knew about it."

"Not me, sunshine," she snapped. "I wouldn't spoil my plans with David by doing anything so silly."

"He's furious about the slur on his beloved hotel. He's usually so reined in – it was quite interesting to see him lose his rag." Josh had a temper himself, so it always amused him to watch when others lost theirs.

"I wish I'd been a fly on the wall. It would be good to see David get hot under the collar about something. I sometimes wonder if he knows what passion is," Layla said wistfully.

"David's father turned up afterwards and calmed his son down. Theo has a soothing effect – he always knows exactly what to say. I don't know why but I really like the man."

"So do I. He has time for everyone." She chose not to mention the artist's materials. Theo was a successful sculptor and could afford a magnanimous gift. Irritation with having no money flooded though her again and she leaned across and patted his knee. "Come on, Josh, you can tell me the truth. I know you're a thief. A good one, since no-one seems to suspect you. A leopard doesn't change his spots. I'm really hard up and need some spending money," she cajoled.

Josh stood up in exasperation and went over to look out of the grimy window. "What galls me is that I would like to have done it, I could have done it and I didn't. I won't be the one getting cash from the stolen goods and with tight security now in place I've lost my chance."

"What did you get for them? We agreed to share all the spoils," Layla said eagerly.

"You are not listening to me," shouted Josh, angrily striking the window frame. "I tell you once and for all, I did not do it."

"Alright. Calm down. I believe you," she said sulkily, not wanting to risk him losing his temper completely – she'd seen it happen and it was frightening. "You and I tell lots of lies but never to each other."

"I heard shouting," said Kate coming in unexpectedly through the kitchen from the back door. "Can I join in? I've got something to shout about too." She threw herself into a chair. The others stared at her in amazement.

"You're home early," said Layla. Trying to defuse the situation, she lit the touch-paper.

"Too right I am! I've lost my job. I've been fired," Kate hissed in her fury. "I spend months of my life working in the fetid atmosphere of that smoky pub, washing up until my hands are red and raw, for a mingy pittance. Today I've been unjustly accused of stealing something and given no chance to protest my innocence.

"You're not the only one," said Josh moodily.

Kate ignored this and went on. "The new pub cook says his pay packet has been stolen, and after a search it's found in my jacket pocket. Someone must have planted it there so I'd get the blame, but I've no idea why anyone would do this to me. I tell Colin I'm innocent but he says I'm very fortunate that he and Amy have decided not to call in the police, and I'm told to leave instantly. Why have I been treated like this? It's so unfair." Kate started to sob and Josh crouched down beside her, putting his arm around her shoulders.

"Kat, my gutsy girl. Don't get upset. They're bastards and it's not worth crying over. It was a lousy job and you know it." He stroked her shoulder.

"But I need the money. I'm already in arrears with the rent on this place." Her tear-stained face was desperate.

"Why don't you ask your father for a loan?" Layla could never understand why Kate was so reluctant to borrow from her wealthy relatives.

"Because he's already helped me with the final electricity demand and a horrible telephone bill. I want to be independent and pay my own way. Years ago Daddy gave me half of everything he owned and I lost it all," she howled. "I don't want to ask him for anything more. I don't deserve it."

Layla and Josh had heard this all before and her guilt trip made them feel uncomfortable. Surprising himself, Josh pulled some twenty pound notes out of his pocket and placed them on the table. "I'll pay this month's rent. I probably owe you more than that anyway when I lived here and contributed nothing." Seeing Layla raise her eyebrows, Josh raised his voice. "No Layla! This is my hard-earned cash from my respectable job as a barman. I'm not the thief and you'd better believe it!"

Kate stopped crying and looked up in amazement. "What are talking about? Who's accusing you of being a thief?"

"Layla has nasty suspicions – but they're unwarranted. I'm innocent this time – though I may not have been in the past! You know about the robbery at the hotel – it's now splashed over all the papers and your brother is very upset. Layla here thinks I did it and I've been trying to get it into her thick head that I didn't. You and I have both been wronged," he said in a mournful voice, darting a wicked smile at Layla over Kate's head.

"There's a difference. You haven't lost your job over it. And Kate has. It's time I went out to earn some money," Layla said decisively. Josh gave her an interrogative look. "No Josh. Not that way. I'm a painter and... I'm... going to paint – not just pictures but people's rooms. A bit of redecorating. It can't be that difficult! Wash down walls and paintwork, rub them with a bit of sandpaper, and apply the paint!" She smiled at the others who were listening to her with doubtful expressions and looking at her soft hands with their long nails. "Don't look so unconvinced. I'll show you. All I need is a bit of start-up cash to buy the necessary equipment – and I think I know where I can get it!"

"Not from me," Josh said hastily. "My drinking money has already been seriously depleted by helping out Kate."

Kate gave him a grateful hug and said to Layla, "Maybe I should come into business with you. Wielding a paintbrush can't be any more tiring than washing up all day." She gave a giggle. "We could become a fantastic female decorating team. We'd get all the jobs where little old ladies don't want sweaty, hairy, tattooed men in their houses." Kate punched her fist in the air.

"What a twisted view you have of hardworking men!" Josh was grinning, holding his head in his hands. "You two are a formidable pair – I feel almost sorry for the clientele in the town – they won't be able to resist you!"

"Our slogan will be: 'We touch up for less!' We could do fast work, cut corners and overcharge," Layla crowed.

Kate raised her eyebrows in mock horror. "That would be daylight robbery!"

They all burst into laughter.

Theo was driving to town in December and braked as he saw his daughter standing alone at a bus stop, bathed in wintry sunlight. She was wearing a long, green scarf and an old jacket with a bag slung over her shoulder. He remembered a younger Kate, when she had been a student, with a similar green scarf that he had given her. It might even be the same one as she had recently dug out an old trunk full of warm clothes left behind when she had gone on her travels.

She turned, hoping that at last the bus was arriving, and her pinched face broke into a smile as she recognised his car. Stopping a few feet from her, he wound down the window and she leaned in, her breath visible in the frosty air. "Daddy, how lovely to see you. Are you going into town?" She opened the door and slid in. "It's so cold out there and so warm in here." She pulled the door closed, leaned across and gave her father a kiss. "Can I have a lift?" An unnecessary request.

Theo felt her chilled lips on his cheek and his day suddenly became more special. "Dear child... nothing could make me happier than transporting my daughter to where she wants to go." He put the car into gear and moved off. His daughter seemed younger – an echo of her golden innocent days. "Where do you want me to take you?"

Kate leaned back in the comfortable seat, rubbing her numbed fingers. "I'm going into the library to borrow some books for my correspondence course, and as my house is so cold and damp, I'm thinking of staying there and doing some work. I might also drop by the job agency and see what's on offer. What takes you to town?"

"I've got a meeting with a promising young architect about our two new classrooms." Theo was a governor of the primary school and he was, of course, referring to Andrew, as Kate knew. "I'm meeting him for a coffee first – why don't you to join us?" Theo had long been aware of Andrew's affection for Kate, though she never noticed it.

"Good idea. I'd like to see Andrew again," she said breezily. "He seems to have disappeared from view."

No he hasn't, thought Theo, *he's just a gentle guy with strong feelings who doesn't push himself forward.* "How's the studying going?"

"I love it. I won't be able to do any teaching until I finish next summer, and even then I won't be fully trained. Right now I need a job – there's only waitressing or bar work, but it pays so badly and to be honest, I couldn't bear to work in another pub at the moment."

Theo knew she must be short of money and that she would not ask for his help. He sighed. "I was so sorry to hear you lost your job, but perhaps it's for the best. You'll have more time for studying. I know you'll be brilliant with children in the classroom one day."

"I'm also worried about Layla – she needs an occupation too. She was talking about getting decorating work but she has no experience. I love Layla but she's not as practical as I am." Theo smiled, finding it endearing that Kate never criticised her friend for not contributing to the household expenses. "I think Layla might become very resourceful, if she had motivation." *And hope.*

After parking the car in town, they strolled companionably to the coffee shop at the rear of the bakery where Theo had arranged to meet Andrew. There was a smell of warm bread and coffee beans and they saw him sitting at a round table. Catching sight of them, he leapt to his feet, a slight blush on his features that only Theo noticed.

Theo grasped his hand. "Good to see you, Andrew. Look what I scooped up at the side of the road, looking cold and bedraggled!" He had his other arm round his daughter's shoulders.

"I may not be smart but I don't look bedraggled," laughed Kate as she went up to Andrew and without hesitation reached up and gave him a friendly peck on the cheek. Theo was amused by the young man's look of embarrassed delight.

Andrew was eager to pull out a chair for her. "Hello, Kate. How's life treating you?"

"The bad news is I got fired from my job, I live in a freezing house and I've got no money. But I do have a wonderful father, some good friends and a few plans, so I'm in great spirits." She gave him a beaming smile and sat down.

Over coffee, Andrew and Theo talked about their meeting with the school governors and the projected building works and then the sculpture that Theo was working on in his studio. "I'm using a ladder at the moment – I need to get on top of a particularly tall piece – a commission for a fountain."

"Can I come up to the barn and see you tomorrow to have a look at it?" Kate asked. "That's one advantage of being out of work – it gives me more time for family and friends. Which reminds me – what news of David; how's business at the hotel? I was sorry to see the bad press about the robbery a few weeks back."

"David's got over that but is worried about low occupancy. There are lots of events planned for the spring but the winter is quiet. He told me he'd taken out your friend Layla a few times."

"Layla mentioned it but doesn't talk much about him." Kate had mixed feelings about her brother with her less-than-respectable friend.

Theo looked at his watch and rose to his feet. "Andrew, we must get on our way to the school. I'll pay for the coffees." As he went over to settle the bill, he heard Andrew speak to Kate.

"What are you doing today?" The tone was casual.

"Some studying in the library and looking for work," she replied with a smile. "Later I'll catch the bus back home."

Andrew cleared his throat. "Actually I'm not busy this evening. Why don't you come out for a pub meal and I could drive you back home afterwards?"

"Sounds a good idea to me. Any pub will be fine so long as it's not The Crown. How about meeting outside the library at 6 pm?" She sounded quite enthusiastic but her reason became clear. "I had no lunch so I'll be ravenous by then!"

Theo hoped that when her appetite for food was satisfied, she might be hungry for friendship. As they walked to the school with Andrew, the older man was aware of a quiet excitement in his companion.

"What made you want to run a hotel?" Layla asked David, who was driving. They had set off early in his car for a day in the city.

"I never wanted to do anything else after our family had a magical and memorable holiday at a seaside hotel when I was a child. I went to college to study hotel management and worked in hotels to get experience. Kate's decision to leave home delayed my dream as I had to buy out her share of the family home and repay the debt. Then I had to raise funds before I could convert it into a hotel and I'm hugely indebted to my father for supporting the project. Theo put his career as a sculptor on hold during that time. Without his inspiration and input it would never have happened. Now it's done and we've created a beautiful place for others to enjoy." David's face lit up and Layla envied his enthusiasm and commitment.

After arriving in the city and parking the car, they had gone to an art gallery. Pacing around, sometimes together and sometimes on their own, they had said little, but afterwards David took her to a late lunch at a restaurant where they chatted about the exhibition and discussed which paintings they had liked and why. Layla told him she had once been at art college and that she was now painting again. She drew a sketch of the head waiter on the back of the menu and hid it under her plate.

Afterwards they visited a large bookshop, where he bought her an illustrated art book about portraits. When she thanked him, he said it gave him pleasure. They wandered along the streets and looked in shop windows. Layla would have liked to have been able to buy some new clothes, which she needed, but she had no money and felt reluctant to put him in a position where it was obvious she wanted him to pay. She sighed as she thought: *I never used to have these scruples. I must be getting soft.*

It was getting dark, and a sleety rain started to fall when they set off on the two hour drive back. He concentrated on the road so it seemed natural for her to do the talking. Layla was adept at keeping things light-hearted but after a while David interrupted her flow of patter and asked, "Why don't you tell me a bit about your life? I've opened up on mine this morning so I think it's your turn."

It was bound to happen – she had known that one day he would ask about her past. She felt weary of avoiding the issue and decided to tell him the bare bones. She took a deep breath.

"I was a single child and lived with my parents in a country a long way from here. I went to the local school where I had a few friends. My father was a graphic designer and used to help me with drawing. I don't remember my mother working – but she didn't do much cooking and often bought take-away meals. I think she was lazy. I remember her as pretty and she liked shopping for new clothes. I think my father had to work quite hard to pay the bills. He died of leukaemia when I was twelve years old. I was devastated. There was no-one at home to talk to anymore. With no husband and no income, my mother became very sullen. She was angry with life and with me. We'd never got on, but when my father was no longer there to smooth things out between us, things got worse. She didn't like having to manage without a man, and within a year she had found someone else and we moved in with him."

"What was he like?" prompted David, his eyes on the road.

"He was horrible. Not violent, but creepy and disgusting. When I came home from school he would be lurking around the hall and would hug me before I had a chance to avoid him and run upstairs. My room had no lock on it and a few times he came in and sat down on my bed and tried to get me to touch him. This upset me and I became very frightened of being alone with him. When at last I had to tell Mum about it, she flipped, thinking I had encouraged him, which is what he told her. She was jealous." Layla had no inclination to lie – she felt like telling it straight.

"I was sent away to stay with a distant relative in another town, which was fine by me. I never saw my mother again. I wasn't very welcome where I'd been sent – the woman made me work in the house to help pay for my keep. I suppose I went off the rails at this point because my schooling abruptly came to an end when I was sixteen. I'd played truant and ducked classes because of bullying at school, and I spent hours in the municipal art gallery because it was free, warm and had some good pictures. My home life was dire. I already had my own passport so I decided to leave, switch countries and get a job and a life."

"Quite brave of you to go off on your own." David listened attentively as he drove but said little. "Your childhood sounds very different from mine. So sad and lonely!"

Layla nodded, thinking how loveless it had been too. "I had a secret ambition to become an artist and wanted to go to art school. Easier said than done. I got on a train without paying the fare, and when I found myself in a big city I needed a roof over my head and a job. After a difficult few weeks getting to grips with a new language, I managed to find work as a waitress." She paused, remembering how acutely miserable and desperate she had been – homeless and hungry – and how she'd been forced to steal to survive.

She was reluctant to discuss this part of her life and became vague, knowing that details would be damaging. "Somehow I managed to get to art school and hold down a job to pay for it." In fact Carlos had paid some of her fees. "I persevered but towards the end of the course I decided to go travelling just before my final exams." Not on her own. "This was a huge mistake." The first of many.

She was getting into murky waters so she steered the conversation back to art. "That's why I want to take up painting again. I mentioned it to your father that day in his studio, and he remembered and sent me the most amazing collection of artist's materials – all top quality. It was so generous and thoughtful of him."

She saw David smile, though he said nothing, so she went on impulsively. "Theo makes me feel special and empowers me. I'm going to produce the best painting I can to give to him."

"He'd really like that. He always encourages creativity and, though I was never any good at drawing, he helped me to develop a real appreciation of art and architecture."

"You've created a lovely hotel where people can find peace."

"My father trusted me with his family home so the business has to succeed, even though right now it's going through a rough patch."

They lapsed into silence. Layla was relieved that she had avoided making any awkward revelations.

David looked across at her as she sat watching the country road unfolding ahead, illuminated by the headlights, surrounded by darkness. Her profile etched itself into his mind. Her expression was serious and there was a tense, closed look on her face to ward off any further probing. *She's evaded telling me painful things,* he thought.

"Are you warm enough?" he asked to break into her reverie. She nodded. Her silence was getting to him. He really wanted to know why she was living in the area, what she planned to do with her life and, most of all, what she felt about him. He liked her – she was intelligent and beautiful, in spite of the heavy make-up. He liked her most when she was natural, spontaneous – even when she swore. She was so obviously a woman of the world – perhaps with a past she was ashamed of. He hoped the reason she was guarded might be because his good opinion of her mattered. She intrigued him and he badly wanted to hold her in his arms. Until now she had given him the occasional kiss on the cheek and he had put an arm round her shoulders. He inhaled her presence in his car like an intoxicating perfume. He wanted more of her mind and her body – but found it difficult to make a move because she was giving confusing signals. Did she want him or his money? Though it might be difficult or even disastrous to ask, he now wanted some serious answers.

When they were a few miles from the cottage he stopped the car on a secluded part of the road, got out and stood for a minute in the cold wintry air. Layla remained inside, waiting. He strode round to her side of the car and yanked open the door. Leaning down and taking her head in his hands, he kissed her full lips. She put one hand on his chest as if to push him away but then passively accepted his embrace. His heart lurched. After a minute she pulled back and he quietly closed the door and, walking round, climbed in to the driver's seat and turned to face her.

"Tell me why you are here," David said in desperation. "Why are you living in that dilapidated house with Kate? Is it friendship for her or lack of money that keeps you here? Or are you running away from something?" Layla shook her head as if she didn't know the answer – or didn't want to tell him. David went on relentlessly, grabbing her arm to make her look at him. "Why do you spend time with me? Because you need my help or because you like me? What are your motives?" Still no reply. He pulled away, saying, "I need to know – because it's tormenting me."

Layla licked her bruised lips and stared at him.

David waited – would it be honesty or deceit?

She took a deep breath and spoke. "Alright. I'll tell you now whilst we sit in the dark because that's where I've spent so much of my life. I was forced into a life I never wanted, but I'm not an innocent. I've lived on my wits and on my beauty. I sold myself. I had to. At first it was to pay for the necessities of life but later for luxuries. I didn't walk the streets. I had clients – I could pick and choose – and this was less dangerous." As David put his head in his hands, Layla said savagely, "So now you know that I was a call-girl, a tart, a whore, you are no doubt disgusted. All those middle-class prejudices are kicking in so you can feel justified in despising me. I'm soiled goods. I'm to be condemned for misleading honest folk by appearing beautiful on the outside whilst being rotten within." Her voice was full of derision.

"Don't you dare tell me how I feel!" David cried out. "You've no idea."

Layla went on relentlessly. "You want to know why I'm here? Josh and I came because we were looking for somewhere to hide and escape arrest. A friend told us which country Kate was in and where she lived. We both liked your gutsy sister a lot, so it seemed a good plan to travel here and see her again. We'd been kind to her when she was down. We thought she might reciprocate when we needed a bolt hole. So our reason for coming here was partly friendship but mainly self-seeking." She sighed. "We needed money and a place to stay until our trail had gone cold and our past couldn't catch up on us. When we discovered that Kate had family and they had wealth and property, I suspect our motives became even more mercenary. I'm disgusted with myself but admit that we thought we could fleece you or Theo and then move on."

David raised his head but said nothing. Her words had horrified him. But at least here was the truth. She had nothing to gain by telling it and it was her honesty that gave him a tiny flicker of hope.

Layla was nearing the end of her outburst of self-incrimination and in a low voice said, "During these past months, in spite of the lack of money, I've grown to like living in the countryside, away from big cities and evil people. I've washed away some of the dirt from my life and started to believe that things might be different, that there's another life I could lead. You and Kate and Theo have shown me respect, love and generosity, and I'm so grateful." David heard her sob before she went on. "I must have changed a little for the better, because I'd never have told the ugly truth about my life before. I used to be the queen of lies! Josh and Kate are real friends who've shared my world and don't blame me. But here Maria distrusts me, Andrew disapproves of me too, and this confession will make you hate me. You think someone like me can't change her ways."

"Will you stop telling me what I think," interrupted David angrily. "You deluged me with a torrent of horror – at least you could give me time to take it all in."

But Layla had more to say and nothing would stop her. "Now you've had all the sordid details, you're feeling revulsion and regretting the time you've spent with a scarlet woman. To complete the record, here are more negative replies to questions about my life: I've never been pregnant nor had an abortion and I'm not HIV positive. Finally, am I happy about myself and what I've done? No I'm bloody well not!"

He could hear the catch in her throat and knew she was crying. Sickened by all her revelations and yet still feeling desire for the woman beside him, David's mind swirled in confusion. Adrift and needing an anchor, he found himself wondering how his father would react and, uncannily, it seemed as if Layla had heard his unspoken thoughts.

"Theo doesn't condemn me – I always get the feeling when I'm with him that he accepts me as I am," Layla said in a tearful voice.

"He doesn't know what you were."

"He does. Kate told him."

David was stunned – he knew his father never betrayed confidences and always showed compassion to people whatever they might have done. He recalled with surprise that Theo had encouraged him to take Layla out for the day.

Layla went on quietly, "We all warm ourselves in the sunlight of Theo's acceptance. I always feel that your father likes me for who I am now and doesn't despise me for what I was. He makes me feel clean again and gives me hope that I can be good. Some of us, including your sister, have been faced with tough choices, made bad decisions and taken the wrong course. Kate has managed to claw her way back to a measure of self-respect, though she's far from confident, even now. I went further down the dark path to ruin, but at least I've stopped and begun to look up towards the light. I'm searching for freedom from shame. Give me credit for that."

As David stared out into the blackness of the winter night, he felt Layla put her hand on his arm as she whispered, "You've never been forced to do bad things or take the easy way out when confronted with really difficult choices. One day you will, and then you'll understand."

David's mouth felt dry as he drove the remaining miles. The day had promised much and ended miserably. Neither of them broke the frozen silence, not even when they arrived. He watched her walk to the door without turning round. After she had gone into the house, he drove home, his mind spinning.

9

The party began well with no hint of the fiasco that was to follow. Kate was throwing a 'House Cooling Party' to celebrate leaving her house at the end of March. Cool it was, in spite of the open fire in the little grate, but everyone was enjoying themselves. All day it had been threatening to snow and she hoped it would hold off until the next day. The paper-thin curtains were closed but the old windows let in draughts, and when guests arrived, chilled air ghosted in through the door. There was plenty of wine and beer – most people had bought bottles with them – and Josh had turned up with a couple of cases of lager.

Kate was not sorry to be leaving. This was her second winter in the damp dwelling and she had always intended to find herself something better before she faced another one. Now she had lost her job and as Layla had not yet found work, the rent was unaffordable. A week ago she had notified their landlord, a neighbouring farmer, of their decision to vacate the cottage. Then they had invited friends to help them celebrate their departure.

The small room was crammed with people and the babble of conversation mingled with the music. Kate looked around her. It was good to have friends in the house – parties had been rare events in recent months. She had spent the afternoon making large quantities of chilli and rice, bowls of which were now in the oven ready for supper. Josh had organised music, having managed to acquire a sound system and some CD's. She didn't like to question him too closely as to how he had got them, and when she had voiced her vague suspicions, Josh had put on his look of reproachful innocence and said accusingly that she didn't trust him. Too right, she didn't!

The doorbell rang again. This time it was Jamie from the farm. "I'm on my own. We couldn't get a babysitter so Penny's had to stay with the children." He gave Kate a hug, saying, "It's arctic out there, and not much better in here. Just as well that Penny's at home – she hates the cold." He cast his eyes around the room. "You've got a good crowd. Here's a contribution." He passed Kate a couple of bottles of red wine.

He stayed to chat with her for a few minutes and when the doorbell went again, he ambled over to talk to friends as she let in two girls, one with her boyfriend. Josh seemed to have invited quite a few of the hotel staff, some of whom Kate knew. David had already arrived and she hoped that his employees would not feel awkward to be at the same party as their boss. But her brother seemed quite relaxed about this and greeted them warmly as friends. She had long been aware that the staff liked and respected David.

When it was time to serve supper, Kate asked Andrew to help her carry it through. The noise diminished for a while whilst guests hungrily consumed the hot meal and then moved on to the cheese and bread laid out on the table. Andrew insisted that Kate sit on one of the broken-backed armchairs and eat too, whilst he stood beside her and held her glass.

Opposite them, Maria, wearing a long wool skirt with a pale yellow sweater, was sitting on the sofa with Josh sprawled on the carpet at her feet. Kate could hear him paying extravagant compliments to Maria who was pink with embarrassment but trying to smile. At one point he grasped her hand and looking up into her flushed face, declared theatrically, "My lovely lady, as beautiful as you are kind, I offer you my undying devotion."

Maria, looking disconcerted but trying to laugh, said, "Josh, I am not your lady. And I suspect I'm not the first to be offered your undying devotion."

She smiled at Layla who was perched on the arm of the sofa.

Kate could tell that Josh had already drunk too much and hoped his good humour would hold up. When Maria said, "Do stop joking," Kate whispered to Andrew that this might not be the wisest response to Josh's declarations of love.

"Why won't you take me seriously?" Josh suddenly demanded in a louder voice, so that others near them turned round to listen. "You are the one I love. You are the first woman I've ever said this to and meant it." Maria smiled warily and looked around her to find someone who would rescue her from the embarrassment of Josh on his knees, protesting, "Why don't you believe me? How many times do I have to tell you I love you? You're the only reason I stick around. What do I have to do to convince you?" He got to his feet, grabbing a bottle of wine from the table and pouring a full glass, carelessly slopping some over the edges. He raised it up and, grinning round at his assembled audience, he turned to Maria, saying, "I toast the health of the loveliest, the purest and" – here he gave a dramatic pause – "the most unfeeling, hard-hearted blonde dame I've ever met." He drank off the entire glass and refilled it with a flourish, spilling yet more on the carpet. He now had the attention of everyone in the room – the handsome rake pleading unrequited love to a virtuous lady.

Kate and Layla were watching him with fascinated horror – they knew what to expect.

Maria, looking even more discomforted now there was an array of giggling onlookers, shook her head and tried to look unruffled as Josh sank again to his knees. "I'm on my knees before you. I offer you my love, my loyalty and my life. Give me some hope." His mock-heroic voice had a note of desperation that only Layla recognised. "Give me a kiss," demanded Josh, suddenly lunging forward and grabbing Maria's slender foot, kissing the point of her ankle bone.

Maria sharply wrenched her foot free and recoiled from him, her patience snapping at last. "Don't do that, Josh. You're drunk."

"You bet I am," Josh ranted on. "And I'm not going to stop. I'm going to drown myself in drink because you are so cruel." As he leaned over to pick up the bottle, he overbalanced and lay there laughing, tears running down his face. Maria made her escape, and went into the kitchen to compose herself. Layla got up and crouched beside Josh, telling him to calm down. She took him outside to sober him up in the wintry cold air. When they returned, Josh retired to a corner with a bottle. Kate sighed – it was like having a time bomb ticking away without knowing how long it would be before it exploded.

An hour later, Kate heard the sound of raised voices and assumed it was a drunken, quarrelsome Josh in a foul mood, very different from teasing, sober Josh. She was mistaken – Josh was still dangerously quiet with a smouldering cigarette in one hand and a glass in the other, but it was her brother who was in an argument with their cousin, Jamie. She could see them on the other side of the room, radiating aggression, standing face to face with Layla between them, like some trio in a drama. Kate knew that Layla had met Jamie a few times but this was something that David had just learned. She went over to try and defuse the situation. David, pale with anger, accused Jamie of deceit and being disloyal to his wife. Jamie, in red-faced fury, responded with a blistering insult delivered with a mix of belligerence and guilt.

"Come on, David, we're having a party here. Cool it." Kate put her arm on her brother's shoulder but he jerked it away and turned on his heel.

"Sorry, Kate. I'm going home. I can't take this," he said striding over to the front door. As he left, there was some tittering from a couple of his employees who had been watching. Jamie muttered an apology and sat down beside Layla. Gradually conversation resumed and the music was turned up louder.

Kate felt someone touch her arm and turned to find Andrew behind her, smiling and holding out a glass of wine. "Thanks," she said, taking a sip. "I need a drink and seem to have lost my glass again. I'm sorry David's left in a huff. He was angry with Layla for flirting with Jamie, who's a married man and should know better.

"He's jealous," said Andrew quietly.

"He needn't be. Layla flirts with everyone and it means nothing."

"I'm not sure David realises that. And he thinks, as I do, that she shouldn't target married men."

"Layla told me that she and David have stopped seeing each other, so I don't know why he came to the party. I think he's obsessed with her."

Andrew decided to drop the subject of David's infatuation with Layla. "I gave Maria a lift this evening and she tells me you've found somewhere to live in town."

"I have and, even better, I've got a job in a newsagent's with flexible hours which will allow me to study," Kate told him. "It's only shop work but the pay's better than at the pub and it will give me time to study. Whilst on my course, I hope to get work experience at the primary school. Daddy's pleased because he's been encouraging me to get back into working with children."

"So when do you start and where are you going to stay?"

"There's a small studio flat to rent near the station. It's being renovated and will be available for me when I move out of here at the end of this month."

Kate saw Andrew blush slightly when he realised that this was not far from the street where he lived. "Do let me know if I can do anything to help when you move. My car will certainly carry more kit than your unreliable bike. What about Layla? Where will she live?"

Kate frowned. "She plans to go away for a few weeks – to see if she can find work in the city. She's hoping to find a job which will give her time to continue with her painting, but I worry how she will manage to pay rent if she doesn't get work."

"Layla can look after herself, I should think," Andrew said, "probably more than you can."

"I know you don't approve of the two of them," said Kate, "but they're not lazy spongers. David gave Josh a job which he's still got, and my father has a lot of time for Layla – they meet up for tea and discuss art." Kate knew that people like Layla and Josh, drifting and uncommitted, disconcerted Andrew. She wanted to show him that there were unconventional things about her too. "I'm getting better at looking after myself," Kate said looking into his eyes and thinking he was not really as ugly as Layla said, "but I'm happy to accept your offer to transport my kit to the new place. I hope to see more of you when I'm living in town."

"May I take that as a promise?" Andrew put his arm round Kate's waist. "I think you've noticed me at last!" He bent down to kiss her but at that moment the front door burst open and about seven or eight men exploded into the party. Kate, who did not recognise any of them, pulled away from Andrew saying, "They look drunk. Here comes trouble," and together they went across to confront the boisterous gate crashers.

Not far away up the lane, Ross waited, lurking in an unobtrusive black car with no lights. He had 'obtained' it in a distant town a couple of days earlier on his afternoon off.

A few minutes earlier the lads from the bar in town had driven past in a couple of cars and on three motorbikes. His boys, Rif and Leo, were with them, having gone to the bar earlier and got talking to Josh's usual drinking companions. They bought a lot of drinks and let slip the news that their mate was throwing a party a few miles away and wanted them all to come along. Fuelled by alcohol and the promise of a rowdy evening, they had set out with Rif as guide to show them the way. Soon after their arrival at the house, Rif, tall and intimidating, planned to insult someone, pick a quarrel and get others involved. Leo, agile and strong, would instigate a fight and the two of them would get the drunken pub-goers to start smashing up the place, before leaving. He expected them to turn up within an hour and climb into the car. Leo would take over the driving and Ross himself would be dropped off a mile or so from the hotel, and they would disappear. He'd probably never see them again.

Ross had worked for Ator for a number of years and had recently transferred from the 'drugs' side of the enterprise to 'harassment'. This was very different work: more devious, often dull, less dangerous but well paid. Contact with his employer was rare and always by mobile telephone, at pre-arranged times and on different numbers, so Ross knew very little about him. His boss had a personal vendetta against Theo, the prime target, but chose to attack him through harassment of his children, making them suffer and ruining their lives.

Ross was disappointed that Josh and Layla had not been more disruptive. The pimp and his tart had been shipped in by Jakob to destabilise Kate, the target's daughter, but it appeared that they had succumbed to the charms of rural life and were in no way creating the problems he had anticipated. Josh was now working in the hotel and trying to lay the owner's ex-fiancée. Ross hoped Josh would use the temazies which he had obtained for him and slip a mickie into the pallid little blonde's drink and then satisfy his lust. Ross himself occasionally used temazies and had sexual fantasies about Kate, who was a feisty girl with a good body. He was disappointed that no physical abuse had been authorised by Ator.

Ross looked at his watch, picked up his mobile and called Jakob.

"Krait here," said Jakob. "Is that Sergio?"

"Yes," said Ross. "Just to say that our boys have gone into the house with the rowdies. I think they'll enjoy themselves."

"Good. One of them will dump the car, I assume?"

"All arranged. What's next on the agenda?"

"You wait for instructions."

Ross felt irritated. He hated the countryside, found the hotel too remote, and restaurant work, even though he was experienced at it, bored him. "Is it possible to tell the boss that I'm fed up with my current assignment and want to move on?"

"No chance," said Jakob who felt much the same. "Anyhow, Ator hinted to me that soon you'll be ordered to deal a decisive blow to the target family. Afterwards you'll be moved on to another location. You are to keep your distance, if possible, from the prime target, who is intuitive and shrewd."

Ross had an uneasy suspicion that Theo already distrusted him. On the few occasions when the older man had looked at him, Ross felt like a rabbit caught in the glare of headlights and knew he had to tread warily.

"One more thing. Ator was not pleased that the accusation of theft that got the daughter fired from the pub did not lead to a prosecution. It should have been handled so the evidence was conclusive."

"Don't worry. Tonight's fracas should cause her a lot of grief."

"Good!" said Jakob ending the call.

Ross continued to wait. Soon Rif and Leo would appear. Leaving havoc behind them, they would drive off into the night.

It was past midnight and the noise was deafening. The gate-crashers were enjoying themselves but the other guests were having a miserable time.

Andrew had been unable to eject the unwelcome newcomers without causing a brawl. Most of them were drunk and some looked threatening. For about twenty minutes they had lounged around, helping themselves to beer and wine and jeering at the nervous guests who had not yet left. They greeted Josh loudly and teased him for being so drunk, whilst he seemed puzzled as to why they were there. They increased the volume of the music until it was deafeningly loud and ignored Layla and Kate's vociferous demands for them to leave.

Andrew had tried to persuade three of them to go, but he was shoved away by an aggressive man with a shaved head who told him to stop interfering or he'd get hurt. The man did not speak with a local accent, so Andrew asked him where he was from and got a punch in the face. Staggering back against the table and jolting some glasses on to the floor, he lunged back at his opponent and grabbed him round the neck. With surprising agility, the stocky man twisted free, caught Andrew off balance and threw him with the ease of a judo expert. As Andrew slammed into the wall, a wrenching pain tore through his shoulder. When he tried to get to his feet the pain left him gasping and, sinking back powerless to help, he could only watch as the situation deteriorated in front of him.

One of the troublemakers saw the scuffle, sniggered and shouted to his mates, "Our friend here wants to smash a few glasses, so let's help him!" Whereupon he picked up a table-lamp, wrenched the wire out, and swinging it by the base along the top of the table, he swept off all the plates and glasses on to the floor. The resulting crash seemed to trigger off a desire to break everything in sight and the cry went up, "Trash the place."

There was panic as the remaining guests tried to leave through the front door but found their way barred by a tall man in a denim jacket, who told them with a leer that he thought it unfriendly to be trying to go so early. One couple managed to slip away through the back door in the kitchen before it was blocked by the fridge rammed against it. Some frightened girls locked themselves into the bathroom.

Bottles of wine were thrown against the wall, smashing and spurting wine on furniture and floor. A chair had its legs wrenched off to use in breaking ornaments and pictures and to poke holes in the plaster and the ceiling. Sofa cushions were split open and the contents hurled around, whilst someone with a knife slashed the armchairs. Sounds of breaking crockery and whoops of delight by the perpetrators were coming from the kitchen. Andrew was outraged but was helpless, whilst Kate and Jamie desperately tried to stop the house being wrecked. They were shoved aside by the thugs, who used chairs to break the front window. The glass shattered and the cold air flooded in. Broken glazing bars with jagged remnants of glass dangled in the black void.

Andrew caught sight of Layla stealthily climbing the stairs whilst everyone's attention was focussed on avoiding the splintered shards of the wrecked window. He had heard a cry of rage from Kate as she watched this senseless destruction but then she caught sight of him lying on the floor and ran across.

"Andrew, are you hurt?"

"Get help! Call the police!" he said to her urgently.

"I tried to but my mobile was knocked out of my hand and stamped on." Distressed, Kate looked around the room. "Where's Layla?"

"She's managed to get upstairs," Andrew said, thinking Kate had more courage. He put out his hand to comfort her and winced with the pain. "Stay here and keep out of their way."

"You've got blood on your face," Kate said as she leaned over him, and he felt her hand move his hair from his forehead to look for the cut. She noticed he was holding his arm. "What's the matter with your arm?" Before he could answer, there was another crash and the sound of splintering wood in the room. Kate said urgently, "Keep still and I'll shield you."

At this point, one of the drunken revellers smashed the last remaining bulb in the hanging lamp, putting the sitting room into semi-darkness, the only light coming from the open door to the kitchen. A howl of delight greeted this and the rampage went on, with the few remaining guests unable to leave, cowering against the walls, shielding themselves.

Layla had made a quick telephone call from the mobile in her room and now crouched halfway down the stairs trying to assess the situation and hoping no-one was getting hurt. She spotted Andrew lying awkwardly against a wall with Kate beside him and Jamie valiantly trying to stop two yobs as they threw books and CD's into the log fire and smashed the sound system. Josh, drunken and enraged, was staggering around trying to find Maria.

Inevitably one of the louts tried the bathroom door and, finding it locked, kicked it in. Three frightened girls including Maria were pulled out into the room. It was when the shaven-headed man grabbed Maria and tried to kiss her that the trashing stopped and an ugly fight began.

Josh heard Maria's scream and threw himself in a fury at her attacker. He was so drunk that the other man's punches soon had Josh on the floor, where he was savagely kicked. Appalled, Layla called out for someone to help him. When two of the louts from the town saw their old drinking pal being attacked while he was down, they got angry and turned on the shaven-headed man and his tall friend. The fight soon got out of hand with the local men full of alcohol and adrenalin, turning on the two strangers.

Josh was still on the ground as Layla watched the fight erupt in the dim room. She saw two of the thugs signal to each other, extricate themselves from the melee and vanish through the front door.

At this point, one of the remaining drunks caught sight of her shadowy face and started to creep up the stairs towards her. Layla backed away, like a cornered cat. "How about a nice cuddle in one of the bedrooms, my pretty one?" he said with a leer, but as he reached out for her, she stood up quickly and lashed out with her foot. She struck his chest, and with a cry he staggered back losing his balance. *Good riddance,* she thought, as she heard him crash downwards.

In the shaft of light from the kitchen she could see that Jamie, fit and strong from the physical work on his farm, was still on his feet and trying to deal with one attacker whist fending off another. She hoped that her assailant had knocked himself out, but with alarm she saw him get to his feet and with a snarl of anger start back up the stairs. The look on his face was frightening and she panicked. "Jamie, help me," she shrieked.

Then something strange happened.

From outside the house two very strong beams of light shone in though the broken window and a loud horn sounded. One of the troublemakers thought this was the police and shouted a warning to the others. Within seconds they had gone, jostling to get out of the door, one limping and another shouting obscenities. Those inside heard running footsteps before car doors slammed and bike engines roared into life.

As a stunned silence descended and as the sound of their vehicles receded, a tall figure silhouetted against the car headlights climbed in through the gaping hole where the window had been.

"Is anyone badly injured?" asked Theo.

Layla was the only one who was unsurprised to see him. She had known he would come, and watched as two girls, who were scared out of their wits, began to cry with relief.

Kate sprang to her feet and ran across to him. "Daddy, thank goodness you're here. Are the police with you?

"They're on their way. But the troublemakers have departed." Theo's calm and measured voice was already having an effect. "Who's been hurt?"

"Andrew's in a lot of pain with his arm. Josh has either been knocked out or he's passed out. They kicked him horribly."

Maria came forward and said quietly, "I've had a look at Josh and he's badly bruised with some nasty cuts on his head. He's starting to come round but I think we'll need to get him to hospital for an x-ray. He may be concussed. We'd better not move him yet."

Layla, who was also aware of the dangers of blows to the head, felt sick with worry about Josh. With a shudder, she recalled the two thugs kicking him.

Jamie, practical as ever, came forward. "I'll ring for an ambulance. Has anyone a phone? Mine's been smashed."

Layla ran back upstairs to get her mobile and, returning, she handed it to Jamie who rapidly contacted the emergency services and requested an ambulance. In the glare from the headlights she could see he had swollen knuckles and a nasty bruise on his cheek.

"How did you know about the trouble, Daddy?" Kate was amazed he was there.

Layla spoke up: "I don't know how to call the police, so I phoned Theo and asked him to contact them."

"That was sensible, Layla," said Theo, giving her a smile of approval before walking over to see Josh, who was stirring and trying to sit up. He bent down and gently said, "The party's over, Josh. The troublemakers have gone. We've called an ambulance for you." He watched as Maria carefully washed a nasty cut above Josh's left eye, from which blood had run down his face, whilst another girl held a bowl of water for her.

Maria looked up at Theo. "Andrew may have dislocated his shoulder and I've told him to keep still. When they arrive we'll get the paramedics to look at him too."

Layla turned to Jamie, still standing beside her. "Thanks for your help. You were great but you're going to have a dreadful black eye."

"No problem." Jamie saw Layla was shaking and he put his arm round her shoulders. "What a shame your party turned out so disastrously. But at least we have only two casualties. There's a lot of damage to the house but I expect the insurance will cover it."

"Kate has no insurance," said Layla in a small voice, seeing Kate gazing around the scene of devastation looking shell-shocked. "But I'm more worried about Andrew and Josh." Josh was sitting on the debris-strewn floor, leaning against a cupboard, his head lowered. "Sorry. Very... very drunk," he was mumbling through swollen lips. "Can't stand up. Sorry. Everything's blurred. Got a bad headache." This time it was Maria who was kneeling in front of him.

"Thank you for defending me and I'm sorry you got so bashed up because of it." Maria gave Josh a gentle kiss on the cheek.

He raised his head and slowly put his hand up to the spot she had touched with her lips. "It was worth it," he said thickly.

Layla was relieved to see him responding. She knew Josh was besotted with Maria, who had always repulsed him but now displayed a hint of something more than the usual concern of a nurse for a patient.

Layla noticed Theo going round reassuring the remaining shaken guests. As always his presence had a calming effect. They all heard the siren of the ambulance, and within a short time the paramedics had Josh on a stretcher to get him back to the hospital quickly to examine his head injuries. They thought a doctor should relocate Andrew's shoulder under anaesthetic and suggested he also return in the ambulance.

The police turned up half an hour later. Rowdy parties that had got out of hand were not their priority but they were surprised at the extent of the damage and took some statements and descriptions of the troublemakers from Kate and Layla and the few shaken people who were still present. The house by this time was very cold and it was still dark, although someone had managed to rig up a light in the sitting room after Theo had switched off his car headlights. The police left, saying they would return in the morning and make enquiries to find out who was responsible.

Finally everyone departed. Theo phoned his son and David appeared soon afterwards. Since the cottage was uninhabitable, David insisted that Layla and Kate return with him to the hotel where he had a bedroom that they could use. Wearily the two dishevelled women got into his car, leaving the ruins of their wrecked home. David murmured some words of comfort to his sister but to Layla he said nothing. Theo had told them that he and Jamie would attempt to make some sort of barricade across the gaping and broken windows and then abandon the sad little house for the night.

A few days later Theo visited Josh in hospital. Maria had telephoned to say that a CT scan had been performed and Josh had sustained a skull fracture though luckily no bleeding was visible under the skull which would have indicated injury to the brain. The doctor had said that skull fractures usually healed well but the patient also had bruising around the head and severe concussion. Josh had been unconscious for nearly ten minutes on the night he had been punched and kicked, though this might have been due in part to the alcohol he had consumed. She explained that trauma had probably caused the blurred vision, nausea and confusion that afflicted him for the first couple of days in hospital. Josh had bad headaches for which he had been given painkillers and, though tired, he found sleep difficult. As she related the details of Josh's medical condition, Theo had detected a note of personal concern in Maria's professional voice.

In the ward, Josh was in a bed in the corner furthest from the window. He had a soft bandage around part of his head, with his dark hair visible below it. He lay still, his head propped up on pillows, with one hand shielding his eyes. As Theo stopped at the foot of the bed, Josh moved his hand away revealing a bruised bloodshot eye and gave a crooked grin through swollen lips.

"Come to look at the drunken idiot who got his skull bashed in?" He waved at the older man, flinching as he did so.

"You look quite sober now," said Theo with an answering smile, sitting on a chair beside the bed.

"More's the pity. I feel terrible. This is the worse hangover I've ever had," Josh groaned.

"The word 'concussion' seems more appropriate, Josh. I'm told you sustained some savage kicks to your head when you were down on the floor." Theo, shocked at Josh's appearance and the pallor of his skin, was angry with those who had inflicted such damage. "It was a vicious attack."

"I don't really remember much about it. I recall coming round and seeing Maria kneeling beside me like an angel of light."

"Maria has been keeping us informed of your progress."

"She even kissed me. A few seconds of heaven to prepare me for the nightmare pain in my head that I've had ever since." Josh grimaced. "I feel sick and dizzy too. I know I deserve it – I behaved dreadfully. I feel so guilty – the whole thing was my fault."

"I don't think that's quite true, Josh," said Theo quietly.

"Yes it is," Josh cut in bitterly. Trying to sit up, he winced and sank back against the pillows, closing his eyes and murmuring, "The light's too bright."

Theo watched him for a minute in silence. Then Josh spoke again with his eyes shut. "Layla and Kate came to see me yesterday. They tell me that the house is wrecked and needs lots of work and money to get it back into shape. It's all my fault. Apparently I told my mates at the pub about the party – though I don't remember doing such a daft thing – and that's why they gate-crashed, got fighting drunk and trashed the place."

"I have my suspicions about that," said Theo drily. "I'm sure the event was more orchestrated than we are meant to think. There were two strangers who may have provoked the fight and encouraged the senseless destruction before they vanished into the dark."

"It's all a bit blurred in my head. I was so awfully drunk." Josh opened his eyes again. "But what I do know is this: somehow I've got to repay the girls for the damage. I don't know how I'm going to do it because I've probably lost my job as well."

"You certainly have not," said Theo. "David didn't see the worst of your drunken behaviour and he would certainly have applauded your attempt to stop one of the troublemakers from mauling Maria. He's asked me to tell you that he's signed you off on sick leave until you recover."

"That's kind of him. I don't deserve it. I would like to ask one thing. Is your son at all bothered about my being in love with his ex-fiancée?"

"Not at all. I think he has some emotional issues elsewhere to divert his thoughts."

"You mean Layla. She really likes him a lot but thinks he's too good for her." Josh became animated. "She's not a bad person, Theo. She's had a hard life and regrets what's happened in the past. She told David all about herself and he's horrified. Layla can be selfish at times but deep down she's loving and faithful."

Theo said, "I know that."

A thought struck Josh. "Layla and I have never been lovers. We're companions who cruise around together. It's almost like having a sister – we quarrel like mad and then laugh together but we've always been there for each other. It hurts me to think that people disapprove of her."

"I don't condemn her, though I might not approve of how she's lived or what she's done. Anyhow she's wants to turn her life around and I'm going to help her to do just that." Theo looked intently at the younger man. "What about you, Josh? How about a change for the good in your life?"

"I've always thought I had the ability to be good. It's just that I couldn't afford to be."

"Why not give it a try?"

"I might try to give up cigarettes. They make me horribly feel sick right now. Kicking the booze would be tricky, but you never know. I really ought to control my temper too. When I've had a skinful I get quite nasty, I'm told." Josh laughed mockingly. "Layla always said that one day I'd get my head stove in. I've been told my skull is cracked so it seems she's right. I hear that Andrew had a nasty dislocated shoulder. Please tell Kate that I'm massively sorry about the fight and what happened to the house."

"Stop beating yourself up with guilt," said Theo rising to his feet. "You need to get some rest now. That's the best treatment for concussion, Maria tells me."

"Tell the dame that I love her. She thinks me disreputable but I won't stop trying to win her." Josh looked up at Theo with a lopsided grin. "Maybe I'm going soft in the head but I know it's the real thing!"

"Who's there?" called Kate, her heart beating anxiously. She had called by the empty house to collect some clothes and heard the sound of movement from the floor above.

Ten days had passed since their disastrous party and although Kate and Layla had tried to clear up the mess and broken glass, they could do nothing about the damage to the walls, windows and furniture. The owner of the property had inspected, and one of his farm hands came to board up the gaping window frames so the house was in semi-darkness.

She heard a door open and Layla's face appear at the top of the stairs. "What are you doing here?" Kate was surprised. "The place is a wreck and it's horribly cold. I thought you were still staying at Homeward House."

"Come on up, the electricity works and I've got a fan heater in my bedroom. It's quite habitable up here, if you don't mind the lack of hot water."

Kate climbed the stairs and they went into Layla's room, which looked surprisingly comfortable – in stark contrast to the ruinous state of the ground floor.

Layla closed the door. "Sit down on the wicker chair that I've borrowed from your room. How about a cup of coffee? I've got the electric kettle from the kitchen – somehow it survived – I found it amongst the debris in the only corner of the kitchen floor that hadn't been urinated on." She picked up a plastic bottle of water, tipped some into the kettle and switched it on. "There's no hot water because the gas is turned off, but there's cold water in the bathroom downstairs. And up here I keep warm enough if the door's closed." She spooned some instant coffee into a chipped mug and a teacup. "I salvaged these survivors from the kitchen. They couldn't break the teaspoons, so I have plenty of those." She gave a bright smile but Kate knew her well enough to detect the flicker of desperation.

"How long have you been here? I thought you and David had made it up and he was letting you stay in one of the hotel rooms until you find somewhere else." Kate, who was comfortable staying with Maria and her mother in town, was dismayed that her friend was camping out in the trashed house.

"Let's just say that David still has problems about being associated with an immoral woman. I used to think lies got me into a lot of hot water but telling the truth has really burned my boats. Your brother is a man of high principles and I don't measure up. So I jumped ship, but not before I liberated some provisions from the hotel kitchen. And here I am. I'm alright though the food's run out and I'm a bit hungry."

"I can buy you some food. Andrew's lent me his car until he's able to drive again. His shoulder was relocated under anaesthetic but it's still very painful."

"Sandwiches would be good. The cooker's broken so there's no way of heating anything." Layla laughed. "It reminds me of old times, Kate, when we were unable to pay the bills and food was scarce."

"I remember – we were living in that attic apartment. And Josh went out and stole some foie gras and smoked salmon."

"And a bottle of champagne."

They both fell silent and drank their coffee. The past was still with them. Layla put her cup down on the floor saying, "Don't worry about me. I won't be here for long. We were due to leave at the end of this month in any case, so I've been hatching a little plan and found somewhere else to live for a while. I've persuaded Jamie to lend me the little one-bedroomed holiday cottage down in the water meadows. It's a bit primitive – but nothing like as bad as this place!"

Kate looked at Layla with raised eyebrows and a face full of disapproval.

"No, I am not involved with your cousin. He's a married man."

"That never worried you in the past," said Kate, remembering the quarrel between the cousins at the party.

"Well it does now. I've been living among you moral folk for too long and some of your scruples have rubbed off on me. It makes life harder but it makes me feel better. I've not asked Jamie if I can stay in the cottage for free. I've offered to give the walls a lick of paint which I can do, instead of paying rent which I can't. It will get me into practice for my proposed venture into decorating. Not sure how I'm going to eat until the business gets up and running but something will turn up! What about you?"

"You're not only one who's resourceful, Layla. I've got a part-time job in a shop which gives me time to study. I've even found somewhere to stay in town. Let's cheer up – it'll be spring soon."

"When I'm out of here, I'll try to get a loan for buying the equipment I'll need," said Layla.

"From the bank?" Kate sounded doubtful.

Layla took a deep breath. Another lapse into truthfulness. "Actually from Jamie."

"Layla! Whatever is Penny going to think about this? She's bound to jump to the wrong conclusion."

"I can't see why he needs to tell her – but he could say quite truthfully that he's lending the cottage to a painter who will decorate it while in residence." She turned to face her friend who was giving her a hard stare. "I am a painter; he's just a friend. That's the truth, Kate."

"How many times in the past have I heard you say that when both of us knew you were telling lies?"

"I'm emphatically not interested in Jamie."

"You may not be. But he's interested in you. You've thrown your net over him and hooked yet another admirer. David got upset at the party because he still desires you. He was jealous when he saw Jamie panting after you. Why do you encourage him?"

"Jamie's a wealthy farmer and he's useful." Layla spoke sulkily, leaning back against the pillows. "And I need somewhere to live."

Kate raised her voice. "My brother is a wealthy hotelier and he's been useful too. I see you still intend to 'take' instead of 'give'. You disappoint me. I thought you were trying to change. I thought you liked David." She leaned against the door and folded her arms.

"Give me a chance. I'm trying to change," Layla snapped back. She jumped off the bed and went over to Kate. "Believe it or not, I love and respect your brother. I told him the truth and look where it's got me. Rejected as unclean!" The bitterness gave way to dejection. "David's a sensitive, kind and honest man. I've not met many of those in my life up till now. I come to this country and meet three – David, his father and your Andrew. That's why I'm still here – they've restored my faith in mankind." There were tears in her eyes. "But it isn't easy living with their disapproval."

"David should learn to accept we all make mistakes. My father never condemns anyone. And as for Andrew – he's not judgmental. And he's not *my* Andrew yet," said Kate with a faint smile. "But I'm hoping."

"I've no hope of a future with David," Layla said desolately.

"Cheer up. Come on – I'll buy you a hot meal. You look famished. We can commiserate together – we have other problems to deal with – financial ones. I've been to see Daddy to ask his advice about a stern letter that I've received from the solicitors who act for the owner of this house. If we hadn't been leaving anyway, we'd be evicted. We're liable for the damage inflicted. As I'm uninsured, I have to find the money to pay the huge cost of the work. Debt looms even larger." Kate sighed.

As they clattered down the stairs, Layla said with a giggle, "Perhaps we can ask Josh to rob a bank for us."

"He's still suffering from the concussion and is off work so I don't think he's capable of it."

"Poor Josh. It was bad luck."

"No it wasn't. He was raging drunk and he lost the fight. But I feel sorry for him."

They left the house and walked across to the car. "Do you think he's serious when he claims to love Maria?" Layla asked.

"It seems so. He's charmed her mother with his exaggerated courtesy. What's even more surprising is that Maria has a soft spot for him. Talk about chalk and cheese."

"More like beauty and the beast," Layla said as they drove off.

"Whereas we're so similar," said Kate. "Sisters in guilt. I'm not sure I have the courage to emulate you and come clean with Andrew about my past." She fell silent, wondering how he might react when he knew the truth. Like Layla she didn't deserve a good man but she didn't want to lose him.

"Things are going from bad to worse," said David, hunched anxiously over his desk. Theo had arrived for their weekly lunch to find the hotel in the midst of another crisis. "Within the past two days a number of guests, some of whom have already departed, have developed severe gastro-enteritis and are suffering from nausea and vomiting," David explained. "A doctor has been called out to treat those still staying here and is concerned about an elderly couple who might have to go to hospital if they don't improve. He says the outbreak of food poisoning is due to harmful bacteria in food and the local health department will have to be informed to investigate the matter. I'm hugely concerned for my sick guests. I'm also aware that if the hotel is closed down, even temporarily, this is certain to damage its reputation with disastrous consequences for the business."

The telephone went and David answered it briefly. He stood up. "Sorry but I have to go. One guest's condition has worsened," and he hurried out. Theo knew that well-being of guests was paramount and his son prided himself on the exceptional standard of hygiene in his hotel. Theo made himself a cup of coffee and sat down to analyse the situation. The mishaps were increasing and this was not mere chance. His family were being targeted and he knew who might be responsible. Six years ago news had reached him that Ator had been released from prison. The man had taken time to re-establish his criminal organisation but he had succeeded. Driven by smouldering hatred for Theo, his depraved mind would seek revenge and it was probable he had ordered his agents to make Theo's children suffer.

Kate had been a victim. Some years back she had been swindled out of the remainder of her inheritance from his trust. She was impetuous and had made bad decisions but she was not a thief. Yet she had been wrongly accused of theft twice – the first had resulted in a prison term, a fact only he in the family knew about, and the second had caused dismissal from her job, though this time a prosecution had been avoided. Recently her party had been invaded by two troublemakers who enlisted local drunks to cause havoc. Her guests were badly frightened, two of them injured and the house wrecked. Kate was short of money, having given food and shelter to her homeless friends for many months. She would get further in debt from claims for damages by the owner of the house. When he'd offered to help, she gently but firmly refused, saying she would pay it off herself. She had visited him two days before and Andrew, whose shoulder was much improved, had come with her. The young architect had been devoted to his daughter for a long while and Theo hoped that she would take his advice to tell Andrew the truth about her life during the five years she had lived abroad. The young man might be shocked but it would clear a path for the relationship to develop without any secrecy.

David was under attack too, in the place where he most wanted to succeed. There had been an unsolved robbery at his hotel which had resulted in bad publicity. Recently a guest had tripped on loose carpet and fallen downstairs, breaking his arm. His injuries might have been worse, but was it accidental? This might not be bad management but planned malevolence. This time guests were ill with food poisoning and the kitchens about to be scrutinised by health inspectors. Introducing bacteria such as listeria, E. coli or salmonella into the hotel kitchen, especially in food that was to be eaten raw, would not pose too many problems for a man of Ator's ingenuity. He would need an accomplice with access to the kitchens, someone on the staff whose presence would not arouse suspicion. Of the few employees who had joined in recent months, Josh had been taken on without references, but Theo doubted he was responsible and he had been off sick for some time. Sergio, on the other hand, with references that checked out, had access to the kitchen and there was a calculating intelligence behind the inscrutable face. But nothing could be proved.

Theo reflected that the hotel disasters were not the only problems in David's life. The troubled young man was trying to come to terms with distressing facts about the woman he loved. He hoped that in time David would be less inclined to make moral judgements and would learn that no-one was immune from temptation. If only his son would focus on his personal life with the same intensity that he gave his business affairs.

Andrew was unaware of the shock he was about to receive. He was back at work but had to rest his shoulder as much as possible. Walking round construction sites was inadvisable so he was at his desk dealing with office paperwork. While he opened the correspondence and glanced at it, he thought about Kate.

The evening before, after he had helped move her few possessions from Maria's home into her little studio, they went to a restaurant to celebrate. During their meal Kate mentioned that David had updated her on the food poisoning problem at the hotel. It seemed that the bacteria had been identified as listeria and it was present in some unpasteurised soft cheese which certain guests had eaten. Most of them had now recovered but an elderly man had been transferred to hospital because doctors suspected he might develop meningitis. Kate was worried for her brother. This empathy with other people's problems endeared her to Andrew. He felt sorry for David for a different reason. His friend had become obsessed with Layla – a woman with a murky past.

The final letter to be opened was handwritten. The envelope was addressed to him at his office and he pulled out a single sheet of paper. The words on it said, "You ought to know that your girlfriend is a convicted criminal. She has served time in prison for theft. She was sacked from her last job for stealing." There was no signature.

Andrew was stunned. He knew Kate had run wild but he couldn't believe she was a thief. Furious with the vindictive individual who had sent him the poison pen note, he tore it up. He felt no anger towards Kate, just a deep feeling of disappointment. He wondered if she would ever tell him about her past.

10

Layla glanced back at the sad little house with its boarded-up windows. She had lived there for almost a year and the place had good memories and a few bad ones. She was pleased to be leaving – a month in one cramped upstairs room with no hot water had not suited her. She was on the move – but not far.

"Penny for them?" said the man driving the vehicle.

"Just thinking back over the past year. I've stayed put for longer than I usually do. I've been on a journey in my head and the urban creature I used to be has become a would-be country lass." Staring through the windscreen at the trees alongside the road with their early spring leaves shimmering in the clear April sunlight, she went on. "Living here has shown me another way to live life – a less selfish way. I'm trying to change."

"I like you the way you are." He shot her an admiring look.

"Thanks, Jamie," Layla smiled at him. "But I'm still dissatisfied with myself. A year ago I had nowhere to live and no place to go – I was running away from my mistakes. Kate took me in, along with Josh, but after the cottage got wrecked, homelessness loomed again. Thanks to you, I've now got somewhere to live and time to make plans."

"How is Josh?" Jamie knew from Layla that the man was like a brother to her.

"He still has headaches and occasional blurred vision. But he's a resilient guy and is back at work at the hotel." *Where David is every day,* Layla thought, with a stab of envy.

Jamie turned off the lane on to a track which wound its way along the edge of a field and through some woodland. "It's quite isolated but you'll come to no harm. There's a bike you can use to reach the outside world – I've pumped up the tyres – and there's a local shop about two miles down the road."

"I'm going to love it. I'm used to my own company. Anyhow there's decorating to do! I've got to earn my keep." Layla injected enthusiasm into her voice though she felt apprehensive.

The Land Rover bumped over uneven ground and came to a halt beside the little stone cottage she had first seen in the autumn before. The windows were dirty and the faded yellow paint on the front door was peeling. It looked more damp and dilapidated than Layla remembered and she wondered if the plan was a mistake.

Jamie noticed her doubtful expression. "It's a fine little place," he said reassuringly. "The roof's watertight and it's cosy when you get the wood burner going in the evenings. I dumped a load of logs in the shed at the back, where the bike is kept." He took her bag out of the car and the boxes containing a few household items, her painting materials and the decorating equipment, and took them all through the gate to the front porch. Pulling a key out of his pocket, he unlocked the door and they went in.

As she looked around, he carried in her stuff, putting it down on a small rug in the front room. The furniture was dusty but there were curtains in the windows and a few books on a shelf. She went through to the kitchen which was simple but had a gas cooker and a Belfast sink, with some cupboards containing crockery and utensils. She put down a bag with a few items of food on a small wooden table.

"It has everything that's necessary for a holiday let," said Jamie, who was standing close behind her. "I've turned on the water. We laid pipes to the water troughs in the fields, so we got this place connected up too. The cooker and water are heated by bottled gas which turns on here under the sink." He bent down and opened the valve for her. "I'll replace the gas canister when it runs out – if you let me know."

He showed her how to fill and light the oil lamp. "Our holiday guests find it quite romantic without electricity. I've left a jerry can of paraffin in the outside shed and two packs of candles in the front room. The bedding is in the tall cupboard in the bedroom and there are some towels too. I've got to go now – a farmer's work is never done. Will you be OK?"

"I'll manage fine – thank you, Jamie, so much."

"Mobiles don't seem to work here but if you bike to the local shop there's reception. So ring me on mine if you have any problem." He paused, putting his hand on her arm. "Best you don't ring me on my home number."

She nodded. There was no need to ask why. His wife might be surprised to find that the painter to whom he had lent the cottage was female! Penny had a job and two lively children. Jamie said she took little interest in their two empty farm cottages and he dealt with any occasional holiday lets. So she would probably never know.

"Jamie, I regard this place as a secret location. Please don't tell David where I am." She planned to be inaccessible, to give David occasion to miss her.

"Of course." He smiled down at her. "I'll let you settle in and later this week I'll drop by with the paint. I've bought some cream emulsion for the walls and found two cans of pale green gloss paint that will do for the woodwork."

"I'll unpack today, and tomorrow I'll start washing down and sandpapering." She followed him out of the door and said in a business-like tone of voice, "I'll make a good job on the cottage and it's very useful to be able to stay here in return for the work. I'm grateful for the loan too – and your help in buying the painting equipment, which I can use for any further jobs I might get. It's a commercial thing – and I fully intend to repay you."

"There are many ways to repay debts, Layla," Jamie said softly, handing her the key and looking into her face. She didn't answer as he bent down and kissed her on the cheek. "Bye for now."

He drove off, waving at her. Layla hoped she had not landed herself in a tricky situation. It was obvious he was attracted to her and, though she tried not to encourage him, she could see he had hopes for an affair. He might have misunderstood when she said she didn't want David to find her. She would make the rules plain the next time they met.

She was hungry and ate a slice of bread and a wedge of cheese. Kate had lent her some money to buy food. She planned to stay for a month and finish all the work on the cottage. She would then contact David and give them both one last chance to resolve the impasse that their relationship had reached. She knew he desired her but could not bring himself to touch a 'fallen' woman. He was too reticent to talk of love but she believed he did love her. Would absence make his heart grow fonder? If not she would have to go. On her own. Josh would stay whilst he thought he might have a chance with Maria. He seemed to be content working in a job with modest pay – it was so unlike him. She could not remember the last time he had gone pilfering – perhaps he was trying to be good to impress the virtuous Maria. He'd even given up cigarettes.

She felt lonely. Everyone's lives seemed to be on track except for hers. Kate, though up to her ears in debt over the house, appeared to be happy living in town, basking in Andrew's devotion. She asked Kate not to tell her brother and father where she was, though she might go and see Theo, whom she liked and who was not judgemental like his son. He had advised her to be honest about herself, so she had made an effort to tell the truth to David – and much good it had done her! Instead of living comfortably with clothes, food and bills paid for by another, she was still without money, job or purpose and was embarking, ill-equipped, on the next chapter in her life. She looked out of the small window and whispered, "David." Why had she become involved with this oversensitive, upright, beautiful, intelligent, impossible man?

She turned and looked at her new home, her thoughts crystallising. She would stay here temporarily until the time was ripe for a final confrontation with the man she loved. Until then this was home and it was rent free. She rolled up her sleeves – she would clean the windows, sweep the floor and wash the sink. The bed needed making up and her few clothes needed to be unpacked. In the evening she would light the oil lamp and make a fire. Tomorrow she would work so hard she would be too tired to worry. She certainly had changed. The question was, could she keep it up or would she revert to her old way of life?

Jakob was sitting in a small hotel bedroom. Waiting for orders. Yet again. He seethed with resentment against the evil man who controlled his life. He wanted to go his own way but was unable to break free. He needed a woman to share his bed and his life, a safe place he could call his own and money to live on. Instead of this restless pointless existence at the beck and call of a dangerous man.

The telephone rang. It was Ator.

Jakob reported on the food poisoning scandal. "It will be impossible to trace where I obtained the bacterium which I passed to Ross. He managed to introduce it to the stored soft cheese. The elderly guest in hospital has unfortunately not died but there have been substantial compensation payouts. As there was to the accident victim the month before, though this may be covered by insurance."

"The hotel may weather these minor storms," Ator spoke in a hoarse monotone, "but what I'm planning will cause the family enterprise catastrophic harm, from which it will not recover." Jakob knew better than to ask for details. He would be told nothing until the order came with instructions delivered discreetly to ensure no link to the embittered man in his hidden lair. He risked one more comment: "Ross is getting restless and wants to move on."

"The man had better stay put if he knows what's best for him," Ator snapped. "Ross has a vital part to play, after which he will be sent on an overseas assignment, far away from the fallout. Anything else?"

"The son is worried about the hotel problems and is still involved with the prostitute who was seen staying at the hotel. The daughter is heavily in debt over the repairs to the trashed house, and her boyfriend and father have been sent anonymous letters alerting them to her criminal record." Jakob knew that Theo was the enemy Ator was trying to hurt and yet all his efforts were directed at the man's children. The old sculptor was clever but surely he was no match for the powerful Ator. Riskily he asked a question: "Why don't you just attack the prime target? He's not well protected and we could nail him."

He was surprised by the ferocity of the response. "We do this my way."

Kate was itching to tell her decision to her father, who had called round to see her studio flat. "I want to work with children and I want to be with Andrew." Her eyes glowed with resolution. "I'm glad I lost that dreary dead-end job at the pub because I've now got energy and a sense of purpose."

"How are your friends?" Theo asked.

"Josh is still working for David and might even become a reformed character. Layla's got some work." Kate stopped, unable to divulge where her friend was staying and changed tack. "But I love it here. Andrew lives nearby and I hope you think his steady character will be a good influence on me." She adored her father and said impulsively, "I love him, Daddy. I really do."

Theo smiled. "I know you do."

"It's such an amazing feeling. I don't deserve him. He's far too good for me," she had said in a rush of emotion. "We get on so well together and like the same things. He's told me about his parents who live in the south. And about his childhood, his home and his time at college."

"Have you spoken to him about your life?" Theo gently enquired.

Kate frowned. "I've told him about my wonderful childhood, though I've not said much about my parents. He knows you well – and likes you and admires your work." She hesitated. "I admit I've not talked much about my travels abroad – the irresponsible years. I'm so ashamed I caused you so much pain."

"Kate, how many times do I have to tell you that I forgave you long ago. It's wiped clean in my mind. But don't let Andrew imagine things worse than they were. You need to be open with him. People who care for each other shouldn't have secrets. It takes courage to admit mistakes and tell the truth, but once you have done it, you'll be free."

"Layla took the plunge, on your advice, and look where it got her. David has avoided her ever since. She's miserable about it." Kate looked worried.

"So is he," Theo said. "She must give him time."

A week later Kate was sitting at a table with her books. She had put in six hours at the shop that day and was now working on a study assignment which had to be finished by the end of the week. The newsagents had discovered that Kate was industrious and, with the other assistant on annual leave, they offered her extra hours. She was tired – but looking forward to seeing Andrew that evening.

She shoved the books aside and went over to her tiny kitchen to check the chicken casserole and to cook the rice. She had not seen Andrew for over a week and, puzzled by his silence, had telephoned him. He sounded distant and preoccupied but had accepted her invitation to come over and have supper.

Life for Kate was less stressful. She had reluctantly accepted a loan from her brother to pay the owner of the house for the repairs and now she had to save from her earnings to pay him back. David had been so kind, assuring her there was no urgency. He tried to give her the money but she insisted it would be repaid, however long it took.

She looked at her watch and then in a mirror. Her hair was getting longer. Andrew said he liked her green eyes.

After the meal she would spill the beans about her rackety life to the man she loved. She was apprehensive and hoped he would understand.

Her doorbell sounded. She took a deep breath and ran to the door. Andrew stood there, tall and comfortingly familiar with his crooked nose and untidy hair. She gave him a hug and he seemed a bit tense, so she asked if his shoulder was still causing him pain.

"Occasionally but I've nearly got all movement back. I'll be playing tennis soon!" He gave her a tired smile. "How's work going?"

She chatted about her job and her studies and then served supper for them both. Whilst they ate he told her about his work and the new classroom at the school which was nearly finished.

"Maybe one day I'll get to teach in it." Kate grinned across to him.

"Let's hope you do," he responded without enthusiasm. His usual warmth and affection were held in check and Kate knew something was wrong.

When she had cleared away the plates, she made them a cup of coffee. They sat at the table and drank it in awkward silence. She stared at the black dregs in her cup and decided to take the plunge into the dark areas of her past.

"Andrew, I've got some things I need to tell you about," she began hesitatingly. He looked up expectantly. "It's about my years away. I've never really told anyone about them – except for Daddy. But I don't want there to be anything hidden between us. Because I really care about you, I want to share these difficult memories."

"Go ahead, Kate," Andrew said softly. "I'm listening."

So she told him. About her departure from home and her selfish desire to go off with all the money held in trust for her. About the cities in which she had lived and disreputable people with whom she had become involved and friends she had trusted. She spoke about Roberto and her disastrous first love affair, about parties and riotous behaviour, the drugs and the drink. She admitted how besotted she had been with Karl, how he deserted her after stealing everything she had, leaving her desperate and impoverished. Layla and Josh had helped her but finally they too abandoned her. She described her travels, poverty and menial jobs, the despicable Vadim and how he had landed her in prison for theft, the horrors of prison life and her release. Finally she had come to her senses and decided to go home but the journey had been long and punishing. She had brought all this on herself.

Andrew said nothing, his gaze averted. As she spoke, Kate became more and more nervous about his reaction, restlessly moving in her chair. Was he appalled? Would he despise her? She went on raggedly, "I was much younger. I lived in places where I didn't understand the language or the culture. I made bad judgements about people who lived outside the law – and they encouraged my wild behaviour. Their freedom from convention made it easy to give in to temptation. My moral values slipped because I had no boundaries."

She faltered to a stop but Andrew was listening and he looked at her, encouraging her to go on.

"I did have some fun during those five years but most of the time I was miserable and guilt-ridden. It was a hideous, jarring nightmare which stopped only when I returned. I wanted to be forgiven. I've tried to change and I need to be honest about my mad and bad life." She stopped – Andrew had risen to his feet. Was he going to leave? "I hope you don't think I'm awful," she whispered.

But he came and knelt down beside her. Putting his arm round her hunched shoulders, he spoke gently. "Dearest Kate, thank you for sharing this with me. I'm so glad you've been open with me. I love your feistiness, your courage and your perseverance." Kate began to cry with relief, shuddering with release of tension. Andrew stroked her hair and traced a tear down her cheek with his finger.

"The other day," he went on, "I received a despicable poison pen letter, which informed me that the woman I love was a thief and had been in prison. I never believed the first accusation and now, without my asking, you have explained the second. I'll just have to get used to having a jailbird as a wife!"

Kate looked up at his smiling face. "Wife? Andrew, what do..." He stopped her mouth with a kiss.

A few minutes later she pulled back and said, "I do love you. You know that."

"I've loved you for years."

"That's impossible. We met on the night I came home about a year ago. I looked so dreadful – scrawny with dyed blond hair. You sat beside me at dinner. I was so emotionally drained I hardly noticed you."

"In fact we met some seven years before that. You were in your late teens. I visited your family home – before it became a hotel. Your brother, who was a college friend, had invited me. You were there but very preoccupied with a smart young man called Toby. You flitted in like an exotic butterfly, alighting briefly before breezing off to a party with the lucky fellow. I recall being stunned with admiration and eaten up with envy."

"How dreadful, Andrew, that I don't remember the incident at all. I don't even recall what Toby was like. How could I not have noticed you?"

"I was very plain and you were so young. There were probably many admirers," he added in a teasing voice.

"I was very foolish then. Hopefully I'm more sensible now I'm twenty-eight."

"And even more beautiful."

"I can't believe you think that! And you're not plain – I think you're gorgeous."

"Love is blind." He kissed her again.

"Do you really want to spend the rest of your life with me?" Kate looked into his eyes, confident of his assent.

"I'm the faithful type but I've waited long enough. Let's make up for lost time and get married soon. I'm old fashioned so I need to speak to your father. Will he approve?"

"He'll be so happy." Kate got to her feet and danced around the room, lightheaded in her elation. "But not as happy as me!"

A few days afterwards Josh and Maria were climbing off his motorbike when David came out of the back entrance to the hotel, carrying a bottle of champagne. He waved and came across to say hello.

"Hi boss," Josh said, thinking that David must find it strange that Maria, whom he might have married, was going out with a drifter like him.

David noticed that Josh's arm was bleeding through his shirt sleeve. "What's up, Josh? You in the wars again?"

Josh grinned at him. "This lady causes me all kind of problems – I'm her personal bodyguard. My arm – and my heart – are bleeding for her!"

David looked mystified and Maria spoke up: "We went down to the river for a walk along the bank and this dog came hurtling across to us, barking. I'm frightened of big dogs, so I stupidly shrieked and Josh did one of his dramatic acts – trying to protect me – but he overplayed it and the dog took a nasty nip out of his arm before scarpering off."

"There's some antiseptic spray and bandages in the hotel medical kit – and you know where that is, Maria. Same place as when you worked here. Help yourself. Must dash. I've been summoned to a celebration." And he went over to his car, got in and drove off.

Outside the staff accommodation, Josh handed Maria the key to his room and she let them in, saying, "You go and wash the wound and I'll go to the reception area and get what I need."

"I adore you," said Josh grabbing her round the waist with his good arm and planting a kiss on her cheek.

"Let me go, Josh," Maria struggled free. "You're dropping blood on the carpet. Shoo, go and take off your shirt and wash the wound." She disappeared and Josh obediently removed his shirt, dabbed perfunctorily at the cut with a wet cloth and then threw himself on to the bed. He had developed another of his nasty headaches – a side effect of concussion. The doctor said he might suffer from them for months.

Maria came back and told Josh to sit up and hold his arm whilst she cleaned it properly and put a bandage on it. She was conscious of his warm naked chest inches from her and with a prim expression on her face said, "All done. I think you'll live."

"Not without you, sweetheart," drawled Josh, capturing her hand. "I'd die without you."

"You are so silly, Josh," Maria tried unsuccessfully to extricate herself.

"You are so desirable," murmured Josh raising her small hand and kissing her fingertips. "I wonder why I find nurses so sexy?"

Maria escaped and went to sit on the only chair. His physical presence disturbed her. "I need some space. And a break from your exaggerations."

"Heartless woman," moaned Josh beating his bare chest with his fist. "I can't have Maria. I'm not allowed cigarettes. But I could do with a drink."

"Josh, it's the middle of the afternoon." The disapproval was evident.

"Did you imagine I meant alcohol? It's water I need," said Josh reproachfully. "Actually, I've got a rotten headache and need a couple of aspirin and a glass of water." He looked at her beseechingly.

"Why didn't you say so before? Where are they?"

"In the top drawer over there. Glass on the shelf."

Maria got up and went over to the basin to fill a tumbler of water.

"You're as bad as Theo – always trying to reform me," Josh grumbled. "He came and had a chat with me in the hotel the other day, while the bar was quiet. Like you he seems to think I need lessons on 'how to be good'. I told him I'd given up my earlier dishonest ways and ought to be congratulated as I've also given up cigarettes."

"Only because they make you feel sick. But keep it…" Maria was looking in the drawer and suddenly stopped speaking. Josh heard her put the glass down sharply.

"What's the matter, my angel?" Silence. "Maria, what's wrong?"

Maria spun round, two angry red spots on her pale cheeks. She was holding a packet in her hand. "You have Temazepam. It's not been prescribed for you. It has a number of uses but it's also the date rape drug. Why do you have it? Is it intended for me, the next time we go out? Or perhaps you've already used it with some unsuspecting woman who isn't prepared to fall into bed with you as soon as you'd like."

"I've never used it, I swear." Josh put his head in his hands. "I don't do drugs any more. I prefer food."

"So why is it here?" Maria was outraged. "You're disgusting. I don't why I've listened to your protestations of love." She was crying. "You almost made me believe them."

"Don't go, Maria. Let me explain." He got to his feet, feeling cold and desperate.

"Don't come near me," she hissed as she tore the door open. "I'll go before you offer me a laced drink. The receptionist can call me a taxi." The door slammed shut on Josh's dreams.

"He's on his way," said Theo. He glanced at the calendar as he put the telephone receiver down. It was 13th May, the day of a fatal family accident many years before. From now on the date would have a more joyful connotation. He looked across at Kate and Andrew who were standing together, with her arm round his broad waist and his arm round her slim shoulders, looking out over the glorious spring countryside.

Kate had telephoned to say that they wanted to come and see him that weekend because Andrew had something important to ask him. Theo knew what this was. Kate had said, "I've told Andrew about my bad years and he still loves me. You were right, Daddy. I had to be honest with him. It's such a relief we no longer have any secrets from each other."

Andrew had formally asked Theo for his daughter's hand in marriage. Theo's heart was full as he gave his consent. Kate gave Theo a huge hug and then took Andrew's hand. "He wants to marry me. I can't get over how crazy he is. But he seems to think it's a good idea!"

Andrew laughed. "It's the best idea I've ever had. It's not new – it's been lurking around in my mind for some time. But Kate only noticed me recently."

"Untrue." Kate shook her head and did a pirouette. "I'm so… ooh happy." She stopped and said to the two men who were fondly watching her, "I want to tell everyone. David first. Let's ring him and tell him to come and celebrate. Now. Daddy, can you call him?"

Her euphoria was infectious and Theo went across to ring his son and tell him to come over and bring a bottle of champagne. David was surprised but heard the persuasive note in his father's voice and said he was on his way. Theo was aware that David had difficulties with the hotel and the fallout from the food-poisoning episode. He hoped his son, who had looked tired and stressed the last time they had met, would put these cares aside when he heard the news.

Whilst they waited for David to arrive, Andrew telephoned his parents and his sister, who were delighted. Kate spoke with Andrew's parents for the first time and he arranged to bring Kate to visit them, staying overnight at his sister's home to break the long journey.

The trio were discussing wedding dates when David arrived. The moment he walked in and saw Andrew and Kate's faces, he knew. When the hugs and congratulations were over they opened the champagne. Andrew and David were close friends, their earlier misunderstanding over Maria long forgotten.

"I've harboured a secret passion for your sister for years," Andrew said. "It's finally ignited a flame in her."

Talking animatedly together, the couple walked over to the other side of the studio, to look at Theo's recently finished sculpture which was waiting to go to the foundry. Theo found himself wondering whether David was contrasting their happiness with the misery of his own indecision about the woman he loved.

David watched them and said quietly to his father, "I'm so pleased. Andrew is a kind and serious professional man, who will be a steadying influence on my mercurial sister. I hope he'll be able to cope with her highs and lows." He sipped his champagne and Theo was surprised to see him smile and say, "Layla once said Andrew was 'no oil painting'. But just at this moment, with his face alight with joy, Andrew looks almost handsome. Kate certainly thinks he is!"

Theo asked, "Have you seen Layla recently? She's seems to have gone to ground and I don't know where she's living these days."

"Neither do I," said David shortly. He shook away his misgivings. "But ten minutes ago I did see Josh with Maria. They had just returned to the hotel and Josh had been bitten by a dog."

Kate had come across the studio to put down her glass and caught the end of this conversation. "Is he alright?"

"He's fine. Maria will deal with it. She's so gentle – I can't see why she's interested in someone as wild and unpredictable as Josh."

"Josh may be outspoken and often outrageous but he's a kind person. He and Layla were good friends to me. Underneath their teasing flippancy, they're loyal and caring people." Kate spoke warmly. "I must tell them about Andrew and me. They are going to be so delighted!"

Theo decided to risk asking Kate about Layla. "So where is lovely Layla? She's not been to see me recently."

"Daddy, you have such a soft spot for her," Kate rattled on unthinkingly. "She's fine, living in a holiday cottage that Jamie has lent her – somewhere on his farm, miles from anywhere. She's redecorating it. I ought to give her a ring..."

She stopped suddenly because Andrew had produced a small box from his pocket and was holding it out to her. "My darling Kate, *I'm* going to give *you* a ring."

Kate, silent at last, opened the box and took it out. Andrew gently picked it up from the palm of her hand, put it on her finger and kissed her.

Theo glanced at David, who was standing still, staring at the ring, his thoughts miles away. There was a stunned look on his son's face as the news sank in that Layla was living in Jamie's cottage. Theo, aware of his latent jealousy, put a hand on his son's arm. David looked up at his father and their eyes met – Theo could see the pain and jealousy. "Think this through first, David. Stay calm. Don't jump to conclusions," he said quietly.

David nodded slowly and forcing a smile for his sister and her fiancé, said, "That's a beautiful ring and I'm truly happy for you both. But I must be off now. Business calls."

Kate, who had been examining her engagement ring, ran over and flung her arms round him. "Thanks for the champagne. You're my favourite brother."

"Dearest Kate, I'm you're *only* brother," came the predictable response as he went out of the door.

Layla was singing as she washed her brushes. This kind of painting was tiring but straightforward – it required no creativity and incurred no frustration. Leaving the brushes in the sink, she straightened up, feeling the ache across her shoulders, and looked around the kitchen. It looked as creamy and fresh as the other rooms she had already completed. There had been no rain for a week and with little humidity in the cottage the paint would dry well. Now the walls were finished, she would start on the wooden window frames and the doors. Tomorrow.

Wiping her hand on her overall, she went through to the sitting room. Glancing at a small mirror on the wall, she noticed a smear of emulsion on her forehead. How much she had changed from the woman whose face had always been fully made-up, with hair brushed and hands manicured. Now her scrubbed face looked pink with health and there were even a few freckles. Her hair was tangled and most of her long nails broken. More important things occupied her mind. Without David, what would she do with the rest of her life?

She sighed. She would give him another two weeks and then let him know where she was and suggest they talk. What would win – his love or his prejudice? While she waited there was still hope. How unwise she had been to allow herself to fall in love and become vulnerable!

The evening sunlight filtered in through the small windows, but soon she would have to light the oil lamp. Now it was May she did not bother with a fire and in any case her stock of wood had nearly run out and she was not inclined to contact Jamie and ask for more. She was trying to avoid any further obligation to him. He had called in a week before to see if she was alright, and to deliver a spare gas canister and show her how to connect it up when the other ran out. She was well aware of his interest in her but managed to fend off any affectionate advances from him by being practical about the gas and focussing on the decorating work.

Amazingly, apart from her dull ache for David, she didn't mind being on her own. It was relaxing, uncomplicated and she had the freedom to be herself. She did not to have to lie or pretend. The cottage was out of mobile range so she wasn't bothered by calls. Kate had dropped by a few days before to tell her the news of her engagement and it was marvellous to see her friend so happy. Andrew was a good person and though she privately thought him a little too staid for Kate, he would be faithful and considerate. Layla had met many men who were neither, so her friend had chosen well. Kate's future was settled – unlike hers.

Hearing the sound of a car engine, she darted into the bedroom to remove her overalls and put on a long skirt and top. Perhaps David had discovered where she was! She heard the car door slam as she dragged a brush through her tangled hair. As she walked into the living room, Jamie was standing there. She was annoyed he had entered without any courteous knock, but reflected that it was his property after all.

"Hi Jamie. Nice to see you. Lovely evening, isn't it?" She managed to keep the disappointment out of her voice.

"Layla, you look well. Blooming and beautiful."

Ignoring this comment, Layla asked, "What do you think of the walls? I've finished all the emulsion except for the little bathroom."

"They look fine," and he glanced round briefly before going across to her and giving her a hug that was a little too warm. "Well done. You're a fast worker."

Not as fast as you are, thought Layla. "I'm going to start on the paintwork tomorrow – the sanding has been done. It was tiring work." She tried to look wearier than she felt.

"How about I take you out for a meal?" Jamie grinned when Layla shot him a wary look. "It's just a meal I'm suggesting. Food for a hungry worker."

Though there was little enough to eat in her kitchen, Layla shook her head and said in a grateful tone, "Thanks but I won't. I'm not hungry and need an early night – to rest my aching limbs!"

"Still deflecting my efforts to chat you up," said Jamie putting on a mock woebegone expression.

"You're a married man with children."

"I know, but you're such a temptation. I can't help myself. What can a man do with you around?"

"Show her respect. And the same goes for your wife. Treat her right."

"Let's have a glass of wine together. No strings." He pulled a bottle out of his capacious jacket pocket. "You get the glasses and I'll light the oil lamp for you."

It seemed ungenerous to refuse, and within a few minutes Layla was sitting on the small sofa with a glass in her hand and Jamie had taken off his jacket and was leaning against the mantelpiece with his wine. The oil lamp on the table shed a golden light.

Layla mentioned that Kate was engaged to Andrew but Jamie already knew, saying, "News travels fast round here. Though your staying in my cottage still seems to be under wraps."

"Kate knows."

"That's risky. She's not always discreet. Unlike her brother – he always plays his cards close to his chest."

"You're right. David doesn't talk much about himself." She could not resist asking, "How is he?"

"I've not seen him much recently. Only once since our little altercation at your disastrous party."

Layla was curious. "You've known him most of your life. Has he always been so reticent?"

"David was always more reserved than Kate, who's the impetuous and reckless one. He's energetic and ambitious for his hotel but can be generous too in a quiet sort of way. You can always rely on David."

"How are you related?"

"We're first cousins. Their mother was my aunt."

"They never talk about their mother. I gather she died in an accident when they were very small."

"It was bad luck. They never really knew her – Kate was just a baby."

"I've heard about a woman called Rachel who was around when they were small."

"Rachel's my mother and she helped Theo look after them. They often used to stay at the farm and play with Louise and me."

"Is that your sister?"

"Yes. She married a farmer who lives the other side of the country – and that's where Mum moved a few years back. She didn't want to stay in the farmhouse when I married Penny, and decided to live near Louise."

"So you inherited the farm from your parents?"

"Dad sent me off to college to learn about estate management but all I ever wanted to do was come home and learn from practical experience. It was just as well I did this, as my Dad died suddenly and I had to take over the running of the farm with Mum."

"So what did David do after he left school?" asked Layla, deftly turning the conversation back to the topic that most interested her.

"David was always keen to live at home and work in the country. He has a strong feeling for the land, even stronger than I do. It's how I earn my daily bread and I don't have too many romantic notions about nature and the soul of the land, but David cares passionately about it. He wanted to share the place with others by opening a hotel. So Theo sent him off to study hotel management, after which he worked for a couple of years elsewhere before coming home to pursue his dream."

"And Kate. Didn't she like the countryside? It's heavenly here, so why did she leave home?" Layla was curious.

Jamie picked up the bottle of wine and went over to fill her glass and then his own. He wanted to sit on the sofa next to Layla but she was lying with her legs stretched out and there was no room. So he sat down in one of the upright chairs before answering, "Kate was a bit wild. She was less academic than her brother and she got on well with kids and intended to train as a primary school teacher. She never finished the course. I think there were too many distractions – she was a pretty thing, had a succession of boyfriends and was always going to parties. She had itchy feet too, and always talked about travelling and seeing the world. She swanned off for over five years and went badly off the rails – but you know more about that than any of us." Jamie looked at Layla with raised eyebrows.

Layla loyally refused to elaborate on Kate's misdemeanours, especially as they were interwoven with her own, and merely remarked, "Kate's buckled down now and has decided to retrain. And David has his beloved hotel."

"It was hard for him when she came back. He'd stayed at home and done the right thing and everyone was making a fuss of her. Theo's managed to reconcile them. He's always been a peacemaker and the whole family adore him."

"Theo's such a star!" said Layla. "He treats me with respect and cares about me. He's amazing."

"Theo cares about everyone. As a child he was the one adult I always felt at ease with and he's marvellous with my children – they love spending time with him."

"Theo used to live with David at 'Homeward House'. Why did he move?"

"His studio burned down and when it was rebuilt, Theo could move up there. David's such a workaholic that he's hard to live with. Probably why his sister didn't want to work for him when he offered her a job."

"Kate told me she wanted to be independent. I admire her for that." Layla waved her glass at Jamie who refilled it. "She said she needed to earn David's trust."

"The siblings are very different. As teenagers she was outgoing and sociable and he was shy with girls."

"But he's so good-looking. And seems unaware of how attractive he is. I find him unassuming, thoughtful and courteous."

"So I gather," said Jamie drily, draining his glass and standing up. "It seems there's no hope you might want to have an uncomplicated affair with a married farmer who lusts after you horribly." Layla shook her head. "So David is the one. Lucky bastard! He doesn't deserve you."

"You've got it the wrong way round. I don't deserve him," Layla said sadly. "I'm a scarlet woman! I'm untouchable."

"More fool him."

"He's so very different from most of the men I've met in my life. Who all seem to want one thing." Seeing Jamie wince, Layla said softly, "Sorry, but I no longer want to be the object of men's lust. I want a man's love. I want David – but he's wrestling with his principles about whether he can put up with a woman with a past. I don't know what will happen, but if he washes his hands of me, I'll have to go." She was near to tears.

"You've told me where to go. Home to my wife. So I'm off." Jamie gave her a smile and Layla stood up to say goodbye. "Come on, give me a hug as a friend – and I'll let you get some sleep." He held out his arms and gave her a big comforting embrace. "I hope my cousin has better luck than me. You've got paint on your face," he said, looking down at her and wiping her forehead with his finger.

At this point both of them heard the door open and, pulling apart, they saw David standing in the open doorway, the black night behind him, his handsome face contorted with suspicion.

There was a moment of frozen silence.

"Before you jump to any wrong conclusions," Jamie said in a normal voice, whilst putting on his jacket, "I'd like to inform you that I'm just leaving. Layla is my tenant, my decorator and my friend. We have just spent the last hour talking amicably about you."

A look of surprise and confusion appeared on David's face, followed by disbelief.

As he sauntered to the door, Jamie stopped as he passed his cousin and looking at him straight in the eyes, said, "You have no reason to be jealous. Layla is interested in one man only – and it's not me!" He walked outside and called back, "Bye Layla! Best of luck with the paintwork – and with the outraged lover boy!"

They heard him start up the Land Rover and drive slowly down the track, the noise of the motor fading into the whispering of the trees as the wind blew through them.

At about the time that Layla finished painting that day, Josh had finished cleaning up the hotel bar and was seated on a stool in the lounge looking moodily out of the window. He had given up smoking but was itching for a cigarette. There were few guests in the hotel – probably the result of bad publicity about the food poisoning. David had told his staff that this was to be expected but that, in time, the affair would die down and guest numbers would start to rise again.

Josh felt tired and he was depressed by the rift between him and Maria. He had tried to call her but she would not speak to him. Why on earth had he allowed himself to get so obsessed about a woman who was so straight-laced and uncompromising? Surely he could cut loose and get the hell out! But strangely the appeal of his former itinerant way of life had diminished. He enjoyed living in the country, he was alright with the work and it was good to have regular food and a roof over his head. He liked the area and the local people but, most of all, he found being in love exhilarating. How could he convince Maria that he not only loved her but respected her? He would never have used the Temazzies that Sergio had given him.

As if on cue, the restaurant manager came into the lounge. "Have you finished drying all the glasses and wiping down the bar?" Sergio could see this had been done but liked to demonstrate his authority over Josh.

"It's all done. Just taking a breather. There are no guests about. I could do with a fag!"

Sergio pulled out a packet from his pocket and silently offered one to Josh, who hesitated and then took one. He got up, went round behind the bar and lit it with a match. Taking a big drag on it, he exhaled theatrically, "I miss these death-sticks. Thanks. I didn't know you smoked, Sergio."

"Only rarely, when I'm off duty. Stub it out and bin it if any guests come into the lounge, will you?"

"Sure." Josh watched Sergio walk through to reception. Dry, humourless man.

He took another puff and dragged the nicotine into his lungs. A minute later, he felt a wave of nausea and with a sigh he flicked the cigarette into the bin. He could almost hear Theo's voice encouraging him to give them up and

Maria saying they were bad for his health. He needed to shut their solicitous chatter out of his head. He lacked sleep and would go and lie down for a while – Sergio could manage without him. Anyhow his shift finished at 6 pm. Tonight he'd take one of those blasted Temazzies. After all they were designed to knock people out – and he needed a few hours of oblivion.

Later that night, in the cottage in the woods, there was silence – the raw emptiness that comes after a heated and prolonged exchange of words. Fatigue had set in, his recriminations had petered out, her arguments and tears had run their course. Somehow Layla had managed to convince him that Jamie's visit had been, on her part at least, innocent. As his hot rage cooled, David realised how much he had missed her company – her velvet voice, her acute perception, her disturbing beauty.

Layla had fallen asleep, leaning against him on the sofa, exhausted with emotion. David looked down at her closed eyes, her full lips and her creamy skin – and he ached for her. His arm was around her shoulders, her head rested against his chest. The room was in shadow – the oil lamp had almost gone out and he remembered its golden light on her face as she told him she loved him. She was full of contradictions: her laughter was like a teasing caress but the expression in her eyes burned him up. The painful truth hurt: she was a woman who had slept with many men but tonight she had refused to go to bed with him. In spite of having told him he was all she desired. He wanted her – but felt unable to commit himself to her and live with the knowledge of what she had been. The dilemma ate away at his peace of mind.

He moved a strand of tangled dark hair from her cheek, pulled her shawl up over her arm and whispered her name. She stirred beguilingly but did not wake. The oil lamp finally extinguished itself and David sat on, unmoving in the dark, with the woman he desired asleep beside him. Sometime later he glanced out of the window. There was a faint rosy light in the sky – surely it could not be dawn yet? The birds were eerily silent. Alarm began to pulse in his head. The glow was coming from the west. Was it fire?

His mind clicked into acute awareness and he roused Layla, who mumbled his name as she woke. "Layla, I have to go. Something's wrong. I think there's a fire a few miles away. The vegetation is dry and I need to find out if it's spreading and coming in this direction."

She was awake now, registering the anxiety in his voice, and said, "I'll come with you." As she put on her shoes, she saw David punching a number into his mobile. "It won't work. There's no reception here."

He took her arm as they left the cottage. "Hurry. My car isn't far away." They ran up the woodland track together, neither of them daring to voice the nightmare suspicion mushrooming in their minds.

Jamie woke up. What had disturbed him? He glanced down at his wife who was asleep beside him, her face pillowed on one palm. He had come so near to being unfaithful to her last night, but temptation had been resisted. Just as well. He might tell Penny that the painter staying in the cottage was David's woman!

He sniffed the air – the window was open – and there was a faint hint of something unusual. He identified it and sat up. Fire. Not in his farm – he would have woken before and heard the animals – but further away. A tiny drift of smoke was carried on the wind. He quietly got out of bed and went over to the window. Over to the west there was an orange tinge to the dark clouds and a shimmer of red along the black horizon. Yes, something was on fire – a few miles away. What was in that direction?

Certainty hit him. He pulled on his clothes, woke Penny and told her. It was after 3 am. By the time he was in the car and on his way, the sky had grown more lurid. He bounced down the rutted farm drive to the main road and turned westwards. A few seconds later a motorbike hurtled round the bend on his side of the road and, swerving to avoiding him, shot off in the opposite direction. Jamie swore loudly and put his foot on the accelerator.

Olga had been dreaming about her childhood, when an alarm went off. She realised almost immediately that this was the intercom from the hotel. It was about 2 am. She was the duty manager on call that night and lived only a couple of miles down the road. When she answered, the panic-stricken voice of Clara who lived in the staff quarters at the rear of the hotel told her of the fire. The fire brigade had been called. Olga leapt out of bed, scrambled into her clothes and rang Francis to alert him. She called the fire service to check they were on their way and only then did she jump into her car and head off to her place of work, Homeward House.

On arrival she had found that most of the guests were already outside in a small huddle, together with Clara and Sonya, two of the staff who lived on site. She was surprised that David was not there reassuring them and assumed he was round the back checking that everyone was out. Olga needed to ascertain that all guests and all residential staff were accounted for.

She was told that Toni, the maintenance man who lived on site, had been alerted by the smoke and smell, and had woken up Patrice, the chef, in the room adjacent to his, and they had both run across to the main part of the hotel where there was much smoke but few flames. They had raced upstairs, woken up those guests who were still asleep and shepherded them out of the hotel.

The fire was now getting hold with flames and sparks on the roof. Olga had still not seen David.

At this point the fire engines arrived and their first priority was to ensure that everyone had got out. All fourteen guests were accounted for and were asked to stand further down the lawn. One of them was in acute shock, two were suffering from smoke inhalation and the rest were shaken but alright. An ambulance was called. The fire chief checked with Olga as to which staff members lived in. David was still not to be found and the owner's flat was in the part of the hotel where the fire seemed to be at its worst. It was with massive relief that they discovered that David's car was gone and realised that he must have gone out for the night – an unusual occurrence.

Sergio was unaccounted for and his car was still in the staff parking lot. This was worrying as the restaurant manager's room was above the kitchen and the smoke in this area was chokingly thick as the fire had spread. Two firemen were sent in to locate and rescue him. Sonya, one of the waitresses, began to cry and Patrice put his arm round her shoulders. Josh had not appeared either.

"What about Josh? Where is he?" Olga demanded amidst the noise of the firemen setting up their equipment.

Patrice replied, "I bang on 'is door, but I get no reply. The door is locked and 'is bike is not 'ere."

Clara chirped up, her voice wobbly with panic. "I haven't seen him. But on his evenings off he sometimes goes into town to go drinking with friends and kips down with one of them."

"Can you both go and look after our guests on the lawn? They look very miserable and cold." Olga walked over to Francis who had just arrived. "Isn't this terrible?" They watched as the firemen began to tackle the blaze.

"Are all the guests and staff out?" he asked

"All except Sergio who's unaccounted for. The firemen have been in to look for him, but it's dangerously hot in that area."

"Where's the boss?"

"Search me," said Olga. "His car's gone. I've tried to phone him but he's not answering his mobile. I've phoned Theo who's on his way."

"They're in for a dreadful shock when they get here," Francis said, wincing as he heard an explosion from the kitchen area and saw flames shoot up into the sky. He realised that Sergio's room was just above and his face registered a look of horror. "I'll go over to the guests and staff and try to calm them." He went across to the bedraggled figures standing on the lawn and gazing with horror at the destruction of the hotel.

The fire had now taken hold and the fire crew who were directing their hoses on to the flames had radioed for further support from the fire service. The new bedroom wing was ablaze and the fire was starting to spread to the rear and to the front reception rooms.

Theo appeared on the scene and strode over to Olga, who put him in the picture and told him that David was off site. He then spoke briefly to the fire chief and was told that one person was unaccounted for – Sergio. Theo asked if the staff accommodation, which had been converted from old stables and was fifty yards from the main building, was in any danger. He was told it was threatened and had been evacuated.

Theo was uneasy and went over to see the staff. Josh was not present, and Toni told him Patrice had banged on his door but it was locked and his bike was gone. Theo suspected where his son might be but he was uneasy about Josh, so he skirted round the blazing hotel, keeping well clear. The smoke and smell was billowing around him as he reached the staff quarters. He took off his sweater and held it over his mouth and nose as he checked all the rooms, finding them all empty except for No 3. The curtains were drawn and the door locked. He thumped on the door and decided to make absolutely sure by breaking into the room. The door would not give way to his shoulder, so he wrapped the sweater round his knuckles and broke a window pane next to the catch. It was pitch dark inside. He glanced over his shoulder at the fire raging on the other side of the courtyard, opened the window and climbed in.

Theo switched on the light and saw Josh asleep on the bed. Amazed that the noise and fumes had not woken the man, Theo shook him urgently. "Get up, man. There's a fire coming this way."

Josh seemed almost comatose but eventually he stirred and mumbled, "Go 'way. Leave me alone." His words were slurred and he sounded drugged. Theo wrenched him forward and pulled him up into a sitting position. Josh was fully clothed and very disorientated. Smoke was surging in through the window. Putting his arm round Josh, he dragged him across to the door and finding the key in the lock, he opened it and pulled Josh outside. The atmosphere was thick with acrid smoke, flying ash and debris. Josh began to cough. A fireman spotted them as they emerged and ran across to help.

"Sorry sir. We were told everyone had been accounted for," he said to Theo as they both pulled Josh clear of immediate danger. Josh was now awake but very confused and horror-struck by the fire.

Theo took him across to a fellow staff member and left him in his care. He went across to give reassurance to the assembled guests who were now sitting on the grass, appalled. After ten minutes with them, he walked over to Olga, who seemed mesmerised by the destruction of the hotel she worked in. "Are you alright?" he asked.

"It's so dreadful. I can't bear to see it." She was almost in tears. He put his arm around her shoulders and stood with a grim face watching the fire consume his old home and his son's dream.

The ambulance arrived and soon afterwards the taxis which Francis had arranged to take the guests to a hotel in town. Jamie turned up and was delegated to ferry some of the employees to accommodation hastily arranged for them.

The smoke from the doused flames billowed around, the firefighters illuminated on their crane, keeping their distance now in the searing heat. Finally, just as the roof over the main part of the hotel carved in with an enormous surging fireball, David arrived with Layla.

He stumbled out of the car, his face a mask of horror as he ran over to where Theo and Olga were standing, their haggard faces streaked with ash. "Is everyone safe?" was his first question. He went white with shock when he learned that Sergio was missing and presumed a victim. He then stared at the spectacle in front of him, all he had worked so hard to achieve crumbling into red hot fragments before his eyes.

As a grey dawn broke and the exhausted firemen were still damping down the blackened walls, rain began to fall. It helped to extinguish the last flames and dissipate the caustic smell but it could not wash away the night's horror.

David sat on the scarred lawn, staring at the ruins of his hotel, his hands clasped round his knees like a child. Layla and Theo watched him, knowing that there were no comforting words that would assuage his desolation.

PART THREE

"He gives strength to the weary
And increases the power of the weak.
Even youths grow tired and weary,
And young men stumble and fall;
But those who hope in the Lord
Will renew their strength.
They will soar on wings like eagles;
They will run and not grow weary,
They will walk and not be faint."

Concerning comfort for God's people
The Bible, Isaiah 40:29-31

11

"You're driving me mad. Stop moping around. Sometimes I think I preferred you when you smoked and drank." Layla yelled at Josh from the kitchen door.

"Don't mention cigarettes to me," Josh groaned, sitting with his head in his hands. "They've caused so much damage." He coughed hoarsely.

"I don't think it's the fags that have affected your health. It's probably smoke inhalation. You were in your room, downwind of the fire for quite a while before Theo dragged you outside."

"Good of him to rescue me. Might have burned to a crisp," Josh said morosely.

"You wouldn't have – the staff quarters were blackened with ash but relatively undamaged, I hear. Unlike the hotel which is a total ruin. What a nightmare! I feel so desperate for poor David."

Josh had got a lift to the cottage, not wanting to spend a whole day in the cramped accommodation which the hotel management had found locally for employees whilst the future of the hotel and their jobs was being resolved. A week has passed since the night of the fire.

"I feel terrible," he groaned. Though sympathetic, Layla was beginning to get irritated by him and could not fathom out why Josh, who was usually upbeat, felt so wretched.

"I can see you might be upset because your job has gone up in smoke or perhaps you're miserable because Maria's decided you're a waste of time. Which you are right now." Layla sounded exasperated. "Whatever made you knock yourself out with the silly drug that she took exception to? What's your problem?"

"Because I'm culpable, Layla," Josh said sharply. "You don't understand that I'm to blame. I threw a lit cigarette into the bin in the bar and then cleared off and went to bed. It's obvious I caused the horrific fire and Sergio's death. I didn't much care for him but I certainly didn't wish him dead. I feel so guilty. I've been agonising over whether I should confess."

Layla looked at him aghast. "Josh, that may not have been the cause of the fire. In any case, it was an accident."

"So it was. But my carelessness means that someone is dead, the hotel is destroyed and everyone's going to lose their jobs. And the boss has lost everything he owns. I'm responsible and I don't feel too good about it. What's even worse is that Maria still hasn't been near me and probably hates my guts." Josh gave another retching cough.

"It may not be possible to pinpoint the cause of the fire, but if you feel that bad, you'd better tell someone. Why don't you talk to Theo? He always knows what's the best thing to do."

"I might do that." Josh threw himself on the sofa and closed his eyes. "When I feel better."

"You ought to thank him for his prompt action. Your lungs might be much worse if he hadn't checked up whether you were still in your room."

"There's another problem. My bike's been stolen. I've no transport and I don't fancy a long walk to Theo's studio."

Layla had already heard about the missing bike and was tired of Josh's complaints. She had her own worries. David was distant and they were further away from resolving the block in their relationship than ever. He was frantically busy dealing with the fallout after the fire. She ached to console him but he repulsed all sympathy. Perhaps he blamed her for his absence on the night his hotel went up in flames.

Father and son were not allowed near the hotel site. So Theo was back in his studio and had resumed working in clay on a life-size figure of a musician playing a cello. Work on this commission had been delayed because of the fire. The preceding two weeks had incurred an exceptional workload on all management staff, and the stress on David was immense. It was heart-breaking to witness the state of what had been a handsome hotel and their beloved family home. An acrid smell lingered over the burned-out wreck like a shroud of misery.

In the immediate aftermath the fire services had made sure that the surviving structure and the damaged walls were stable and safe so that a team wearing protective clothing could enter and conduct an examination. There was extensive water damage to any parts that had not been destroyed by flames and heat. The fire department and the insurance company had called in forensic investigators to determine how and where the fire had started and whether the cause was accidental or deliberate. If it proved to be a case of arson, then evidence would need to be preserved and collected as soon as possible. Until this was established they were treating the area as a crime scene. Theo had felt deeply uncomfortable about the fact that he and his son were barred from it.

At an initial meeting with the forensic team it had been explained to Theo and David that although much of the evidence had been destroyed, it would be possible to conclude what caused the fire and where it began by conducting a thorough search and testing for accelerants using hydrocarbon analysis. David was informed that the most common indicator of arson was the presence of some sort of fuel such as petrol, diesel, acetone or alcohol which an arsonist might use to speed up the burning process when starting a fire.

The fact that a member of staff was still missing, presumed dead – a victim of the fire – had increased the seriousness of the crime if it was arson and not accidental. The forensic investigators had not yet located any human remains but they were still searching.

Theo had been surprised to have a visit from Josh a couple of days before.

"I had to come over and thank you for your perseverance in locating me on the night of the fire. Second time you've come to my rescue." The barman was now out of a job but this disappointment did not account for the conscience-stricken look on Josh's dark features. "Theo, I feel dreadful about it but I think I might have caused the fire by throwing a lighted cigarette into a bin in the bar. It was stupid and irresponsible and I've done real harm to a family I've grown to like and respect."

Theo had suggested he should pass on this information to the forensic experts and that if this was the cause, he would not be held culpable since it was accidental and not intentional. Looking hugely relieved, Josh said he would do this.

Theo was having a quiet afternoon working creatively and focussing on something other than the tragedy. But his overriding concern about his son's state of mind kept intruding and it was only with a massive effort of will that he managed to make any progress on his sculpture.

Some while later, hearing a telephone ring in his sitting room adjacent to the studio, he paused. David, who had been staying with his father since his flat and all personal property had been destroyed, was next door dealing with various problems and urgent matters. The call was answered. Theo picked up his tool and went on shaping the shoulder that was to hold the bow. He needed time now with his model, a young student called Mark, who would be returning for another session the next day.

The connecting door was thrown open and Theo, seeing his son framed in the doorway, knew that he was about to hear more bad news.

David's pale face and tense posture indicated yet another nasty twist to the disaster. "This is the final straw! I've just received a telephone call from the police. It seems that I am now under suspicion of arson and wilfully destroying my own hotel."

This was what Theo had feared. "David, calm down. They are conducting an investigation and will consider all possibilities. The truth will come out."

David spoke in a taut, clipped tone. "It has now been established that the fire started in my flat at the back of the hotel. They have found irregular pooling marks on the floor in my kitchen which show traces of an accelerant, placed there intentionally by someone. Clearly they think this was me. They informed me they are now to conduct a background check on my business to detect any signs of debt or problems which might suggest a motive for arson and insurance fraud. They also discovered that a window in my living room had been left open which caused ventilation and spread flames – and this might have been done on purpose. By me!"

Theo walked across the studio towards his son. "This is only conjecture. They are well aware that someone else could have started the fire."

"As if it isn't bad enough to lose everything – my home, my hotel, my livelihood – I am now accused of causing it!" David went on without appearing to have heard his father. "I'm not sure how much more of this I can take."

Putting his hand on his son's arm, Theo could feel the tension quivering through him. "Let's go next door, sit down and talk this through. We know something they don't – that you didn't do it. If it was arson, then we need to consider who might have done it – a member of the staff or a complete outsider. We should do what they are doing – look for motives and opportunity."

"Good idea. That's sensible," said David jerkily as he sat down at the table, trying to keep a lid on his emotions. "I feel like someone who's lost a child and is accused of its murder."

"It's not as bad as that." Theo was making some coffee. "Nothing like as bad. But whilst we're on the sad subject, have they found any traces of Sergio?"

"Not yet, but his flat was over the kitchen and the fire was intense in that area." He grimaced. "What a ghastly way to die."

"One of the fire investigators told me fire would have to reach an extremely high temperature over a period of time to completely destroy a human body and this would not have been the case with the hotel fire. So perhaps Sergio was not in his flat and is not dead."

"His car's still in the staff parking area. Where could he be? If he were alive, he'd have turned up by now. The publicity has been horrendous."

"Unless he doesn't want to be found," Theo spoke meditatively. "Anyhow, let's wait for confirmation from the fire investigators on that one. Is there anyone else who might have deliberately started the fire? Arson is usually an act of revenge or vandalism.

"You're asking me if there is someone I employ or know who would wish to damage me so much that they would set fire to my hotel. I can't think of anyone who would do that."

"It's been established that the fire started in your flat so we need to think about who had access to it. Anyone entering your flat in order to start fire would have to be certain that you were absent and unlikely to return soon."

"Normally I'm in and out all day long because that's where my office is. But on that particular day," David went on bitterly, "I left in a hurry because I was angry and suspicious and wanted to get over to the cottage that Jamie has lent to Layla and have it out with her. I hadn't seen her for weeks and, as you recall, Kate let slip where she was. Stupidly I forgot to inform the duty manager, Olga, that I would be out for a few hours and, even more unwisely, I may not have locked the door. I can't remember."

"A golden opportunity for someone to gain entry... Who would have seen you leaving the hotel that evening?"

David thought about this. "I suppose the receptionist, Emily, might have seen me cross the front hall, and anyone working in the bar or restaurant could have seen me through the window going to my car – I tend to leave it in the guest car park at the front rather than in the staff parking area at the rear. Guests may have seen me. It could have been started by a rogue guest."

"Guests don't know about the layout of the hotel, nor do they usually hold grudges against the owner, and they were all in their rooms when the fire started and therefore in danger."

"How lucky that we had only fourteen guests in the hotel! A full hotel would have taken much longer to evacuate. I feel terrible that I wasn't there to help."

"So how many hours were you gone, David?" Theo asked gently, knowing he was touching on a raw nerve.

David groaned with exasperation. "I was away for a long time. A few guests were still dining so I must have left some time after nine o'clock. And it was past three in the morning when I returned to face the nightmare scenario."

"So you were gone for about six hours. Clara phoned Olga whilst Patrice and Toni started to wake the guests and get them out. Olga says she remembers it being about 2 am when she left her home to drive here. So the fire must have started between 9 pm and about 1 am – and, it seems, in your flat. Have they definitely ruled out an accidental cause?"

"Their fingers are pointing at me. It fanned out from my flat. I could have set it up and then gone out. I can't prove that I didn't." David sounded defeated.

"And they can't prove you did," Theo said succinctly. "What could they possibly think was your motive?"

"Debt. In theory they're right – the hotel does owe money to the bank. We mortgaged the property in order to raise the funds to enlarge and build the new wing – which is now destroyed. It would have taken another few years of trading to pay off the loan but we were in profit and had some sensible projections to repay within a period of time. Recently unlucky problems have reduced guest numbers but we would have recovered. Now the hotel is no more, I've no way of paying off the loan without insurance." He paused and looking at his father with dawning realisation, slowly said, "If it was arson and if I can't prove my innocence, then the insurance company would consider it fraud and refuse to pay out. I could be bankrupt. I could go to prison."

"You could be dead – and there were moments when some of your staff thought that you were! But you're very much alive and you need to fight this intelligently. Don't get discouraged."

Kate was carefree. It was nearly midsummer and the countryside was green and fragrant. She had finished her morning at the newsagent and, taking an afternoon off from studying, was going to visit her father. Andrew had lent his car to her. She never minded taking the bus or biking but it was luxurious to drive. The external world seemed to reflect her own inner glow and in spite of the horrible tragic fire a few weeks ago, she could not repress the elation welling up in her, a feeling of contentment and purpose. She was engaged to be married to a man who knew about her past and accepted it. She was training to teach primary school children, with a part-time job to make ends meet and had a studio flat to live in. All was well with her.

But not for her brother, who was engulfed in misery. Her sadness over the loss of her family home – as she saw the hotel – was tempered by the fact that she had not lived there for a number of years. Naturally she was upset by what had happened and by the subsequent bleak despair in David. She had tried to sympathise and to pull him out of his black mood but all her efforts were rebuffed.

Kate wondered if her brother would be at the studio – she would not mind if he wasn't there. She didn't want to be reminded of the forensic investigator's suspicion that the hotel proprietor had committed arson. She pulled up outside the studio and, as always, was captivated by the amazing view across the valley from the hillside. She avoided looking down at the place where the black ruins of the hotel were visible, and walked over to the large wooden barn door which was never locked. She opened it and went in.

The sunlight streaming through the window flooded across the spacious studio and there was stillness and peace. Theo's domain was always filled with light. She went across to the door to the annexe and knocked – there was no reply so she opened it and peered in. No-one was there. She was disappointed – wanting to see her father and share her enjoyment of the lovely day. Where was he? She wandered over to the window and looked out. A figure was lying on the grassy slope – it was David.

Delighted to see her brother relaxing in the sunshine, Kate opened the door into the garden and ran down to join him. "Hi, David! Isn't this a glorious day?" She bestowed a wide smile on him.

Her brother sat up, his face downcast. "Hello Kate. What brings you here?" he asked listlessly.

"I came to see you and Daddy," she lied brightly. "Where is he?"

"He's up at the foundry today, working on the patination of a new casting of the stag. Won't be back for hours, I expect."

Kate flung herself down on the grass beside him and said, "I've taken the afternoon off and borrowed Andrew's car." She bit the bullet. "How are things, David?"

He was silent for a few seconds. "Terrible, Kate, if you must know. Every day I expect to be arrested for arson. It's a desperate situation. I've racked my brains to try and work out why someone would want to burn the hotel down. I wonder who has it in for me – perhaps Josh, because he thinks I've made Layla miserable or he's jealous. I don't know."

"You know very well that Josh and Layla aren't an item," Kate said scornfully. "Layla always treats him like a brother and Josh is languishing in unrequited love for Maria. Anyhow Josh isn't vindictive and I don't think him capable of arson."

"Dad doesn't like to bad-mouth anyone but he thinks Sergio might have been involved since no trace of him has been found. I don't agree because I can't for the life of me see what his motive might be." David put a hand to his head. "I'm so tired of it all. There's so much to do, so many issues to deal with: compensation for the guests who were so badly shocked, redundancy payments for the staff, the insurance claim in abeyance, constant questions and interviews, and all the hotel finances and records being pored over by investigators. There are bills to pay and no money! Francis and Olga have been wonderful but they too are worried about their future. It's such a dreadful mess."

Kate lay back and let this wash over her – she had heard it all before and was ashamed to be feeling resentful that her day was polluted by all this misery!

David needed to get his act together and be less negative. Irritation welled up inside her. It was selfish to be annoyed because her high spirits had been dragged down but she could not help it. She sat up and grabbed her brother's arm. "Stop it, David. It's like a dirge. You've got stuck in this 'poor-ol'-me' syndrome."

David was stunned into silence and flinched his arm away. Kate went blundering on, knowing she was making things worse but unable to help herself. "You've got to stop agonising about it all day long. It now appears no-one died in the fire. This arson thing won't stick – Daddy say's they can't prove it was you. You've got to pick yourself up and get on with life. Confront the problems and deal with them. And get some sleep – you look exhausted."

David leapt to his feet and looking down at his sister with an angry flush on his face, said, "Thank you for your valuable advice. How kind! So like you – so thoughtless! You are incapable of comprehending my situation. I've lost everything, have huge debts and might end up in prison for a crime I didn't commit. I'm in despair as to what to do. My relationship with my father has become strained, my emotional life is in turmoil and now I have my sister carping at me!"

Kate stood up and as soon as he took a breath, she retaliated. "You accuse me of not understanding and not being sympathetic. You forget I too lost everything including my freedom. I was at the bottom of a huge hole and didn't know which way to turn. But I came home, admitted my mistakes and got on with life."

"You did indeed come home," jeered David, "but your problems had been self-inflicted. Then your two unprincipled friends arrived here and disrupted our lives. One of them has destroyed my peace of mind and the other may well have destroyed my hotel!" He knew this was unreasonable.

"You're paranoid," retaliated Kate. "You're a stressed, overworked obsessive. All these wild accusations! You don't realise that you've messed up Layla – she loves you and doesn't know what to make of your attitude. You can't decide whether to forgive her for having a scandalous past or whether to throw her back into the gutter from where she came."

"You and Layla made your choices and then expect people like Andrew and me to turn a blind eye to your faults and your past." David lost his temper. "Well done, Kate! Your life is back on track and Andrew is clearly a nobler fellow than me."

"You bet he is," yelled Kate. "I know what it is to feel guilt and he knows how to forgive. Something that you have yet to learn! You always envied my happy-go-lucky attitude and were jealous of my freedom. You forget it was your choice to stay at home, to slave away, build your castle and make your pile. Now that tragedy has struck and you've lost it all, you're envious of my happiness, my secure relationship and my peace of mind. I've managed to free myself from a preoccupation with possessions. There are more important things in life."

With an angry exclamation, David turned and stalked off down the hill. "That's another lesson you need to learn," Kate shouted at his retreating back. "Love is more important than anything!"

Annoyed with herself for becoming embroiled in a sibling row, Kate retreated into the house. She took a few deep breaths to calm her pounding heart, and feeling guilty that she had given her brother a piece of her mind, she wondered how her father handled his sensitive, touchy son. She decided to leave Theo a note before she left and tell him about their quarrel. She trusted him to pour oil on troubled waters – he always did.

Layla put down her palette, leaned forward to pick up a jar containing white spirit and began to clean her brush. It was early evening and she was hungry. She started to pack up to walk back to the cottage. The temperature had become cooler – she was wearing a green painting smock over a pair of white cotton shorts that Kate had given her. Her face was freckled and her arms and legs were no longer pale – she had never spent so much time outdoors in her life as in the past couple of months.

As she made her way back through the trees, carrying her boxed easel and other kit, she felt vaguely apprehensive. Perhaps it was her usual preoccupation with where she should live and what she might do. After more than a year in a rural environment she had grown to love the serenity of the natural world. She didn't want to leave but the man she loved was in a dark and indecisive place and did not want to include her in his plans for the future. She needed to find work, pay her way in the world and be independent.

She had finished the cottage paintwork a couple of weeks before and was pleased she could return to painting canvasses. The weather was clear and warm and the daylight hours were long. She felt her work was improving and taking new directions that intrigued her. She hoped to try her hand at portraits soon, but for the present her subjects were trees and she tried to capture their spiritual and light-infused quality. The few people who saw her work said it had a mysterious appeal. She had even managed to get a local gallery in town to put two of them on display and had been surprised and pleased when one of them sold. It had enabled her to buy food.

She had now met Penny and had spent an entertaining day making colourful pictures with the two children. They had invited her to share a meal with them at the farm and during the evening Jamie asked if he could commission a painting of his farmhouse to send to his mother, who had lived in it for many years and whose sixtieth birthday was imminent. Layla said she would be delighted and would do it for free, but they insisted on a fee.

She glimpsed her little cottage through the trees and realised how much she liked living there. It would be hard to leave and move on into an uncertain future, but she had to go. Layla had offered to pay Jamie some rent from the proceeds of her sale, but he wouldn't hear of it. She had also discussed her plans with Theo who was encouraging and supportive. How different from his son, whom she had seen only twice since the fire.

As she got closer, she saw a figure mysteriously detach itself from the shade of the large beech tree beside the cottage. It was as if her thoughts had materialised into reality – for there was David.

David had spent many sleepless nights and when exhaustion finally did bring some oblivion, his dreams were full of people asking him questions and demanding answers that he could not give. He woke feeling persecuted and disorientated. He was aware how short-tempered he had become recently and this irritability had resulted in a horrible row with his sister, some unwarranted remarks to his father and a general inability to communicate with people and relate to those around him. He ought to move out of his father's home and live on his own. He was unable to concentrate, and anxiety nibbled at the edges of his mind. Theo had suggested he see a doctor to help him cope with stress but David had angrily refused, fearing that a doctor might tell him what he knew already – that he was falling apart.

Five nights ago, the solution had come to him. It was clean, alluring – and completely irresponsible! He would go away – far away. Escape from tiredness, torment and the fear of losing his freedom. As the idea swirled around in his head, he was attracted by this simple solution. He should do it before they arrested him and took away his passport. He would miss his father but always love him. He had been deeply committed to his hotel but it was now gone. He would go too.

It was vital to keep his decision secret. He would tell only his father and not until the day of his departure, and he would not be dissuaded. He began to make preparations, quietly withdrawing some of his savings and purchasing travellers cheques that would make him untraceable. A new passport to replace his burned one had just arrived; his credit cards had been with him. He had bought a few items of clothing but his paintings, books and personal belongings had gone up in flames. He would take his car and travel without baggage. At last he would break free, have his chance to see the world and leave his cares behind. This was something he had to do. On his own.

He was now ready to slip away but knew he must tell Layla. Tomorrow he would be gone so he had to see her today. Dreading the confrontation and knowing it would be painful for them both, he drove to the cottage and parked at the back. When he discovered she was not inside, he was relieved to have time to collect his thoughts. So he sat down under the beech tree to wait for her return.

Tiredness crept up on him and he slipped into a doze, waking with a jerk when a shaft of the declining sun fell across him through the trees. Had Layla come back whilst he'd slept? He stood up and as he took a few steps towards the cottage, he heard her calling his name from the other direction. He turned and there she was – coming through the trees – a small figure, bare-legged in white shorts and a cloud of dark hair around her face. Her skin glowed in the evening sunlight and there was a smile on her face. David stood still, his heart aching.

As she came close, his limbs unfroze and he went towards her, a feeling of compression in his chest. "Layla." He managed to utter her name.

"Hi, stranger!" she said cheerfully without any hint of reproach. "Have you been here long? I've been painting, deep in the woods."

"Let me carry those for you." He averted his gaze, taking the easel, canvas and folding stool, leaving her to carry only the bag of paints slung over her shoulder.

"Thank you." Layla reached up as she said this and gave him a soft kiss on his cheek. His arms were encumbered and he felt awkward. "So how are you?" she went on. "I'm hoping no news is good news."

This time the reproof was there, however slight. "I know I've not been in contact," he admitted. "There's no excuse – except that I'm still in a bad place and seem to be out of touch with everything happening around me."

They reached the cottage and went inside. The interior was dim and there was a faint fragrance from some wild flowers in a jam-jar on the table. David put the painting kit down, quietly closed the door and turned to watch Layla, who set about lighting the oil lamp. He watched her as she removed the glass shade, wound up the wick and lit a match. Her skin looked dusky and sun-freckled and he knew if he touched it that it would be warm and smooth. He took a deep breath.

"Layla, I need to talk to you."

"I didn't imagine you'd come here to be silent. Though I wouldn't have minded if you'd come because you needed to be with me or because you desperately wanted to kiss me. But talking is good too. At least I hope it is." Layla turned up the flame and went across to scoop up a shawl off the back of the sofa which she wrapped round her hips. "Time to cover up. It's getting cool." She stood there with her arms folded loosely across her chest, in an attitude of expectation with a gentle smile on her face.

"I want to explain about the terrible situation I'm in. My life is about to take a new direction," David began. "I need to tell you about it."

"I'm listening." She waited. Averting his face from her gaze, he told her about the aftermath of the fire, the guilt he felt over Sergio's death, the painful loss of everything he had worked for – all things she already knew about – and finally mentioned the fact that he was suspected of starting the fire and each day dreaded he would be arrested and charged. "It is arson and they have evidence to show it started in my flat."

"That's ridiculous – you were the owner. Why on earth would you destroy your own hotel?" Layla was shocked. "Anyhow, you were with me here. I can vouch for that."

"It makes no difference. One can start a fire in advance that will get going slowly. I could have set it up before I left. As for motive – the business was in debt and they think I'm trying to defraud the insurance company."

"Nobody who knows you is going to believe that! They're wrong and you must prove them wrong."

"I can't, Layla. They have damning evidence. It was no accident. I've racked my brains to think who might have been that malicious – and I can't come up with anyone."

"What does your father think?"

David chose not to answer this. "Whether they lock me up for something I didn't do or whether they let me off the hook, either way I'm finished! The insurance won't pay out for arson and I've lost everything – including the family home and possessions. I have nothing left." He could not suppress a note of self-pity.

"David, calm down. You are focussing only on material things. I used to do the same – and it's a huge mistake. You may have nothing left in material assets or wealth, but you possess so much more." David looked at her questioningly and Layla continued, "It's staring you in the face. You have family and friends who love you and who care. That's of real value. With their support and encouragement, you can pick yourself up and start again."

David sat down on a chair, putting his head in his hands. "It's easy for you to say this but it's not that simple. I feel I'm drowning."

Layla went across to him and put her arm round his shoulder. "You should stop moping and be thankful that no-one you loved was injured or killed. Of course the fire was terrible and what you've been through is painful, but there are worse things that can happen. It's unlike you to despair." He was acutely aware of her warmth beside him and the temptation was strong to accept her unspoken invitation to let her help him through it. "I speak from experience," she said. "There are always troubles in this world and you need to learn to cope with life's knocks."

Slowly David raised his head – she had given him the opportunity to bring up the burning issue of his defection. And departure. He stood up and took hold of both her elbows in his hands and looked straight into her face. "That's what I intend to do. I'm setting off on a new path – a voyage of discovery." He saw a flash of hope in her eyes and knew he had to quell it instantly. It would be unfair to mislead her. "I'm going away. Alone."

"You're running away..." He could see the tears welling up in her eyes. "What about me? Don't you feel anything for me? Don't I matter at all?"

"Layla, you know I care about you." He could not bring himself to utter the word 'love' – it would make things much harder. He inwardly cringed as he uttered the lame excuses, "But I've nothing to offer you now – no home, no security – and if I stayed, I might end up in prison. I need to get away. I want to go."

"Losing everything is not the end of the world. Not finding love within you and in others – that's the ultimate tragedy," Layla said, making an effort to hold back the tears and remain calm. "David, when we first met, I admit I was interested in your wealth and the protection it might afford me from my flaky, insecure existence. But since then I've come to know you and discover things can be different. I've learned to love this part of the world as you do. Theo has encouraged me to change so I've tried to tell the truth instead of lies, tried to be kind instead of selfish. I feel better about myself. But though Theo accepts me as I am now, you still see me as I was. I believe you do care for me but you cannot accept or forgive what I've done. If you could, there'd be a future for us – together. I could come with you."

David closed his eye and shook his head, shutting out her face, blotting out her persuasive words. He would not succumb. "I have to go. On my own. To find myself," he reiterated.

"What are you looking for, David? You don't even know! Is it truth you seek – or peace? You may not find them – instead you may meet evil people, see bad things. It's a wild world out there – don't I know it! You've never been away. You're such an innocent; you'll be in danger."

"Better my innocence than your experience," David snapped back, detecting the note of anxiety in her voice but angry with her for suggesting he couldn't look after himself.

"So we're back again to your big hang-up, to what really sticks in your gullet – my past! My wicked life is the excuse you need to stay uncommitted. My love is a tarnished thing, of no value to one who seeks purity." Layla began to get angry. "This is such a selfish decision – and a cowardly one. It will give a lot of pain to your father and your sister."

"Kate and I had another nasty row. She won't miss me." He fidgeted, needing to get away before his resolve broke.

"I will miss you, David. You're so stubborn. You see life and love in front of you and you refuse what's offered," she pleaded.

"You're wrong. I'm setting off to *experience* life. Maybe one day I'll come back and we can swap notes," he muttered.

"Maybe I won't be here!"

There was a brief silence. "Layla, if we meet again things might be different. Who knows?" He leaned over, kissed her chastely on the forehead and went across to the door. He suppressed a shudder of regret. Tomorrow he would be gone.

"When are you leaving?" She looked forlorn.

Shrinking from telling her the cruel truth, he lied, "Soon." As he went to the door, pain swelled in his chest.

David emerged into the deepening twilight, feeling apprehensive as if he'd left the safety of a familiar shore and set off on a voyage to the unknown. Looking through the window he saw the amber light from the oil lamp illuminate the woman he had forsaken. He turned away, closing his ears to an insidious whisper telling him he had made a monumental mistake.

Theo knew who was speaking, even though it was many years since he had heard that rasping voice. He was unsurprised that Ator had discovered his telephone number and finally made direct contact. It was inevitable that revenge and hatred long suppressed would surface eventually. Ator considered the recent extreme measure a decisive blow against Theo's children. The depraved man, proud of a monstrous act which he saw as victory, had an urge to gloat over his enemy. The exultation was evident. Chilling. Theo said nothing. What had been done was infernally shameful. Lack of response would undermine the other's malicious enjoyment. Words would be wasted, communication was impossible. So Theo quietly cut the connection – silence was powerful. The early morning light dispelled the memory of darkness. In the stillness he heard his son moving about in the adjoining room. He knew what was coming.

Layla's sleep had been invaded by dreams and shortly after dawn she woke and lay listening to the birds singing. The feeling of hope this engendered lingered for a few seconds but evaporated with the recollection that she had lost the battle for David. His life was out of control and the possibility of happiness was slipping away. Loneliness engulfed her. She needed to talk to someone who would understand and tried to telephone Theo, but strangely at this hour his number was occupied. In a panic, she called Kate, who blearily answered and then listened, quickly focussing when she heard the desperation in her friend's voice.

Layla told her about David leaving to go travelling, voicing her fears. "I kept hoping that he would ask me to go with him – but he didn't. Your brother is so unworldly and inexperienced that I'm worried he won't survive."

"I did," Kate reminded her. "I made bad decisions, had nasty moments, but I came home in the end. Don't fret. He loves you, I'm sure. He'll come back soon."

Layla didn't think so. She was not comforted. She ended the call and faced the problem of what to do with the remainder of her life.

David was standing in the middle of the studio gazing out of the window at the beloved countryside he was about to leave behind. Theo's eagle eyes immediately noticed a canvas bag on the floor in the corner and a small rucksack beside it. "Are you leaving today?" he asked quietly.

David swung round. "You've guessed."

"All week I've been watching you making what you thought were discreet preparations and in the past two days I've seen you saying goodbye to everything and every place with your eyes. Of course I know."

"You won't think it's a good plan but it's the only one I've got." David was defensive.

Theo was careful to keep any reproach out of his voice. "What I think probably won't make any difference. You've not asked for my advice."

"Because I knew you wouldn't approve," David retaliated. "Theo, you may think I'm irresponsible but I've done all I can do: put in hand all the staff redundancy notices and payments and agreed compensation to be paid to guests whose possessions were lost in the fire. There should be enough funds in the bank to do that. Olga and Francis can deal with any remaining issues and settle any outstanding invoices – and we have agreed sadly that their employment will terminate in a month's time. I've left some notes and a letter for them. Without insurance the hotel is finished. I'm superfluous so I'm jumping ship."

"May I say that skipping the country whilst under suspicion of arson might fuel suspicions?" said Theo mildly.

David ignored this. "It's not only the hotel that's gone. Our childhood home is gone. The family's lost everything."

"We haven't lost our memories or our future – fire can't destroy those."

"It's extinguished my reason for staying here. Please understand that I've made up my mind – I'm leaving. Now." This was said resolutely. "Can you understand why?"

"You want freedom from responsibility, work pressure and the miserable stress caused by the fire. And you might be arrested for arson."

"Exactly so, Theo. And I really want to see the world. I never did go travelling."

"You never wanted to. There were opportunities to do so but you chose to stay. Just as Kate chose to go. You both had the choice. You still have the choice."

"Please can you say goodbye to Kate – we had a horrid quarrel the last time we saw each other, and I regret it. I'm sorry, too, I can't stay for the wedding but I'm sure it will be a wonderful day. I hoped it would take place at Homeward House but sadly it can't now."

"How are you travelling?"

"I'm taking my car, though I might sell it along the way." David smiled wryly. "I'll probably need the money!"

"And are you going alone?" Theo was aware that David had been out for a few hours the previous evening and suspected he had gone to tell Layla of his plans.

Looking guilty and trying to suppress a tremor in his voice, his son muttered, "Yes, on my own."

"Are you being fair on Layla?" Theo asked bluntly, concerned for his protégé.

"Probably not. But she's better off without me. She'll get over it," David said harshly.

"But will you?"

"Please leave off, Theo. I've made my decision. Right or wrong. Layla's not the only one who's hurting."

"Where are you heading for? How long will you be gone?" Theo calmly put the big questions.

"I've no idea. I'll go where the wind blows me. I might be away for a few years. Who knows?"

"In that case all that's left for me to do is give a few words of advice: be courageous and truthful and kind to others."

"Thanks. But I want to leave with your goodwill," said David solemnly.

"You have my blessing and as always my love," Theo said gracefully. "Do you think you'll come back?" This child needed to spread his wings and stretch his imagination before he could find his way home.

"Probably. Possibly. When I've found what I'm seeking."

Theo smiled, "I'll send you news of home." He gave his son a giant embrace and felt the young man's desperate hug in return. "Keep in touch from time to time."

Averting his eyes and saying, "I can't make promises but I'll try," David slung the rucksack over his shoulder, picked up the bag in one hand and, giving his father an anguished wave with the other, went out.

Theo stood still, eyes closed, as his son left on his search.

12

The incessant rain pattered on the car roof whilst the driver peered through the arc of visibility created by the car's windscreen wipers and tried to focus on the road ahead. He was driving too fast, to put miles between him and all he loved, to get so far that he could not change his mind and they could not follow. The torrents of rainwater would wash out his tracks and, if he was lucky, eliminate all traces of his past.

On the day of his departure, David travelled a long way, stopping only once to buy something to eat and drink. Long after dark he found a small hotel and his exhaustion soon plunged him into oblivion. The next few days followed a similar pattern – deep regenerative sleep followed by long journeys each day to put as many miles as possible between him and the stress of his last month at home. He was on the run, escaping from the clutches of those who would accuse him of something he hadn't done and inflict on him punishment he didn't deserve. After a week he slowed down, left the main routes for smaller roads and began to look around him.

He gradually became aware of the changing landscape and vegetation. As he passed through towns, he registered the different architecture in buildings and began to notice the people walking in the streets. At first he didn't bother initiating casual conversations with those around him in restaurants and cafes. After a while loneliness made him attempt to communicate with people he encountered, but with no common language there was mutual incomprehension. He appreciated it when people were friendly and felt rejected when confronted by resentment. Indifference, his or theirs, isolated him. His sister had better social skills and made friends easily, even when language posed a barrier. His father always put people at their ease and was a good listener. Late at night, David ached with loss. And he tried not to think of Layla.

He stayed in a pleasant town for three days and began to unwind. He was now ready to go to an internet café and send an e-mail home saying he was alright, in good health and still heading south. He did not want to tell them where he was, as this seemed irrelevant because soon he would be somewhere else. He received two e-mails, both from his father, giving brief news without mentioning the impact of his departure on the progress of the forensic team investigating the fire. David was grateful for that. It felt strange having no occupation, no deadlines, no commitments.

Theo's words had been full of common sense and encouragement with no trace of censure. He missed his father's unchanging affection and dependability. But he wanted to learn, to meet people and experience things that he would never find at home. He needed to find meaning and purpose. He climbed into his car and drove on.

A month later, he met Alicia. The girl had noticed him sitting on the dusty steps of the fountain in the main square of her town, and wandered across.

"Hello. How are you?" She stood looking down at him, her arms folded, a pleasant smile on her lips, curiosity making her bold.

David, who had been watching the water slide down the stone sculpture, turned when he heard her voice. He looked up at the figure before him, blinking in the sunlight.

"My name's Alicia. I'm a student." She said this in accented English and sat down beside him, crossing her brown legs and smoothing her cotton skirt over them. He sighed. He wanted to be left alone.

"I'm David." Brevity had become a habit.

"I'm studying English and it's good for me to practise. May I talk to you?" David nodded without much enthusiasm and she continued chattily, "What do you do?"

He didn't reply because it suddenly occurred to him that he didn't have the answer to her question.

She was persistent. "What are you doing here?"

"It seems I'm on holiday," he said vaguely, "travelling around." He did not wish to elaborate, to be defined.

"Where are you heading?" Again she tried to get specifics.

"I've no idea." He smiled at her, finding he enjoyed being evasive.

It was her turn to blink.

It had happened again – she was captivated. Women had told him he had an attractive smile and yet he was always surprised when the evidence of this appeared in the eyes of yet another casual acquaintance. It was exasperating. Particularly when he wanted to be left in peace.

"So you don't really know where you're going, David, and it seems you have no plans." The girl gave a cheeky laugh, took a breath and said, "I need a lift to my parents' farm – it's only an hour away. Would you like to buy me a cold drink and drive me there?" She was unembarrassed by her presumption.

"Should you be talking to a total stranger like me?" He put on what he thought was a steely expression but merely succeeded in giving her the full impact of his striking good looks. "Are you sure I'm trustworthy?"

"No, I'm not sure," she stammered. Then, gaining courage and tossing her hair, she grinned at him. "But you look kind and I take the risk."

She chattered whilst they had a drink in a bar, telling him about the town, her studies, the local food and other inconsequential things. As they drove she gave him directions and kept looking at the car and its driver with a thoughtful expression.

When they were nearly there, she surprised him by asking directly, "Would you care to be my boyfriend?" Seeing his wary look, she continued, "It's only pretence. My parents keep saying they want me to meet a nice boy but always disapprove of the young men I go out with. So if I can tell them you are a boyfriend, it would please them. You have nice car. You are nice-looking and polite." She paused whilst David winced at her repeated 'nice'. "Please."

"I can't do that, Alicia. It's a deception. We've only just met and I'm giving you a lift home before I journey onwards." He didn't want involvement.

"You could stay for a few days. The farm is very pretty. There is good food." There was a note of entreaty in her voice. She wanted his help. But David decided he would deliver her safely, meet her parents and get on his way.

It turned out that it wasn't Alicia who needed help. When they arrived and had bounced down a dirt road to a small farmhouse, he could see that the place was beautiful but run-down and badly in need of repairs. When they stopped, a small woman appeared in the open doorway. Though by no means old, she walked with a stick and hobbled across to embrace her daughter. Alicia normally took a bus when visiting her parents and always walked from the bus stop nearby. So her mother was surprised to see Alicia arrive by car with a strange man driving her and even more curious when she discovered he was a foreigner. But she greeted him with genuine warmth.

Alicia explained to him in English, which the woman clearly did not speak, that her mother had a problem with walking as a result of an accident some years before. They followed her into the house, where David was offered a glass of fresh lemon and water. They took this out on to the terrace, where a dark-haired man rose to his feet from a wooden chair – this was Alicia's father. Unable to see him clearly because he was silhouetted against the bright sunlight in the garden beyond, David felt there was something strange about him, and then as the older man tentatively offered his hand in greeting, it became obvious he was blind.

The parents' incapacities explained why the farm was looking so unkempt. Over a simple meal with much laughter and little comprehension, Alicia explained that she often took time off from studying in the town to come home and help her parents with the farm. The cows had been sold and now only the chickens remained and a few fields of crops and vegetables which needed only sunshine and water until harvesting. Her mother could manage the chickens and selling the eggs, but her father could manage nothing. Sowing and harvesting the crops were done by Alicia and a cousin who lived nearby. Life was hard.

And yet they seemed content and at peace – the couple cared deeply for each other and for their daughter, which was obvious from their affectionate touches and a gentle teasing tolerance. The father said he loved listening to music and liked to sing too. After the meal, whilst they all sat on the terrace, he gave them a couple of songs in a pleasant baritone, his only accompaniment being the sound of cicadas in the nearby undergrowth. David was charmed by the trio and discarding his plan to leave promptly, it seemed completely natural to accept their invitation to stay overnight in a small spare bedroom.

The next day, whilst Alicia was picking beans in the field adjacent to the house with David helping her, she explained that the room he had slept in had been her older brother's room. Six years before, he had left home and gone to seek work in a city in another part of the country. He had never wanted to stay in what he considered was dull rural poverty and had made a life for himself elsewhere, rarely returning to see his parents and managing to suppress any feelings of obligation to help them when his father had lost his sight. Alicia mentioned briefly that a younger brother had been born very handicapped and had not survived beyond the age of four. She appeared to have no feelings of animosity towards her older sibling nor any bitterness about the plight of her parents and their dependence on her.

After a midday meal of bread, salad and eggs, David offered to help repair the barn roof and fix a broken hinge on the door. The hot afternoon wore on, and when he'd done what he could and put the ladder away, he splashed his face with some water and looking round, he saw there were weeds between the rows of beans, so he picked up a hoe. His mind slipped into neutral doing this work which felt comfortingly familiar, reminding him of many days spent working on Jamie's farm when he was in his teens.

Alicia was helping her mother mend a hole in the fencing of the hens' enclosure. Her father was kneading bread which would be baked later. He did the tasks that he could manage without any frustration at his inability to do more. As evening came, David put down his hoe, feeling stiffness in his back. Alicia's mother appeared, smiled at him and asked the inevitable question which needed no translating. He had done a day's work, he was pleasantly tired and hungry so it was natural for her to offer and him to accept a cool drink, supper and another night's rest in the farmhouse. Alicia was grateful and she amused them all during the meal telling them anecdotes about her fellow students, switching from her own language into broken English and back, to encompass them all in her lively good humour. They drank local wine and David tried to teach her father a song in English.

Their guest stayed for a week – doing what he could to help. Emptying his mind into the physical labour, absorbing the sunshine, eating and sleeping – and listening to Alicia's chatter and her father's singing. They accepted his help gracefully and gratefully – and he felt comfortable with them and worked willingly, recalling his father who often spoke of the immense satisfaction in doing things for others.

He respected the family. This modest couple might have been sad about one son's defection and the other's death, or bitter about his blindness and her lameness, but they were not. They calmly accepted the cards that life had dealt them and lived without resentment. Reflecting on his own recent problems, David felt humbled by their example.

But he had to move on. He liked Alicia but didn't want her to think he was lingering for her. He had stayed and helped because he enjoyed their company and because their home was tranquil. But their mutual affection began to remind him of his own home and family and he had to suppress the temptation to turn back.

The next day he said goodbye. He hoped Alicia would one day find a man who would value her, love her and perhaps help her run the farm for her parents. He wasn't the one.

A few days later he drove into a sprawling city and found a bank and somewhere to get internet access. He checked his e-mails rarely as he didn't want beguiling news from home to wrap its tentacles round him. But now he found a longer letter from his father and after a quick glance, he realised it was about the fire investigation. His heart sank.

He fortified himself with coffee and began to read. Theo told him that he was no longer under suspicion of arson and that the focus was now on Sergio. This surprised David because he believed the restaurant manager had died in the fire. Theo explained that human remains had not been located and evidence of certain things that should have been in Sergio's flat if he had died there – such as his mobile phone – was missing. The police had started to investigate his background. When one of the references he gave when applying for the job was discovered to have survived in a fireproof filing cabinet in the hotel office, they made a check. They tracked down the person who had given the reference and found that a description of the person known to the referee was very different from the man that staff members described. When they checked the registration number of Sergio's car, which had been left in the car park giving credence to his being in the hotel that night, the address given by its owner was found not to exist.

More recently another piece of the jigsaw had fallen into place; this was the total disappearance of Josh's motorbike. When interviewed, Josh said he usually threw his keys down on the table in his room but these had not been found, even though the staff rooms had been relatively undamaged. It was suggested that Sergio might have started the fire, stolen the keys and made his escape on Josh's bike. When Jamie heard of this, he volunteered the information that whilst turning on to the main road on his way to the fire that night, he had been passed by a hunched figure on a motorbike speeding in the opposite direction.

Theo wrote that as yet Sergio appeared to have had no motive for the crime but the fact that he had not perished in the fire and had never turned up afterwards was being viewed as suspicious. David should no longer feel in any way culpable since it was clear that no employee had died. His father concluded by expressing his hope that his son was well.

The guilt David had felt over Sergio's death was dispelled but he now had to suppress his anger against the person who was responsible. He sent a brief response thanking Theo for the information, saying he was fine and had been working on a farm for a few days.

He then headed for the coast. Arriving at a port, he checked into a small hotel for a couple of nights and, leaving his kit in the room and his car parked in a nearby street, he ventured out to find a place to eat in the seedy surrounding area. When he emerged, it was dark and rainy and he returned directly to the hotel. It was only the next day that he discovered his car was gone and with it his computer that he had left in the boot. He was furious, and spent a frustrating few hours in the local police station trying to explain about his vehicle and its theft. The officers were uninterested in his problem and pessimistic about finding the vehicle. Feeling unsettled by the loss of his familiar travelling companion, David felt vulnerable. Now he would have to face the countries through which he would travel without the protective metal carapace of his trusty car. Where would he go to next?

He wanted to experience nature in the raw and the lure of wide open spaces. It was time to embark on a voyage across the sea to countries with different cultures and terrain, somewhere wilder. In Africa he would learn to cope with isolation.

That he was already far from home made him feel slightly off balance and knowing that he was heading even further away, he suppressed his anxiety and went across to the offices of a shipping company and booked a ticket for a ship leaving in two days. His details were with the police but he had no hope his car would be found. It was probably hundreds of miles away by now – as he would be soon.

On his final evening he left his dismal room and decided to check on his e-mails. Sitting at the grimy computer that the hotel lent to guests, he found two messages in his inbox.

The first was from his father. This contained another update on the fire investigation, but as Sergio had never been traced, this was winding down and the matter was now under scrutiny by the insurance company. Theo did not raise false hopes about whether the fire might be covered by insurance but passed on the news without comment. He mentioned there was to be a major exhibition of some of his bronzes at a prestigious art gallery and that he was working hard to produce new pieces for this. He had put forward a design and drawings for a large corporate commission and had won it. Hoping David was well and learning much about new places, other people and about himself, Theo ended by affirming his love and support, and saying that he would always be happy to speak to him if his son ever felt liked calling.

David was pleasantly surprised to have an e-mail from his sister, who rarely communicated. Kate, in her outspoken way, wrote she was concerned about how he was coping with the itinerant life. She teased him for being so reticent about where he was and what he was doing, and hoped he would keep in touch with them better than she had done. She now knew how worrying silence was. She went on to say that her marriage to Andrew had been fixed for the spring. She gave the date and said they would both love it if he came back for the wedding, suggesting that he could fly home for a few days and then set off again afterwards. David knew he would not return. The lure of home was strong but it would be a backward step. Freedom from cares and responsibility beckoned and the horizon seemed azure with possibilities. He chose not to reply – it was less cruel not to respond than to say no.

He was delighted that Kate was marrying one of his closest friends and realised he felt envious. Their loving and trusting partnership contrasted so painfully with the fractured relationship that he and Layla had abandoned. David had long suppressed his feelings for her but there were moments when he ached for Layla. He had rejected her love and had no right to feel disappointed when he heard nothing from her and no news about her from Theo or Kate. He had not asked for any.

The next day he sailed for Africa.

David travelled through the Sahara and the Sahel, heading south. He chose to avoid urban areas, preferring the wide open spaces and journeying through arid desert lands. He finally reached the immensity of the savannah – vast grasslands, moving endlessly in the wind like undulating waves, dotted with islands of acacia trees and taller vegetation, under skies of intense blue. There were miles and miles of dusty tracks and brown rivers, endless hills and far horizons, in a land of hot sun where thousands of animals moved and lived and died.

It proved difficult to explore using local buses as they inevitably went from town to town. When he wanted to visit game reserves, David discovered he was required to use their transport and drivers, and the best way to experience the game parks was to stay in tented camps. This was expensive but he decided to take the opportunity and hire a Land Cruiser and guide. His savings were dwindling but he reckoned he could get a job somewhere soon to augment the funds he needed for travelling. He could find work in a hotel or restaurant – he had the training.

He met a pleasant man called Alec who was travelling around on holiday and wanted to have a week on safari in a huge game park, so together they organised a vehicle with a guide and took off into the bush. The driver, who was also their guide, was a local man of morose countenance known as Caleb, though he said his real name was Fumo. He was knowledgeable and knew where to find the wild animals they wanted to see on the vast plains. They spent two days staying in tents in a comfortable camp with another party of four individuals in their own vehicle. On the game drives they were delighted to see many of the giants of the savannah – giraffes, elephants, hippos and buffalo, as well as the more elusive such as cheetahs, a leopard and a rhino. Then they moved on to a smaller tented camp in a more remote area where they were the only guests.

On the second evening, just before dusk, a Jeep arrived driven by a tall man who was a game warden. He and Caleb knew each other, but whereas their guide rarely smiled and said little, the other man, whose name was Enzi, was friendly and likeable. He had worked for the game park for a number of years and was dedicated to protecting the wildlife and conserving their habitat.

That evening, the four men ate together, served by two lads who cooked and ran the camp, and there was much laughter, talk and beer. Caleb suggested they spend half a day walking in the bush to which they both agreed, and then, since they were going in the direction he intended to patrol, Enzi asked if he might accompany them. Caleb seemed disgruntled about this but reluctantly agreed when his two clients expressed enthusiasm. They were briefed to wear dark clothing and bring hats and water bottles.

The next day Caleb drove them to a remote area that few tourists visited, which was on the edge of the game park, not far from a river and waterhole. Here they parked and set off in single file; he and Alec took their cameras but Caleb and Enzi took guns in the unlikely event of needing to defend themselves against a charging animal. Enzi went first with his .375 heavy calibre rifle over his shoulder and Caleb took up the rear.

It was hot and very dusty. The dry season was coming to an end and rains would come soon. Animals would be found near the dwindling supply of water. As they walked along, David felt quite vulnerable without the safety and speed of the land cruiser. They skirted round a clearing where there were some buffalo, keeping downwind so as not to alert the animals to their presence. One of the buffalos – an old male, Enzi told them quietly – lifted its head as if he sensed their presence, but took no action. These animals were dangerous and as they walked away with their backs to these unpredictable creatures, adrenalin surged through David. After a couple of hours during which time they had seen a number of less dangerous wild animals – mainly gazelles, zebra and wildebeest – they stopped and Caleb told them that there were elephant in the area which they might see. They were just about to set off on a path that would eventually bring them back to their vehicle, when not far off they heard the sharp crack of shots. Caleb dropped to the ground and silently indicated to his clients that they should do the same, which they did. Enzi crouched down like a panther about to spring and slipped the rifle off his shoulder to hold it across his chest.

A thundering sound drummed through the ground and the four of them watched as five elephant crashed through the bush about two hundred yards away and headed off in another direction from theirs. David heaved a sigh of relief, but wondered who had been shooting at the wildlife since this was strictly forbidden unless it was in self-defence in a life-threatening situation. After a minute they moved forward cautiously, keeping low, to see what had happened. David looked at Enzi and Caleb and whilst the game warden seemed fearless, their guide was wary and nervous. After a few minutes, they heard voices and again Caleb motioned them to lie down. Enzi alone remained standing. They could see through the trees what appeared to be a wounded or dead elephant lying on the ground a hundred yards away and three men near the animal. One of them whooped and took out a huge knife.

"Poachers," Enzi hissed. "We can catch them!"

Caleb put out his hand as a warning, knowing he would lose his licence if he endangered his tourists. "They are armed. Dangerous men. We must leave. Not letting them see us."

"We're both armed," said Enzi quietly and determinedly. "They seem to have only one weapon. They're poverty-stricken meat poachers. We outnumber them. I must try to arrest them."

David could see the three men start to work cutting the flesh of the magnificent animal and felt his anger surge. He could understand why Enzi was so outraged.

Caleb gave Enzi a mutinous look and pulled at Alec's sleeve. "No. We go now. Very quiet," he whispered urgently. "You too," and he indicated David who was crouching nearby.

David was about to protest but Caleb glared at him, saying, "This is Enzi's job not mine. I go now. You come with me or I not responsible for what happen."

Alec, lying prone on the ground, looked frightened as he assessed the situation and realised that someone might get hurt and there was a chance it could be him. Caleb turned and started to crawl stealthily away and Alec followed him. Stricken, David realised that the odds were now against them and he gave Enzi a desperate look. Fear flooded through him. The other two had melted into the undergrowth and the urge to follow them was immensely strong.

Enzi put a hand on his shoulder and said softly, "This is my fight, my job, not yours. Go." And, to his disgrace, David went, crawling silently away on his belly, leaving a brave man to face up to his convictions.

He heard a few days later that Enzi's mutilated body had been found and the poachers had vanished with their booty. This was a land where the harsh laws of nature were all too evident: kill or be killed, eat or be eaten. He felt sick, disgusted by his shameful desertion of a fine man who had needed – but not demanded – his support.

He spent seven months in Africa, and on the brink of departing, he looked back on his time and he recalled his initial feelings of freedom and hope engendered by the huge continent and how these were dispelled when his courage had failed him. Then images of Enzi and Caleb invaded and his memories became polluted. He needed to move on to banish his guilt.

Months later, in Asia, David awoke, emerging from disturbing dreams full of noise and confusion. He remained lying on the bed, relishing his escape and trying to reduce his heartrate. The sunlight, glancing through the window from the wind-ruffled water, stippled across the walls in a constantly moving pattern of light. David watched it and tried to achieve a sense of calm. He had managed to move away physically from yesterday's danger but his mind remained in a state of agitated panic.

There was a quiet knock at his door. As he sat up, the door opened and a young man with a smiling face proffered a plate of food with a glass of tea. David was thirsty and accepted this gracefully. As he drank the tea, he looked back over the traumatic past two weeks.

He had come to this beautiful region on the recommendation of a couple he had met on a train. Knowing the area was politically unstable but unable to resist the temptation to see the renowned mountains and lakes, he had travelled for three days to get here. Within an hour of arrival, near an old bridge over the river, he had been bitten by a dog whilst trying to prevent the ravenous animal from attacking a child who was carrying a loaf of bread. After the dog had run off down the road, a man who spoke some English explained that the dog might be rabid, something that had not occurred to David and which filled him with horror. Apparently there were thousands of stray dogs roaming the streets, many of which were infected.

The family of the boy, who soon arrived on the scene, had volubly insisted on accompanying David to hospital to get the wound cleaned and have the vital rabies immunoglobulin administered and immediate vaccination. The cost of this treatment made a significant dent in David's limited local currency. When the boy's father understood that the foreigner had just arrived in the city and had nowhere to stay, he persuaded him to spend a few days relaxing in one of the many rented houseboats along the edges of the lake, and recommended one run by his relatives, a couple called Anil and Mala, who would look after him well.

On his departure from the hospital, with his wound treated and an appointment made for further vaccinations every five days, he had gone down to the heart of the city to get to a bank and then find the houseboat that had been suggested to him. He was now used to travelling on public transport.

David was taken out to the houseboat in a local boat called a shikara, and was delighted to arrive at an attractive, though slightly dilapidated, wooden vessel, which was modestly comfortable and relatively inexpensive. The quiet young couple, who had welcomed their guest with deferential smiles, lived forward and David's cabin was a large roomy one at the stern with a wooden balcony looking out over the peaceful lake. In the higher altitude it was much cooler than the sweltering heat of the plains he had recently left and was an ideal place to recover after his nasty encounter with the rabid dog.

The first morning he had woken early and wandered out on to the stern deck outside his room. The lake stretched out before him, a wide panorama of peaceful, sunlit water, surrounded on all sides by snow-capped mountains under a clear sky. Small craft plied across the lake leaving inky trails through the silver surface of the lake. There were many houseboats on either side of the one he was staying on and David realised that he had found the perfect haven for a month or two.

As he watched, some birds flew overhead which he thought might be duck. His observation of them was disrupted by a splashing sound as a tiny, battered wooden shikara appeared round the stern of the next houseboat, with a small boy of about ten paddling it. As it passed below where he was standing, the boy flashed a disarming smile and in a few broken words of English asked David if he wanted to be taken ashore or out on to the lake. The suggestion was appealing and within a few minutes, David was seated on a threadbare cushion under a small, torn sun canopy and they had set off into the middle of the lake, where the boy suggested an early morning swim. The lad said his name was Kiran and that he lived by ferrying people to and fro. Any money he earned he took home to his mother and his sisters. His father was dead. He was now the head of the family, he said with his eyes shining with pride and responsibility.

When they were in the middle of the lake, Kiran stopped paddling and looked expectantly at David, who was feeling nervous about diving into the sleek, gunmetal dark water. He had never been a strong swimmer and he recalled the time when, as a child, he had fallen into the weedy water of a green pond and thought he was drowning. The fear and revulsion he had experienced then washed over him again. He smiled at the boy who was watching him and, dipping his hand into the chill early morning water, murmured that it was too cold. Kiran nodded politely and got the boat moving.

A companionable friendship developed between the stranger and the boy. Kiran came by each day and took David around the waterways, lakes and river, showing him glorious, colourful gardens built by ancient conquerors, elegant fountains and, in the city, old palaces and wooden mosques. David paid him double what the lad asked for, though this was still very little. They developed an arrangement: David taught the boy a little English and Kiran showed the foreigner the waterways and the sights.

Five days after the dog had bitten him, David was obliged to return to the hospital for another unpleasant vaccination, the second of six. Although he was assured by a doctor that the rabies immunoglobulin he had been given on the day of the bite was 100% effective against rabies, he had nightmares about developing the symptoms of infection and the disease which would cause death from respiratory failure within seven days. Kiran collected him by the lakeshore in his shikara and then, in an effort to divert his client's attention from worries about rabies, he took him into another part of town along a narrow and less attractive canal to meet his family.

After about half an hour, David saw a young woman beside the river washing clothes next to a large basket, with three small girls scampering about helping her. Kiran pulled the boat into the bank and after they got out he introduced his foreign client to his mother, Sushma, and his three sisters. He indicated that the basket contained not laundry but his baby sister, called Punim, a name which meant 'full moonlight'. Kiran explained that his infant sister was sick. His mother was a shy, beautiful woman whose solemn dignity was combined with a weary acceptance of the task of bringing up four daughters with no husband to provide for them. Kiran had told David that she took in washing and did laundry for wealthier neighbours. Her son was clearly the only other earner in the family. The smallest daughter was quite small and probably less than a year old, so the death of the father must have been a recent event. Discreetly, without saying anything, he handed the woman some money – crumpled notes she tucked carefully into her clothing as she gave him a despondent smile.

During the next week, they visited six of the nine old bridges which connected the two parts of the city, and David spent hours lying on the cushion, trailing his fingers in the cool water whilst Kiran paddled the small craft. He dreamed of Layla and wondered how his family was. Though he felt disinclined to search for a place with internet connections, his thoughts often strayed to the familiar landscapes of home and the people he'd left behind.

When he went back to the hospital for the third vaccination, the sky was overcast and the air humid and heavy. Afterwards, feeling uneasy, David wandered back down through the town towards the lake, where he was to meet Kiran who would row him back to the houseboat. He stopped beside a street vendor to buy some fruit and chose some nectarines, cheerfully paying the inflated price the man wrote down on a scrap of paper. Carrying the fruit in a plastic bag, inhaling their warm aroma, he walked past a dilapidated government building with a courtyard enclosed by rusty railings inside which there were a number of police and people in military uniforms milling around.

He recalled with absolute clarity what happened next – the images were burned into his mind. He was passing a small grocer's shop, its metal shutter folded up to display tins and packets piled up to entice customers, when a small truck came hurtling along the street with two people in the back, one of them standing up. A few seconds after it passed him, there was some shouting and gun shots immediately followed by a violent explosion. David shrank back into the shelter of the shop and as dust surged towards him, a brief moment of stunned silence was broken by cries and shrieks emanating from within it. He knew the area had suffered from severe political and terrorist unrest for a number of years and that thousands of people had been killed and injured but until that moment he had found it impossible to believe that insurgency and violent protests were a real threat in what appeared to be such a gentle and peaceful city.

He ran back towards the mayhem to see if he could help and was soon engulfed in a nightmare of confusion, fear and panic. He saw bodies lying in the compound, two of them badly mutilated and ominously still, and another being lifted and carried toward the building. People were screaming, staggering around in distress or crouching down in shock. One of the men in the speeding truck had lobbed a grenade over the railings into the compound, causing death and destruction. A woman in a headscarf was standing in the street outside wailing, with two frightened children clutching her clothing. Needing to do something positive, David took her firmly by the arm, shepherded the trio to the shelter of a doorway on the other side of the road and tried to calm the wailing children. He noticed the faces of those in the street near him – shocked, frightened – and two women had their eyes closed in rejection of the brutality blasted into their consciousness.

Two Jeeps had arrived, and some soldiers with guns jumped out and began to take charge. The wailing of sirens announced the imminent arrival of ambulances. David decided that as a foreigner who didn't understand the language there was little more he could do and began to walk away. In fascinated horror he took a last look at the courtyard and his eyes focussed on a severed arm lying at the foot of the railings. He vomited and lurched away in revulsion, running back past the grocery and the scattered nectarines which lay smashed on the scarred pavement. White-faced, he had stumbled back to the waterfront and asked Kiran to take him back to the houseboat.

The family aboard had been distressed to discover that their guest had witnessed such an appalling incident and tried to compensate by talking to him in soothing tones and plying him with meals and drinks. They politely refused to discuss what had happened – it was if as they did not want to acknowledge the reality of the violence they all lived with alongside the beauty. Even Kiran avoided the subject. In deep shock he had gone to bed.

Feeling exhausted, David remained in his room on the houseboat and slowly the morning light on the lake and mountains worked its soothing magic. He was unharmed. He was safe. But he was lonely, needing comfort from someone who cared for him. He was missing his father's companionship and, as he now admitted, Layla's love.

As he tried to recall the tender warmth of Layla's eyes and irrationally to banish the memory of her face when they had parted, his reverie was interrupted by yet another knock on the door. It was Anil again. "Kiran is here. Do you wish to go in his boat?"

"Not today, thank you," said David tiredly. "Perhaps tomorrow."

"I will tell him, sir. Would you like some fruit?" Anil asked softly, sensitive of the bruising effect of witnessing a terrorist attack. The locals were accustomed to these sad and disruptive occurrences but the few tourists who came to the region were shocked by them.

"No thanks, Anil. Please tell Mala that I don't want any food at the moment. I slept badly and need to rest." The young man nodded, retreating silently, and David closed his eyes again. He lay there and tried to fix his thoughts on another experience, in another continent, to restore his faith in humanity and in the order of nature, amid the chaos of human cruelty and folly. He remembered Alicia and her parents, and was comforted.

David realised that sleep was impossible and getting up from the bed, he went on to the balcony and gazed out over the silver sheen of the lake and the tiny islands that appeared to be floating upon its surface with the encircling mountains as a majestic backdrop. So much beauty and yet such brutality in the midst of it! David had always thought himself as composed, but recently he had a tendency to see-saw between highs and lows, between tranquil contentment and discordant anguish. His calm, rational approach to life had been undermined not only by fire, loss and frustrated love, but now by violence, poverty and death.

David would have left the area and travelled on to try and put the horror behind him, but he had to stay for the remaining vaccinations. Kiran still came by each day with suggestions of things to do to divert his client's sombre state of mind. His idea of a picnic afloat appealed to David and the next day they set off in the boy's shikara. He found the stillness and beauty not only a bizarre contrast but also a calming antidote to the pandemonium of the street bombing he had witnessed. It followed the pattern of contrasts and contradictions he was discovering in his travels – in the midst of huge suffering he had witnessed both calm stoicism and hysterical panic.

As he listened to the plop of Kiran's paddle and the soothing babble of the water, David cast his mind back over the year since he had left home.

An earlier tragic episode clouded the good memories of his time in Africa. Amid the beauty of grasslands, trees and wildlife, Enzi had been cruelly hacked down in a brave, almost foolhardy, attempt to bring poachers to justice. And yesterday, in Asia, in a serene land of mountains, lakes and flowers there had been a bomb attack and he had witnessed a similar act of pitiless violence and sudden death.

Invoked by these thoughts, his father's words drifted into his consciousness, telling his son to have courage to act against wrongdoing, humility in learning from others and to show compassion to those he met. David had imagined himself voyaging unruffled across oceans of miles, learning serenity and wisdom from a dispassionate observation of all he encountered. But the water had become turbulent. He had encountered suffering and injustice. His self-possession was becoming eroded by tragedy and the harsh reality of man's inhumanity to man.

He sighed for the loss of innocence. Layla had warned him of the dangers; she had offered to travel with him and share their experiences. But he had turned her down and ended the relationship. Thinking about love reminded him that Kate and Andrew were now happily married.

A month before her wedding, Kate had e-mailed, pleading with him to reconsider and come back to be part of their special day. Maria had agreed to be her bridesmaid. She had casually mentioned that Josh, who was still working in the area, would be there and that Layla, who had been abroad for some while, had promised to be at her best friend's marriage. With some reluctance, as he would miss seeing not only his family but also Layla, he had replied that he was now in Asia and could not afford the time or the money to travel back so far. He had resolved to avoid the dislocation of rapid air flights, spanning in a few hours what had taken him many months of unhurried wandering. This was the truth but it was also an excuse – he was not ready to go back.

Kate had recently sent some photographs of the wedding, wistfully mentioning her disappointment that he had been unable to come. He had opened up the attached photographs on the screen to view them. In one group shot he found Layla, her dark hair piled up on her head, standing beside a bearded man whom he did not recognise. She was smiling, half turned to her companion, her hand on his arm. A sharp pain swept through him from the shock of seeing her with someone else and the awareness that he still cared for her. He struggled not to feel jealous and resolved not to find out what she was doing and where was she living. She might have reverted to her former profession and he couldn't cope with that thought. One day he would rid himself of the image of Layla, erase her from his memory and meet another woman, less tainted and less fickle. Less like a knife in the gut.

He had closed the photograph and logged out.

Kiran's boyish voice broke into his thoughts. "Do you want to swim?"

"No. Please take me back." His abrupt words made the boy fall silent.

The following day, David sat on his balcony hoping that Kiran would come rowing past. He had told Anil he wanted to read a book and was not to be disturbed but perversely he now wanted to go out on the lake, to listen to the lad chatting away in his pidgin English, forget the voices from his past and deny the lure of home. He decided to go ashore to get some exercise by walking in the city.

He went through the houseboat to where the family lived to ask them to lend him their small shikara so he could paddle himself. But the wooden craft was gone and hearing the sound of crying, he found Mala squatting in the area where she cooked the meals, rocking back and forth, with her face in her hands. Thinking she was hurt or ill, David crouched down and without thinking put his hand gently on her shoulder. "Mala, what's the matter? Are you ill?"

The woman flinched away from his alien touch. Aware she had rejected his genuine concern, she looked at him with her dark eyes full of tears. "Sorry. I am not sick. Just sad."

"Why are you sad? Can I help?"

Mala, whose English was very limited, just shook her head, and said, "No. No. Sorry."

That afternoon, when Anil returned, David discovered that some of his wife's relatives had suffered a tragedy. They too had a houseboat available for rent and lived aboard with their young family. Anil explained that one of their children had fallen overboard and drowned early that morning, and he had gone to give them some support in their grief. "It is very sad, sir. But it happens sometimes when so many of us live on the water. Not everyone knows how to swim. But the boy was only three and the water is deep."

"Please tell your wife how sorry I am about this child's death." *What a sad waste of a life,* he reflected. A moment's carelessness or inattention by the parent and a beloved little one was lost. A human life taken by the dark waters of the lake. He shivered. If ever he had children he would be vigilant.

David was surprised that Kiran did not return for three days and had to ask Anil to arrange a boat for him to go ashore and attend the hospital again for another vaccination. He missed the boy's friendly company and wondered why he now kept away. At the hospital, there seemed to be some sort of protest in progress, with a large crowd of people outside with placards. He was unable to read the foreign script or find out from anyone the reason for the demonstration, though he saw the men were angry and many of the women distraught. Whilst in the city, he called in at an internet access office and decided to tell his father about his travels in Asia including a brief account of the terrorist bomb outrage. It took some while and it was by far the longest communication he had yet sent home. The process was cathartic and he felt better for sharing the burden and the pain with someone who loved him. Perhaps one day they would talk about it and try to make sense of what seemed senseless. His father was so balanced and always saw things from a broader perspective.

The following day, Kiran turned up. David was reading in his room aboard the houseboat when he heard the boy calling him. He went outside to the aft balcony and there was Kiran, below in his small, battered shikara, beckoning him. A few minutes later, he was settled on the cushions and being paddled away across the lake. The boy seemed quieter and more serious, so David asked him what the matter was.

"My baby sister, Punim," Kiran began, his eyes filling with tears. "She dies – four days ago. My mother, she is very, very sad. My sisters, they are crying all the time."

David remembered the infant's tiny face, lying open-eyed in the basket he had peered into when he had met the family. Now she was dead. A few days before a small boy had drowned. The death of innocent children was so unbearable. He sat up and motioned the distressed lad to stop paddling.

"Kiran, I'm so very sorry. What a terrible loss for you and your family. Why did she die? I didn't realise she was so very ill."

"She was not too ill. But my mother take her to the hospital, to the place for children, because she has cough and a fever. She is given injection but she gets much worse. Soon after she dies. It is a bad, bad hospital. Many babies and children die there. The parents get very angry, but what can they do?" Kiran banged his small fist on the side of the boat and looked out over the water, his face dark with anger and pain. David ached for the boy in his grief.

When they returned to the houseboat, David pulled out all the local currency from his pocket and thrust it into the boy's hand in payment for hiring the shikara.

"You give me too much," said Kiran handing back half of the grubby notes. "I take only what I earn."

"No, please keep it. Give it to your mother, for your sisters." Kiran silently took it back, nodding his head from side to side. "You soon go?" he said.

"Yes, soon. But I won't forget you. Ever." On a sudden impulse, he took off his gold watch, which he knew the boy admired, and gave it to Kiran. "Here's something for you to remember me by."

The boy's pinched face lit up as he took the watch and looked at it with pride. "Thank you, sir. It's a very, very good watch." He put it to his ears and listened to its subdued expensive tick. A smile crept over his face as he momentarily forgot his family tragedy. David knew that Kiran would almost certainly have to sell it soon to help his mother, though he doubted that the lad would get a good price for it. The boy had no need for accurate timekeeping – he had no agenda, no necessity to know what hour of the day it was.

That evening Anil explained to David that the state-run hospital had a very bad reputation resulting from a high number of infant deaths, largely because of shortage of staff and inadequate medical equipment. "The conditions inside are shocking and many children have to share beds and risk infection from others. There is only one nurse available for thirty patients. Many newborn babies die. It is so bad that angry parents make protests outside the hospital, accusing it of negligence. But nothing is done," said Anil. "I would never take my children in through the door."

David was outraged. "How shameful. Someone in government should compel the hospital to deal with the problem."

Anil looked puzzled by this remark and giving a small smile and the sideways nod that so often accompanied his remarks, said, "That is the way things are here."

Death was interwoven closely with life and the local people accepted this without question. They shrugged their bony shoulders and smiled, acknowledging the uncertainty of life and the inevitability of suffering.

A week later David received the final dose of preventative vaccine for rabies and he decided to leave the beautiful but haunted land and move on to another place. He had been travelling now for well over a year and his cash was shrinking. Soon he would need to go to a country where he could get a job and earn some money to enable his peripatetic life to continue. He decided he might try to find a travelling companion and moved to a traveller's hostel in the city where he would be sure of meeting others who were heading east or west.

Kiran was stoic about David's departure. His tourist clients came and went but he had to stay and work on the lake, hiring out his little shikara for inadequate wages for the foreseeable future. David wistfully said goodbye to his little companion and managed to obtain the address where he lived with his mother and sisters. Kiran confided that his ambition was to learn to read and write but David knew that the long hours the boy had to work to help his family would allow little time for education.

Kiran said he would always remember his foreigner for the gift of the watch. But the boy would expect never to hear from him again.

As he headed further east, David hoped time would be kind to Kiran.

13

Kate looked expectantly at the door of the restaurant and checked her watch. She noticed the date – she and Andrew had been married for almost a year. In a few days their first wedding anniversary would be a double celebration. Her face took on an inward look as she imagined the tiny child growing within her. She looked down to see if there was any indication but her stomach was as flat as ever. As she tried to imagine her abdomen swelling up, a strange feeling of protectiveness surged up.

"Spilt coffee in your lap?"

Kate's head jerked up and found Maria standing beside the table. "No. Actually, I'm just checking to see…" She paused for effect and then continued with a smile, "…if there's a bump."

Maria blinked in surprise. "You're not pregnant?"

"I am. We're over the moon."

Maria gave her friend a warm hug. "That's wonderful news – I'm so pleased for you both." Her face shone with delight as she took off her coat and sat down. "When is it due?"

"I'm about two months gone, so it'll be an autumn baby."

It was a rainy Saturday in late March. The two women often met for lunch whilst Andrew was playing squash with a work colleague. After ordering, Maria asked Kate how long she had known.

"I've suspected it for a while – but we only got confirmation a few days ago. I can't believe that someone as reckless and selfish as me is going to be a mother. What a responsibility!" Kate shook her head in amazement.

"Stop running yourself down. You've been a hard-working, dependable person for some time now. Being a parent will ensure that you become unselfish," Maria said firmly.

"Being considered a reliable citizen is almost as amazing as being pregnant. Daddy seems to think I've metamorphosed into a trustworthy person."

"Have you told him yet?"

"Last night we drove out to Home Barn and gave him the good news. He was so calm and unsurprised that it was almost as if he'd known."

"The first grandchild will be very important to Theo."

"All his grandchildren will be equally special," said Kate, visualising her father holding a tiny baby in his huge hands whilst another small child sat on his knee. "Andrew is so pleased. He patted me on the head and said I'd turned out to be a good wife after all!" They both laughed and ate for a while in silence, until Kate remembered the other thing she wanted to tell Maria. "There's some other good news Theo told us."

Maria looked up. "What's that?"

"He's returning after all this time." Kate hoped that this would please her friend. "He wants to live and work here."

Maria said warmly, "That's wonderful. You must all be so relieved. When did you hear from your brother?"

"It's not him who's coming back. I meant Josh, of course. Sadly there's still no news from David. It seems that Theo and Josh have kept in touch whilst Josh has been on a training course for catering management. That's going to finish this summer and he's hoping to get a job locally. Of course we all know why he's so keen to come back. He makes no secret of it."

Maria looked embarrassed. "There's no understanding between Josh and me. I told him to go away, sort out his drink problem and get a proper job. That was eighteen months ago. I've not written or spoken to him since, though he persists in sending me funny postcards."

"Josh has a great sense of fun. Go on, admit it, Maria. You miss him. If only a little bit. He still adores you."

"I can't think why. I've never encouraged him."

"Perhaps that's the reason. He's not used to being turned down. His quest for the unattainable is what keeps him interested. Can't you unbend a little? He's not so very bad," Kate said persuasively.

"On his own admission he's a thief and a liar and a drunkard." Maria sounded prim.

"Daddy says he's changed for the better. He might even become acceptable." There was no response from her companion, so she went on. "I've missed him and his optimism, flamboyance and uncritical affection for his friends."

Detecting a note of censure, Maria was defensive, "You think I'm too harsh on him. I did care about him. I enjoyed his company – and he's attractive. But he was also deceitful. And unreliable. He hurt me."

"Maria... Forgive and forget. Dump Hugh, that dreary doctor you've been seeing, and welcome back the joyful Josh."

"I'm not going out with Hugh anymore," Maria said. "He's a dedicated and caring man but you're right – he's a bit dull!"

"But Josh isn't. He's anything but dull. He's gloriously alive."

"I think he did love me." Maria's eyes grew soft at the memory.

"You bet he did. And still does. That's why he's coming back – to see if there's any hope. Think carefully, Maria. If you drive him away this time, he may not return. Josh may be unpredictable in his behaviour but he's been faithful to you. He's a lovely guy. Give him another chance."

"If Theo likes him, I suppose he can't be all bad!" Maria got to her feet. "I'll think about it. Come on. The rain's stopped. Let's pay and go for a walk."

As they strolled along the street, Kate told her friend about a promotion that Andrew was hoping for, and about the continuing saga of the designs for the proposed rebuilding of the hotel, which had been rejected by the planning

186

authorities, were resubmitted and had now been approved. Maria mentioned she had to take time off from her work to care for her mother whose health was worse. She might terminate her nursing job at the hospital and take on agency work, which would give her more flexibility and allow her to accommodate her mother's needs.

"Things sound a little sad at home," said Kate, looking up at the skies which had now cleared. "You need Josh to cheer you up!"

Theo looked at the midsummer sky through the roofless ruin of his old family home. The charred smell had finally gone and the ash had blown away. Two years had passed since the fire – weeds and grass had grown up around the wrecked building, abandoned for so long. He gave a sigh for the ruined hopes of his son who had left soon afterwards and not come back.

Now at last new plans and activity brought hope for renewal. Most of the site had been cleared. The rear kitchen wing had gone altogether but part of the new wing was still standing, although badly scorched. The main house had been badly damaged but the thick exterior walls and some internal ones remained. The staff accommodation in the old stable block at the rear was undamaged though filthy with neglect. Workmen from the demolition gang had removed rubble, charred beams and burned chattels. The roof had been considered dangerous and was demolished in the weeks after the fire. A few paintings had been rescued before the fire had taken hold but almost all the contents had been destroyed.

What had not been extinguished in the fire was the most precious thing of all – human life – and for this Theo was profoundly grateful. People had lost their jobs, his son had lost his hotel – but these were things that could be remedied. If there was the will to do so. Kate was enthusiastic but from David there was silence.

Theo heard a car coming down the drive and watched as Andrew drew up and stopped. His son-in-law climbed out of his car and walked towards him. Theo gave the younger man an affectionate hug and together they surveyed the scene.

"At last the demolition work is done and we can begin the rebuild." There was a note of excitement in his voice. Andrew and his firm had been working on the new plans and specifications for some considerable time.

"It's been a long haul and I'm keen for the project to start," said Theo. The long, drawn-out negotiations on the matter of the insurance claim had finally resulted in a substantial pay-out and funds had now been received. In the absence of any instructions from his son, and since he held David's power of attorney, he had decided to rebuild. Some months before he had approved the drawings and an application was submitted to the planning authority. A detailed specification had been drawn up and when full approval had come through, suitable building contractors submitted quotations for the work. He and Andrew had chosen the firm who were to start the following week.

"I hope David will approve of what we're doing, if ever he comes back," Andrew said.

"*When* he comes back," Theo corrected, giving Andrew a reassuring smile. "I have every confidence in my son's ability to survive. When he does return, he will understand we needed to move on. I'm sure he'll be inspired and re-energised by your designs."

"It seems strange to think that in one year all those drawings and dreams will have become a reality and that this time next summer we might be standing here gazing at the new Homeward House," Andrew said, looking at the ruined walls and fire-damaged façade but seeing in his mind's eye a vision of the new building.

"And David might be here with us."

"I'll tell you who *will* be here," said Andrew with a grin. "Your grandchild!"

"How is Kate? Not getting too tired, I hope?" asked Theo, aware that his daughter was in the middle of an active summer term at the school, on her feet all day.

"She's fine. There's a small bump now and she looks beautiful. The baby's not due till late October, and she tells me she wants to work until halfway through next term. I still find it hard to believe I'm going to be a father!"

They strolled across to the huge beech which had survived the sparks and heat, and still stood, magnificent in its summer foliage. Dwarfed beneath it was a small portable cabin that was to be the site manager's office, with a space for the architect's drawings and specifications. Andrew's firm had agreed that he would be on site regularly to oversee the project and he showed Theo the schedule of works, which they discussed.

Before he left, Andrew said, "Kate and I have been talking about getting somewhere else to live. Now we've both got salaries, and with a baby on the way, we need somewhere with a bit more space. I'd love to live in the country but we can't afford that yet. We're looking to rent on the outskirts of town."

Theo leaned against the huge trunk of the beech and smiled at his practical son-in-law. "What's your dream, Andrew?"

"I want to be a good father. And become a successful architect. But I do have a dream. I hope one day to design and build my own home."

"If you want something enough, you need to focus on it. Believe in yourself. If it's a good dream and if you work hard, it will happen in time."

"Thanks for your encouraging words, Theo. But just now my attention and energy are centred on this project and I have to go back to the office and get things moving. The building contractors start in five days."

After Andrew left, Theo looked at the overgrown garden, neglected since the fire. He sat on a lichen-covered bench and gazed around him at the bright sunlight filtering through the leaves. For many years he had lived in this peaceful place surrounded by ancient hills. He had seen the seasons pass and watched saplings grow into mature trees. He felt in tune with the serenity of the natural surroundings. He belonged here. So did his children, who had once run through these woods in a time of innocence.

Light and laughter, he hoped, would emerge from darkness and fire. But not yet. A cloud passed over the sun and the shadows under the old tree deepened. Theo's thoughts flowed like a river, plans swirling in his head. He would have patience.

The demolition firm were loading the last load of debris into a lorry to be taken away and dumped. The afternoon wore on and Theo remained where he was. The workmen finished and drove off. The place became quiet with the sound of birdsong and the quiet rustle of wind in foliage.

Eventually Theo stirred and directed his gaze to the front of the ruined building. He had heard what he was waiting to hear – the sound of a motorbike on the gravel drive. He watched a tall young man emerge from behind the bushes and stride towards him. He stood up and raised a hand in greeting.

In a distant city Layla stood back and surveyed her work and its presentation in her allocated space within the main studio. This was her show at the end of the two-year course and her work would soon be assessed. She felt anxious and hoped it would it be good enough for her to pass and achieve a Diploma in Higher Education in Fine Art. Two weeks before she had completed her module entitled Critical Studies and Research Methods, which explored the historical dimension of her chosen area. This was portraiture and Layla had been exploring this theme in her practical studio work, culminating in this exhibition.

Layla flipped her hair out of her eyes and adjusted the height of a pair of charcoal sketches of the faces of two children. A large portrait painting in acrylic was the main centrepiece of her exhibition and as Layla scrutinized this huge work again, the eyes of the old woman stared back at her, looking back through the years of a long life at the young woman she had once been. She had a secret conviction that whatever the outcome, she had produced something good. She pulled out a small camera and took a couple photographs of her show to send to Theo. Without his support none of this would have been possible.

She had been lucky to get a place on the course and it was the credits for her degree course, abandoned some years before, which had persuaded them to accept her. After years of living on her wits but without constraints, Layla had found it hard to go back to studying, focussing on goals and keeping set hours. But she was keen to learn and found great satisfaction working creatively again. She spent hours in the studio and enjoyed the company and stimulation of other students.

She switched off the lights, waved at a couple of others who were putting finishing touches to their shows and left the studio. As she walked across to the coffee shop, Layla felt light-headed. She had done it. She had resisted the temptation to go back to her former way of life. Her time in the country with Theo and his family had changed her and though there had been a period of despair when David had left, she had picked herself up and, with her 'adopted' father's help and encouragement, she had succeeded.

She was immensely grateful to Theo for advising her how to obtain a loan to pay the course fees and for assisting with her maintenance costs whilst she studied. He had kept in regular touch and they had met up a few times when he was in the city on business seeing the gallery that marketed his sculptures. She had told him she hoped one day to be able to repay him but he merely smiled and said he was "investing in art and creativity". Tonight she would write to him and let him know that her course was completed.

"Hello there. Is your show all ready?" Peter leaned down and gave her a kiss on the cheek. "Can I join you?"

"Of course," Layla murmured with a fleeting regret that her private moment of elation had been interrupted, and hoping he would remove his hand from her shoulder.

Peter, a tutor on her course, had been very attentive for some weeks and because she had consented to go out with him a few times, he regarded her as his 'girlfriend'. As a mature student Layla was nearer his age than others on the course. She was popular with her fellow students but Peter glared at any of them who approached her whilst he was with her.

"What are your plans now?" he enquired after he had ordered a coffee.

"I want to catch up on sleep," Layla answered promptly.

"I mean your plans for the future." Peter lowered his voice, covered her hand with his and looked into her eyes. "I'm hoping that I might be a part of them."

"Whoa, Peter," said Layla breezily, "give me time to catch my breath – I like you lots, but just now I want to savour the end of term and keep my options open."

"I just want you to know that I'm here for you," he said, patting her hand.

"That's so kind." Layla removed her hand to drink her coffee. "I've got a big decision to make in the coming weeks."

"What decision?" Peter's face glowed with hope.

"If I pass, I'm considering whether I might progress on to the final year of the BA Fine Art degree." She could see Peter was pleased at the prospect of her remaining in college for another year, but his face fell when she went on. "But there is the option of deferring for a year before continuing, and I might do that as I've some unfinished business to deal with. I'll let you know but now I must dash to meet up with the others for a celebratory drink. We'll be going our own separate ways soon, so I want to say goodbye."

"Not to me, I hope." There was a note of desperation in his voice and Layla felt weighed down by his possessiveness.

"Course not. I'll be here until I dismantle the show. Then I plan to take a holiday and stay with some friends." She longed to go back to the one place in the world where she had found love and contentment and see the only family that cared about her.

"If you want me to drive you anywhere, I'd love to help."

"Thanks, Peter." Layla put some money on the table to pay for her coffee, picked up her bag, bestowed one of her dazzling smiles on him and darted outside.

Peter was becoming too devoted – she had to discourage him. She headed for the accommodation block and some sleep. Back in her study bedroom, she caught sight of the small card depicting crossroads that Theo had sent her, in which he had written, "Seek advice about the right path to take. Go forward with confidence. And humility. Don't stand still or slip back." She could still hear his fatherly voice in her head, saying to her the last time they had met, "Trust me, you'll be a happier person if you do what you love doing and if you are kind to others along the way." Next week she would paint a picture to give to Theo. He'd loved her last one.

In another country, a taxi drew up at an airport Departures and a stocky man emerged. He scowled at the taxi driver as he paid the fare, and picking up a black holdall, he strode into the check-in area.

Jacob was simmering with fury as he queued. He had been working for one of Ator's profitable enterprises in a country where he'd been able to siphon off a small part of the income generated in cash. He was careful about this pilfering – if discovered retribution would be harsh – but Ator was far away and his surveillance less efficient. Jakob hoped his 'private fund' would one day grow large enough to allow him to cut free, disappear to another part of the world and live comfortably without being at the beck and call of a man he hated.

But he had been summoned back to the base of operations and asked to resume persecuting the family that had long been the target of Ator's venom. Two years had passed since he had ordered Ross to set the hotel on fire and get the son suspected of arson. Ross had now been redeployed elsewhere, the hotel was a total ruin and the proprietor had done a runner and disappeared. Now his boss's attention had reverted to this family and he wanted Jakob to leave his cosy set-up and carry out more covert harassment. Why didn't Ator rub them out and be done with it? Obviously he relished a slow, relentless revenge.

He passed through security, scowling at one of the team who gave him a body search. It would be necessary to keep himself invisible from the family and he remembered feeling uneasy on the only occasion he had encountered Theo, a few years before, when he had come to spy out the land and taunt him with bad news about his daughter. He recalled a penetrating intelligence beneath the big man's calm demeanour and longed to know the reason for Ator's vendetta against him. As he boarded the aeroplane a curious thought struck him: might Theo be the one who could cause Ator's downfall – and would it be worth switching allegiance? He must keep such traitorous thoughts hidden from his employer.

Some hours later, after landing, he found a quiet area and dialled the contact number, and speculated whether on this assignment he would meet the person who had employed him for so many years. Would the man look as reptilian as his voice sounded?

The ringing tone ceased as the call was answered. "Yes," hissed Ator.

"Jakob here. I'm in the country."

The warm summer evening witnessed another arrival. "Hey Theo, long time no see!" Josh drawled as he shook the older man's hand warmly. "I've missed you and yours."

"Welcome back, Josh." Theo noticed he was looking less gaunt and his pale skin was tanned; he was wearing jeans, a yellow shirt and had a crumpled linen jacket. His hair was as untidy as ever and the grin just as jaunty. "You look well – all that hard work must be good for you."

"I've had a bit of a holiday in the sun – I needed a break after college finished. Then I thought I'd come and see how things were going back at the ranch." Josh looked across at the burned-out building. "Sad to see the hotel still a ruin and everything so dilapidated. It was such a fine place. I thought by now things would have got moving. But nothing's changed since I was here over a year ago at Kate and Andrew's wedding. Now *that* was a good party!"

"You know Kate's pregnant, I suppose?"

"Yeah. No way could she resist telling me the brilliant news."

"She's still working in a school. Andrew's had a promotion and is project manager for the contract to build the new hotel. He was here earlier."

"The last time we met, you were making plans to rebuild. What caused the delay?" Josh threw himself down on the long grass and Theo sat down.

"It's been a long haul. David hasn't been around to help in the consultations but we're finally there. Planning permission has been granted and the finance is arranged. The most damaged parts have been demolished and the site is ready for the building contractors who start next week."

"So you managed to get the stingy insurance company to pay out. That must have hurt them! Does David know you've won the battle?"

"He doesn't keep in touch that often," said Theo carefully.

"Which means that you haven't heard from him..." Josh was quick to assess the situation. "And you're all worried by the silence."

"Not unduly. David's a resourceful man and he'll have his reasons for the lack of communication. He was in Asia the last time we heard." And he told Josh what David had written at that time.

The shadows began to lengthen as they talked, Theo on his bench and Josh sitting on the ground at his feet. Josh mentioned he had been in Asia some years before. "That's where I began to steal, mainly because I was hungry. Then it became a way of life and I embarked on my career as a thief. More money for less work. I was clever and avoided being caught, but it was risky, often scary and I had a few close calls."

"Did you feel guilty?" Theo asked.

"I knew it was wrong but suppressed guilt. I want you to know I've stopped now. I kept the promise I made when we last spoke that I wouldn't steal anymore. Though I admit I've been tempted."

"I believe you'll continue to resist the temptation. Stay strong. Don't steal again."

"I won't, Theo. I've turned my back on it. I want to thank you hugely for all the support and financial help you've given me over the past year or so. I'd never have got my act together to become an honest citizen without your encouragement."

"Delighted to help. So you completed the Catering Management Course?"

"Restaurant Management too. You'd have been proud of me, Theo. I've been so focussed."

"I *am* proud of you, Josh," Theo said with a smile.

"I turned up at most of the lectures, did all the practical stuff and didn't get distracted by all the lovely girls on the course. As you know, there's only one lady I'm fixed on and she lives near here."

"Maria is fine – still single, though I believe there is an eligible doctor who is showing a bit of interest in our lovely lass."

"He'd better clear off my patch," growled Josh. "I'll behave well – I'll just throw him in the river!" They both laughed. "Do you think I've still got a chance with her?"

"If you are open and truthful with her. No more lies. I ought to tell you that her mother is quite unwell and Maria has her work cut out looking after her and keeping working."

"The girl's incredible! I must see her tomorrow. Somehow." Josh groaned theatrically. "I can't wait anymore."

"Don't ambush her without warning. That's my advice. Where are you staying tonight?"

"I've no idea... On your sofa?" Josh grinned.

"It seems so. I'll make you one of my rustic meals."

"Good, I'm ravenous."

"You always are."

"There were times in my life when food was hard to come by, so I take it when it's offered. With gratitude."

Theo rose and they started to walk back to the drive where he had left his truck. "I see you've got another bike. I hope you're less reckless on it these days. Falls can hurt!"

"Thanks for the warning – it makes me think you care what happens to me. You're like a father – how I used to imagine a loving father would be. It feels good."

"I do care about you, Josh. Tell me what happened to your parents. You've never spoken of them."

"Not much to say. I don't really remember them – my real father pushed off when I was about three. We were evicted from our home and had to move to a cheap, grimy apartment. A succession of men passed through our lives and left me with bruises and my mother with addictions. She became a heroin junkie, cheating and stealing to get her dope money, and died a few years later from an overdose, or it may have been septicaemia from a dirty needle. My little sister, Carla, and I were put in care which wasn't a whole lot of fun. But we did get some education and for a while I quite enjoyed school. Then I got in with some bad lads and became disruptive and disobedient. I ran away when I was fifteen – the care home must have been pleased to be rid of me. Carla was adopted – on account of being a lot prettier than me – but I lost trace of her years ago." Josh stopped abruptly and shrugged his shoulders, muttering, "I hope she's happy, wherever she is."

Theo felt saddened at this tale of a loveless childhood. "Come home with me, Josh. Put the past behind you." He got into his truck.

Josh climbed on to his bike and roared the engine into life. "You go ahead, Theo. I'll follow on my trusty machine and try not to fall off into the ditch on that rotten road up to your barn. At least I'm sober."

The air was heavy with August heat and Kate, now seven months pregnant, was sitting on a packing case waiting for Andrew to arrive back with another load. They were moving into a small terraced house with more space and a second bedroom for the baby. On the edge of town it was within walking distance of a small park, and Kate hoped to have it ready well before the birth. She was tired and her back ached. Andrew had taken to rubbing her back each evening and gently stroking her bump.

She heard the van pull up outside and the sound of voices. Josh was giving them a hand with the move and put his head round the door – "Good to see you taking a load off your feet, dear one. Your brawny husband and I are just about to come staggering in with the sofa, so you'll be able to shift your lovely derrière on to that – much more comfortable!"

Kate laughed and heard them grunting as they carried it through the front door and into the room. When it was in place, Josh collapsed dramatically on to it and lay there breathing heavily. "No room for me, then?" said Kate.

"Always room for you in my heart and on the sofa." Josh leapt to his feet and scooping her up, he carried her across and set her down.

"Watch out, that's my wife and baby you're lugging around." Andrew was amused but also concerned.

"Too right. Precious cargo." Josh bent down and whispered to Kate, "You're even heavier than the sofa."

Two hours later the final pieces of furniture had been collected and the small house was full of boxes and bags. Exhausted and hungry, Kate and Andrew were in the small kitchen unpacking some plates and cutlery, waiting for Josh who had dashed out to buy pizzas and a bottle of wine.

"Tonight is going to be the first night in our new home," said Kate as she reached up to put some bowls in the cupboard. "It calls for a celebration."

"It's unlikely that we'll be able to celebrate in bed. I'm too weary," murmured Andrew, putting his arms round his wife's belly. "You are getting magnificently large, darling Kate."

"I felt the baby kick. He must have heard you!"

"Enough of this canoodling, lovebirds. Time for that later." Josh had returned. "Now it's time to eat. I'm starving." He banged the pizza boxes down on the table, grabbed three glasses from a box and opened the wine bottle. "Just as well it's plonk with a screw cap as we've no chance of finding the corkscrew!"

They all sat down and ate. "Josh, we are so grateful for your help," said Kate with her mouth full. "And for the pizzas."

"I have an ulterior motive. I expect lots of meals round this table in the future. By way of gratitude."

"You're the chef these days – you can cook them," Andrew remarked.

"I'm not a chef. I'll be a catering manager when I get a proper job. In fact I've got some news: I applied for a position running the canteen at the secondary school in town and they've offered me an interview."

"Josh, are you really qualified for that? Have you had enough experience?" Kate was sceptical.

"Listen, kid, I've already had two jobs in this field – one in a hotel as a placement during the course and I'm now helping out temporarily at a restaurant here in town." He radiated confidence, saying, "I've done the training and I have the required skills."

"And what are those, Josh?" Kate asked, sipping water instead of wine.

"According to the manual, you need to be well-organised and methodical. You'd be amazed how I've improved in this direction. Secondly, you need to be able to motivate and manage staff – no problems there. Thirdly, strong customer service skills are required – I need a bit of practice there but I'll pick them up quick enough," said Josh, ticking them off on his fingers. "Fourthly, you need tact and diplomacy – that's something I might have to swot up on."

"You certainly will," interrupted Andrew with a laugh.

"Fifthly, stamina is essential – I've loads of that, clearly after today's effort. Sixth, the ability to keep calm in a crisis is vital. No-one better than me in that respect – if I'm sober." Here Josh took an enormous swig of wine and Kate spluttered. "Finally, you need strong communications skills. I'm a brilliant talker, so a natural for the job!"

"No false modesty then. You might be able to blag your way into it with a bit of luck," said Andrew.

"Just you wait," Josh grinned wickedly. "They'll give me the job because I want it and because I'm the best. Those kids will love me and my food."

"If they don't get put off first by your lean and hungry appearance," Kate giggled.

"I want to stay. I like this place. It's starting to feel like home – something I've never had before. I'm making headway with the ice-maiden who's finally taken pity on me. I think my beloved Maria has forgiven me."

"I hear you're a firm favourite with her mother. Maria says you've been besieging them, visiting her Mum after you finish work and before she gets back from the hospital."

"Win the mother and the daughter will follow. That's my plan. I'm wearing her down. I'm melting her heart. She's gonna be mine."

"Like the job."

"I do need it." Josh looked anxious. "That's one of my angelic Maria's unreasonable demands. I have to have a proper job before she'll marry me."

"Josh, have you popped the question?"

"So many times." Josh sighed dramatically. "Soon she might take me seriously. Here's hoping!" He drained his glass and got to his feet. "Another of her preposterous requirements is that I cut down on the alcohol. That's why I was stingy and only bought one bottle. So I'm horribly sober with too much blood in my alcohol stream. Maria would approve. How I love that divine, demanding woman!" Josh bowed to his audience. "I must go. I've got a late shift at the restaurant. Be gloriously happy in your new home." And he left.

Theo watched as the lorry lumbered down the lane to the main road, its roof just brushing the branches of the trees along the track. The leaves were beginning to take on some autumn colour. The foundry had just collected some pieces which were ready to be cast into bronze. He had recently finished three sculptures – two commissions and another one of a pregnant woman. He had, of course, used his daughter as a model during the summer holidays and he had hugely enjoyed talking to her during the sittings. Her happiness in her marriage, pregnancy and job were a joy to him.

He went through to his adjoining cottage and put the kettle on before switching on his computer. With a cup of coffee, he sat down to check his e-mails. As he glanced through the five new incoming ones, his son's name leapt out at him. David – at last! The jolt of relief was as strong as if a charge of electricity had passed through him. Theo eagerly read through the words that ended many months of silence.

Dear Theo,

You must wonder why I've not been in touch for so long. The truth is that I've been living up in a remote village in the mountains four days' walk from the nearest town. I've been staying with a family, learning the language and working with some of the local men to build a new school here. The children are delightful, often timid but eager to learn. There is so little money and although many of the materials have been donated, there are no funds for labour, so the construction is done by villagers after they finish their usual work and by two volunteers, of which I'm one. The other is a gap-year student who had been trekking around the area and turned up here. We are both committed to the project which is now nearing completion. I wanted to stay in one place and had no inclination to leave until a week ago. I've found living in a small community, many miles from civilisation, is hugely satisfying – and cleansing. I've been dog tired most of the time with all the physical work and the altitude, but I love it. In a modest way I think I've made a difference and helped the local people. You should see my hands! They're calloused and scratched, but my arm muscles are impressive! Ari, the other foreigner here, has twice walked out and had a week off in the town. On both occasions, I asked him to send you an e-mail just telling you I was alright and not to worry about me. He was a bit vague (it might be the 'weed' he smokes) and gave me the impression he had done this. I've now discovered that he didn't bother, so I hope you've all not been too concerned by the lack of any communication.

I am well – and moving on again. I'm heading across to the Americas and have a working passage aboard a ship, so I'll let you know when I'm there, though it may take a few weeks. Thanks for your e-mailed letters – you are so wonderful at keeping in touch, even when your wayward son never responds. I am so happy about the news that Kate and Andrew are to have a baby – do give them my love. It was good to hear what's happening about Homeward House and I'm grateful that you are taking all the decisions. My earlier life seems so remote and almost irrelevant – sorry! Perhaps I've finally got things in perspective. I admit that life, at times, isn't great – it's exhausting, often lonely and occasionally risky. Anyhow, I've developed an appetite for wandering and want to meet more people and see more places. Time to sign off. Don't give up on me – I may come home one day when it's right to do so. I love you – and miss you.

David.

Not as much as I miss you, thought Theo. It was two years since David had departed. He forwarded his son's e-mail to his daughter, who would want to hear the news that her brother was alright even though he had no plans to come home. He was reminded that another of his protégés had contacted him to say that she was returning to see them all. She was due to arrive tomorrow.

Some weeks back Layla had sent him a triumphant message, saying she had finished her diploma, her work had now been assessed and she had passed. She was planning to come and stay for a few weeks before going abroad to live cheaply and paint portraits; she would decide whether to continue studying fine art to degree level after deferring a year. She had little money but had acquired a tent and was wondering if she might camp on the land at Homeward House. He had responded promptly, telling her that Josh also had turned up, had got some temporary work in town and was staying in his old room in the abandoned hotel staff quarters. If it suited her, she could take one of the other rooms and share the kitchen and living room. She had shared accommodation before with Josh so Theo had no worry about suggesting it without consulting him. They would have no rent to pay as the whole area was a building site. If she didn't mind the noise and disruption of the construction work during the day, she was welcome.

Layla had been swift to accept his kind offer and would be arriving the next day which was a Sunday. A friend called Peter would be giving her a lift. Theo had arranged a picnic lunch to celebrate her return and had invited Josh, Kate and Andrew, Jamie and his family, and Maria to join him at the barn. His children, his waifs and strays were returning to the fold and he was pleased. But the future was uncertain for many of them.

Seventy miles away in a remote, disused quarry, Jakob leaned over the open boot of a stolen car. He had trigged up a ten gallon tank on two blocks of wood which were bolted down, and had drilled two holes – one through the side of the tank about an inch from its base and another hole through the base of the boot, near the bumper. He inserted a plastic pipe with washers into the hole in the tank and to this he had attached a lever ball valve which was also bolted down. A pipe was fitted from the outlet of this valve through the hole in the car boot base.

Jacob straightened up to ease his back. Now he had to bolt a piece of wood on to the lever and drill a hole in the free end. Finally he tied a length of rope through this hole and passed the free end forward to the front of the car. He closed the boot and got into the driver's seat, checking that the empty five gallon plastic jerrycan was on the passenger seat, together with the binoculars. He then drove to the nearest garage.

As he put diesel in the car's tank and then filled the jerrycan, he thought about his plan. It had been easy to figure out the password that Kate used for her e-mails – the one word on her mind day and night: "Andrew". The first piece of information he obtained was about her brother and his whereabouts and this had been passed on to Ator. Five days ago he had hacked in and read about Josh's return and Layla's proposed visit. He discovered that a Sunday meal had been arranged at the sculptor's barn for all the family. This presented him with the ideal opportunity to carry out Ator's orders. He had already made a reconnaissance trip to the target area and he would drive there tomorrow morning. He screwed on the top of the jerrycan, paid up and left.

In the evening, having poured the contents of the plastic can into the larger tank in the boot, he drove to another garage and repeated the process. His preparations were complete so he returned to his motel and slept.

Theo had set up a table on the stone flags outside his barn in the warm September sunshine. His nephew, Jamie, was playing with his two boys who were kicking a ball about in the field below while his wife, Penny, was sitting at the table.

Layla, who had arrived the day before, looked about her with a sigh of contentment. "You can see for miles. I'm so glad to be back here. I've missed you all."

Kate, wearing a straw hat, was leaning back in her chair with Andrew beside her, his hand in hers lying on her prominent belly. "The baby's due at the end of October," she said to Penny. "Only six weeks to go."

Theo looked delighted to have his young people around him, and turned to Layla. "I hope it's alright living so close to the building work. Josh seems to cope with it."

"It's fine. He left on his bike to go into town and collect Maria before you picked me up. I'm surprised they haven't arrived yet."

"Josh is always late," said Kate with a laugh. "Nothing to worry about."

"Obviously the lady has relented," said Andrew. "He's got her back on his bike."

"What Josh really wants is to get a ring on her finger." Layla was surprised by the determination Josh had demonstrated in his pursuit of the woman he loved and wistfully regretted that David had shown no such devotion to her.

Talk turned to Homeward House and Andrew put them in the picture on the progress of the work. "We're hoping to have the roof back on the existing structure before the autumn rain kicks in, though it will be months before the new building is ready for that." Everyone was aware that Andrew's drive and expertise were vital to the project.

When Kate relayed the latest news from her brother, Layla kept silent, noticing that Theo was watching her with concern. She gave him a bright smile.

The sound of a bike on the lower road was heard and soon they could see the dust as Josh negotiated his way up the steep track. Theo rose to his feet to greet them as they appeared round the corner of the barn. Maria looked somewhat wind-blown but happy with an enigmatic expression on her face. Josh was ebullient as ever, flashing his teeth in a wide smile.

"I have delivered my lovely Maria safe and sound. Doesn't she look beautiful?"

"Good to see you, Maria," Theo said as he gave her a kiss on the cheek, "and you too, Josh. What kept you?" He anticipated the answer from the triumphant expression on the man's face and the mysterious smile on the woman's.

Josh put his arm round Maria in a very possessive way. "If you really want to know, we stopped at the bridge and walked down to the river bank where on my knees I proposed to this lovely woman for the seventh time. I'm happy to say that Maria has just done me the honour of accepting my hand in marriage. At last." He bent down and gave her a long kiss. Behind his head, Maria waggled her fingers and the ring glinted in the sunlight.

A chorus of delighted shouts greeted this announcement; everyone except Kate got to their feet, and much hugging and hand-shaking ensued.

"I used to dream of a place where peace reigned, where there was lots to eat and a pure woman who would love me," said Josh. "Now I've found it. And her."

"So what made you decide to finally accept this reprobate, Maria?" Jamie asked.

Before Maria had time to think of an answer, Josh spun round, blurting out, "That's the other bit of good news. I've got the job. Isn't it amazing? I've made a vow never to drink to excess. So I've fulfilled the criteria. She had to say yes!"

"That's not so, Josh," protested Maria with a smile.

"The truth is she's been infatuated with me for ages but just wouldn't admit it," said Josh, grinning at everyone. "She's not so besotted with my bike, though, and I've promised I'll get a car when I start to earn a decent wage."

Kate giggled as Josh bent down to kiss her forehead. "I can't believe you're going to be a married man."

"And in the future a father as well – I want lots of kids. They can play with yours," Josh said impetuously. He blew a kiss at his fiancée. "Maria, are you happy with this plan?"

"Have you decided when the wedding will be?" asked Theo

"As soon as possible. I can't tolerate any delay. I've waited too long. If that's alright with you, dearest heart?" Josh asked looking into Maria's eyes. "You do love me extravagantly, don't you?"

"I do, darling Josh."

"That's alright, then. Let's eat. I'm as hungry as can be."

Some hours later Maria insisted that Josh drive her home so she could tell her mother about the engagement. They left, Josh descending slowly and carefully on his bike with his beloved cargo. Everyone strolled round the barn to the driveway whilst Jamie and Penny called for their sons who were collecting conkers. Layla refused the offer of a lift from Andrew and Kate, saying she would walk back down the hill in the sunshine. Theo kissed his daughter, saying, "Take care and rest up for the next few weeks. You'll be in my thoughts." Andrew helped Kate gently into the car and reassured his father-in-law that he would do all he could to ensure that his active wife didn't do too much. Then they drove off.

On the road below, about half a mile away, Jakob got swiftly into his car, throwing the binoculars on to the passenger seat. He pulled into the narrow road from the grass verge where he had been waiting for over an hour and drove off quickly in the direction of the town. It was a secluded country road; only one car had passed him about twenty minutes earlier and Josh and his girlfriend on a bike five minutes before. About four miles further, at a place in the road just before a sharp left hand bend, where there were some trees on the left and a ditch on the right, Jakob slowed down and picking up the rope from the rear of the car that was lying slack on the central armrest, he gave a sharp tug. This swivelled the lever on the valve a quarter turn and opened the pipe from which ten gallons of diesel gushed out below and behind his rear wheels. He could hear the engine of the other car getting closer along the road behind him as he turned the corner and accelerated away, leaving a dangerous pool of diesel flooding across the road. He would like to have stopped and viewed what had happened from a vantage point but knew he needed to get away fast. In a few hours he would dump the stolen car and disappear. He would easily discover what happened.

Kate was happily thinking about Josh and Maria, when Andrew started to brake for the corner ahead. He caught sight of the black shadow across the road in the shade of the trees and thought it was water – perhaps the nearby river had broken its bank. He braked steadily, conscious of Kate's condition, and then gasped with horror as he hit the liquid and the smell of diesel filled his nostrils.

With a shriek Kate bent forward covering her belly with her arms as Andrew tried to keep control and failed. The car skidded, spun round in an arc and slid backwards into the ditch on the far side of the corner. There was a jolting thud as the car came to a sudden stop with the front angled up into the road. Andrew recovered first from the jarring impact and, frantic with worry, leaned across to his wife asking if she was hurt. Kate whimpering and white-faced, whispered she was not in pain. The car had not been travelling fast on impact and miraculously the two occupants were unhurt though badly shaken

Andrew climbed out, ignoring the pain in his neck, and within a minute he had helped Kate out and put her gently down on the bank. She was shaking with shock and they needed help fast. Then he heard another car in the distance coming down the road. Running back along the verge to try and warn the driver, he waved his hands and shouted as a big Land Rover came towards him, slowed and stopped yards from the diesel spill. To Andrew's immense relief, it was Jamie and his family.

Within half an hour, Penny had driven Andrew and Kate to the hospital in the Land Rover, whilst Jamie waited for the police, who blocked off the road. Soon afterward the fire engine arrived to disperse the diesel. The police had their suspicions that the spill was too big to be a mere accident but resolved to check with local farmers and tractors. Theo had been contacted and had driven into town. Andrew was suffering from bruising and whiplash; Kate, almost hysterical with fear for her baby, had gone into premature labour.

One evening two weeks later, Theo, Andrew and Layla were sitting at the kitchen table in Andrew and Kate's small house. Andrew was looking grey with fatigue.

Theo looked grim as Andrew explained that the police had contacted him and confirmed that the diesel spill was a malicious, probably random, act on the part of someone who had now disappeared. "I told them that as far as we know there's no-one who has a grudge against us and who wishes us harm. They say the culprit may never be identified. I'll take him apart if I ever discover who he is."

Theo took a deep breath and said in a measured voice, "I ought to tell you that there may be someone who does want to harm our family." The others looked at him in surprise as he went on. "I'd been hoping I wouldn't have to tell you about this but now I think I must, because we need to be vigilant. Over the past few years some bad things have happened which I know to be the work of someone who has hated me for a very long while."

"Who is this person?" said Andrew with a savage look.

Theo leaned forward, putting his hand on Andrew's arm, and said calmly, "Kate needs to hear this too. Layla, would you see if she can join us?"

Layla got to her feet and quietly left the room. Two minutes later, the two women returned and both sat down at the table, Kate beside her husband.

Kate sighed with weariness. "Nathan's finally dropped off. He's so tiny but he's feeding alright. It's so wonderful to be home at last – the hospital was so noisy."

Theo had to rein in his anger. His grandson had undergone a traumatic birth and weighed just four pounds. Kate had a tough time but remained in hospital whilst her premature son was in the special care baby unit. Andrew, who spent many days going back and forth to the hospital whilst his neck was in a collar, had collected his wife and baby that afternoon, and Layla had come round to help prepare the house and give her friend some support.

"Dear one," Theo began looking with concern at his daughter, "I don't want to worry you unduly but the time has come for me to tell you a bit of family history. You're not too tired?"

"No, Daddy, I'm just glad to be here with all the ones I love most, and with our child," she said turning to stroke Andrew's cheek.

Theo turned to Layla. "It may surprise you to know that David and Kate are adopted."

Layla raised her eyebrows as Kate said, "I've known all my life – but I never think about it. Daddy has always been my father. I did tell you, Andrew, some while back."

"You may have wondered what happened to their mother," Theo continued. "Kate and David are the children of Rachel's sister and her husband, who both tragically died in a car accident when David was aged three and Kate was only six months old. There was some suspicion at the time that it was not accidental but nothing was ever proved. Their parents had been very close and dear friends of mine and there was an understanding between us that if anything should happen to either of them, I would be guardian to their children. Rachel and I debated what to do and it was decided that I should adopt her nephew and niece and that she would help me bring them up. Rachel and her husband had their own children, Jamie and his sister Louise, and so Kate and David lived with me. Rachel helped me so much whilst the children were young and before she was widowed."

"That's why we spent so much time on the farm with our cousins," said Kate. "We had a glorious childhood – we lived in Homeward House but spent a lot of time running free at the farm. I can't think why I was so keen to go and leave it all," she muttered.

"As I recall you were much influenced by a couple of friends at college who persuaded you that freedom was to be found elsewhere, doing alternative things in other countries," Theo said gently. "I've had my suspicions about who put them up to it."

"It was *my* decision to leave, Daddy."

"As it was your brother's. Far horizons are very tempting. But you came back and now you are a wife and a mother." Theo went on, without looking at Layla, "David may return too. I hope he does."

"The story goes much further back than all this, way before you were all born, when I was in charge of a large enterprise. A man called Ator once worked for me in a senior position – he was clever, single-minded and industrious – but he became self-important and greedy for power. Conspiring to take over my job, he was disruptive and managed to get some of my employees to side with him. This plan didn't work, so he tried to destroy all I was working for through dishonest financial transactions which feathered his nest but undermined the stability of the whole company. When I discovered this, I confronted Ator, fired him and called the police. Trying to elude arrest, he stole my car to escape. But he drove too fast, had an accident and tragically killed an innocent person. The vehicle was engulfed by flames but he got out alive, though his face was horribly burned. He spent some time in hospital and an even longer time in prison. He has been out for some years, and I believe he has enlisted others to help him build up an organisation which generates big money from criminal activities. I believe he lives in near darkness because his eyes were so badly damaged. He probably blames me for his disfigurement and wants revenge." His listeners were staring at him in dismay.

"He is careful and covers his tracks, using others to threaten those I love. His agents were responsible for some of my Kate's woes whilst she was away from home. They caused the accidents at the hotel and incited others to wreck Kate's and Layla's party and trash their house. Sergio was no doubt one of them, particularly given the fact that the hotel was destroyed by arson. Branded by flames, Ator often uses fire as his weapon. The earlier blaze at my barn was no accident either."

Kate had turned pale and Andrew's craggy face looked grim. Theo rose to his feet, and putting a hand on her shoulder and looking down on them all, said, "Don't be afraid. Trust me. I know all about him and though he's trying to destroy my world and harm my precious children, I will not let him."

There was silence round the table as everyone realised there had been a long campaign of malice against the family.

"Ator takes pleasure when others suffer. But his power is waning. He is sick and has fewer agents to carry out his plans," Theo said calmly. "He smoulders with hatred and we still need to be vigilant."

Kate shakily got to her feet, saying she wanted to see if Nathan was sleeping alright, and Andrew went with her.

When Jakob heard that the couple had survived relatively unscathed, he was annoyed but strangely relieved. He had become less comfortable with these strikes against a family he was beginning to respect. Now he had met Ator, he detested the man so much that he might risk disloyalty. He had risen up the pecking order and was now trusted enough to be admitted into Ator's bunker-like office and to report in person rather than by telephone. He had known that the evil man had some sort of physical deformity but the first sight of his face was still a shock. Ator had been horribly disfigured by burns.

Jakob's enthusiasm for obeying orders and harassing the target family was decreasing. He was also discovering where Ator was vulnerable and how his operations could be undermined. He continued to dream about a life free of bondage. His thoughts turned to Theo, someone who held his family together without coercion and threats.

The new project had lost momentum because two of the main players were tired and preoccupied. The building contractors had been working for three months and needed constant input and monitoring, but the architect was on site less often and had missed a couple of meetings. He had to give time to his wife and their infant son.

Theo was worried about Kate, who seemed to have lost her enthusiasm about the rebuilding of the family house and hotel. A few weeks before the traumatic accident that caused the premature arrival of her son, Kate had confided to him her dream for the future of Homeward House. She had said, "We have so much and there are many people out there with so little. We could create a retreat for families or orphans or people who have problems and need respite care in a peaceful place. If David decides to live his life elsewhere, we don't have to run it as a hotel. It could be a holiday residential centre for families and young people. Andrew would be in charge of the buildings. Josh could be the caterer, Maria the resident nurse. I could organise lessons, and Layla, if she stays, might give art classes. And we could all live there together – there'll be lots of space." Theo had smiled at, but approved of, her idealism.

He had just been speaking to his son-in-law on the telephone. "The baby blues have gone on for too long," said Andrew, sounding weary. "Kate can't cope well and lacks confidence in her ability to look after Nathan. It's unlike her to be so negative. She says she's tired and wants to sleep, and seems disappointed that motherhood is not as wonderful as she'd imagined it to be." Theo was sympathetic and had given words of encouragement.

Ten minutes later, he was telephoning Maria, who was aware of the problem and said she thought that Kate might be suffering from postnatal depression and would need much family support. "Andrew has only recently recovered from his whiplash injury and is now up at night trying to be with Kate who is reluctant to feed the baby. He's working hard with the huge responsibility for the hotel rebuild but he's getting very overtired and stressed because he thinks Kate does not love her son enough and this might harm the child."

Theo agreed that Kate needed support and Andrew was under a lot of pressure; he told Maria he would help as much as he could. Maria warned him that Kate might be unaware of why she felt this way and that she should see a doctor. When he had set this in motion, Theo wrote to his son and gave him the news, adding that the family were in need of his help and asking him to consider returning home and becoming involved in the new project.

Josh and Maria were married on a windy November day with friends and family around them. It was a quiet ceremony but a happy one. Maria's mother was now seriously ill and wished to see them married before she died. Devoted to Josh, she was pleased that her daughter and son-in-law were going to live with her. Maria was nursing her almost full time, having taken leave from her job. Josh was walking tall with a career, a home and an adored wife.

At a celebratory meal in a restaurant afterwards, Theo leaned back in his chair, emanating goodwill but inwardly apprehensive. His family was growing: he had 'adopted' Maria long ago and now her husband Josh had become part of the family, in the same way that Andrew had joined when he married Kate. But his daughter and her husband were going through a bad patch. Kate, normally resilient, was acutely depressed and Andrew had to take time off work to help look after the baby. David was still overseas and Theo was worried about the people he was mixing with at the new workplace he had mentioned in his latest email. He was concerned, too, for Layla who was sitting beside him, her eyes troubled.

Layla had been unsettled all autumn. She was undecided whether to continue her fine art studies and was taking a year off to travel and paint. She seemed vague about her future plans and had told Theo that Peter, the tutor in her college, had asked her to marry him. When asked if she loved him, Layla had shaken her head and said she wasn't yet ready for a husband, a home and security.

Theo turned to Layla and lowered his voice, saying, "I've heard from David. He's now in South America, where he's got a job. Unusually, he's given us the name of the city he's living in and the bar where he works. He seems to be in no hurry to return home. Which is a pity."

Layla took a sip of wine and said, "David's a loner. Since learning about the hateful Ator, I'm fearful for you all, especially your son. He's far away. I hope he's become more streetwise."

At this point Josh stood up and delivered a short speech. He was eager to depart with his lovely bride and soon afterwards the couple left for a few days in a hotel. A nurse had been arranged to take care of Maria's mother. Two hours later, Layla also departed, but with little intention of returning any time soon. Theo had assured her that she was adopted into his family and would always be loved and welcomed home.

But Layla was restless. She would move on to search for what her siblings already had – love.

14

The bar was in a seedy area of town, the décor was tawdry and the clientele dubious. David felt dispirited as he wiped down the bar and put away the glasses. Soon the evening customers would start coming in to 'El Molino' and then he would be on his feet in a smoke-filled atmosphere for eight long hours. He had arrived in the country strong and fit from his months of physical work on the building project in the mountains and his working passage aboard a small merchant ship. But for the past two months he had been working long and late hours in the bar in the centre of a huge city. The twilight in which he toiled depressed him. It would soon be time to move on but first he needed to earn enough money for the journey north. He had felt fulfilled working in a small community with people he respected but now he found himself working with people he did not like, for customers whose way of life he did not approve. A job had been hard to find without a work permit but this job provided a small room in a nearby 'hostal' and he had needed somewhere to stay. It was a means to an end – to enable him to travel on.

Agustin, the owner of the bar, strode in, barked a few orders at him and disappeared into the back office. David grasped that the other barman would be late for work and he had to manage the first hour on his own. To get this job David had been obliged to do a rapid recall of basic Spanish which he had once learned years before. He heard the two waiters, Vincente and Tomás, arrive at the back entrance and chat as they put on their clean white shirts. Agustin's widowed sister was already seated at the till at one end of the bar. She was the cashier and all money was handed to her by the barman or waiters. She said little and her sullen pinched face did nothing to enliven David's mood.

He began to fill the beer fridge with bottles. As he did this familiar task, he was reminded about the many stock-takes he had done in his hotel and his thoughts turned to home, thousands of miles away. The day before he had received one of his father's regular e-mails and read that Kate and Andrew's son was called Nathan and that Josh and Maria had recently got married. He found it strange that Maria, to whom he had once been engaged, was now married – and to Josh, someone whose background was so alien to hers. Most surprising of all was Theo's remark that he considered both Josh and Layla as 'adopted' into the family which already included Andrew, his son-in law and Maria, who had long been regarded as a daughter. There had been no news of Layla, although she had been at the wedding and then left the country. Theo had attached a photo of the small wedding. Glimpsing Layla's face in the background, David firmly repressed the sense of loss.

The bar opened for the evening and David had no further time to think. After a couple of hours, the other barman, Ignacio, arrived mumbling his apologies, and David managed to sit down and grab something to eat from the trays of tapas that were available.

Towards midnight, Valentina and Isidora came in and sat at a small table next to the bar, arranging their skirts to casually reveal their legs to the drinkers and drunks perched on stools at the counter. The waiters were busy outside so David served them their usual cocktails and flashed them a smile. They were prostitutes but Agustin allowed them in as they were attractive, entertaining, and because customers liked them. Isidora was a slim, dark-skinned girl with short, dyed blonde hair and an alluring smile. Valentina had more generous curves, a pair of magnificent eyes and a cloud of tangled dark hair. Her mellow voice and warm laughter reminded David of Layla, who had once been in the same profession. He knew from Valentina that coercion and poverty had pushed her in a direction she hadn't chosen and didn't like. The same had been true of Layla, who had managed to break free. He wondered where she was now.

There was a sound of laughter and cheering. Joaquin had come into the bar with two of his gang, who accompanied him as bodyguards. Most of those who frequented the bar were associated with his organisation. Those who had reason to fear him did not choose to drink there. His scheming eyes darted round the crowd checking out the clientele and when he saw Valentina, Joaquin cut a path through the room towards her. For a fleshy man he moved with surprising agility and reaching the table, he sat down and bestowed on her a jubilant smile that had a hint of menace, whilst he placed a large hand possessively on her knee. The woman had told David that she found Joaquin repulsive but had to pretend to be attracted to the thug because her pimp had given her instructions to be compliant. A working girl had to oblige her client and her protector so she gave a throaty laugh and put her arm round his neck. David quietly served the important customer his usual drink and judiciously kept silent. He'd soon discovered that it was unwise to be too talkative in this bar; silence was safer.

Valentina and Joaquin moved to sit at an outside table and Isidora followed when Agustin joined them from his office behind the bar. Isidora and Agustin had an 'understanding' and David had learned to be discreet because anything he did or said to one of them would be passed on to the other. Within the hour both men had left with their women. The staff at El Molino toiled on into the early hours and it was almost 4 am before the bar closed and David fell on to his hard mattress and into an exhausted sleep. In the morning he vaguely remembered dreaming about a dark-haired woman – Layla or perhaps Valentina. It troubled him that he couldn't quite recall which one it was. The sun slanted in through the narrow window. It was too hot to draw the threadbare curtain. He craved for a cooler climate and lay there thinking about his trek through the mountains a few months back, about the grandeur, the space and the immensity of silence. As the sunlight played on the stained wall of his room, he recalled the clarity of the light that had shone through the unglazed window on to the floor of the small dwelling where he had spent a month with Rafael.

Soon after arriving in South America, he had set off trekking in the mountains and, wandering from the track one afternoon, had encountered the old man collecting water at a stream. The hermit invited him to share a meal and take a night's rest with him. The place had a stark beauty and the man had a wise face. So he extended his stay.

Rafael had lived all alone for years in the sierra with a few goats and the occasional visitor. David contributed the meagre rations he had been carrying and they ate simply and sparingly. He tried to communicate in his rusty Spanish, though words were often unnecessary. The old man would work silently at his small vegetable patch or tend his animals, or sit for hours not speaking, just contemplating the solitude, content with his own thoughts. At first this silence made his guest feel awkward but within a few days the long gaps between the halting conversations became comfortable and then desirable. Rafael radiated contentment and demonstrated to his visitor that true freedom was in acceptance. David gained quiet satisfaction in helping the old man mend the roof before the wind and wet weather came, or dig over another patch of the rocky, hard ground. His restlessness decreased but he could not supress his obsession with travelling and his urge to see beyond the next horizon.

He left when he felt there were no more jobs he could do that would justify him sharing the few resources the place offered. He would never forget Rafael's lined and weather-beaten face and those calm eyes that followed him down the track as he walked away. The hermit had been an inspiration.

Within a week he had arrived in a huge city, and looked for work to save the money he would need to travel onwards. Less dry and dusty than the harsh altiplano, the city was vibrant and enjoyable. His Spanish improved and with better communication he made a few friends and shared some meals. The majority of inhabitants worked long hours for poor pay and in their midst were darker elements of society whose occupations were less honest and more lucrative. Here was extortion, violence and hatred. The city gangs were involved in it and vied with each other for supremacy and the rich pickings that protection rackets afforded. The only job he could find brought David into contact with these scum.

Someone rapped on his door and called his name. He got off the bed and opened the door. It was Luis, an unsavoury character who controlled three hookers, including Valentina. David had no idea why he might want to talk to him. The man spoke in Spanish: "You keep away from Valentina. I see you talking with her in El Molino. Don't speak to her anymore."

"That's crazy. I'm the barman – I work there."

"She talk to you. I see she like you, pretty boy."

"We chat in the bar sometimes. She has no interest in me." David tried to sound unconcerned.

Luis pointed a long, grimy finger at him. "Don't mess with my whores. They have no time for friends – they are working girls. Stay away or you won't be pretty boy for long." Luis spat on the ground at his feet and, with a sneer, turned and ran down the stairs.

David stared after him. He was attracted to Valentina, he had to admit. Was his interest in her that obvious? He resented the slimy pimp's threats but knew he had to tread carefully, especially as Joaquin was one of Valentina's clients.

And he had arranged already to meet Valentina at midday.

It was after 5 pm when David emerged from the small hotel where they had spent the afternoon. Valentina had been flirting with him for weeks and had finally suggested that they meet up "to get to know each other better". She told him she was disgusted by the men she was obliged to have sex with. David was the man she desired so he would not have to pay. He had resisted until now when, flattered by her attention and aching for some intimacy to dispel his loneliness, in a moment of folly he succumbed to temptation and arranged an assignation.

It was a sordid encounter, ensuing from her desperation for affection and his need for a woman. They used each other. In the daylight and unclothed, Valentina looked much older and her plump, dimpled flesh slightly repelled him even before they lay down on the bed. Afterwards she stroked his cheek and said that her small son, who lived with her family in the country, had eyes the same colour as his. She kissed David, something she never did with clients. He had to stop himself from recoiling. There was only one woman whose kisses he had cherished; Valentina's meant nothing to him.

When he had satisfied his appetite, David felt sickened by what he had done. There was no love between them and his skin itched with shame. She sold her body for money and he was no better. He burned with self-loathing.

David left the hotel first, as he had to start his shift at the bar at 6 pm when Ignacio went home. He emerged into the narrow street and carefully looking both ways he set off. At the corner a man was buying a newspaper from a street vendor and, averting his head, David ran down the street and jumped on a bus. Returning to his room he had a shower to try to wash his sweat and her sticky perfume off his skin but he couldn't wash away the stain that darkened his mind. Not only did he feel unclean but he felt uneasy. As he walked to work, he hoped that the two women would not call in tonight because he doubted that Valentina could be discreet. What if Joaquin found out? Fear sank her claws into his mind.

He had to leave the city. He would make careful preparations and then take off. Until then he had to keep the lid on his wretched mistake. And on his own self-disgust.

David quietly packed his kit into a rucksack, but hesitated as to what to do with his passport and money. He decided to conceal them in the rucksack which he had arranged to leave at the house of some friends – a married couple who lived in another part of the city, from where he planned to depart by bus early the next morning. Carrying them on his person at night would be more risky. Taking a final look round his room he locked the door and he surreptitiously left the building with the rucksack. It was the afternoon siesta and few people were about as he made his way across the sweltering city. At one point he had a prickling sensation that someone was following him and he turned round, but saw only a slight, dark-haired woman, her back to him, watching two urchins playing in the street.

When he arrived, Andrea was at home with her children whilst her husband, Raul, was at work. Carefully stowing the rucksack under the stairs for him, she gave David a cold drink before he left. His face betrayed anxiety about his clandestine departure.

"Take care," she said in Spanish. "We will expect you later and Raul will take you to the bus station at dawn." As he left the small house, a taxi cruised past with opaque windows and David made a mental effort to stop himself from imagining threats. He was unsure if it was wise to go back to the bar but he did not want to lose a week's pay, due to him after his shift that night. Before then he had to see Valentina and say goodbye. Reluctance, heavy as a stone, dragged him down but he could not leave without telling her he was going. He longed for the freedom of the road where he would not feel threatened or compromised.

He arrived at the café where they had arranged to meet, went in and sat at a small table – he did not want them to be seen in the street. Feeling edgy, he ordered a beer and shortly afterwards Valentina breezed in, hair flying, lips pouting, to meet her handsome foreigner. He got to his feet and she reached up and gave him a kiss. He ordered coffee but she wanted a drink. They sat down and she started chatting about a strange foreign woman she had met the day before. David was not listening, wondering how to tell her he was leaving.

He put his hand on her plump arm and she stopped speaking in mid-sentence. Taking a deep breath, he began in his simple Spanish, "Valentina – I have made a terrible mistake in letting myself become involved with you. I like you very much but I've made no commitment to you and I feel in danger by continuing our friendship. I have to leave."

"Please stay here, David. I promise soon to leave the city. We can be together, live a normal life. Don't leave me," she pleaded with tears in her eyes.

David tried to explain he felt guilty for misleading her. "Valentina, you are an attractive woman and I was flattered by your attention and your invitation to sleep with you. If I gave you the impression that I loved you, I regret it very much."

"You men are all the same," she said bitterly, folding her arms. "You do not care if you hurt us women. You take what you want and you leave. It is the story of my life."

"You must leave. I know I've hurt you and I'm sorry. But Luis has already threatened me and should Joaquin discover our affair then I'm dead."

"I only slept with you once. This is not an affair." She prodded his chest with a scarlet fingernail. "You used me. Now you are frightened."

210

"I've treated you badly, Valentina. Please let's end it now and remain friends."

"When are you going?" She had accepted the inevitable. "Have you told Agustin?"

"I plan to leave tomorrow and I've told no-one except you and a couple of friends."

"Keep it that way. I won't come into the bar tonight. I'll say goodbye now." They both stood up. She leaned across and gave him a lingering kiss, hoping to make him change his mind, but when he did not respond, she tossed her head angrily and walked out, calling over her shoulder, "Adios, gringo." David felt he had destroyed any illusion she might still have that were any kind and trustworthy men in the world.

A few minutes later he left and headed back to his last evening working in the bar. In a few hours he'd be gone. He was running away – again.

It was after 3 am. David cleaned the bar after the last customers left. Vincente and Tomás had left and the door was now locked. Agustin had been in earlier for a couple of hours and paid his staff, and had gone to whichever gambling club he frequented on a Friday. His sister, who had been on her cashier stool most of the evening, silently removed the cash from the till and put it into the safe in the office which she then locked. The woman lived in an apartment in the next street and whilst she picked up her bag and coat, David hurriedly pushed a brief note to his boss under the office door. He felt bad about leaving him in the lurch but the man would soon find another barman. He shut off the lights and they left the premises, Agustin's sister carefully locking up. It was his usual habit to see her safely home before returning to his own place nearby, but when she had disappeared into the door of her apartment block, he turned away and headed off in another direction. He was not going back.

Arriving at the plaza where there were still a few people around, David was relieved there was no-one he knew and set off to Raul and Andrea's house, along the same route he had walked earlier. He felt slightly jittery for no particular reason. He started to relax after a few minutes, until he turned into another road and was horrified to see Luis lurking outside La Barra de la Noche, a night club, talking to another man. David darted down a badly lit side street, hoping that he had not been seen.

He ran swiftly, his heart pounding, and soon became aware of running feet behind him. Some way ahead, he saw a car pull up and three people get out, a woman and two men who began to walk towards him. David stopped, panic flooding through him: Valentina had asked two friends to punish him for deserting her. Then his pursuers caught up with him and he spun round to confront them. A knife glinted in the dim light of an upstairs window and David, unarmed and suddenly angry, prepared to fight for his life. One of his assailants leapt at him giving him a huge punch that sent him sprawling on the ground. He heard Luis's spiteful laughter and raised an arm to defend himself from the knife the man held poised over him. There were shouts from down the street and as Luis glanced up, David quickly rolled to one side to miss the downward thrust. A searing pain in his shoulder told him he had not been quick enough to avoid the blade. He could hear running feet approaching and knew he had no chance. A savage kick in the ribs was followed by a stunning blow to his head, and his world exploded into blackness.

In another part of the world, Theo was in his studio watching the dark clouds eat up the blue sky. It was morning and he was thinking about his children. Kate was severely depressed, Andrew was exhausted, and he ached with longing for David who was alone and out of touch. He could not protect his son from the wild world. A premonition engulfed him that, thousands of miles away, David was in mortal danger. He closed his eyes, willing his son strength to cope with whatever he encountered. He stood there for an hour focussing on him, trying to dispel the blackness and let the light break through.

Then he walked through to his cottage and sat down to e-mail his son:

Dearest David,

I have been thinking of you and feel apprehensive that you may be in a dark place. I hope you will find protection and come though stronger than before. Do not be afraid to ask for help – there is no offence in weakness and no shame in admitting it. Keep positive and keep relating to people. We all need each other.

Regarding news from home, another week has passed and my grandson Nathan is growing well – he is now a sturdy baby who smiles at us all when he is not crying for his next meal! He is much loved. However, Kate is overtired and often feels low. Andrew is overstretched because he is hugely involved in the building project and also needs to give a lot of time and support to Kate. Homeward House is rising from the ashes and much work is needed to ensure that everything is in place for the new family enterprise when the building works are finally completed in a few months' time. Josh is still working as catering manager at the school and Maria has found nursing work. I had a letter from Layla the other day – she tells me she is painting portraits and planning a new venture.

I have completed two large commissions, which have both been cast into bronze and will soon be in situ. I have now begun work on a sculpture that I hope will grace the gardens of the new Homeward House. The family persuaded me to do this and though I am enthusiastic, I'm not showing my maquette to anyone. The design will be my surprise.

Wherever you are, I think of you continually and love you deeply. I hope you will come back one day – when you are ready.

Theo

That Saturday afternoon, whilst her son slept in his cot, Kate forced herself to send a short e-mail to her brother. She had her misgivings about the new project and did not mention the waves of black despair that washed over her from time to time, but gave him some news about Nathan. She ended by saying:

> Dad was so pleased to hear news of you. It makes a change to know which corner of the world you are in. Why are you working in a bar earning a pittance? Come home – we have a plans for the new Homeward House that we want you to become involved in. I could use your help and experience. It's been so long. Nathan is beginning to say things and he wants to meet his uncle. Haven't you had enough of travelling yet?

In the evening of the same day, Josh, who rarely sent e-mails, decided to send a few words to his old employer:

> Hi David, long time no see. I never thought I'd settle down – marriage was not on my agenda. It's so life-changing. And so sweet. Cannot imagine how Maria puts up with me. Your dad has been such a great encourager and I now have a career and a home. I might even have children. My life's coming good. Why don't you keep in touch or, better still, come back? Your family miss you massively.

> Josh

That night, as he sat in a dreary hotel bedroom tapping into his laptop, Jakob received a message back from one of Ator's overseas contacts.

> Word has it that the gringo who worked at the El Molino bar was attacked in a dark street and left to die. There was no need for me to arrange an accident. The fool got involved with the crime boss's whore and was punished in the usual way. I assume the matter is closed.

Jakob recalled David throwing him out of his hotel and was not unduly bothered that the man had met a lonely and painful death. He deleted the e-mail and moved on to the next.

The following morning, bells tolled out around the city for the Sunday mass. The sound of them penetrated into the conscious minds of those awake in their beds, infiltrated into the dreams of the sleeping and, perhaps, some of the patients lying unconscious in the city hospital.

A young man who had been there since the early hours of Saturday morning stirred for the first time since his admission. The light streamed in through the window but because the man's eyes were bandaged, he remained in darkness. Pain had arrived with consciousness and he groaned. A nurse, who was checking a patient in the bed opposite, looked up and walked over. The man tried to speak but his lips were swollen and split and he managed only an unintelligible whisper. She sent a message to the doctor on duty who came after an hour, examined the patient and left some instructions. The nurse tried to get the man to drink a few sips of water and made him comfortable.

A young woman, sitting quietly in a chair in a waiting area along the corridor from the ward, was informed that her friend had woken up. Since it was almost the time for admitting visitors, she was allowed to enter the ward and sit beside the bed. Watching the patient as he lay, she saw him move one of his legs and purse his lips as this unleashed pain. Gently she picked up one of his bruised hands and held it between her two but remained silent. His fingers grasped hers and he tried to turn his head in her direction but this made him wince. Scared and disorientated, he mumbled in English, "Why is it dark? Who are you?" Perhaps she did not understand as she made no reply, just stroked his hand rhythmically. He relaxed and after a few minutes he appeared to have fallen asleep.

David was alive. That was enough.

The girl is drowning. He is the only one who has seen her fall off the wooden boat, but he is unable to move. Fear grips him as the murky green waters of the lake suck her down. He remembers his father talking about compassion. Suddenly his limbs are freed from their paralysis and he swallows his horror as he dives into the dark water to try and reach her. Punim has gone; Kiran is crying, crying. And now this one is sinking down, small limbs waving like seaweed – he swims further into the swirling depths after her. His lungs are being torn apart. He emerges into the light amid the wind-rippled grass of the endless plains and there is Enzi, black skin and strong limbs gleaming in the sunlight, his calm eyes surveying the scene, making a brave decision to go forward alone, leaving Caleb cowering in the bushes. He too finds himself crawling away, unwilling to challenge the evil that will hack down his friend. Theo's words echo in his head: "Have courage." He stops, turns and begins to follow in Enzi's footsteps.

Then Alicia emerges from the barn and walks across the courtyard dappled by the evening sunlight filtering through the old olive tree. She sees him in the shadows and opens her arms – the temptation to stay is strong. But the future beckons him and she cannot persuade him to stay and settle down.

He walks away again, looking over his shoulder as Rafael serenely watches him pick his way down the rocky path from the hermit mountain. There is more to learn, more to see. He recalls Theo saying, "Be truthful." He has not told Layla the truth and has caused her pain.

Again he is running away. He tells Valentina that he does not love her but the truth hurts. He is trying to escape down a dark street and his lungs are rasping. A slice of pain cuts through him. And another. He is broken. Blackness with bells tolling.

A pinpoint of light grows. Love is all there is. Theo is just out of sight, listening for him, loving him and leading him back. Back from dreams to reality.

The next day the dressings were removed from one of his eyes, and David was able to see. He was told about his injuries – a deep wound to the shoulder, which was stitched and would mend well, two broken ribs from being savagely kicked, a cut and severe bruising above and around his eyes from another kick to his head, and the resultant concussion. He had been unconscious for over thirty hours. He asked about the woman who had visited him. She had gone and not returned; no-one knew her name.

He had a visit from the police in connection with the serious assault he had sustained. Muggings were common and if a local were involved and no fatalities resulted, they were often not investigated. Because a foreigner was targeted and had the good fortune to survive, they felt obliged to visit the victim and ask a few questions. David, who knew the identity of his assailant, kept his silence – he had been in South America long enough to know that to reveal this would put his safety even more at risk. He hoped that Luis believed he was dead – he could think of no other reason why the man would have left him in the street.

He was surprised to learn from the police that a woman with two male friends had intervened and prevented his attackers from finishing him off. They had picked up the victim and taken him to the hospital. He felt guilty because he had assumed that Valentina, in addition to Luis and Joaquin, had been angry with him and decided to teach him a lesson. Now he realised that she had probably saved his life. He wondered who had paid for his medical care – knowing that there was rarely free treatment in Latin America and that ambulance drivers often demanded cash. He would ask the doctor.

However, it was not Valentina who came to visit him the next day. To his surprise it was Andrea. She had received a scrawled note which told her that David was in the city hospital having been badly mugged. She was frightened for him and pleaded with him to leave the city and the country as soon as he was able. Raul would help him do this, but she did not want her husband to be seen visiting him as she was afraid. He was relieved to be reminded that his bag was safe – and his passport too.

Two days later David was discharged. He still had a bad headache but was able to walk alright even though his ribs were causing him pain. He enquired about payment for his treatment. Apparently the cash in his pockets, his week's wages, had been sufficient to enable some basic care from the doctors, but after the first day in hospital someone had arranged for his medical bill to be paid. Who was doing this? It baffled him. Surely no-one from home knew about this. Home... The word was soothing. Had his father's protective arms reached round the world? When he was better he would contact his family – he needed healing and love.

Vulnerable as a weak animal, he crept out of the hospital and took a taxi to Andrea and Raul's house. He trusted them but he knew he had to leave and go somewhere to recover his strength. His friends were sympathetic and looked after him for another day but were nervous about harbouring him. They look relieved when he declared himself well enough to travel, though unsure if he could put on his rucksack with his shoulder wound still bandaged. Raul took him to the bus station and David bought a ticket for a town near the border. Soon he was on his way heading northwards and in considerable discomfort. The bus jolting meant he was in agony with his broken ribs, but he took some painkillers, swigging them down with water Andrea had given him as she said goodbye. They were kind people and he was grateful, but now he was on his own again.

Theo watched his grandson sleeping, and bending down, brushed the boy's tiny forehead with a gentle kiss. He was at Kate and Andrew's house for supper and they had been discussing the developing plans for the family hotel and activity centre which they hoped would open in the autumn. Kate seemed tired and listless, and Theo noticed Andrew watching her with a worried frown. To cheer them up he suggested they find a new name for the hotel venture. Kate came up with Safe Haven Hotel, Andrew put forward The Phoenix, and Theo suggested Homeward Bound, which retained half of the original name. No decision would be made until Josh and Maria had been consulted as this was a family enterprise. Tactfully no-one had mentioned the members of the family whose absences had now become prolonged. David had been gone for a long time and Layla's visits had been fleeting and few.

The day before, Theo had received a short e-mail from his son in which David said he had been mugged and had sustained a few bruises. He was staying further north on the coast, helping out in a beach restaurant. It was a beautiful area and he had started sketching in his spare time. He had met some other backpackers and would leave with them. Theo doubted that his injuries had been that slight but was delighted to hear that David would be travelling with others – it was a new development. His self-reliant son usually journeyed alone.

With a final glance at Nathan, who had yet to meet his uncle, Theo left the bedroom. Innocence needed protection but he knew that Ator's power was waning, his health deteriorating and his ability to harm Theo's family diminishing. No further attempts had been made on those nearest to him, but those far away were still at risk and Theo hoped that soon they would come back into the fold. It had to be their decision.

He went downstairs to supper.

Some weeks later, in a colder part of the world, Layla put down the brush, looked at the painting in front of her and sighed. The portrait was technically good but it lacked 'soul'. In a similar way she was physically healthy but emotionally empty. Her last project, now concluded, had been exhausting though highly satisfying. But the achievement of her ultimate goal had receded again and she felt dejected. She missed her adopted family far away back home, surprised that she, who had always regarded herself as itinerant, could consider anywhere as 'home'.

Putting down her palette, she got up and allowing her sitter a few minutes to relax and move about, she crossed the room to look out of the window. She needed a new challenge and the blue hills in the distance beckoned her to another adventure. She went back to her easel, knowing she must concentrate on her painting. She had managed to obtain this commission, which was financially very useful, and had to finish it before she was free to move on. Layla turned, smiling encouragingly at her subject, Mario, who returned to his seated pose, and she returned to the easel and resumed work.

"How did you get that?" Jasmine leaned over, brushed the sand off a warm shoulder, and ran her finger down the red scar. The two of them were on their own, lying in the sun, while the other three were swimming in the sea.

Her companion sat up and said, "I was working in a bar and I got mugged by two guys one night on the way home." He looked across the beach to the sea and she looked at his profile and wondered why he was so reticent.

"How frightening, Dave. Did they rob you too?"

At last he looked down at her. "Only of my peace of mind. They didn't take anything. Three people came to my help and the thugs took off. I ended up in hospital and left the country as soon as I could."

"How simply awful. I don't blame you for running away." He did not react to her comment but lay down again on his front and closed his eyes. They had been travelling as a group for about three weeks but Jasmine knew very little about him. He was a bit older, a good listener and seemed to like their company but never talked much about himself. The problem was that he didn't respond to her obvious desire to get to know him better.

It was hot, so she fished a bottle of water out of her bag and drank some. Then she leaned over David and dribbled some on to his back, giggling as she did so.

He didn't move and murmured, "That's nice."

She bent down and whispered into his ear, "So are you. But do you think I am? Do you find me attractive?"

He rolled over on to his back and gazed up at her for a few seconds. "Yes, very," he said in a serious tone of voice. She looked puzzled – if he found her attractive, why wasn't he taking advantage of her evident partiality to him?

He was almost *too* good-looking. A sudden thought struck her and, frowning, she asked, "Are you gay?"

"No, I'm not," and he gave one of his devastating smiles that made her want to kiss him.

"If you fancy women, Dave, then why not me?" Jasmine pouted at him as provocatively as she could.

It was his turn to sit up and look perplexed. At last she had got under his skin and made him question why he held her at arm's length. She went on relentlessly, "The only other explanation is that there must be someone else."

He stared at her, as perception followed by pain passed across his face, his inward eye focussing on another but sadly not on her. Jasmine knew that she'd got it right. She swallowed her disappointment and managed to say, gently, "Clearly you miss her a lot. Why don't you tell her you love her?"

"I've lost her." The words were uttered with bleak self-loathing. "I'm such a fool."

Jasmine was startled by the passionate bitterness she had aroused. "I'm so sorry," she whispered, getting to her feet, feeling awkward. "I think I'll have a swim." She set off down to the water's edge to join her other friends in the sea. She looked back longingly at the still figure sitting upright, staring into the distance. He hadn't even noticed she'd gone.

Though the bus was crowded, David felt lonely. The companionship he had enjoyed for three weeks had convinced him that self-imposed isolation was not conducive to well-being and he had found that dependence on others was a positive and not a negative experience. But his fellow travellers had needed to return to their homes and jobs, and after a last meal together at a restaurant, the next day they went their separate ways. In the usual manner they had all swopped addresses whilst knowing it was unlikely they would ever meet again. Jasmine, whose seductive offer he had rejected, was returning to college and, as she said goodbye she gave him a hug and said, "Go find her. You need love in your life."

He looked out of the bus window as it climbed up the side of a wide valley and had a sudden realisation that the gaping void in his life could only be filled by one person and that he had to find her. He must find Layla. Where in the world was she? Perhaps she no longer thought about him and was with another man, living another life, forever severed from him. It had been his blindness and his prejudice that had driven her away. But there was hope and he would search for her.

He had to contact those back home who might still keep in touch with Layla. Surely his sister or Josh would know where she was – they had been such close friends. Sudden urgency gripped him and he could not wait to leave the bus to look for a café where he could send an e-mail to them and make the first move in trying to track her down. Was she alright or even still alive? He felt almost sick with apprehension and, filled with new purpose, on an impulse he got off at the next place.

He knew as soon as the bus departed, leaving him stranded in a small dusty town, that he had made a mistake. It was midday, blisteringly hot and the streets were deserted. All the shops were closed. The sun's heat seemed compressed between the walls of the buildings and its harsh light reflected off the road. He felt trapped in the limbo between his starting point and his destination, his past life and his future, in a small narrow country sandwiched between two mighty continents. He was thirsty and picking up his rucksack which he still found uncomfortable to put over his injured shoulder, he started walking to see if he could find somewhere out of the sun and get some water.

As he passed a large, dilapidated building without windows, he noticed a door ajar, and from the darkness within he heard a strange whimpering noise. Thinking it might be an animal in pain, he stepped inside. For a few seconds he could see nothing as his eyes adjusted to the dim interior. Then in the far corner he heard some scuffling followed by a human cry of fear. Dropping his rucksack, he darted forward and saw two men attacking a woman. With a yell of fury he pulled one of them away and threw him to the floor. Ignoring the pain from his injured shoulder he swung a punch at the second attacker who staggered back. In a red fury with this assault on a defenceless woman, David kicked the man who doubled up with a grunt of pain. He heard steps and spun round to defend himself from the first man, but was surprised to see him back off and run toward the open door, followed by the other, who shouted an insult as he disappeared from view. David, breathing heavily, crouched down to reassure the woman who was cowering on the floor and wailing in distress.

He spoke to her in Spanish but she responded with a stream of confused words which he could not understand at all. She was a young indigenous woman and he had read somewhere that such women were often targeted, raped and murdered in this country, and sometimes their bodies were mutilated. In horror he realised that this might have been her fate, had he not intervened. He helped her to her feet. Tears were running down her face but she seemed unharmed, though in shock. Slowly in Spanish he said they should go to the police and report the attack. She must have understood this because a look of fear crossed her face and she shook her head and became agitated again. He put his hand on her arm but she backed off and ran across the shed and darted out into the street, leaving David on his own.

Slowly he walked back towards the shaft of sunlight mottling the floor in the open doorway, hoping she would get back home safely to her family. When he reached the door, he looked around for his rucksack which he had dropped in his haste to help the victim of the assault. It had gone. He frantically searched the dusty floor but it was nowhere. One of the two attackers must have grabbed it as they fled. This was a disaster! He had been warned about pickpockets in bus stations so he had hidden his roll of cash in a special compartment in the rucksack. They would find it no doubt. His passport was gone too. He had no credit card since he no longer had a bank account with any funds in it. All he had now were the clothes he wore and a little local currency in his pocket.

He emerged into the bright, relentless sun, still stunned by how quickly his situation had changed. Within a few minutes he had ceased to be an independent backpacking traveller and was now destitute, without money or food, stranded in a town the name of which he didn't yet know. He was still thirsty. No doubt he could find some water but soon he would be very hungry.

As he wandered along the streets, he realised things were bleak. How could he e-mail his father to ask for a loan and request it be transferred to a local bank if he were unable to produce identification to get the funds? A new passport could only be obtained from his embassy in the capital city, which was a long way away. He had no money or means of getting there. He resolved to ask for help from the police when he reported the loss of his passport and money, but when he located them, all they did was issue him with a written police report noting the theft of his passport. As he expected, they were not interested in a gringo who had been silly enough to lose his rucksack and all his money. He would need to be resourceful. He was on his own.

Jakob leaned forward, looking at the screen with satisfaction. His hacking skills had improved and he'd managed to crack Ator's password with just half a day's work. Now he had access to Ator's online documents and had uncovered the hidden details about his finances and network. It was only a matter of time before he found a way to divert funds into his own private account and then withdraw them. He had also discovered that Ator now had few agents and his 'projects' had declined in number. It appeared that the iron control his boss had once wielded over his enterprises was slipping, his power diminishing and his territory shrinking. Soon it would be time to jump ship.

His employer's health had deteriorated and he needed more assistance, so Jakob had been trusted with greater responsibility. Finally his loyalty was being rewarded. He would continue ingratiating himself and worming his way into the centre of operations until it suited him and he was ready to make his move. Meanwhile, to prevent suspicion, he complied with the sick man's commands.

When Ator called him in to his dark bunker it was clear his hatred of Theo and his family was still festering. He ordered Jakob to make plans to destroy the target family, who were again thriving in spite of all he had inflicted on them. In his sibilant voice he had given instructions: "Harassment is no longer enough. I require a permanent solution." He handed Jakob an envelope. "Take your time, plan carefully and set this up to avoid any possibility of tracing the resulting outcome back to me. Be vigilant. He is clever. Be cleverer." Jakob knew that 'he' meant Theo.

A few days later, he managed to hack into Kate's e-mails again and discovered with annoyance that David was still alive and in a specific location. Jakob would find out what contacts Ator had in that area to see if an accident could be arranged. Then he would turn his attention to the rest of the family. There was still a possibility that he might change sides and warn Theo. He wanted to keep his options open as the power might be shifting and he needed to be on the winning side.

David ditched his scruples, grabbed the bread and ran. He darted down an alley listening for any shouting or pursuit. But his theft had gone unnoticed, so he pushed the loaf down the front of his dusty shirt and walked another couple of hundred yards before stopping beneath a scrawny tree and cramming some bread into his mouth. The previous day, after walking for five blistering hours, he had reached a small, dusty village. No-one in this country seemed to understand the notion of hitchhiking. Finding a roofless shed, he had slept there for the night. Early the next morning he had woken up cold and thirsty, but managed to drink from a public standpipe; he no longer bothered whether it was pure or not – there was no choice. Whilst splashing some water over his dirty hair and sunburned face, the smell of newly baked bread had wafted to him, making his stomach contract, and he realised that after two days without eating he was very hungry. He located the shop and had circled round like a famished predator before snatching a loaf. He had been reduced to begging for food in the last town he'd gone through – and now he had resorted to stealing.

He left the village and after about an hour of walking along the road he sat down in the shade of a wall and ate some more of the bread, savouring the sweet taste of the dough. Hunger was a powerful motivation to commit crime, he reflected. Poverty drove honest people to break the law. He wondered if deprivation had ever forced his sister, or Josh or Layla, to steal in order to eat. Finding Layla was a priority but simple survival was more urgent.

A lorry lumbered past in front of him and he looked down the road, wondering how far it was to the next town and where he might spend the night. It was surprisingly chilly at night despite being so hot during the day. He found sleeping rough less dangerous in the countryside than in the towns and he was less likely to be threatened. He wasn't worried about being robbed because he had nothing. He took a few mouthfuls of water from a plastic bottle which he had found discarded in a trash can and refilled many times. Water, at least, was free. He calculated that he had another sixty miles to go to the capital, and set off. It was strange to be unencumbered and free of worldly possessions, living on bread and water. He put one foot in front of the other and slowly made progress towards his goal. He had no time constraints.

A few cars passed him and then there was a lull. He no longer bothered to try and get a ride, merely trudged onwards, his mind either in neutral or thinking of his family. And Layla. A truck passed him and then slowed down, pulled over and stopped. A voice called out to him in Spanish and then in English. "Do you want a lift?"

Two hours later he was in the city and the driver kindly dropped him off at his destination – the embassy. Within a few hours his life underwent another seismic change. At the consulate he explained the loss of his passport, money and baggage. He was told that a new replacement passport would take up to eight weeks to process and issue. Since he could recall his passport number and had a crumpled copy of the local police report of its loss, it could be cancelled and he could be issued with an emergency passport within a few days. They let him send an e-mail to his father and loaned him enough money for a meal and a night in a modest hotel, where he had the first shower for two weeks and the luxury of sleeping in a bed.

It was two days before he managed to obtain the correct documents to prove his identity and enable him to go the bank which he had designated to his father and collect the dollars. He changed some into local currency and sent an e-mail to Theo thanking him and reassuring his family that he was safe and in possession of the funds. He did not tell them about his weeks as a vagrant beggar. But he asked if Kate knew where Layla was.

He received a comforting message by return from his father and felt the words lift off the page and fly into his heart. Raphael's words came back to him: "In the end, you will go home to the one who loves you most, the one that frees your mind." *Soon,* David thought, *but not yet.*

He would defer his decision until he had news of Layla, and would need to seek work to repay his father. In the meantime, he relaxed, bought himself some clothing and had a few good meals. While waiting for his emergency passport to be issued, he was free for a few days. His injured shoulder no longer pained him and his broken ribs had healed so it was time to see something of the country other than its dusty roads. He recalled Layla had once told him about the ancient Mayan temples and pyramids in the depths of its tropical rainforests, which she had always wanted to visit. He decided to take a tourist bus and spend a couple of days wandering through the famous archaeological site. He bought himself a secure travel pouch, a sketch pad, pencils and a small rucksack before he set off. Travelling light had become a habit. So had resilience.

Kate was hugely relieved when her father told her that David had been in touch and had arrived in the capital city. He had received the remitted funds and was alright. She had been so worried about him. Her mood had lightened recently and she had begun to take real pleasure in looking after Nathan. The black clouds of depression had receded and she began to involve herself again in the hotel project that took up so much of Andrew's time. Two days later, she had an e-mail from her brother asking if she knew where Layla was and how he might reach her. Kate knew Layla's e-mail address but decided to contact her friend first, tell her where David was and ask if she wanted him to know where she was. Layla replied the next day saying she was just about to go travelling and did not wish Kate to pass on her e-mail address. Somewhat saddened by the news that Layla no longer cared about her brother, Kate sent a brief message back to David: "We're all so pleased you are safe and well. Sorry, I don't know where Layla is at the moment." Which was the truth.

David's heartrate returned to normal as he gazed at the breathtaking panorama before him. The rainforest canopy through which he had ascended stretched out on each side as far as the eye could see. He had climbed up steep ladders to the top of the tallest temple pyramid, over two hundred feet from the ground. From the platform, rippling green forest extended to the far horizon, broken only by the stone roof combs of four other Mayan pyramids, like ships on the ocean. It reminded him of the sea of grass that had stretched before him in the wide savannah in Africa. He might never come here again but he would never forget the awe-inspiring breadth of the natural surroundings.

He wondered if Layla had ever managed to find her way here and fulfil a dream. He glanced down at his sketchpad and realised he could never capture the essence of this place in a drawing. He had travelled for a whole day to get here and though it was in a remote part of the country, there were many visitors and foreign tourists. As he descended the narrow ladders, passing others going up or down, suspended between the earth and the sky, he had a feeling of dislocation, as if this was a hiatus between the past and the future. He had kept himself away from his family, trying to prove that he was self-sufficient. Isolated, whether he was in the middle of a crowd or alone on a mountain, all he wanted now was to find his way back home and admit he needed love and companionship. People mattered more than places.

An hour later he climbed to the top of another pyramid, which was known as the Temple of the Great Jaguar. This one was less tall and below him he could see a wide clearing and the remains of a palace. He listened to a couple of tourists talking near him, one of them speaking slowly in a deep voice that reminded him of Theo's. He longed to see his father and wondered why he had for so long perversely refused to make a telephone call home. That morning he had glimpsed the date on a newspaper; it was early September, three years since he had set off from home to escape from his wrecked dreams and see the world. A large bird flew overhead as an inner voice prompted him to wing his way home. The time had come.

Dizzy with the momentous decision he had made, he glanced downward. Amongst the crowd of people wandering around gazing at the ruins, he saw a small figure dressed in white on the far edge of the great square below. It was a young woman with dark hair who looked a little like Layla. Knowing this was irrational, David became convinced it was her and started to scramble down the steep steps whilst shouting out her name to catch her attention. The woman was some way off and had started to walk away down a path towards the trees. Desperate not to lose sight of her, he took his eyes off the steps and missed his footing.

With a desperate cry he slipped and fell heavily, slithering to a rest near the bottom of the pyramid. Two tourists tried to help him and thought him mad when he tried to walk, as so it was obvious his ankle was broken or sprained. Wincing with pain and disappointment, David was unable to follow the woman.

Later, after a visit to a doctor in the nearby village and with his foot bound up, he lay in a small hotel room listening to the night sounds of the rainforest animals. He could hear the dense music of the cicadas and a distant howler monkey. He had, of course, been mistaken and had spotted someone who resembled the woman he now knew he still loved. It had been wishful thinking – the local women *all* had dark hair. In any case, Layla never wore white.

His path was at last clear – he would go home to his family who, it seemed, needed his support. When he was back, he would continue his search for Layla; Josh might know where she was, and if not, perhaps one day she might visit them. He calculated he had enough money for an air ticket and resolved to get home as quickly he could. In spite of the injury to his foot he would make the long journey and limp home.

The next day, as he hobbled out to catch the bus back to the capital, he passed a bread shop. Two local women were standing outside with their children, looking hungrily at the bread for sale. On an impulse, he went in, bought five large loaves and, coming out, handed them to the surprised women. It was a small gesture to try and make amends for his theft five days before. It made him feel better to give something back.

15

Theo was waiting, his large hands loosely clasped in his lap, seated on his favourite bench overlooking the small playground. The children had just come out of school for the day and their mothers had brought them here to let off steam before going home. Theo enjoyed watching them whilst feeling protective of their innocence. A dark shadow fell across him and he knew without turning his head that Jakob had arrived. Two days ago the man had contacted Theo, saying he had something important to discuss, and a meeting had been arranged.

"Strange place you picked for a private business discussion." Jakob stared moodily across at the sunlit scene.

"I recollect that you wanted to speak to me and it was my choice where to meet." Theo spoke calmly but his fists were clenched. "Why don't you sit down?"

The excited cries of carefree children echoed round the park. "Noisy brats," growled Jakob, sitting down at the other end of the bench and putting on dark sunglasses. "You know whom I work for." He spoke abruptly. "I've obeyed his orders and put up with his infernal temper for years. He used to be very powerful but now he's weaker. His health is getting worse and his business empire is crumbling." He paused but Theo kept silent. "I know you and your family have been a thorn in his flesh for years and the target of his hatred – though I don't know why. I admit that on his instructions I've done damage to your children. But I suspect that underneath your mild exterior, you are a powerful man and I might do better by doing a deal with you."

"So what's your proposition?" Theo's voice had a sharp edge to it as he remembered all that his family had suffered.

"I know where Ator is, where the hub of his enterprise is located. I am in possession of detailed information that will help you to break him and bust his organisation. All I want in exchange for this is immunity from prosecution and a large sum of money."

Theo looked reflectively across the grass at the trees, their leaves shivering in the wind. "I already know all about Ator. I've been acquainted with him for a great many years and have always known his power was temporary. I don't propose to give you anything, except perhaps some good advice as to how you could change your life for the better."

Jakob's face darkened. "I don't want that," he snapped. "My information is worth paying for. You underestimate what I can do for you. Or what I will do to you if you refuse."

Theo stood up quickly and Jakob felt disturbingly small as the big man towered over him, the light from the sun behind him casting a luminous halo round his body. In a stern voice Theo said, "You can do nothing to me. Tell that snake you work for to stop threatening my family."

Jakob leapt to his feet, his face distorted with anger. "You'll regret this," he snarled.

"I won't – but *you* will." Theo spoke firmly, standing still as Jakob stormed off down the path and disappeared into the shadow of the trees.

At her desk Kate leaned back in her chair and stretched. She had at last emerged from her depression and had regained her energy. Nathan had been asleep for a couple of hours but soon he would wake and start crawling round and her quiet time would come to an end. She had been working on the final arrangements and staffing requirements for the new business. The venture had been delayed for three months due to the building works taking longer than scheduled. Curtains had been made and carpets chosen, the furniture was ready for delivery and all the kitchen equipment and dining room crockery and cutlery had been ordered. They had purchased all the linen and towels, identified potential suppliers for their provisions, and soon they would have to interview candidates for the remaining jobs and work out staff rotas and duties.

The opening of Homeward Bound Hotel had been rescheduled for early December and featured in many brochures. They already had some enquiries and a few bookings. It was advertised as a country hotel for families and groups, with the emphasis on adventure, sport, learning, arts and crafts. In addition to all the bedrooms, reception and dining rooms, guests had the use of a gym, a games room, a studio and craft room, badminton and tennis courts, a lecture hall, a television room, a crèche, an adventure playground and a fleet of bicycles. In a year or so, there would be an indoor swimming pool and a kitchen for cookery courses.

They had managed to rebuild without going much over budget. Because the bedrooms and the general decor of the public rooms were not as sophisticated or luxurious as they had been, there had been enough to stretch to most of the extra facilities, but now funds were running short, and a bank loan had been required to finish the works and provide funds to get the business up and running until a clientele was built up to create profit. This might take more than a year. Kate worried about it and often wished that David were around so they could use his experience in running a hotel. Fortunately two of his management staff, including Olga, had been persuaded to return and their input and advice had proved invaluable.

She heard Nathan begin to snuffle which preceded his being fully awake and noisily making his presence felt. As she got to her feet the doorbell sounded and she remembered she had invited Maria for tea. Dashing through to the kitchen, she put on the kettle and then went to open the door.

Maria stood on the doorstep, her blonde hair tangled by the wind, looking even paler than usual. "What kept you? Had you forgotten I was coming?" she said as she stepped inside and put down her bags.

"Of course not," lied Kate cheerfully. "I've been working hard on hotel stuff trying to get lots done before Nathan wakes and clamours for my attention. So I haven't baked a cake, though I think we may have some biscuits." She grinned at her friend. "I must come clean and admit I completely forgot!"

Laughing, they both walked through to a very messy kitchen. Kate loathed housework.

"What have you been doing in town?" Kate asked as she made the tea and found a couple of clean mugs. "You look tired."

Maria sank on to a chair. "I've been shopping for things we still need in our cottage."

"Do you like living in the country or is it too remote and quiet? I'm keen to know."

Maria and Josh had left the terraced house they had been living in since her mother's death. Two months before, they had moved into one of two cottages that had been created by converting the staff accommodation of the original hotel. The second cottage was almost finished and ready for Kate and Andrew to occupy.

"I love it there," Maria exhaled in pure pleasure. "The beauty, the peace and – when work is completed on the hotel – I expect there'll be some quiet too."

"Until the hotel opens and all the guests start coming. Not to mention that soon you're going to have some very noisy neighbours." Nathan had started wailing in the next room.

"That will be different from the noise of a construction site. And in any case, there'll be some privacy behind the fence and trees." Maria took a sip of her tea and put her feet up on a chair whilst Kate went into the next room and returned with Nathan. The boy looked warm, well-rested – and hungry.

Kate handed him to Maria and went across to prepare his supper. "Have a cuddle with Auntie Maria, Nathan, while I get you some food."

"I suppose I had better get used to having a baby on my lap." Maria kissed the soft hair on the top of Nathan's head.

"How are you feeling?" said Kate peering myopically at the label on a jar, having mislaid her glasses again.

"At last I've stopped throwing up – and now all I have to look forward to is blowing up like a balloon over the next few months. They tell me I'll start to feel marvellous – soon. Can't wait!"

"So you will. You'll bloom and grow and look even more beautiful. Though it gets a bit heavy and tiring in the final months." Kate put the bowl on the table, lifted Nathan from Maria's lap into a high chair and began to spoon food slowly into his mouth. When he started to whinge, she let him have the spoon to feed himself and waited for the inevitable mess.

"I wonder whether it will be a girl or a boy." Maria gently touched her abdomen. "I really don't mind – and neither does Josh. He's over the moon about being a father and has already chosen names. It will be good having you next door to us as it's a bit isolated during the day when Josh is at work, though

I'm enjoying a break from nursing for the first time in ages. And it's been such a lovely summer."

"Not long now and Josh will be working just across the yard from you. It'll be my Andrew then who has to commute into town to his practice. Though recently he's been spending a lot of time on site to ensure all is going to plan. It's been such a big responsibility."

"Josh is very keen to give up the school job and start work in the superb kitchen that Andrew's designed at the hotel. He's longing for a new challenge – catering and cooking for adults and children on holiday."

"We must expect a slow start, Maria. It'll take time to drum up bookings. Weekends and holidays will be busy but we'll have to try and fill up weekdays in term times with residential courses. Art classes are usually in demand but I'm beginning to doubt whether Layla wants to run them. I've not heard from her for ages. I hope you can manage to combine being a new mum with helping organise the hotel crèche and being available should any guests need medical attention. Daddy has no doubt that you'll cope marvellously."

"Theo never expresses doubts about any of us."

"Daddy's been brilliant as the mastermind behind the whole project. Always so encouraging. Always so energising."

"I don't know what any of us would do without him."

Nathan, his face smeared in food, crowed in delight as if agreeing and banged his spoon rapturously on the chair.

The warm September sun cast a peachy glow on the stone walls and the bronze lustre of its late afternoon rays were reflected in the window panes. The blackened stone had long since been repaired, sandblasted and re-pointed and the outside wall was now as it had been many years before, when the house had first been constructed. Theo stood looking across from where the new landscaping work was being undertaken on the other side of the drive. He was pleased. He loved his place – it had always been his home and it would be his home again with his family around him.

Andrew's new design had incorporated the old walls and front façade that had survived the fire and were structurally sound. These had been part of the original house and their restoration and utilisation within a scheme for the whole rebuild had been one of his main stipulations, after the decision had been finally taken by the family to construct another hotel on the same site. Andrew's firm were again appointed as architects. Theo was relieved that Andrew was a professional who listened to the wishes of the family, of which he was a part. Theo was sad that David had not communicated nor shown any wish to become involved although he had given his father power of attorney before he left three years ago. The insurance monies attributed to David had been allocated by his father to the new project.

Theo had been instrumental in orchestrating the architects, the building contractors and the family, tactfully blending their different ideas to keep the whole project on track and moving forward to his ultimate goal. The builders had now completed the exterior of the buildings and all the major internal works. The project manager of the building firm had subcontracted out the decorating which would soon be completed so that the furnishings and carpets could be installed. He was confident that by mid-November all the contractors would have finished and the new business could occupy the premises to have a month to train up staff, work up the management structure and order in supplies before Homeward Bound Hotel opened its elegant new doors to guests.

Theo saw Josh and Andrew emerge from round the corner of the building and stand talking beside Andrew's car. They had been inspecting the work in the new kitchens to ensure that all the new equipment had been installed. Josh would be in charge of all the catering, food and beverages in the new hotel. Theo was gratified that the man had turned himself around from a feckless, dishonest rogue to a committed and trustworthy member of the family team. He had even managed to keep his drinking and temper under control. Andrew had been tireless, working long hours and with total dedication to get the whole project finished. Disappointed by the delays, he had told his father-in-law that it was inevitable they would hit some problems.

Kate had decided not to return to teaching after her long recovery from postnatal depression and had thrown herself into working on the hotel project with renewed enthusiasm, handling decisions regarding interior décor and also planning the staff they would need. If David ever returned, he would clearly be a part owner of the new enterprise, though Kate fretted he might not approve of their aim to be modest, reasonably priced and family-orientated with less focus on luxury and exclusivity. There had been little time or money to spend on marketing, but Kate was an optimist and resolved to find the right person to promote the hotel. Olga's experience was proving useful and she hoped to persuade a retired Francis to return to handle the accounts side of the business.

The workmen were now leaving at the end of their day and soon the place would become still and peaceful. Theo watched as the two men finished their discussion and Andrew got into his car to drive home whilst Josh turned to walk back to the cottage, hungry for his supper. Maria had given up her nursing job and was involved in identifying suppliers of the equipment needed for the activities and sports. Josh was enthusiastic about the adventure playground they hoped to construct. He was already talking about how his child would play with Nathan in the years to come. Andrew saluted as he drove past him down the drive and Theo waved back. The other cottage was now ready and before long Kate with her husband and child would be living here too.

Soon Theo would be moving back into a spacious apartment at the top of the 'old' house with wonderful views over the gardens and fields. He would keep his studio in the barn for the present but looked forward to living with his family around him. The new sculpture for the hotel had long been finished and the foundry had cast it, done the patination and would deliver it in a week's time. A few yards from where he stood facing the front entrance was the stone plinth ready to receive the bronze.

Theo strolled across and up to the new front door, with its gleaming varnished wood and glass panels, letting in light to the spacious front hall and reception area. The transformation from destruction to restoration was almost complete. He turned and surveyed his world, his blue eyes looking into the distance, hope in his heart but with an awareness of danger. The site fell quiet, and the only sounds were the wind through the trees, a few birds and the muted noise of some distant cows as they walked to the diary for evening milking.

Theo sat down on the top step in the evening sun, his face serene but his whole body alert with expectation. Some time passed. Then he heard the sound of someone walking up the drive.

Jakob had been stealthily circling round the hotel site. He had been dismayed to find that the devastation he had brought about only three years before had been eradicated and that a gracious new building had re-emerged from the ashes. What was it about this family – why were they able to rise up again after the crushing blows they had been dealt over the years on Ator's orders? He was still smouldering with anger after Theo's rejection of his offer of collaboration and annoyed because Kate had changed her password so he could no longer tap into all the family information. As he prowled like a predator beneath the trees, trying to devise what he might do to inflict serious havoc, he caught sight of Theo sitting at the top of the steps to the hotel entrance. He quickly concealed himself behind some shrubs.

Theo was looking down the drive and then, swivelling his head round, he fixed his penetrating eyes on the exact place where Jakob was hidden. Feeling supremely uncomfortable under such intense scrutiny, even though he was convinced that he could not be seen in the shadows, Jakob kept motionless, inwardly churning with malevolence as he planned how he would harm this family. After a tense minute Jakob saw Theo's gaze turn back as if he was expecting someone to arrive. Then he too heard the sound of footsteps crunching on the newly laid gravel of the drive.

A gust of wind made the trees shimmer and the sunlight flickered through their leaves on to the scene. Like some ancient Greek drama unfolding before him, Jakob ground his teeth as he watched the return of the lost son.

The wayfarer came round the bend in the drive and saw his father on the steps of a much loved home that he believed had disappeared forever. David stopped in amazement. When he started to run, Jakob noticed that he had a limp. Theo stood up and slowly opened his arms to enfold his son. After a long embrace the two men drew apart and looked at each other. In spite of his hostility, Jakob was touched. He was also envious – no-one had ever welcomed him with such love. He had no home, no family. He belonged nowhere.

The two men sat down together on the steps and began talking. Jakob could hear the murmur of their voices and he watched resentfully until he could bear it no longer, then he turned and crept backwards away from the reconciliation he had tried so hard to prevent. His contacts had failed to track down David and eliminate him. It was infuriating to see him arrive home after all this time, just as his sister had done a few years earlier. Both had been made to suffer but were back under their father's protection and this meant that from now on it would be much harder to reach them. Their experiences in the wicked world might have taught them to be more wary but he would discover where they were weak and vulnerable and find a way to annihilate them. This would be done not because Ator required it, but because he, Jakob, wanted to destroy what he could not have.

Seething with vindictiveness, he made his way round the edges of the garden to the rear of the hotel. The workmen had gone but he could hear some music. He remembered that Maria and Josh now lived in a part of the old staff block, set back from the main buildings. He looked around but could see no-one so he approached cautiously. There were two entrance doors and peering in through the windows at one end, it was apparent that this part was unoccupied. Further along, towards the other end, a window was open and it was from this room that the music was emanating. He crept along the front wall and after glancing behind him, he peered in. The blonde woman, Maria, was laying a table for a meal, her back turned toward the window, and as she moved, something in her stance made him realise she was pregnant. He knew Theo adored Maria and regarded her as a daughter. Here was an unprotected pregnant woman and an unborn child in an isolated cottage. This was a possibility.

He heard a door open and moved quickly back from the window, cursing under his breath. His anger and frustration had made him careless.

"What the hell are you doing here spying on my wife?" Josh stood threateningly on the path a few yards away and he looked furious. Jakob recalled that the man had a quick temper and hoped that after all this time Josh would not remember who he was. They had met only once in a dimly lit nightclub in another country, about two years after Karl had ruined Kate. On Ator's instructions.

Jakob held up both his hands in a gesture of submission and put a smile on his face. "No offence meant. Just wanted to know if the place was occupied. Good to have someone living here after all this time."

"And who the heck are you?"

"I haven't been here since before the big fire a few years back. I used to stay at the hotel."

Josh spoke brusquely. "I used to work here and now I come to think of it, you *do* look a little familiar. But in any case this building is private property and the new hotel is not open yet, so I think you should leave. Now."

Maria had come to the door and was standing behind her husband. She was staring at the prowler, a puzzled frown on her face.

Jakob was uncomfortable with their scrutiny – each of them might at any moment recognize him. "Sure, I'll be on my way – sorry to have intruded." He turned and walked away towards the car park, even though his car was not there. He would avoid returning to the front of the hotel – he didn't want to interrupt the touching reunion between father and son. He needed to vanish fast.

"And don't come back," Josh called after him. Jakob smiled thinly as he slunk away – he had been told to clear off and the insult rankled. He had never liked Josh. When a man had a wife, he should learn it was unwise to make enemies.

An hour had passed and still David and Theo sat and talked. The sun was low in the sky and the autumn dew had caused a chill in the air when eventually Theo rose to his feet saying, "Thank you, David, for telling me where you've been and whom you've met. And most of all what you've learned about yourself. I'm overjoyed to have you home and that you're glad to be back. We must tell Kate and the others – they'll be so surprised."

"And pleased too, I hope," said David, standing up. "I'm sorry that I've been rather uncommunicative on my travels."

"They'll forgive that, I'm sure. As I have."

David looked around him in wonder. "I cannot believe what's been achieved – it's like the fire never happened. It all seems miraculously restored to former glory."

"Not quite. I think you'll find that although the front of the building is similar, there's a very different structure behind. You'll see we have gone for clean, simple lines both outside and within, and the fittings and furnishings are modest but comfortable and more practical for a family hotel. Would you like to have a quick walk round or shall we contact Kate now?"

"Let's ring them right now. I'd like to see Kate and Andrew and to meet my nephew."

Theo nodded approvingly. His son had his priorities right, at last. Love comes first. People before possessions. He hoped David had learned to be less reserved and more trusting. The family needed to have a shared vision.

That evening they were all together at Home Barn. Before leaving the hotel, Theo had telephoned Kate, and her exclamation of delight when she heard the news was audible to David. She said she would let Andrew know and be on her way. Theo then rang Josh and Maria, who were equally surprised and who promised to join them. Josh offered to get a meal put together.

Kate, who had just bathed Nathan and made him ready for bed, got him dressed and extravagantly ordered a taxi to drive her straight to the barn to greet her brother and show him her son. Andrew, who had the car and was at a business meeting in another town, arrived a little later, by which time Josh and Maria were there. Kate had been so happy to see her brother but she was also anxious for his approval of what they were doing with the new hotel project. He reassured her that he was amenable to whatever they had all planned and that he would love to see the new buildings and business plans during the following few days. That could come later – for now he just wanted to be with his family.

Josh was cooking a celebratory supper for them in the cottage kitchen and as he worked away, something triggered in his head about the stranger that afternoon. Maria had told him that she had seen him on the day that Olga had been showing her round the hotel a few days prior to her starting work as a receptionist, and the man had walked angrily through the entrance hall and had flung himself out of the hotel and into his car, accelerating noisily down the drive. Her new employer, David, had come out a few minutes later, with his face as black as thunder to ensure the man had gone. Maria had a good memory for faces and she was sure it was the same man.

Josh had an uneasy suspicion that he had met the man before. Suddenly he made the connection – the face of the intruder outside their house was the same as the shifty guy called Krait whom he and Layla had once met in some bar in a foreign city. He had given them the information which had led to the bungled robbery for which they had almost been caught. He had also told them of Kate's whereabouts and suggested they travel to her country and see if she would harbour them whilst things died down.

After the meal, David, with his nephew Nathan asleep on his lap, told Maria and Kate the graphic story of how he had injured his leg falling down a pyramid.

Josh discreetly called Theo aside and told him that he recognised the person who had been lurking about the hotel that day as a man he once knew called Krait. "Maria says that he's the same man she and Olga saw leave the hotel a few years back before she started work there. If it's the same guy, is he a threat?"

"Indeed, he might be," Theo said grimly. "His other name is Jakob and he's cunning and malicious. I first met him here on the day Maria saw him and more recently I had a meeting with him in town. I'm sorry to say that when I refused a proposition he put to me, he became angry and made threats. He works for Ator who, as you know, has a long-standing grudge against me, so we need to be vigilant."

"Well, if the jerk comes anywhere near Maria or me again, I'll take him apart," Josh said angrily.

Theo put his hand on Josh's arm. "If I were you, I'd just call the police – or me."

Two days later, Kate received an e-mail from Layla. After recounting her recent travels on the American continent, she said she was still painting and had recently finished a portrait commission of a local politician's wife. She hoped Nathan and the family were well and asked Kate to give her love to Theo, and to tell him she was alright and still following his advice. Towards the end she wrote:

> In spite of considerable effort, I've been unable to track down your brother, although I discovered we were in the same country at one time. I cannot give you any reassurance as to whether he is alright. Have you had any news of him? I don't know why I bother about a man to whom I haven't spoken for over three years. I have other fish to fry and other things to occupy my time. David's a loner with inflexible principles and prejudices – and he's never going to stop

despising me for what I once was. I don't think he cares about me anymore.

That's not true, thought Kate, as David had mentioned her name the day before, rather too casually. With elation, she tapped out a reply:

David's back. Amazingly he came home two days ago. It's so wonderful to see him. He has a bad limp from a recent fall and looks thinner, but it's in his head that he's really changed. He seems to be much calmer and more composed – and less reticent. He's told Daddy a lot about what he's been doing but we've not had time yet for a deep sibling chat. He's thrilled to meet Nathan and very pleased that Josh and Maria are going to have a child. He asked after you! I said very little except that you were well and living overseas. I didn't tell him that I had tried to enlist you as the new teacher for the art classes we are planning to run at the hotel, because I still don't know your thoughts on that. Layla, do come back home and see us all. There's still a chance!

The fine weather continued into early October. David was staying with his father and had been enjoying spending time revisiting the area he had lived in for most of his life and grown to love. David's old habit of keeping his father at arm's length seemed to have evaporated and the pair of them were more comfortable together than they had been for years.

Theo saw that his son was waiting. He had made no decisions about the future, though he had been updated about the new family venture by those who were keen to have his approval and know whether he wished to be involved. David confided in his father that he felt strangely removed from it all and had tried to work out whether this was because he had managed to distance himself from his ambition to become a successful hotelier or because he had finally learned that he could step back and let others take decisions without wanting to control things. Theo didn't try to hurry him into commitment because he knew the resolution had to come from David.

Only once had his son asked him about Layla and where she was, and Theo had answered truthfully that he did not know but that from time to time she got in touch. David had nodded and changed the subject.

The day came for Kate and Andrew to move into their newly renovated cottage adjacent to Maria and Josh's. The evening before, with Nathan asleep upstairs, while they were packing up the remainder of their personal possessions, Kate voiced her concerns about her brother.

"I'm worried that David isn't happy about our decision to have a very different kind of hotel from the earlier one. He doesn't say so but he doesn't seem very enthusiastic either."

"He seemed quite impressed with the new building when I took him round it. He was amazed how much has been achieved and how close we are to having everything ready for the launch of the new business. He's been away for three years and he's trying to assimilate all that's happened in his absence." As he spoke Andrew was piling books into a large box.

"I mentioned to him that we badly need someone on the management team who has experience, which he's definitely got, and that we hope he'll join in and perhaps take over the marketing and promotional side of things. He listened, seemed interested, but he didn't say he would." Kate sounded exasperated.

"He didn't say he wouldn't either. Give him time, Kate. He's only just got back."

"We don't have a lot of time. He's been back almost three weeks. If he doesn't want to come aboard then I've got to find someone else to fulfil that role. He seems to have completely changed from the ambitious workaholic that I used to know as my brother."

"I don't think he's adverse to involvement," said Andrew. "He's just more relaxed and wants to think about it all. He might even decide not to stay."

But Kate was fretting about plans. "If he does, where's he going to live? I've suggested to him that after Daddy moves into his new flat in the main house, he could occupy the barn cottage for a while. Or perhaps we could build a cottage adjacent to the new games room – though that's not an option yet. We need to generate some money."

"Stop worrying. Let's concentrate on getting the final items packed up for our move tomorrow," Andrew said, taping up two packing cases ready for the removal van in the morning.

What Kate didn't discuss with her husband was her concern that only once David had enquired after Layla. It seemed he was no longer interested in her. Perhaps Layla, too, had finally turned her back on him.

Kate had unpacked the basket and was now sitting under the tree with Nathan in her arms. He had been crawling around on the rug but now he was quiet and had almost dropped off to sleep.

David was sprawled on the grass with the old summerhouse behind him. "Great idea of yours to have a picnic!" He gazed upwards at the foliage above him. "The leaves are only just starting to turn. I've really missed the magnificent autumn colours that we get here."

"It's warm for mid-October. Perhaps we're having an Indian summer," Kate said. Nathan had fallen asleep so she gently laid him down on the rug and pulled the corner over him.

It was midweek. Andrew and Josh were both at work and Maria had gone into town to an appointment at the antenatal clinic. Theo was in the hotel talking to the project manager and had said he would join them soon. Brother and sister had been chatting and David had been telling Kate about his travels in Asia.

Kate opened a can of beer and handed it to him and David got to his feet and strolled over to the edge of the pond. He noticed the rickety plank bridge had disappeared and the water was covered with a film of bilious-green algae. He shivered in revulsion and turned back. "Do you remember how we used to play down here as children? And how afraid I was of the water and how hopeless I was at swimming?"

Kate smiled and glancing down at Nathan to check he was still fast asleep, she quietly got to her feet and walked over to her brother. "That's right – you hated the water and I seem to recall that you once fell in. There was a wobbly old plank that we used to run across and you lost your balance."

"I also remember that on the night you returned from your travels I came down here to the pond in a fit of jealous temper because I thought you would disrupt everything. Theo found me and made me return to the hotel and welcome my prodigal sister. I behaved rather badly," David admitted.

"After I came home I tried so hard to win your respect. I didn't want to disrupt your life."

"Then a year later there was the fire and my world fell apart. Now I'm the one who's been away and come home. And I, too, don't want to disrupt *your* plans, Kate. This is your project," he said gently, indicating the hotel through the trees.

Kate gave him a pleading look. "David, it's a family project and we all want you to be involved." She took hold of his arm and led him to where he could see the new building gleaming in the sunlight. "Look over there. It's ours. Please, David, we need you. We want you to be part of this. It's not about ownership. This is a joint venture and we all have to work together to make it successful."

David looked down at his sister affectionately, touched by her sincerity. "Perhaps I might get involved. I hardly know what else I'd do."

Kate gave a shout of delight. "At last, you've shown some interest."

At this point, they both heard a rustling sound and turned round, guiltily remembering the sleeping infant. Kate ran across to the rug beneath the trees and cried out, "Nathan's not here. Where's he gone?" The note of panic was evident and David ran across to help her find the small child.

"He must have woken up and crawled off – we'll find him." He ran to search under the surrounding trees and bushes. He could hear Kate frantically running round the clearing calling her son's name and getting more and more frightened. The child was nowhere to be found. He heard Kate cry out and saw her standing at the edge of the pond, staring in horror at a sinister gap in the green slime that covered the surface, wailing, "No. He can't have crawled this far, surely. He can't have fallen in!"

Kate became hysterical and jumped into the pond, and began frantically groping around beneath the surface to try and locate Nathan who, she was convinced, had disappeared below the surface. Watching in horror as she became more and more distressed, David pleaded, "Kate, come out. He may very well be somewhere else – safe in the undergrowth."

But by this time, Kate was crying uncontrollably, "It's my fault. I left him on a rug and now he's drowned." She was floundering around, tears streaking down her face, when she suddenly lost her footing and slithered underneath. Banishing his fear of the slimy green water, David dived in to save his sister.

He could see Kate thrashing around below the surface and he grabbed her. Steadying himself by thrusting his feet into the soft, sucking mud on the bottom, he pulled her up and dragged her back to the bank. His sister was in total shock, choking in her panic, so he picked her up, staggered out of the pond and put her down on the ground. She was completely distraught and gasping for air. "Find him! Find him! I don't want to live if Nathan's dead," Kate moaned, rocking herself back and forth.

David stood beside her, his hand on her shuddering shoulder, miserably aware of the impact this tragedy would have on all their lives. He knelt down beside her, putting his arm round her. Then he heard it. The world stood still.

A thin wail, a baby's cry. When Kate heard it, her head jerked up, hope replacing despair. The cries grew louder and David leapt to his feet, but at that point they both heard footsteps on the path and a woman's voice calling, "I have him. I've got Nathan."

To their stunned surprise, they saw a figure dressed in white appear through the trees, carrying Nathan in her arms. Kate tried shakily to get to her feet but her legs wouldn't hold her and she sank to her knees, holding out her arms for her child, crying, "Nathan! Nathan!"

The woman arrived in the clearing, went up to Kate and gently put the wailing child into his mother's arms. The decibel level of Nathan's screams increased as his mother hugged him to her wet clothing and bent over him, kissing him and saying tearfully, "My darling, you're safe. My precious boy, I love you so."

"I thought you never went swimming," Layla said calmly to David, talking across the huddled figure of the reunited mother and child between them.

"I thought you never wore white," he responded in quiet amazement, his eyes fixed on her as if she was an apparition that might disappear.

Theo could hear his grandson crying as he walked quickly down to the summerhouse beside the pond. As he entered the clearing he saw a tableau in front of him. Kate, her wet hair plastered round her face, was kneeling on the ground, holding and hugging Nathan who was crying lustily. David, also dripping wet, was crouching down on one side of his sister, with an arm around her shoulders, looking up at Layla who stood on the other side of Kate, her hand resting on the baby's head. Layla and David were gazing at each other.

A few minutes later, the family grouping had changed. Kate was sitting in the summerhouse on a bench with the rug draped round her shoulders. Theo was holding his grandson, who had become quiet in his grandfather's arms. Layla was sitting beside Kate – and David was leaning against the wooden wall, watching them, his clothes plastered to his skin.

"Nathan didn't wake up and crawl away. He was abducted," said Theo. Kate looked horrified, David mystified. "Tell them what happened, Layla."

"I'd finished a portrait commission and decided to come and pay you all a visit. I landed this morning, hired a car at the airport and set off on the long drive here. When I arrived in town and went to your house, Kate, I discovered you had moved and your neighbours told me you were now living here. When I came up the drive and saw the resurrected Homeward House, I was stunned with surprise. I knew you were rebuilding but I had no idea you had completed the work. I pulled up and was just getting out of the hire car when I saw a man emerge from the trees on the other side of the drive. He was carrying a child and he looked very furtive. When he saw me, he froze and it was at that moment that I recognised him. I was certain, even though I've not seen him for a few years, that it was Krait."

"Whom we know as Jakob," interposed Theo.

"The baby was whimpering, and from the awkward way the man was holding him, I realised that he wasn't the father. I went over and demanded what he was doing there and if the child was his. While he was hesitating I looked at the baby and realised he was Kate's little Nathan. So I grabbed him. Nathan let out a scream of fright and I ran with him towards the house. Krait started to pursue me, but at that moment..."

"I came out of the front door," Theo said.

"Theo saw the situation and let out a roar of anger," continued Layla. "Krait stopped in his tracks, spun round and ran back towards my car. I'd left the keys in the ignition and he jumped in and started up, reversing savagely round, and then drove off at speed down the drive. I was left holding the baby. Thankfully."

"I told Layla her unexpected arrival had come at a very opportune moment and suggested she immediately bring Nathan down here because I knew Kate would be distraught." Theo gave Kate a look of worried concern.

"I thought he'd crawled into the pond and drowned. It was the worst moment of my life," said Kate, still looking pale and strained. Layla gave her a hug.

Theo looked down at the boy in his arms and then at his beloved daughters, saying, "I made a quick phone call to the police alerting them to the attempted kidnapping and the theft of a car, and then I called Andrew, who will already be on his way here. I reassured him that his son was safe but that he should get here without delay to comfort Kate who had had a nasty shock."

Layla stood up. "As I understand it, Kate now lives near here so why don't we all go back to her house so she can change out of those wet things. She needs a hot drink too. I expect David can borrow some dry clothes from Andrew." She smiled warmly across at him and Theo saw an answering smile illuminate his son's face.

Theo set off first, carrying his precious cargo. Layla tucked Kate's arm in hers and as they passed David, she leaned up and with her free hand plucked a piece of duckweed out of his hair. "You look dreadful – cold, slimy and muddy," she commented, a mischievous glint in her eyes.

"But you look wonderful," David responded as he set off up the path behind them. "And I'm not cold. Not at all." *Quite the opposite.*

Ator was in a vile mood. He was ill. The treatment for his cancer had meant that he had to leave his bunker to go to a private clinic and he felt dispirited on his return. The tablets could only dull the pain that ate away his resolve and his strength. Worse than that, he was bitter and disappointed that many of his enterprises had slipped away from his control and a number of his agents and operatives had stopped working for him and no longer reported for orders. But his predominant feeling was of anger. He had discovered from his financial controller, Jammet, who had been fired yesterday, that Jakob had been slyly siphoning off funds from two sources of income and that someone, probably the same treacherous Jakob, had been copying files from the database. Until now he had considered the agent loyal but clearly his deception posed a grave threat.

Two months before, Ator had become aware that his centre of operations had become too vulnerable and decided to relocate to another country. A suitable place had been found and converted, new equipment had been obtained, and tomorrow he would be travelling there. Jakob did not know this and Ator had been very careful to give no verbal or written hint of his plans to most of his agents.

There was a knock on the door and Ator pressed a button to open it. He already knew who it was, from the camera located in the outside office that enabled him to view any potential visitor. The door clicked open and swung shut behind the newcomer. A tall, bearded man stood waiting for Ator to speak. He knew better than to make any greeting or initiate any discussion.

"Ah, Laslo, is everything ready? Have you dealt with the files I put out to be destroyed?"

"They are all incinerated as you ordered. The remaining equipment is clean and ready to transport. It will be collected by Robson this evening. I have confirmed your car will be here ready for your departure at seven o'clock tomorrow." Laslo spoke quietly, without inflection.

"And Jammet? He knows the plan. Have you done as instructed?"

"I've ensured that Jammet will not be speaking to anyone."

Ator nodded, completely unmoved by the demise of a man who had worked for him for three years. His thoughts turned to hated Theo and his family. He had enjoyed playing with his victims like a cat with a mouse, but now it was time to kill them off. Having discovered that his life would be curtailed, he had to move decisively to cut short theirs before he became too weak to organise it. "What's the latest from Jakob?" he rasped.

Laslo's eye's glinted. "He communicated a few hours ago. He says that tomorrow he has a plan to eliminate the members of the family who live on site in adjacent converted cottages. It seems the kidnapping and extortion he planned didn't quite come off. Do you want to deploy me?"

"Wait first to see if he is successful and then, whatever the outcome, I want you to deal with him. I am displeased with Jakob. Report back on both counts through the usual channel." Ator leaned forward, wincing with pain, and picked up a package, which he gave to Laslo. "Here are your further instructions regarding the target family and I trust you will carry them out.

Two weeks today. If you do, there should be no need for any further operations against them. You are to vanish in the usual way. Report to me afterwards and be on standby for a different assignment." He turned away, the interview at an end.

"There is one slight matter." Laslo was hesitant.

Ator swung round. "Yes?" he snarled.

"The target's daughter, Kate, may remember me from my encounter with her a few years back which resulted in a prison sentence for her. She knew me as Vadim."

"Then keep out of her sight. Don't fail." He looked coldly at Laslo, who was well aware of the price for failure in Ator's organisation.

After Laslo left, Ator's shoulders sagged. Though weakened through sickness he would drag himself up and try to revive his influence and power during the time he had left. But for the present he had to retreat abroad, and do this discreetly. His disfigured face no longer bothered him but it was distinctive and people tended to remember deformities, so he always travelled in a car with dark tinted windows, and employed a driver. He would go, leaving another to implement the final solution he had devised for his old adversary and his children.

It was late afternoon and two figures were walking slowly along the edge of a field, silhouetted against the yellow stubble, bathed in the amber rays of the declining sun. They had been outside for hours delighting in the small corner of the world to which they both felt most attached. They were happy to spend time together, catching up on each other's lives and trying to explore how they now felt about each other.

They had been talking about their travels and escapades but most of all about some of the people they had encountered. David preferred to try and forget those who had harmed or tried to kill him, but he wanted to share with Layla his encounters with those who had enriched his life and changed his perceptions, telling her about Alicia, Enzi, Kiran, Rafael, Jasmine and, with difficulty and guilt, about Valentina.

Layla had told him about Peter and his proposal of marriage, her student friends, about her fine art course, her work as a portrait painter, and about Mario and others she had met and painted, including the sad politician's wife, Beatriz. She told him about Josh and Maria's wedding, when she had last been here with her precious adopted family. "It's so wonderful that Josh has turned his life around and found love."

David stopped walking and looked down at Layla, holding her hand. "I'd like to think that I too have turned my life around and changed my attitude. You talk about fidelity and I am so ashamed. I admit I was unfaithful to you – with Valentina and, in my mind, with others. Please forgive me. I've been so intolerant and I'm sickened when I think of the wounding words I spoke to you."

Layla reached up and put her hand on his chest as if to feel the beating of his heart. "I have been faithful to you, David, during your long absence. And with little hope that you would ever come back to me. I too have changed from the woman I was some years ago. Theo told me that my past could be wiped clean if I genuinely felt remorse about it. Coming here was a chance to start again and be a better person. As a symbol of my new life, I often wear white, though I occasionally hanker after flamboyant red," Layla laughed softly. "And I forgive you."

David bent down and gave her a gentle kiss, holding her tight against him. "Thank you. I don't deserve it. It feels good to get rid of guilt. Kate used to be trapped in it but she did her penitence and moved on. We both ran off from a loving parent to travel the world, went astray and got broken. But we managed to get home, mend our lives and start afresh."

"Whereas Josh and I journeyed downwards from deprivation into crime and then escaped to this place where Theo encouraged us to change. To our amazement we were welcomed. We all took different paths but ended up here – together." Layla looked around and sighed with happiness.

"I'm not going to let go of you this time." David tightened his grip.

"Good. But now we should walk back. Kate and Andrew will wonder what's become of me." Layla was staying with them in their cottage, whilst David was at the Home Barn with Theo. "I forgot to tell you that the police found the hire car, abandoned with my case in it, and tomorrow I can collect it from them. I wonder if Jakob has gone for good." She looked a little apprehensive.

"Let's hope so." David tucked her arm in his and they resumed walking. "Do you know, Layla, I think this may be the very same field in which I first saw you."

"When I was the scarlet and muddy woman." She couldn't resist saying it and when she saw him wince she whispered, "Sorry."

"How's the leg?" She changed the subject, noticing he was limping slightly.

"Much better. I seem to have come a long way from the Temple of the Jaguar where it happened."

"So you did go to the Mayan pyramids at Tikal," she said with a strange look. "So did I. Quite recently. How extraordinary!"

"We might even have been there at the same time, unaware of the other's presence. That's where I slipped and messed up my leg. I was thinking of you and took a step to oblivion, lost my balance and fell all the way down the steep steps," David said with a smile.

"So this limp is my fault, is it?" Layla raised her eyebrows.

"I merely want to show you what effect you have on me even when you're far away."

"What about when I'm right beside you?" she asked provocatively.

This time the kiss was long and passionate. When they drew apart she said mysteriously, "Perhaps I've been closer to you than you realize."

Theo was on the third floor of the hotel in the apartment that was almost ready for his occupation. His spacious new domain was light-filled with wide views over the grounds at the front of the hotel, the fields and hills beyond. He would soon be in residence and the move from the cottage would take place in a fortnight. He planned to spend less time in his studio creating sculptures in the future and more time with his family.

In the interim there was a potential problem that needed to be addressed. He had just concluded a telephone call and received some interesting information from one of his contacts: Ator had discovered that the authorities were pursuing him and was about to leave the country. His menace was less potent but Theo did not underestimate him – Ator's malignance would fester and he would continue to pose a threat. So Theo had arranged for a security firm to keep watch on the nearly completed hotel. That afternoon he had met three of their personnel and shown them round the buildings and grounds: two tall, silent men who emanated strength and reliability and, in charge of the operation, a calm, resolute woman called Angela. The team had their instructions and would be unobtrusive in performing their duties to protect Theo's family.

As the big man looked out of the high window, he saw two figures in the fields below, arm in arm, walking slowly back to the house. He hoped they had managed to put the past behind them and make the right decision for their future – together. He loved them both so much. All his children were infinitely precious to him. And they were still in danger.

16

Jakob darted forward keeping in the shadows. This was his opportunity He had been lurking in the hotel's grounds and woods for some days now. He had a van, in which he was camping, parked carefully out of view in secluded woodland a few miles away. He was furious that his plan to kidnap Theo's grandson had been foiled. He was so surprised to see Layla appear just in front of him that he had hesitated and let her take the initiative. This was a bad mistake but he managed to take her car and escape. She had recognised him and so had Theo, which meant he should already have gone. But he was rattled – his hopes of getting a large sum of ransom money gone – and was determined to hit back before he had to go. If he succeeded Ator might reward him but in any case he would get huge satisfaction in causing Theo anguish.

Ator's preferred weapon was fire and he had already used this to destroy the barn and the hotel. This family had an uncanny habit of rising up again from the ashes – but Jakob knew that the loss of one of Theo's children would be irreparable. He wasn't rash enough to attack the studio with father and son both in residence. No-one was yet living in the hotel but the rest of his family were now installed in two converted cottages nearby. The men left for work in the morning and their women stayed behind. He needed access to one of their dwellings so he'd waited. That afternoon he saw Maria and Kate with Layla, who was staying with them, leave their homes to go for a walk with the baby. They might not be gone for long so he had to hurry.

Behind the cottages the land sloped upwards to a small area for parking, from which a track wound down to the main drive. Their small gardens were on each side of the dwellings, with a small yard to the rear. Jakob discovered that just above this yard was a small ledge, made to contain two propane gas bottles, one for each cottage, which were enclosed in a wooden fence. There had to be a gas pipe which fed the propane into the kitchen for the hot water boiler and cooker. There was no-one around so he crept into the yard behind Maria's cottage, located the rubber pipe, and also a small ventilation grill in the kitchen wall through which he could easily push the pipe when he had cut it.

That night, at around 3 am, he would first go round to the front of the cottage, ease open a window and place a small tea-light candle in the sitting room as far as possible from the entry point of the gas pipe, closing the window carefully afterwards. Then he would silently make his way round to the back, cut the gas pipe, ensure that it fed into the ground floor and let the dense, heavy gas seep in and build up. After about half an hour, it would reach the candle in the next room and there would be an explosion and fire. The sleepers above, the pregnant Maria and that loser, Josh, would be trapped. The occupants in the adjacent cottage might also be caught in the fire as it spread across. He would be well clear and watch to see it ignite, before slipping quickly away to his vehicle and making his exit. Noting what he would need to bring to sever the pipe and prise open a window, Jakob left, threading his way stealthily through the woods, along a field and up a deserted track back to his van.

Tomorrow they would be dead and he would be miles away.

Theo strolled into the clearing, leaned against the tree and waited. Within a few minutes, he saw Jakob emerge and cross over to his van, parked discreetly under the trees. As he reached it, Theo stepped out and said quietly, "Hello, Jakob."

Jakob froze momentarily and then jerked round to see his most hated adversary standing a few yards from him. His eyes narrowed but he said nothing.

"Perhaps you call yourself Krait these days, or something else. So what brings you here?" Theo said pleasantly.

"I'm doing no harm, just parked in the countryside to enjoy a walk," sneered Jakob. "There's no law against that."

"You are, in fact, trespassing on land belonging to my nephew, Jamie. But that's nothing compared to your proposed plan to cause a gas explosion and fire in my daughter's cottage."

"I can't imagine why you think that," said Jakob folding his arms in mock surprise, whilst flicking his eyes round to see if anyone else was with Theo.

"You're not the only one who keeps watch round here." Theo's soft voice was intimidating. "From now on there will be many eyes keeping guard over my loved ones. You won't succeed in gaining access. You will be caught and punished. Is it worth it?"

Jakob shrugged casually, pretending ignorance, but Theo could see the tense fury in his face. "I don't know what you're talking about."

Theo suddenly shouted, "Oh yes you do!" and strode forward until he stood in front of Jakob who had shrunk back against his van. "Three times is too much. Why don't you realise that fire can't destroy love? Or hope!" he thundered. "My children have been set free but you are full of bitterness and greed. Evil Ator has poisoned your mind in the same way he's infected others. But I've discovered that he himself is a sick man and has left the country. He's abandoned you. His power is diminishing and he's trapped in a living hell. What about you, Jakob? Where are you heading? The same place?"

Jakob flinched, white with anger. "Leave me alone," he hissed, his face bleak. "Let me go."

Theo could hear the despair in his voice and spoke more kindly. "You don't have to live like this. You think you can run away but you need to face up to who you are and what you've done. You can change – you can be set free not only from Ator but also from your own past and what's eating you up. I could help you start a new life."

"I don't want your help," Jakob screamed dementedly at him, wrenching open the van door and throwing himself into the driving seat. He started the engine and Theo stepped back to let the raging bull accelerate out of the clearing.

When the sound of the vehicle had receded and all he could hear was the wind rustling through the leaves, Theo heaved a sigh. Jakob had made his choice and rejected his offer. He could not win them all.

It soon became apparent that Jakob had vanished from the scene. Two days later, when he had received confirmation that the man was no longer a danger, Theo decided to speak to Josh and Andrew, but not their wives, about the averted threat, to demonstrate they should be vigilant. He did not want to frighten the pregnant Maria nor Kate who had been deeply upset by the attempted abduction of Nathan.

He had already spent a few hours one evening telling David about Ator and his campaign of hate against the family. David was amazed to discover who had been responsible for the barn fire, the house trashing, the food poisoning episode, the car accident and the arson attack which had destroyed his hotel. He felt cold when he realised that, apart from his father, those he loved most in the world might have been severely burned or even dead. He told Theo that it made him even more determined to stay, join the family enterprise, and work together to ensure its success. And their safety.

He located his son-in-law at the hotel, discussing the final snagging list with the contractors. When Theo took him aside and put him in the picture, Andrew was horrified to hear about Jakob's aborted plan, but was reassured when Theo told him that there was a security firm in place keeping the whole premises and grounds under surveillance. Theo warned him that although Ator had retreated to another country with his power eroded, he might be a continuing threat for a while.

Theo left a message on Josh's mobile to ask him to come up to the barn for a private word when he got back from work. It was dusk when Josh turned up.

"Hi, Theo! Good to see you. Is David around?" They walked through the studio to the cottage.

"He's taken Layla out to dinner in town. Borrowed my car too. That's why I got you to come here."

"Perhaps he's going to pop the question," grinned Josh. "It's feels so right to have them back here."

"I think the same. Glass of wine?"

"Sure. So what's all this about?" He sat down on a chair and looked expectantly at Theo.

When he had handed the glass to Josh, Theo told him about the defeat of Jakob's ugly scheme for the destruction of the cottages and their occupants. Josh slowly put his glass down, his face dark with the anger boiling up in him when he realised that his beloved Maria with their unborn child might have been died. He jumped to his feet. "What an unbelievably evil plan. I'd like to tear him apart!"

"Calm down, Josh. Control your anger."

"Where is he? I'll kill him," Josh shouted.

"You can't do that. Anyway, there's no need. The man's already dead," Theo said in a measured tone.

"Good riddance," Josh exclaimed. "Who did it?"

"Jakob was killed by a hit and run driver yesterday. About three hours from here. He had just got out of his car and was crossing the road. The police say the other car was travelling at speed and that the victim was killed instantly; they haven't found the driver. I'm certain it was no accident. Ator punishes disobedience and failure harshly. Jakob would have been frightened and desperate." Theo closed his eyes briefly as if in pain.

Josh took a swig of his wine and kept his thoughts to himself. His adopted father was the most compassionate person he'd ever met and he didn't want to upset him by slandering a dead man.

Layla glanced round the restaurant at the other diners. "Look at that couple over there – so very silent with each other, but it's a peaceful silence not a resentful one. They have a story which has moulded them and it shows in their faces. I like to capture a little of that when I paint people."

"My father says you have a talent for portraits," David said as the waiter cleared away their plates.

"Theo's gloriously creative and is much respected as a sculptor so I've always been touched that he takes an interest in my art."

"He's interested in us all, and he loves to help."

"You helped me too. I found out it was *you* who gave me the artist's materials right at the start. I'd always thought it was Theo."

"It was he who suggested it. And it gave me huge pleasure."

"It helped me so much. I started off painting landscapes but soon decided that portraits were more challenging. People are less perfect than nature – perhaps it's the flaws in humans that make them such fascinating subjects. At college I decided to focus on portraiture, and with hard work and Theo's financial help I finished the fine art diploma course. In the past year I've managed to get a few portrait commissions." She paused. "David, you're not listening."

"I am. But I was distracted by your eyes – dark tawny brown," he said looking intently into them, inhaling her perfume and her beauty. She was wearing a pale cream dress and her dark hair was tied up in a loose knot on her head.

"Burned umber, in artist's paint colours," Layla said with a smile. "Yours are cobalt blue."

He blinked. "Are they? Anyhow, do go on."

"I'm trying to make up my mind whether I'm going to stay and run art workshops at the hotel – which Kate wants me to do – or whether to go back to college for the final year and get my B.A." Layla gave David a penetrating look. "It rather depends on you."

"That gives me hope," David smiled. "I'm undecided too. On my travels I learned a lot from some amazing people. It would be exciting to find work overseas which would help others and be meaningful to me. Alternatively I could achieve that here in a place I love, since everyone wants me to be part of the Homeward Bound project."

"So why not stay?"

"My failing has always been that I don't delegate, and want to do things my way. I was ambitious to succeed. This is a risky venture – idealistic and challenging – and it won't be easy to make it work. I'd have to learn to be part of a team and be assigned a role. That's hard for me. But Theo is upbeat about it. He sees the bigger picture and has it all worked out so I think I might give it a try. What about you, Layla?"

"I'll stay if you stay or go with you if you go. Your family are my family. They adopted me." Layla leaned across and took his hand in hers.

"I love you," David said. At last.

"I'm so glad you've said it." She laughed. "It took you long enough."

"It was Jasmine who made me face up to the truth. After I'd had a horrible experience in South America."

"When you were attacked and ended up in hospital..." Layla started stroking his hand.

He looked up, a puzzled frown on his face. "Did I tell you about that?"

Layla looked serenely across at him. "I love you, David. I have done for years. I waited until you gave us a clue as to where you were. Then I took the initiative."

He gave a gasp of recognition, whipped his hand out from beneath hers and grasped her by the wrist. Layla looked startled. "It was you. At the hospital. My eyes were bandaged. I had a visitor who held my hand and stroked it in just the same way. You were looking after me."

She did not deny it but decided not to tell him about how Kate had told her the city he was in and the name of the bar where he worked, nor about how she had tracked him down, shadowed him, enlisted two people to help, and how they had been too late to prevent the attack but had managed to break up the fight. She did not want him to know of her desolation when she thought he might die and how they had carried him bleeding to hospital. She did not want to break the magic of the evening by telling him this now. Maybe another time.

David stood up, still holding her wrist and pulled Layla to her feet. Then, to the delight of everyone in the restaurant, he went down on his knees and said simply, "Marry me, Layla. I can't live without you."

Laslo could hardly believe his luck. The entire family would be assembled for a celebration lunch. He had managed to dispose of Jakob and now here was an opportunity to carry out the second part of Ator's instructions.

There had been few workmen in the hotel during the past week and Laslo had found it easy to gain access without being seen. He located the room which gave maintenance access to the ducts and pipework for the internal ventilation system, and made a small aperture, to enable him to introduce the lethal poison which Ator had supplied him. From here he would release the ricin into the ventilation system which would circulate it round the hotel and feed into the dining room below. There was a timing device on the small cylinder which would cause a thirty minute delay before the toxic mist began to seep in through the ventilation ducts and outlets. This would give him enough time to make his exit from the building and get away from the scene. Within six to eight hours, those exposed to even minute amounts would start to develop symptoms, and death would occur within three to five days. There was no antidote for ricin and no reliable test to show that a person had been exposed to it. He had hidden the cylinder carefully, ensured that a small downstairs window was unlocked and planned to return when the target family were in the hotel.

Within three days the opportunity had arisen. He saw preparations for a party and assumed that the family would be present. Laslo decided to conceal himself near where he would gain entry, waiting for the moment when all of them were eating in the dining room. Some members of family were in the kitchen helping with preparations. There had just been a delivery of wine and food because the hotel was not yet open and had no provisions. As Laslo sidled round a corner, Kate – the only member of the family whom he had ever met – appeared and caught sight of him.

"Just checking all the boxes are unloaded," he said briskly and walked off towards the van, round the building and out of sight. Kate had stopped in her tracks and Laslo hoped she would not immediately remember when she had last seen him and who he was.

Recognition of Vadim took her only a few seconds. Kate gave a shout and ran after him but he had vanished. She heard the delivery van drive off and assumed he was the driver. Within minutes she found Theo, who had moved in the day before to his new apartment in the hotel, and told him.

"I've just seen Vadim – the man who landed me in prison. He's vindictive and deceitful. What on earth was he doing here? It can't be a coincidence." Kate looked worried.

"Leave it with me, Kate. I'll deal with it. You just go ahead and ensure all is ready for our family lunch party." Theo gave his daughter a reassuring smile and she gratefully left it in his hands and went downstairs.

A couple of hours passed and the family began to assemble in the newly decorated reception area and lounge. Josh was making final preparations for the buffet lunch in the dining room with Kate, whilst Layla and David were dispensing drinks. Maria, now heavily pregnant, was seated and chatting to Jamie and Penny, whose boys were having fun running up and down the new staircase. Andrew was with Nathan, holding the boy's hand as he took some faltering steps, lurching against his father's legs and giggling. Everyone was pleased that Theo was now living amongst them and there was the exciting prospect of the hotel soon opening for business. The patriarch, however, was nowhere to be seen.

When Laslo put on his gloves and slipped out of the empty bedroom, he knew the family were together in the reception rooms below. He sidled noiselessly along the dim corridor to the unused cupboard, where he had hidden his deadly canister, and crouched down to reach for it. As he pulled it out, a door opened and a shaft of light lit up the corridor. As Laslo spun round, holding the small canister, he saw a tall, commanding figure standing silently a few yards from him in the pool of light.

"I assume what you intend to use comes from Ator," Theo said quietly to the intruder. "Give it to me."

"Who are you?" Laslo sneered, knowing precisely who he was and glancing down the corridor to see if his escape route was clear. If he threw the canister at Theo, it would probably break and Laslo might have time to get out before the toxic mist spread. But Theo would soon die, his family would come looking for him and they too would inhale the poison which would be fatal.

"I am Theo. My family are under my protection and I won't let evil men harm them."

"You can't stop me. Ator's poison is powerful," Laslo snarled furiously.

His rage was nothing compared to Theo's anger, as he roared, "Not as powerful as me! His campaign of hate stops now. Give me the canister."

With a savage thrust, Laslo hurled the canister at Theo's head and took off down the corridor to escape. With effortless grace, Theo leaned forward and caught the canister as it sailed through the air.

Laslo stopped in horror when two uniformed security guards appeared in front of him. Turning round he saw with relief that Theo was holding the canister and handing it to a tall, blonde woman.

"Be careful with this, Angela," Laslo heard him saying as the two guards firmly took his arms. "Take it to a laboratory and get it destroyed. Deliver our friend here to the police and I'll make a statement to them later." Theo turned to Laslo. "You will be punished and I hope you mend your ways. You still have time. Though Ator's getting weaker and has little time left."

Lunch was over and all the family were still sitting at the table. The sun shone through the tall windows with a warm afternoon glow. Theo rose to his impressive height and, looking around with a wide loving smile, he began to speak:

"Dear children, there is much to celebrate today. We are all so happy that David and Layla are to be married. Some of us have known for a long time that they love each other. Kate and Andrew have moved to live alongside Josh and Maria. My grandson is over a year old and he's a sturdy, loving child. It's delightfully evident that Maria and Josh will soon become parents."

He looked affectionately across at Maria, who blushed, and Josh, who said, "Can't wait!"

Theo's eyes shone. "Our new venture, Homeward Bound Hotel, is soon to open – as a family hotel to provide pleasure, relaxation and a break from the cares of the world. We'll work together as a committed team and overcome the inevitable problems. Yesterday I moved in to my new abode to live here with you. As you know, I've created a sculpture for the garden. It's been cast into bronze, delivered here and set up on its plinth. May I suggest we put on our coats, go out and unveil it?"

When they were all outside, Theo strode across and pulled off the canvas cover to reveal an exquisite sculpture of a majestic eagle, wings outspread, with a small boy sitting on his back with one small hand raised up. The boy's face and curly hair were unmistakably Nathan's. There was a moment of quiet appreciation as they all surveyed Theo's latest creation against the peaceful green backdrop of trees and fields stretching away to the distant hills.

Kate's voice broke the silence. "Look. Nathan's standing without help. He wants to go and see." Everyone swung round to look at the small child as he took his first steps forward, his arms outstretched to embrace a whole new world.

Acknowledgments

My grateful thanks go to: David Backhouse, Tildy Beach Valli, Tony Collins, Luke Jeffery, Douglas Harding, Jenny Monds, Henri Nouwen, Charmian Ryan, Ella Spratt, Maria Timperley, Diana Wright, and to my family: Michael, Julie, Jack and Claire for their loving support.

About the Author

Eve Bonham is an author of three books. "Madness Lies and Other Stories," a collection of sixteen short stories, was published in 2008. Her first novel "To the End of the Day," came out in 2011, with a Polish edition in 2012 and a Kindle edition in 2013; it relates the dramatic events of a day in the lives of two female friends.

Eve studied English and Irish Literature at Dublin University. She was an English teacher in Bangkok, a fine art auctioneer in London (at the family firm, Bonhams), a picture framer in Wiltshire, a jewellery wholesaler and knitwear retailer in Bath, and has been a lecturer and a journalist. She has sailed extensively, competing in sailing races across the Atlantic and Round the World, and travelled alone overland in remoter parts of Asia, India and South America. She married, lived in a Breton village in France for fourteen years, brought up two children and moved back to England ten years ago. In 2006 she became a Christian, which profoundly changed her life. Three years ago she decided to tackle writing a story about love and loss with an underlying Christian perspective. "The Lost Journey Homeward" is that book.

She now lives in rural Dorset with her husband, Michael, writes for several hours a day, works part time for a property company, assists with community projects, and involves herself in village life. She reads good books, listens to radio, paints watercolours and plants trees. She is currently writing flash fiction (short stories of under 500 words) and doing research for her next book – a novel to be set in Dorset.

Website
www.evebonham.co.uk

Facebook
Eve Bonham – Writer

Twitter
Eve Bonham

Also by the Author

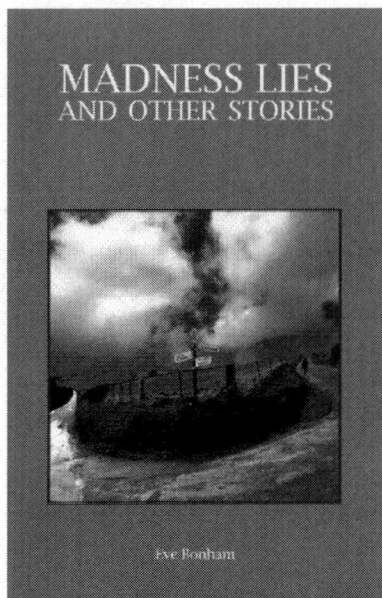

Madness Lies and Other Stories

ISBN: 978-0955931505
Dryad Books (2008)

16 stories, with cartoon illustrations on each title page. 'Eve's subjects are people who change things, causing lives to take a different direction. The experiences she has had trigger her ideas and the people she has encountered inhabit her tales. Invention and imagination do the rest – she writes with sparkle, humour and compassion. She is a serious devotee of the short story as a pithy, punchy and powerful form of fiction.'

To the End of the Day

ISBN: 978-1846245824
Book Guild Ltd. (2011)

Two women, two lives, lived separately but in a state of emotional dependency on each other for many years ... but now on the verge of what?

Anna, a writer with a first book about to be published, and Lizzie, a former actress, have viewed themselves as adoptive sisters, closer than blood-related siblings, ever since their schooldays when they lived under the same roof. Now in their fifties, they meet up for the evening with their husbands at Anna's French home, then the next morning separately make their way across the English Channel for their own very different reasons. Reasons that become clear in the course of a single day as each relives in vivid flashbacks their volatile friendship and the events that have both brought them together and pushed them far apart over the course of four decades.